The

SHADOW PATRIOT

· S O N S   O F   T H E   N E W   W O R L D ·

JONATHAN'S
STORY
II

D1528478

The

SHADOW
PATRIOT

·SONS OF THE NEW WORLD·

JONATHAN'S
STORY
II

·JAMES SHORT·

For Marianne,

Who took my heart and didn't give it back.

PROSPECTS AND DOUBTS

WAS HE BEING followed? From his vantage point on top of the warehouse, Jonathan scanned the harbor, the cobblestone boardwalk, and the connecting street. His years as a smuggler gave him a second sense of the presence of hidden eyes. A wind nipped at his face. Was that him? A man in a green Jaeger uniform at the end of the street stared in the direction of the warehouse. He was too far away to make out his features. Was the Jaeger captain he stalked for the murder of Amelia stalking him? Improbable, yet… Another Jaeger joined his fellow countryman, and they walked on just as Josiah drove around the corner in a second wagon to pick up the extra merchandise.

"What are you looking at?" Daniel called out, then added, "Emma is afraid for you." His sister had stopped speaking after seeing her parents burn to death in the great fire. Daniel often put into her mouth what he wanted to say.

"I am just looking at a new ship docking down the way."

Jonathan returned to their shelter. He had caulked and carpeted the casing that once housed a treadwheel crane to keep out the wind that penetrated the spaces between the loose boards. He made arrangements with Pollux. the warehouse manager, to have a warming stone delivered to the roof every evening. He visited the orphans most afternoons, bringing hot tea with sugar and milk. The children were isolated, but they were safe from the dangerous world below.

When Jonathan left the roof of the warehouse and Emma and Daniel, the dangerous world became his world. He used the cover of war profiteer to spy for the Continental army in British-occupied New York City. He used the cover of a spy to stalk the murderers of Miss Amelia Goodwin, the woman he was to marry. He had wounded the Hessian major Christoph von Wurttemberg on a country lane north of the city and killed the British captain Hogwood on a deserted road north of Philadelphia. Von Wurttemberg returned to Germany to recover so now was beyond his reach. That left the Jaeger Captain Hoffman stationed somewhere on Long Island. Hoffman had gained notoriety by leading successful raids into Connecticut. It was just a matter of time before Jonathan found and confronted the Jaeger captain with his crime. Perversely, schooled by his friend Benedict Arnold before the war in the ways of smuggling and trade, Jonathan was accumulating a fortune as a merchant in the cutthroat mercantile world of occupied New York.

The reason was French wine, difficult to obtain now England and France were at war. Captain Rodrigo, who had sold Jonathan ten panniers of wine, returned with more of the product. They met again at a tavern operated by a half-deaf proprietor. Meredith James who commanded a small flotilla of whaleboats that intercepted traffic in the Long Island Sound also attended the meeting. Half pirate, half King's man, little happened in that body of water James was unaware of. In a low voice, Rodrigo confided that he had more panniers of French claret, burgundy, and champagne to sell. This signified to Jonathan that Rodrigo had a cache probably on the eastern shore of Long Island. Jonathan purchased the entirety of the cargo, two-thirds on credit.

James guffawed at the foolishness of the agreement. "The next time you are giving away your goods, Captain Rodrigo, consider first the man who protects your interests in this part of the world."

The proprietor of the tavern raised his head at the sound of James's loud gruff voice.

"Any other merchant I would refuse," Rodrigo continued in a low voice. "But with the merchandise in our friend's possession, I will sleep at night peacefully as if I already tucked the guineas under my pillow."

"And you, Mr. Asher," James addressed Jonathan. adding an evil stare to his threatening voice, "will also sleep peacefully if you disappoint. Very peacefully, if you catch my drift."

Jonathan did not disappoint. After fighting another indecisive battle at Monmouth, General Clinton who had taken charge of the King's forces abandoned Philadelphia and shipped the army—17,000 additional customers—back to New York. Again, as with coffee, Jonathan found himself with the right product at the right time. The British liked their parties, balls, and fetes well lubricated. He sold out of his inventory in an afternoon, and although he still presented to the world the humble aspect of a man occupying the station barely above a teamster because he drove his wagon, fellow merchants began to calculate his profits and seek ways to ingratiate themselves with him.

Realizing wine would give him entrée to the pockets of hundreds of well-paid British officers in the environs of New York. Jonathan made a proposal the next time he met Rodrigo: "I don't want to just sell whatever you have left over after your other deliveries. I have a thirsty army of 22,000 men here. I will invest more of my own into the venture. The *Danton* is docked near my farm, just begging to be stolen and made into a privateer even though the rudder and steering gear is hidden away. Find a buyer for the *Danton* or sail it down to one of those islands where they are always short of building material, dismantle her, sell the wood, melt and beat the iron fittings into nails and hasps and hinges, take your percentage and use my part of the proceeds to supply me fine wines and champagne and don't forget coffee. We will have a vigorous trade. I am aware of the risks and accept them."

Jonathan was near certain that Rodrigo would sell the *Danton* to a privateer, an immensely profitable undertaking, especially in Southern New Jersey. However Rodrigo disposed of the *Danton*, Jonathan was confident his friend would divide the proceeds honestly.

This arrangement turned out better than a Mexican silver mine. Less than a month later, Rodrigo delivered another fifteen panniers of claret, champagne, and burgundy, over a thousand bottles, which he claimed

Jonathan could sell for 8000 pounds. Rodrigo spent an afternoon going over the names of the different growers and what Jonathan could expect to sell each vintage for. Latour, Lafite, Margaux. Veuve Clicquot, Louis-Roederer, Piper-Heidsieck, Haut Brion, and Taittinger now entered Jonathan's lexicon. The names raised eyebrows and opened pockets. Four bottles of Veuve Clicquot fetched more than two hogsheads of rum.

The transactions were necessarily discreet. For, as expected, the customs men came around sniffing out an opportunity for an exorbitant bribe or an outright seizure of the valuable inventory, the possession of which was treasonable except by them. Jonathan welcomed three pairs of customs men on three consecutive days. He showed his papers from Castor exempting his goods from a requisition and then let them examine his stock. The manifests detailed that his inventory consisted only of the port. In peacetime, you could bring in port at lower duties, and in wartime, you could import it without committing treason. Although the champagne, claret, and burgundy were not bottled like port. The fluid inside did not look like port. Nor did it taste like port; yet the customs men agreed with Jonathan as to the legal nature of the substance. Jonathan had carefully labeled on the cases the buyers of the "port" including Major John André, William Franklin, and David Matthews, and if these great men thought the substance in the bottles was port, well then, who were they, mere customs men without entrée into these exalted circles, to disagree. Gifts of several bottles of "port" on the side to the customs men facilitated their judgment.

Harder to please was Castor Blanchard, the assistant

commissary general, in all things insatiable. Not only in greed and appetite, but in the love of the game. He could think in numbers faster than any man that Jonathan had ever encountered. His game now was to take over Jonathan's wine business. He could not do that without discovering Jonathan's sources. In the meantime, Castor used every opportunity to bully Jonathan.

"And where is my portion of the sale?" The commissary demanded in the interview after Jonathan returned from Philadelphia. The two chairs that supported Castor creaked and groaned as he shifted his great bulk while waiting for an answer.

"If I recall correctly, I gave you thirty bottles in advance," Jonathan replied. This confrontation was not unexpected.

"You misunderstood. That was only an advance."

Jonathan stood his ground. "You made quite a profit off a piece of paper."

Castor shook his head. "What I don't understand is why you paid me for the pass. And why you paid the ship's captain for passage, and God knows how many others to get your merchandise to Philadelphia. Yet you could have disposed of the merchandise here without going through that trouble or expense. In fact, you could have sold to me for the same price you sold to Major André and would have still made a substantial profit."

"Major André had placed the order and was too important a client to pass over to supply others."

Castor shook his head. "Why did you go to Philadelphia?"

"To fill an order of an important client as I stated."

"We'll leave your lies to the side for the moment. As you know, unlike the other commissaries, I been granted the privilege of supplying hock and porter on a limited basis. I have five hundred pounds to invest in your wine trade." This privilege, like most of his advantages, Castor had won at the gaming table. "Also, I acquired influence over their dispensation over two positions—water commissary and cattle feeder—that I might consider handing over to you." These were British sinecures that paid well and involved no work

Jonathan replied: "What I possess in my inventory presently is only a few dozen bottles of second-rate Madeira, which I'm sure would not interest you. I will consider your offer if I receive better quality merchandise in the future."

"May I remind you that I done you too many favors for you to stint me a small one in return."

"I have no merchandise now worth your investment so I can't consider an offer so grossly unfair to you." Disputing with Castor was like dueling with a man who keeps changing weapons.

"Don't word me, Mr. Asher. I expect my share when you receive the next shipment. I have half a mind to not do this dance, rescind your immunity from requisition and seize your inventory for my use."

Castor did prevail to a limited degree. Jonathan resigned himself to selling a pannier of 50 bottles from the next shipment to the commissary below cost. Not enough to make the commissary happy, but enough to stave off his threats so Jonathan still could keep his goods, wagon, and team from seizure. Curston, Castor's bully boy, at this time reappeared—his job obviously to ferret out Jonathan's connections. Lucretia Baldwin, Castor's intelligencer, had begun to patronize the millinery across the street from the home and business of his brother, William, who was an optician. The milliner, Elizabeth Littleton, was yet another responsibility. He had promised the milliner's friend, Mrs. Millicent Dalton, to look after her, for in British-occupied New York, no one survived without protection.

Jonathan accommodated himself in the little treadwheel crane house lying down on the sheepskin rug. This was an excuse for the children who craved human touch to snuggle on either side of him. Daniel played a game pretending to be somewhere else in the world—on a ship, or an island. Emma would hug him as tight as she could as if she wanted to keep him from his dangerous world. Even Daniel seemed happy that the narrowness of their abode necessitated closeness, which the children equated with protection.

Jonathan said his goodbyes to the children a half-hour later and opened the door that led to a ladder inside the warehouse. He felt a stab of a guilty conscience on leaving. They shouldn't be so dependent on him. He tried to console himself with the thought they had survived the horrible death of their parents, they would survive whatever might happen to him.

He remembered the Jaeger on the street corner. He would bring a spyglass for the children tomorrow. He would ask Josiah who was waiting in the warehouse below with a wagon whether he had a close look of the Jaeger. That brought up again the disturbing question: is the stalker being stalked?

CHAPTER 1

November 1778

THE SAILOR GRABBED Jonathan's arm as he exited the tavern and jerked him into an alley. "This way, sir. This way. Don't resist the hand of a well-wisher." When they were completely hidden in the shadows, Jonathan's abductor whispered. "You soon be a wanted man."

"I am already in many places, good and bad, sir, so if you please, release me," Jonathan said after controlling the brief rush of panic. "I've an appointment in half an hour," he added. Although his brother, Gulliver, had sacrificed himself by falsely confessing to the murder of Captain Hogwood, Jonathan couldn't shake the feeling that the matter was not settled. The men under his brother's command had been incensed at the hanging of their lieutenant. They were certain he had been sleeping in his quarters when the murder took place. His confession made no sense to them. Perhaps, they were homing in on the real reason. Jonathan's unease now had become personified in a man with a strong grip, a rolling sailor's gait, and the reek of rum.

The large hand squeezed painfully. "Got no time for formalities, sir, such as I be not this and you be not that. We are morsels about to be stewed in the same pot. I'm doing you a favor. They are after me, meaning you are next."

"What are you implying, sir?" Jonathan shook his arm free.

"Want me to proclaim it to the world." The sailor seized and squeezed his arm again, whispering, "Let's just say I mix with the jacks and seadogs and the shifting ballast in the taverns and listen and listen while they spin me their woes which is every sailor's lot. I find out where they been, what they carrying, the sea worthiness of their vessels. Information which has certain value to certain people in certain quarters."

He drew Jonathan closer, engulfing him in a cloud of rum vapor. "What value you ask? One pound and ten shillings, keeping me in rum, which I cannot live without. I give what be of consequence to a whaleboat captain who exchanges my one pound ten shillings of information for one pound ten shillings."

"This has nothing to do with me," Jonathan exclaimed angrily.

The sailor belched and continued, "Meredith James just caught the captain with papers and other such stuff unhandy to have in his possession. At this very moment, sure the captain is deciding between doing the gallows' dance as a spy and traitor to good King George or giving up his contacts, me among them, and pardoned for his sins against the crown. Loving my rum so much and thereby loving my life, I know what I'd do. Doubt me at your peril. You see, I be your guardian angel, and you mine. You are to help me escape in time of need as I must do for you. That's what they told me when I complained about working by my lonesome."

"Guardian angels don't extort each other," Jonathan whispered harshly, gritting his teeth. Meredith James' hold on Long Island was an unpleasant obstacle to his pursuit of Jaeger Hoffman. Little occurred on Long Island that escaped the notice of the piratical militiaman. Meredith was already suspicious of Jonathan so if he entered the domain of the King of Long Island Sound his movements would be closely followed.

"Guardian angels do what they have to do to get their rum." The sailor's grip tightened as if in preparation to wrenching Jonathan's arm from its socket.

"I might believe you if I were informed about your existence." Jonathan clenched his fist in preparation for the inevitable fight.

"Somebody must forgot," the sailor replied unconcerned. "The damnable thing is I suspicioned this perilous situation came about on account of an intelligencer in Washington's camp who kens who isn't what he seems in the city. So, friend, how do we handle this?"

Murdering his guardian angel immediately occurred to Jonathan as the simplest solution. Unfortunately, he still carried a troublesome conscience. "Can you row?"

"In circles." The sailor lifted his other arm which terminated with a knotted sleeve at the elbow.

Jonathan left a message with his brother's wife, Nancy, that he would be gone for a few days and then visited the

Gatling residence next to his warehouse and gave Thomasina, Josiah's wife, money to take care of the horses, she being the only one of the twenty-four awake. Jonathan felt a stab in his heart when he thought about Emma and Daniel. He had just purchased a small brazier. He told Thomasina to give it to Pollux at the warehouse and inform him that he would be away for a few days. Pollux would know what to do with it. If for some reason Jonathan couldn't return, perhaps he could persuade William and Nancy to take the children in, paying them with the deed to their house. He would figure it out later. This one-armed, inebriated guardian angel now required all his attention. He could see no clear way of dealing with the fellow spy beyond escorting him to Washington's camp near Middlebrook and demanding that Hamilton explain why he put his cover into the hands of an unreliable sot.

Jonathan remembered seeing a small, abandoned bumboat turned upside down on a dock on the East River with its oarlocks still in place, although the wood was too rotted to transport cargo of any weight. Next to the bumboat had lain two splintered oars. If the craft and the oars hadn't been scavenged for firewood yet, they might suffice for the two of them on a smooth crossing into New Jersey.

On viewing the pitiable craft, his one-armed guardian angel swore he had shipped in worse and anyway a drowning was a better end than a hanging for drowned corpses didn't have such horrible expressions. Jonathan launched the boat with his passenger settling himself comfortably in the bow and began rowing around the tip of Manhattan Island toward the cliffs of the Jersey shore. A thick fog rolled in as he passed Manhattan, and Jonathan could only maintain his bearing by rowing at a right angle to the tidal current.

"A smuggler's night," his guardian angel companion observed.

"Not quite that. Smugglers like to see where they are going," Jonathan replied in a whisper.

Suddenly, the sloshing of oars and the voices of a half dozen ladies, giggly and drunk, and possibly quite lost came out of the fog.

"Bumboat full of trulls. Been a while since I cuddled with one of them daughters of Eve," Jonathan's companion commented wistfully.

Jonathan shipped his oars and let the boat drift away from the voices.

"What's that?" the sailor asked, hearing several splashes a little while later.

"Something being thrown overboard," Jonathan said grimly. A naked white body floated past them a minute later. The silhouette of the ship approached then faded gradually, erased by the fog. More splashes sounded. "This doesn't make sense. There shouldn't be prison ships hereabouts."

"Poor buggered souls," the guardian angel whispered, perhaps out of respect for the dead. "Guards don't want the trouble of burying them so just dump their carcasses with nary a prayer."

Jonathan rowed on. After beaching the boat on the Jersey shore, they found a trail up the cliff and stumbled on a road that seemed vaguely familiar to Jonathan. They were in the ambiguous territory just south of Paulus Ferry and safe for neither side.

An hour later a voice boomed out of the darkness, challenging them, "Who goes there?"

They stopped. "Who goes there," the voice repeated. Not knowing whether the challenger was a King's man or a patriot or a cowboy or skinner, Jonathan and his guardian angel ran a hundred yards and hid in a ditch. The caller wisely didn't follow.

Taking a path that detoured around the voice, they unaccountably found themselves walking down the street of a village. Jonathan assumed they were in the Town of Elizabeth, which lay supposedly in Continental territory. They then heard a man grumbling in German from the upper window of a house. Another man pissed against a barn, swearing drunkenly.

"Halt! Wer da?" They were confronted a second time. A gray outline of a man with a leveled musket stood twenty yards in front of them. It was too risky to ascertain whether he was a Hessian or German-speaking Continental soldier.

The sailor unsheathed his knife making the soft sliding sound of metal against leather.

"Quickly, this way," Jonathan said, and they ducked between two houses. A shot rang out behind them. They sprinted into the thick fog. The guard again wisely did not follow.

They traveled in disgruntled silence into the morning, circling the outskirts of the township of Union and keeping their distance from the farmhouses they happened upon. Jonathan had spent a month wandering and working in this area after giving up preaching so when the fog finally lifted in the early afternoon, he recognized the spindly creek, the field of tree stumps, several dozen of which he had cut himself, and the burnt pile of wood that was all that remained of the farm of a family that had allowed him to sleep by their fireplace. They were not far from Middlebrook. Still, Jonathan was cautious. He wanted to avoid being seen by either side, and as Arnold had said, there are roadways, pathways, backways, and smuggler ways. Where possible, he used the last. His companion, swearing continually under his breath for being obliged to walk drunk more miles than any Christian should be required to walk sober, followed.

At a turn in the trail, they suddenly came face to face with Hector perched on top of a fat horse, whistling a jaunty tune, his overlarge tricorn hat pulled down low. The boy started and paled when he saw Jonathan. He had identified Gulliver, Jonathan's brother, as the man who had killed captain Hogwood because of his strong resemblance to Jonathan. Gulliver had gone along and confessed. A moment later the brave boy forced a smile at what might be a vengeful ghost. "You, sir?" He managed to say.

"Visiting your grandmother, Hector? How is she?" Jonathan asked, wondering at the propensity of this boy to be found on the infrequently traveled trails in the dangerous territories between the two armies.

Hector seemed momentarily confused then brightened and said, "'Tisn't one, 'tis t'other. My Brunswick grandmother is middling, some days better, not like my Germantown grandmother who's middling, some days worse."

"Good day to you, Hector," Jonathan said.

"Good day to you, sir." The boy rode off at a fast clip toward Perth Amboy.

In the very late afternoon, they approached the encampment of the Continental Army, chosen because of its strong defensive position and named Log House City. The land had been cleared for a square mile and each brigade occupied a low hill complete with officer cabins and parade grounds. Jonathan had no intention of striding into the camp, renouncing his loyalty to the king and rejoining the army. Delivering his "guardian angel" eliminated the danger so long as the man kept his mouth shut. However, he wanted to speak to Hamilton to clear up a few things.

Discovering a partly ruined shack in a stand of white oak and chestnut trees a quarter-mile from Washington's camp, Jonathan directed the "guardian angel" to convey a request to Hamilton to pay him a visit that evening, but otherwise, tell no one else about his presence.

"Me lips are sealed," his guardian angel said and sauntered off through the field of stumps that separated the wood from the camps, speculating out loud about the Continental Army's stock of rum. Jonathan spent a few minutes trying to figure out what to do next, but the fatigue of having walked twenty-five miles won out over worry and he slipped into a doze.

"Major Clark, what in the bloody damn hell are you doing here?" Jonathan cried out and jerked himself awake.

Sitting bolt upright, he glanced around at the splintery walls of the shed. He did not see Major Clark, the Continental spy that operated in the surroundings of Philadelphia, and who had nearly broken his jaw after providing a pass into the city. Nor did Jonathan see anyone else, yet he was certain somebody had been there in the shack. He rushed outside and then to the edge of the wood which gave out onto a view of Log House City. A small figure was running up the incline of one of the regimental hills holding an oversized tricorn hat in his hand.

The small voice of Hector was heard hailing the guard and he passed by without being stopped. Almost immediately the boy fell in with a stout woman exiting the camp carrying a large basket of laundry to be washed in a creek at the bottom of the hill. From their easy manner together, Jonathan guessed Hector was her son. The woman dumped the laundry next to several tubs simmering over fires while she listened to Hector. Her load was full of officers' uniforms. She continued working, feeling inside each jacket before consigning it to the pot of boiling water. The boy stood back expectantly. The woman retrieved what appeared to be a letter from one of the pockets of a uniform jacket and put it in the folds of her skirt.

"So that's how the information is passed," Jonathan whispered to himself. Hector and his mother worked for the British. The spy, possibly an officer close to Washington, left the information in an inner pocket of his jacket. The laundress retrieved it and gave it to Hector to deliver. A boy, especially one visiting an ill grandmother, would not be bothered on his way through the lines even if he didn't possess a pass, much less searched. If another laundress washed the clothes, the information, probably coded in an innocuous-seeming letter would be set aside or destroyed.

Hector's mother suddenly put her fingers to her lips and bent down to hear her son better. She straightened and glanced around as if trying to pierce the thick foliage with her gaze. Giving another laundress a coin and her basket of soiled clothes, she started walking in the direction of Jonathan's shack. Jonathan retreated into the cover of a stand of gooseberry shrubs twenty yards away. When the laundress neared the doorless entrance, she scraped her upper lip with her bottom teeth and drew a pistol from her skirt.

"Show yerself, Mister," she demanded. "I want to talk to you." After a moment's hesitation, she peered inside.

"I saw him. I heard him snore," Hector insisted. "He was the same man I saw hanged for killing Captain Hogwood, the one I accused—the merchant from New York. And now he is here. I swear to it."

"If dead men come back to life, your father got a lot of explaining to do for not availing himself of the opportunity," the laundress said to her son.

"Maybe, there were two of them that looked alike. But this fellow seemed more like the man riding with Captain Hogwood, and the man they hanged wore a uniform, so I think they hanged the wrong one." Hector was near tears.

"The man confessed to the murder, so he warn't the wrong man. If this fellow were a damn rebel, he'd not be hiding away from his friends. Likely he were just a cowboy looking for easy pickings," the mother said. "Wait until tomorrow afore you leave with the letter." They walked back together toward the camp.

"Why did you betray my identity to a sailor who can't hold his liquor or his tongue?" Jonathan posed this question before any greeting.

Hamilton's eyes flashed. He had arrived at the shed in the gray predawn looking leaner and more predatory than the last time Jonathan saw him. "Given that with your personal vendetta sooner or later you'd be compromised as a source, I thought it wise to have somebody looking out for you. You can't go around murdering British officers and expect to escape notice."

"We dueled," Jonathan protested.

"And the British captain ended up dead, which put Captain Clark who was operating effectively in the area at great risk. He was forced to move south, putting him an inconvenient distance from us."

"There is one less British soldier for you to kill. That is probably my greatest contribution to the cause of liberty thus far." Jonathan hoped to be dismissed.

"No, Mr. Asher, 'tisn't. Because our enemy is so eager to inform us of their successes and our defeats, the gazettes with your advertisements are usually the first intelligence to reach us, and we measure all subsequent information against what you have sent. If we hear a rumor that such a regiment is moving, and we have it from you that they just requisitioned a certain quantity of hard biscuit, the rumor becomes fact, and, additionally, we can often tell from the amounts on the orders how long the campaign is planned. Et cetera, et cetera," Hamilton articulated "et cetera" with a great deal of exasperation. "But we do not believe you can fulfill your present function much longer given that you're more interested in vengeance than the cause of liberty. We, of course, are cultivating other sources to replace you. Still, for the time being, you are useful. Just don't kill any more British officers. It complicates matters."

"Like all human beings, I come with provisions. I ask not a shilling for risking the gallows. Soon, I will respectfully resign from my duties. My business isn't finished yet. When it is, I'll retire from this damn war. This double game has been bad for the nerves, bad for digestion, bad for the pocketbook, and worse for honest intercourse with people that I would like to have honest intercourse with. In the meantime, I have information of a most urgent nature." Jonathan related the story of the laundress and the boy. "All we have to do is find the traitor who is hiding the information in his laundry," Jonathan added.

Hamilton nodded. "Very good. We will catch him, break his code, and send out our own letter, then when the damage is done, hang him."

Jonathan showed Hamilton the path the boy took in case they wanted to follow him, mentioning that he is probably keeping a horse with a loyalist in the town of Middlebrook. While they were speaking, Hector suddenly appeared running down the hill past the guard.

"The mother is working the boy to death in this spying business," Jonathan commented.

Hamilton hit his forehead with his palm. "Christ's blood. I know why she sent him out so soon. We must stop the boy now."

"Isn't it better to discover the traitor?" Jonathan asked.

"No, we must stop the boy, now," Hamilton insisted. "General Washington left today with just a few guards to visit West Point. 'Twould be the easiest thing in the world to snatch him up."

Hamilton set out and blocked the boy's path. "I want to talk to you, lad."

Hector turned and bolted in the other direction, only to be confronted by Jonathan. Sliding under Jonathan's arms, he sprinted toward the camp. Hamilton pursued. The boy ran past the guards screaming, "Murder! Murder! Murder!"

"Catch that boy!" Hamilton called out. The guards leveled their muskets. "Don't shoot me, you dolts!" Hamilton screamed. "Grab him!"

The boy jumped off the path and slid down toward the creek.

Debating with himself whether it was a mistake to stay in the open, Jonathan backed just beyond the edge of the trees to observe the proceedings. Not quite hidden, yet it would take somebody with sharp eyes to pick him out.

Six guards joined the chase. Hector eluded them, ducking and dodging, slipping through their hands as if greased. Soldiers and officers poured out of their tents and cabins and stood on the hillsides watching the commotion. His mother, the laundress, ran down the path crying.

"The boy has papers. He's a courier for a spy," Hamilton shouted. Finally, near the stream, Hector was surrounded. It was then Jonathan noticed Benedict Arnold, who must have been visiting from Philadelphia, standing in the crowd, leaning on a cane.

"Come on, lad, let's see what you have in your pocket." Hamilton approached, holding his hand out.

Hector looked around wildly, then crouched as if to spring.

"Come on boy. You have nothing to be afraid of if you're straight with us," Hamilton said in a kindly manner like a father reasoning with a child.

His mother pushed her way into the circle.

"Don't!" the boy screamed as Hamilton measured a step forward.

"Dear, tell them I made you do it," the laundress pleaded.

The boy took out a pocket flintlock pistol and waved it around wildly. "Don't come near me, I swear I'll shoot you." This was an absurd threat. Three guards had muskets pointed at him.

"Let's just see what's in your pocket." Hamilton measured another step. He was almost close enough to grab the trembling hand with the gun.

The mother pleaded, "Do what the colonel says, Hector. Show him what you have in your pocket. They won't do no harm to a widow and her son."

Suddenly, Hector straightened out of his crouch, a mischievous grin coming into his face, and he retrieved from the pocket attached to his belt a small note a few inches square. "This is what you want," he yelled in his high, thin voice.

"That's a good son." The laundress now stood next to Hamilton. "Give it to Colonel Hamilton. They won't hurt us; I swear on your father's grave."

"Your mother is right," Hamilton said. "We mean you no harm. We just want to see the paper."

"Take care of my family," Hector yelled, addressing someone in the crowd. "You owe us that. And…" Glancing around in a panic, the boy whose eyes must have been keen spotted Jonathan. "There he is." The boy pointed to where Jonathan stood. Jonathan drew back quickly several more feet into the foliage.

Hamilton lunged for the gun.

"Stay away! Stay away!" the boy cried as he dodged him.

Jonathan was uncertain if anyone else had looked where Hector had pointed, and if they had, whether he would be recognized at such a distance.

"The ghost of Captain Hogwood's murderer is watching us," Hector shouted. "Over there in the woods."

This made no sense to the bystanders, and anyway, their attention was riveted on the gun the boy held in one hand and the note in the other.

"He was hanged and now is come for me."

"Please…" The mother begged her son. "Think what you're saying."

"If he isn't a ghost, ma, the wrong man was hanged. The right man is out there hiding in the woods like I told you." Hector wildly waved his gun. "He is a merchant from New York. He is the reason I do this. Take care of my family," the boy again addressed someone in the crowd, chest heaving with sobs. "Remember my last words and take care of them for I am no longer able. You owe us that." He bent down, quickly picked up his oversized tricorn hat which had fallen, and placed it on his head.

"Come on boy. Hand the note over," Hamilton said. "No need to lengthen this out."

"Yes, Colonel, no need." Before anyone comprehended what he was doing, Hector put the note in the hat's fold, pressed the barrel of the pistol to the note, cocked the hammer, and pulled the trigger.

Utter silence followed the crack of the pistol. Then

the mother screamed, rushed to her dead son, and hugged him rocking back and forth.

Jonathan turned away as heard a familiar voice following him: that which Benedict Arnold used to shout over high winds and rough seas. "Jonathan? Is that you, Jonathan?"

Jonathan slowly and carefully made his way back to New York, turning over and over in his mind a list of the reasons why he wasn't to blame for Hector's suicide. He felt the same heartsickness that he had at the death of Dermot and the Indian children. To nobody but Hector was the cause worth the sacrifice of his life. Yet he was too young to understand the principles or the larger loyalties. The cause for him was not the king, but simply the side his family had chosen. He was a brave innocent. The Continental Army and the King's militia were filled with many like him who fought on the side family and friends had chosen for them. They seemed to be the ones who died first.

Emma and Daniel were also innocents, thrown out into the world with nothing. The basics of survival—food, clothing, warmth—had been their main concerns. Jonathan smiled at the thought of how they appeared now: much less scraggly in their warmer clothes, with clearer eyes and more flesh on their bones. The old treadwheel casing which served as their shelter was weatherproof. For cold nights, Jonathan had a bin made in which heated stones could be winched up. He wondered whether they had begun to use the brazier. Emma was still afraid of fire. Then his thoughts strayed back to Hector. His heart ached for him—a brave boy in a dangerous world. He attempted to soothe himself during the return to New York City with the thought: *at least Emma and Daniel are still safe. At least they are still safe.*

CHAPTER 2

JONATHAN OFTEN WORKED the entire night. The British officer class was partial to long evening entertainments while putting away generous amounts of the finest vintages that they were too drunk to appreciate. It wasn't unusual to receive a request at 2 or 3 in the morning. In the first dawn's light, Jonathan often returned to his brother's house on Jacob Street. Amity reigned in the millinery across the way. No need to look for trouble there. Miss Elizabeth went about running the shop with no interference from her unscrupulous brother, Percy. Jonathan came to regard Mrs. Dalton's request to protect the milliner more as an attempt to encourage a courtship he wasn't certain either party desired. However, to be true to his word, he kept an eye on the establishment and the milliner, which wasn't a hardship, Miss Elizabeth being unconsciously beguiling in the way she went about her daily routine.

Jonathan had become fond of his brother William and his freeborn black wife Nancy. They truly cared for him—a luxury in the cruel chaotic world that war creates. Spying, obliging Jonathan to present a false front to the world was the loneliest and the vilest of vocations. Even after a long night of visiting taverns, delivering merchandise, and collecting money, Jonathan often would arrive at the house on Jacob Street at first light, bearing freshly ground coffee beans, warm rolls, fresh berries, or whatever else he could buy off the early morning vendors. It happened to be the magical properties of coffee that furthered his acquaintance with Miss Elizabeth.

Elizabeth was habitually an early riser, although from the glum expression on her face as she swept the porch of the shop, never a willing one. As he was leaving his brother and sister-in-law one morning, Jonathan noticed the droll unhappy face peering out the door. She waved and uttered an approximation of "Good morning, Mr. Asher," although as usual, she avoided looking him in the eye.

Jonathan, diagnosing her malaise as a lack of stimulant, returned to his brother's parlor, and borrowing the last cup of coffee, crossed the cobblestones, rapped on her lintel, and said to the surprised face which was attempting a smile, "Drink this, madam."

"What is this you are offering me, Mr. Asher?" Elizabeth asked suspiciously.

"Coffee," he said, thrusting the cup into her hands.

"I've been warned about the beverage," she said, holding the steaming brew underneath her nose and sniffing dubiously.

"I know, madam. Young ladies shouldn't accept dishes of coffee offered by gentlemen. It unhinges their faculties and makes them into rebels." He winked at her.

She stared momentarily shocked, almost giggled, then touched her lips to the rim of the cup and made a face.

"Sip again," Jonathan urged. "The taste will grow on you."

"Such luxury, Mr. Asher." She frowned. "Anything is bearable with familiarity, even a toothache, to be sure." Elizabeth had the Irish habit of ending all sentences as if they were questions.

"But I wouldn't be at all prosperous selling toothaches," Jonathan replied.

"Sedition must be worse than a toothache, yet many men buy that." Elizabeth cautiously smelled the coffee again.

Jonathan enjoyed the various expressions that played on her features. "I wouldn't know having never bought nor sold sedition."

She sipped again, regarding him uneasily. "Maybe with the next taste my tongue will be reconciled to the bitterness."

It was. A half of a cup later, pleasure gradually flowing into her countenance, she admitted, "Well, I confess this is more pleasant than a toothache or sedition. You are different than most gentlemen who enter my shop, Mr. Asher."

"How so?" He asked.

She took a sip before replying. "You do not boast or puff yourself up as is the custom of soldiers or those amassing their fortunes. You are circumspect and you observe whatever is around you, almost as if you were always expecting an enemy."

"I don't think I am treating you as such."

"Oh, no, you've done me a service few men would or could. I talked to Nancy, and she said you were the kindest man she had ever met. Yet, I know you can be a violent man. Am I the only person who is aware of that secret? A good man and a violent man. I am half afraid of you."

"When I see a wrong done, my temper prompts me to act." Jonathan wasn't certain he wanted to pursue this topic of conversation.

"How is it you haven't joined the King's forces where so obviously the rebels are engaging in the great wrong of treason? Nay, I see you more as a man of fixed principles than of tempers."

"I have friends on both sides, and I have a fixed principle against trying to kill men I like." Jonathan reflected that this would have been true had not the death of Amelia cast him firmly on the side of the rebels.

Elizabeth stared at him while she considered this sentiment. Jonathan wasn't sure of her verdict until she rewarded him with one of her rare smiles and handed him the empty cup. "Thank you very much, Mr. Asher, for the dish of coffee. I believe the people who warned me about the vice of coffee were mistaken, to be sure."

A week later on a similar morning while talking to his brother and Nancy at the entrance to their shop, Jonathan noticed Elizabeth appearing three times at her door, pointedly not glancing across the street.

"I wonder who she is waiting for," Nancy commented, handing him a cup of coffee.

He took the cup and a small bag of coffee powder and walked across the street. He rapped on the door. He could hear Miss Elizabeth inside hesitating, and it was borne in on him that she wasn't used to this kind of attention. When she appeared, he could see that she had taken care with her appearance. She had a darkish complexion of what was called black Irish, round eyes that were an autumn brown, and an open face like Amelia's where her feelings had no place to hide. A nervous twitch tugged at the corner of her mouth.

"Coffee, Miss Elizabeth?" Jonathan asked.

She blushed as she took the cup. "Thank you, Mr. Asher. I think I am becoming indebted to you for this vice."

"Small vices are like the smallpox inoculation," Jonathan said, watching her features relax as she raised the mug to her lips. "A little bit of illness prevents a murderous disease; a small vice prevents larger vices."

"And what larger vices are you thinking might be tempting me?" She asked in not the friendliest of tones.

Jonathan realized that maybe his attempt at wit had gone awry. "The great vice of hating the morning our Lord hath made."

"I do happen to have fresh rolls from the Palatine baker down the street, so I do not think I will dislike this morning altogether," she said, a hint of conspiracy and merriment sparkling in her eyes.

The afternoons were less endurable. His real work began midafternoon after catching up on his sleep and visiting Emma and Daniel. It was then Jonathan visited Provost Cunningham and collected food meant for the starving Continental prisoners. He did not need the money from selling the foodstuffs that should have gone into the mouths of the starving men, however, Colonel Hamilton decided that Jonathan could provide useful information for the Deputy Continental Commissary of Prisoners John Pintard who was barred from entering the prisons of the Provost House or the Sugar House. Jonathan reported on the state of the crowding of the cells: one quarter, one half, three quarters, full, overfull, how diseased the prisoners seemed, how much Cunningham was stealing from them.

On a recent visit to pick up foodstuffs, Cunningham challenged Jonathan: "I was told to amend my behavior by that fool Pintard. I asked what behavior I needed to amend. He accused me of dumping the porridge meant for the prisoners on the stone floor and forcing them to lick it up. Now you saw me accidentally spill a bucket. You may have misinterpreted what occurred."

"I saw an accident as you said." Jonathan agreed with everything Cunningham said except for the price he would pay for the merchandise.

"How did Pintard get the idea it wasn't?" Richmond, a large dark presence, shifted in his chair. This seemed like a threat.

"I don't know how he would get that idea."

"I suspect you told him." The provost marshal put on his glasses and glared at him. This was hypocrisy. Provost Marshal Cunningham boasted frequently of his cruel treatment of prisoners.

"I doubt it came from my lips. 'Tis possible I may have mentioned the spillage in passing at a tavern, and it eventually got around to Pintard, but I found nothing unusual in a bucket spilling, so likely didn't pass it on. Others must have also observed the spillage and come up with that interpretation."

Cunningham's voice rose. "In the future, I don't want the way I run this place to depend on whether you're in your cups or not."

"Like the captain of a ship you are the absolute master here," Jonathan commented blandly. A false conceit of Cunningham was that he had absolute power over the conditions of the prisoners like a captain had over the welfare of his sailors.

"Don't forget the benefits you have acquired in our enterprise." Another conceit of the provost was that in selling the starving prisoners' food he was dispensing patronage.

"I thank you for the opportunity," Jonathan said.

"I do not detect gratitude in your voice. I feel you lack interest in our enterprise. Is it that you now have a more profitable venture? I do not mind a man making what he can out of this damn war. No, not at all. Just don't get in the way of my advancement."

So, starving prisoners is the tool of your advancement, Jonathan thought.

There was a long pause before Cunningham asked: "Did you ever find that French-speaking fellow I owe a debt to? I believe he was in your line of work."

This sought-after individual was Jonathan himself who, disguised as a French-speaking bully boy for hire, had accosted Cunningham and forced him to release a young French aristocrat he was secretly holding as a hostage. Jonathan responded, "No, I haven't."

"Not a clue?" An eyebrow raised. "The wines you sell come from France."

Jonathan shrugged. "That is the product most in demand so that is what I stock."

"And who brings you the merchandise?"

"You understand the need for discretion regarding my sources, but I assure you he is not the fellow you're looking for."

"I do understand better than you think. I have imprisoned at least twenty-five smugglers here over the last several years. All had a similar need for discretion. Unfortunately, it did not serve them well."

"Your prisoners were smuggling merchandise out of New York for the benefit of the rebels, not smuggling in for the benefit of those fighting for the King as I am doing. Don't interrogate me about how I know for what happens here isn't very secret."

"Richmond," Cunningham pointed to the glowering presence in the corner, "warned me off arresting you. He said you work with a dangerous man. I want you to know I fear nobody, and if the time comes to welcome you as a guest here, then I will gladly. In the meantime, don't bruit about your misinterpretation of the conditions here."

The dangerous man could only be his business partner, former slave, and former valet, Gabriel.

"Understood," Jonathan confirmed.

CHAPTER 3

"To what do I owe the honor of your presence, Mr. Blanchard?" Jonathan asked, rising from his desk.

Although as a rule, Castor would not pay a visit to anyone below the rank of colonel, Jonathan wasn't surprised when the commissary blotted the doorway of the office in his warehouse. The coolness that had always existed between them had turned frigid on account of Castor's dissatisfaction with his percentage of the wine trade. The commissary was dressed in battle gear, that is what he wore at the gambling tables—powdered and perfumed, his stockings, breeches, waistcoat, and frock coat requiring an acre of the finest cloths of reds, blues, and emeralds, setting him off like a fat jewel.

Castor eyed a chair, apparently debating whether it could sustain his weight. Concluding that it could, he squeezed his twenty stones through the doorway and settled himself down. The commissary, as was his wont, let the question dangle for a moment before asking. "Is anybody else present, Mr. Asher?"

"No, we are quite private," Jonathan assured him.

Castor nodded, moving his nub of a chin above the thick necklaces of fat. "That is good, Mr. Asher, for my business with you is of a private nature."

"I am listening, sir," Jonathan replied, his pulse quickening.

Castor grumbled and harrumphed, then continued, "As you are aware I tried to discover the reason why a clever merchant like you undertakes dangerous and unprofitable enterprises. 'Tis prudent to expect the worst from my fellow man. That way I avoid disillusions in life. Yet you, Mr. Asher, have reminded me that perhaps I'm not cynical enough."

"Indeed? Pray, go on, sir," Jonathan said wondering what gambit the commissary had in mind.

"Do not think I make a claim to moral superiority," Castor went on, settling into the same posture he used at the gaming tables. His great bulk was immobile as a granite boulder, his small eyes active. "I just maintain that such a claim is spurious in the majority of men. The only truly good man in my acquaintance is my brother, Pollux, and in him, you can see how cringing, craven, and repulsive goodness is."

"I never considered myself better or worse than the run-of-the-mill of my fellows so how has my wickedness exceeded your expectations?" Jonathan asked, adding a mocking undertone to the words.

Castor dangled another long pause, then said, "You are fortunate in my possessing a tolerant disposition when it comes to the failings of others. An honest man would see you hanged by your neck. But what would I gain by that? A commendation for my loyalty to the Crown? Liberty, loyalty, honor are just fine words used to hide the true passions we don't want to admit to ourselves. As you know I asked myself the question why you insisted on traveling to Brunswick and on making that unnecessary journey transporting the panniers of wine to Philadelphia. As a rule, when I have a question, I don't stop inquiring until 'tis answered."

Castor stopped and let a full minute pass before picking up his thread: "I am ignorant of the reason you killed Captain Hogwood. Obviously, from the length you went to pursue him, 'twas a personal grudge. Not a debt from a gaming table because, regrettably, you don't game. No, maybe he seduced a lady that interested you or who was a relation like a sister? Or he cheated you in a large transaction? Unlike me, you hide your unforgiving nature. Whatever it was, his murder was a calculated act that necessitated planning and travel, not a mere outburst of passion."

At the mention of the murder of Hogwood, Jonathan felt a jolt of panic, which he quickly attempted to cover with an expression of astonished innocence as he had done many times before when interrogated by customs officials.

Castor spent a minute wheezing to catch his breath. "In my opinion, 'tis not politic to murder enemies. I always found it more advantageous to destroy them by slowly sucking the marrow out of their bones, perhaps better said salvaging what I can from a ruined life as one will salvage all items of value from a wrecked ship. Your motivations don't interest me. I only want my discretion in your service rewarded. A thousand pounds is adequate—I estimate such a sum is not so great a burden with your present good fortune—and you can pay in weekly install-ments of a hundred pounds."

Castor's real intent, of course, was to take over entirely the business of selling Rodrigo's wine. Jonathan had observed Castor at the gaming table bluffing dukes and generals with ease. Castor could flush admissions out of his opponents like a dog flushes birds out of hiding, often frightening them by the tactic of assuming he knew more than he did. After observing a sea captain's red fingertips, he might ask, "What is the value of the cinnabar that you stowed with your ballast?"

Was this a bluff? Resisting the urge to wipe his sweaty palms on his breeches, Jonathan tried to reason it through: *There were no witnesses who saw us together other than Hector. If I had been followed, the shadower would have known why I had killed Hogwood, therefore Castor would have made that part of his threat.* The trap lay in questioning Castor about his sources or too quickly and vehemently protest-ing that another man had already hanged for the crime, which would create the danger of an argument where he might let slip a detail of the murder that would condemn him. The commissary had boasted once that he could find out more about a man by the questions he asked than the answers he gave.

"I never murdered any captain or for that matter any person, and if I recall correctly, while I was in Philadel-phia, a man was already hanged for murdering a captain," Jonathan replied, deciding to keep to statements, not ques-tions, and refraining from touching his nose. Danton had told him a liar always touches his nose. Castor would be aware of that giveaway and, at this moment, was observing him keenly with his small cold gaming-table eyes.

The great bulk of the commissary in the chair seemed to congeal into something even harder than a boulder of granite. "A boy came across you and Captain Hogwood. The lad unfortunately died, although not before passing on the information to his mother that the murderer of Hogwood had a broken tooth you could see when he smiled."

"Broken tooth or no; you cannot be referring to an incident I was involved in." Jonathan's thoughts raced trying to figure out what Castor was up to by ignoring his brother had confessed and died for the murder. As for the broken tooth, he didn't hear Hector discuss that with his mother so it could be a ploy by Castor to create the appearance of evidence.

"You left Philadelphia in the company of Hogwood," Castor stated. "You attacked Hogwood and cut off his arm with the tomahawk you customarily carry. You returned to the city four days later."

"Again, Mr. Blanchard, you are ignoring that a man already confessed," Jonathan said, blessing and grieving his brother in his thoughts. "I have no earthly reason to kill a captain in the British army." Jonathan challenged Castor to a staring contest, which he lost.

"Lieutenant Samuel Brave was the man hanged. A courageous militia officer from all accounts. I had Curston search out his grave and dig him up. Curston said there was a strong resemblance between you and him, but he couldn't be sure unless he killed you and dug you up two months afterward."

"He confessed. I did not confess for I did not commit the crime."

"He confessed to save your life, which leads me to believe he must have been your brother."

"My brother is an optician on Jacob Street. If you need a fine pair of eyeglasses, he would be happy to oblige. You see, Mr. Blanchard, this is all farfetched. Pollux would not give up his life to shield you."

"I won't argue what is already established: you are the murderer of Captain Hogwood. Your reasons don't matter." Castor smiled slyly. "Perhaps this… Perhaps that… The question is how much for my discretion."

Jonathan kept telling himself: *This is all supposition. He is bluffing. I can't be condemned for a murder another man confessed to. I can't. Hector is dead so he couldn't have identified me by my broken tooth.*

Still, Castor, the master gamer, maintained a disconcerting air of absolute certainty.

"Is there anybody else in Philadelphia you believe I may have murdered?" Jonathan inquired.

"You were stalking Captain Hogwood. You twice visited Brunswick where he was stationed. Carting your coffee and my sauerkraut forty miles to Brunswick wasn't a profitable venture, yet you did it. You understand when a man does something that seems against his interest, I find out why."

"Carting your goods to out-of-the-way places is exactly the reason why I give you a better return than you can get for yourself," Jonathan argued.

"You don't make money off me," Castor retorted. "You do, however, take advantage of the fact that your wagons cannot be requisitioned. That is one of your games. Importing black skin into New York with your African partner is another, which puts you beneath the ordinary scoundrel."

"But murdering British captains is not, Mr. Blanchard. 'Twould be against my interest, as you say." Jonathan suppressed a smile when Castor didn't contradict him. The commissary realized his bluff was crumbling. All he had was a handful of facts—Jonathan was in Brunswick, then Philadelphia when Hogwood was murdered, the boy's last words about the captain's murderer being a New York merchant coming back to life—and the uncanny ability to weigh the odds that an individual can satisfy the criteria and not be the murderer of Hogwood. He likely made up the fact that Hector had identified him by the broken tooth. Thus, Jonathan reminded himself, the commissary was guessing, and the boy was dead so nothing could be verified.

"'Tis a pity I have to turn you in and forgo our commercial relationship." Pity was the sentiment Castor least familiar with.

"'Tis," Jonathan agreed, wondering if Castor had another card to play. "You made quite a profit off of the last pannier of champagne I sold you."

"Or I could not mention it. In that way, you will not be forced into a trial." Castor folded his arms which were approximately the thickness of a grenadier's thighs.

"The trial already took place," Jonathan said. "In any event, I have enough trust in British justice to not fear a trial for a crime that somebody else confessed to and was hanged for committing. And I do not think you will want to start proceedings which will do you no credit. You have been over exercising your imagination in this affair, Mr. Blanchard."

"I never over exercise my imagination," Castor replied coldly.

Jonathan shook his head in disbelief, although Castor was correctly describing himself. "Good day, Mr. Blanchard. You cannot possibly possess evidence that I committed a crime which I didn't commit, and another man hanged for."

"Well, you see that's the thing, Mr. Asher," Castor said, showing every indication of permanence in the chair. "Because he was the only witness against you, you made the mistake of pursuing the boy all the way to the rebel camp where his mother was working. I imagine you planned to kill the boy when the opportunity arose. Why else would you be hiding on the outskirts of the rebel camp where they would welcome the murderer of a British captain?"

"Why would the boy condemn me if he were part of the rebel camp?"

Castor sprung his trap. "You should have asked me, Mr. Asher, how could I be certain he was the same boy as the one in Philadelphia. You didn't for you knew he was."

Jonathan fought back. "That signifies nothing. Your witness is dead unless there are two boys, which proves your accusation baseless."

Unfazed, Castor continued: "The boy pointed you out to his mother. She caught sight of you. Would you like her to have a closer acquaintance with you?"

"I don't see what that will serve," Jonathan said. "But

do what you please." He believed he had been too far away to be recognized, then he recalled that Benedict Arnold had hailed him.

Castor slowly smiled, enjoying the trap he had set. "Out of consideration for her feelings, I wanted to keep her out of this. Your intransigence forced my hand."

Castor left. Jonathan attempted to marshal arguments against secondhand testimony in murder trials. Unfortunately, the anticipation and anxiety Castor created had begun to fuddle his reasoning.

A minute later, the laundress walked into the office— stouter and grayer than he remembered—followed by Castor. She approached Jonathan, and walked slowly around him, examining him closely.

"I can't say he were the man I seen," she announced when she finished, her voice cracking.

"When you observed him entering my warehouse, you swore he was, Mrs. Ormond." Castor angrily gripped her arm. "Smile for her, Mr. Asher, and show your broken tooth."

Jonathan shook his head. "Only if you smile for her also and show your broken tooth. We can line up all New York merchants and order them to smile. I wager half have broken teeth."

She shook her arm free and faced Castor. "I can't say with certainty the gentleman is or isn't. Nay, I am not sacrificing a stranger just because I am wanting to avenge Hector's death."

"And if I proved to you he had specifically gone to Philadelphia to hunt Captain Hogwood?" Castor flushed angrily and began to pant heavily. "Nor was he present in this city when your son met his end."

The laundress was not intimidated. "I might tend to say 'twould be more likely. Not with certainty, sir. Nay, I am not saying even that. Now that I view him close, this man has the face of a good soul. The devil I seen possessed the face of death and evil. Hector was right. He and I was seeing a ghost."

"Ghosts only exist in fevered imaginations. Faces are faces, not evil or good. You claimed you'd know him anywhere, madam. Now you say you doubt," Castor pursued with a hard cold voice.

Mrs. Ormand heaved a sigh ending in a small cry of grief. "I'd know him by feeling my blood curdle on seeing the devil, I'm sure. You are the one making my blood curdle, not this gentleman, sir."

"Then view Mr. Asher from a distance like you did at the warehouse yesterday so you can ascertain again the condition of your blood," Castor commented sarcastically.

"No matter two rods or fifty. I got eyes sharp as a hawk's. As I said I know'd him anywhere. This man is not the devil I seen," she stubbornly insisted.

"I'm sorry your son died so unfortunately," Jonathan said.

"He's in a better place." Hector's mother sighed again. "I miss him for he were the eldest, and he were the one who kept me company after his father died. I miss him terribly. You know what 'tis like for a dear one to die," She addressed Jonathan. "I seen the grief in your eyes when I talk about my grief. He," She indicated Castor, "got the face of a man who never loved so could've never lost a dear one."

"You pretend to know me, madam, yet you know not the murderer of your son who sits in front of you!" Castor wheezed.

Hector's mother stood her ground. "Who killed my Hector? 'Twas the bugger at the edge of the wood who stood staring at him, to be sure. 'Twas the rebel Washington. 'Twas the King. 'Twas the scoundrelly Congress. 'Twas the Parliament. 'Twas his father who got himself killed in his loyalist regiment by the first bullet in the first battle he ever been in. 'Twas me who thought to avenge my husband's death on the whole goddamn Continental Army, and 'twas the man who gave me the means. Where does it end, sir? This person is a stranger. He shows the face of a soul who also suffered loss in this damn war, not the face of the devil. Isn't that true, sir?"

"Yes," Jonathan affirmed, aware that Castor had controlled his color and wheezing and now regarded him with renewed interest.

"So, you ask me to condemn him for what? To satisfy a personal vendetta. I am not taking your money, Mr. Blanchard," the laundress said.

"What was the name Mr. Benedict Arnold called out?" Castor asked.

"Expect me to remember clearly anything else that day? All I saw, heard, smelled was Hector's body in my arms. There were nothing else in the world."

"I have reports that it was Jonathan the name Arnold called out. His name is Jonathan."

"You're trying to make me remember what I don't remember."

"I say he was the man who your son saw with Captain Hogwood before he was murdered," Castor restated in a deadened voice.

"So, you say, but you wasn't there." The laundress stood nose to nose with Castor. "Truth be, I were close enough to feel him in my belly yet were too far away to see the devil clearly. If this gentleman here were the one at the edge of the wood, I am certain I'd feel his presence roiling my innards. But I don't. No matter what, I won't condemn him because you believe he were the man I seen."

"Mrs. Ormand, I take unkindly to being misled," Castor said in a sweetly threatening voice.

"Nay, you're the one misleading." She let out a hysterical laugh. "And even if you're thinking of punishing me—what can you do? You know my grief. You know my poverty. Good day to you, sir."

After she had left, Castor turned to Jonathan and said, "Poor woman. She believes she has nothing to lose so she makes a fool of me, yet she has three other children."

"If I…" Jonathan began.

"If you what, Mr. Asher? Am I about to hear a threat from your lips? Do not, Mr. Asher. You have no power over her circumstances. Still, I must say, bravo, Mr. Asher. You did murder the captain, and you did not lose your nerve. You made a study of me. Bravo. Bravo. I am enjoying this game immensely, and I will be sad when it ends. But 'twill end, I promise you. You need to win with the cards you hold every time; I only need to win once. The thing now is to find the nature of the disagreement between you and Captain Hogwood. I believe when I do you will hang."

After Castor left, Jonathan briefly lost his composure. His hands became shaky. His thoughts scrambled for an escape from his predicament—Castor would lay as many traps as was necessary to undo him. He must leave. He must. As he calmed, Jonathan considered the cost of such a move. He could make excuses to his brother and sister-in-law and would likely see them again after the war, but abandoning Emma and Daniel and Miss Elizabeth seemed to him an irrevocable betrayal. A half-hour later, when Jonathan had completely regained control of himself, he realized that like Castor but to a lesser degree he enjoyed the game.

CHAPTER 4

JONATHAN DID NOT recognize at first the woman trudging along the muddy Post Road five miles south of Kingsbridge. He was on his way to make a delivery to the Hessian camp that guarded the northern approach into Manhattan. He was risking traveling alone because some Jaegers from Long Island had been transferred there and he hoped Captain Hoffman was among them. Jonathan could not set foot on Long Island without Meredith James becoming aware, which made a secret operation there unfeasible. It was within the realm of possibility that James at the behest of Commissary Castor would murder him. Millicent Dalton, also alone, a woman, and on foot, was running an even greater risk.

When she stepped out of the way to let him pass, he stopped the wagon. "It seems we are heading in the same direction, Mrs. Dalton. If you would be so kind as to do me the favor of keeping me company."

Mrs. Dalton raised her sweat-streaked face, showing hostile moss-green eyes. She did not make her usual effort to appear cheerful. "I assure you, Mr. Asher, you want not to take me where I'm going."

"I know of no place south of Harlem River that would inconvenience me," he replied, willing to force the issue. She had no protection aside from the goodwill of those whom she encountered along the way, and he needed a distraction from his thoughts dark with the forebodings of Castor's next move.

Millicent Dalton made an effort to straighten herself. "I'm going to the battlefield of Fort Washington. My brother Thomas is buried in the cemetery nearby. I need somebody to talk to, and he was always the brother who listened to me."

"That lies along my route," Jonathan said, refraining from commenting on the oddness of the errand. "And I'm not about to abandon Elizabeth's dearest friend to the dangers of traversing these roads alone."

Mrs. Dalton gave a small shrug, managed a weary smile, and climbed into the wagon. "Well, this compromises my ladyhood no more than the pitiful dusty figure I'm showing to the world presently. I thank you, Mr. Asher, and my complexion thanks you for the brisk wind is making me as burnt as a Mohawk, and my dress thanks you for surely 'twould become tatters between hither and yon, and my feet who are not experienced wayfarers give thanks to you also." Looking at the sacks of flour, casks of sauerkraut, dozen bottles of Madeira, and a pannier of burgundy, she said, "I thought you only traded in coffee and Madeira, not foodstuffs the starving poor folk lack."

"Occasionally foodstuffs come my way," Jonathan

replied. "I don't actively search them out, and they are only a small portion of what I sell."

"Then you're only responsible for a few souls starving," Millicent shot back.

Jonathan clenched his teeth to avoid an unpolitic reply. The fact that she hadn't hired a conveyance signified that, like so many others in wartime, Mrs. Dalton and her husband were slowly drifting towards destitution.

Millicent. Dalton heaved a sigh. "I apologize, Mr. Asher, for repaying your kind act in such a peevish manner. You caught me in the foulest of moods. The Spencers were so kind to give me Saturday midday to Sunday evening off so I could be with my husband, and then my husband's parents sent a message demanding he visit his ill mother. And how I hate this war. Hate it! Hate it! I cannot even take sides. This brother, Thomas, he died defending Fort Washington. He had nineteen bayonet wounds in him. I know because I buried his body. Nineteen! I came here when I learned about the siege. I thought I might stop it, stop something, at least stop Thomas from being killed. I arrived too late. A comrade, a fellow Continental stripped naked like the other prisoners, said Thomas had surrendered. The Hessians were not satisfied with those they had killed—they wanted the completest revenge for their dead, and so they bayoneted him nineteen times. I should hate them and the king who hired them and pray for Washington's victory, you not think?" Jonathan's companion again gave a dismayed sigh.

"But I have a brother who is a loyalist—Trevor—an honest and good man by the account of all who ever had dealings with him. He was born so sober that we used to tease him as a boy by calling him the Presbyterian. He worked from first light to the hours after dusk when most boys his age were climbing trees and skipping stones in ponds. From his boyhood of blisters and calluses, Trevor saved enough to purchase a small farm. He lives on Long Island with a wife and two daughters. When the Sons of Liberty got wind of his leanings, they dragged him from his house, from his sobbing wife and children. and tarred and feathered him. It took him four months to recover. Do you know what it is to peel tar from live skin?

"When I saw what they done to Trevor, I went to the tavern where the Sons of Liberty were celebrating their brave victory over my brother. As soon as I entered, I picked a plate off the nearest table and hurled it at the leader of the Sons, a jolly, cruel, pudding-bellied man. I went towards him, picking up every trencher, plate, and cup, and bowl, and goblet, and tankard that I could lay my hands on, even from those who were still eating, and threw them at his fat face. The brave Sons subdued me and carried me outside.

"I thought they were going to tar and feather me and began to despair. Then Terence, my husband—he was not that then—who had seen the fracas plunged in, fists flying. Fortunately, his friends rallied to his cause. They held the field, which was me, and the damn Sons fled. There was a small runlet of water where the Sons had dropped me, so I call the incident the battle of Millicent Creek. Thank God, Terence believes a god-fearing man can be neither Whig nor Tory."

"Any decent man detests war," Jonathan said automatically while trying to square her story with the knowledge of her familiarity with a brothel.

Mrs. Dalton eyed him curiously. "I have a third brother who is in the Continental Army. In his last letter, David said he had become a lieutenant and that he would avenge Thomas and that he'd gladly die if he could do so honorably before the eyes of General Washington. So, when I see a man like you who fattens himself with profits from the war, sometimes I can't hold back the venom I feel in my heart and the bile rising from the pit of my stomach."

Jonathan sympathized, but a spy necessarily must explain himself with a lie. "I can choose a side and fight, choose no side and not dirty my hands in this business and starve, or I can do the only thing I know how to do and engage in commerce and not starve."

"I'm not sure I'd act differently in your stead, yet..." Mrs. Dalton managed a weak smile. "Never mind. For some reason, I feel I can speak the part of my mind to you which I daren't to others, so you, Mr. Asher, are the unlucky recipient of my opinions—even the unflattering ones about you."

Jonathan laughed. "I imagine your valiant husband receives his share of your opinions."

Mrs. Dalton allowed herself a low chuckle. "Mr. Dalton is valiant without a doubt. You might imagine I was somewhat bruised, battered, and wet after the fracas with the Sons. Terence took me home in his coach. I thought that was that, but the next day he found out where I worked and visited me while I scrubbed the floor. I thought he was after what a lot of men of the upper station are after with a girl who scrubs floors. I did not realize Terence wouldn't know how to play with a lady's affections. He is upright and honest and made his intentions known by proposing marriage to me the next week. Because I try to be genteel in speech, he believed I was a daughter of a family of high connections fallen on hardship, not a daughter of plain laboring folk. Even when he saw my hands…" She peeled off one glove blushing as if she were unbuttoning her bodice, showing the hand of a maid—reddish, strong, not unbeautiful, but not at all the hand of a lady.

"Did I tell you he is also kind? His parents did not approve of me, at first. No girl from my station would be good enough for their Terence." She sighed. "Good enough is not what you are, but what you do, and they will realize that soon. They are softening and in time, I'm sure I will be loved like a daughter. We married within the month—that was almost two years ago." Mrs. Dalton closed her eyes as if she were trying to remember.

The thought occurred to Jonathan: *If her husband's parents had known about her connection to a brothel, they would have gone further than mere disapproval.*

They drove on in silence until they arrived at a cemetery just off the Post Road at the foot of a hill. Millicent alighted from the wagon and sat by a grave with a warped wooden marker. She talked and paused as if hearing answers.

After a quarter-hour of conversing with her dead brother, Mrs. Dalton returned. "I thank you for your patience and your kindness, Mr. Asher. I have a particular problem. I asked Thomas what to do. Unfortunately, he preferred not to give an opinion." She looked back at the graveyard. "I hear you and Elizabeth share a morning dish of coffee. I thank you for protecting her. I also asked Thomas whether it was the right thing to tell you about her."

"I would like to believe she takes as much pleasure in my company as I do in hers, although her unique combination of lioness and mouse frequently bemuses me," Jonathan said dryly. "I hope your brother approves."

"Don't raise your eyebrows at me, Mr. Asher, I'm not mad," Millicent protested, laughing. "Thomas and I were very dear to each other. He hides in my head until I come here, then I hear him speak. I know that 'tis my own thoughts speaking, but we were so close that I'm certain I get most of what he would say right."

"Then he would approve of my coffee with Elizabeth?" Jonathan asked.

"He would certainly disapprove of my meddling. I did encourage you, Mr. Asher, and I hope I did the best thing for my dear friend. Elizabeth always sneaks your name into our conversation each time I visit her. She deserves the best man in the world. Believe me, a gentler heart exists not despite the Irish she displays in her temper. I don't want to see her harmed in any way, and I can't decide whether…" Her voice trailed off.

"Assuredly, I am not the best man in the world. Nor the worst. I do try to be better for her," Jonathan said.

"Can anybody expect more? We always want perfect matches for our imperfect selves and friends." Millicent frowned. "Thomas has put me out of humor. Occasionally, he does."

"Well, the next time you converse with your brother

about me, bring me along so I can make my case," Jonathan said and found himself smiling at her pretty, freckled face. "I hear there is a new peace initiative giving the rebels everything they wanted in the first place. Perhaps we can put this war behind us."

This news put his passenger into a better humor. She talked about her life as a maid. After working at the millinery, she went into training to be a lady's maid, and starting when the Spencers' daughter was fourteen, she became the child's bosom friend and confidante. That ended three years later when, inexplicably, the mistress took a dislike to her, and one day Millicent found herself chopping onions in the scullery, and then in the laundry, up to her elbows in lye, washing rags. After a year, the mistress relented, and she became an all-work maid in which position she stayed until the daughter married and insisted Millicent become the nursemaid to her children. "I tell Mr. Dalton that he needn't be afraid of the household economy. I believe I could run the whole household myself. He says that he married a lady, not a servant, and I mustn't think like that."

"He desires the best for you," Jonathan said.

"I suppose so." Millicent nodded as if she were half persuaded. She then explained that the children of the older daughter were jealous and also wanted her as a nursemaid and since they were living now under the same roof, she had six charges. For the next hours, Millicent imitated their voices and mimed their antics, confirming Jonathan's opinion that she possessed the aptitude for absorbing the mannerisms and language of those around her, young and old, low station and high. Jonathan found himself laughing.

He returned the favor by making Mrs. Dalton laugh telling stories about his French mother, Madame Corinne as she liked to be called. How she faced down a bear who had invaded the post with a ladle, a pot, and a stream of French invectives until the animal could no longer endure the insults and fled, or how she had kept his sister Andréa from falling into a fatal sleep after eating a poisonous plant by teaching her to sing a naughty French song of how a sailor lost his pants, and how Madame Corinne only spanked him once and cried more than he did.

At one point, Mrs. Dalton said, "Children are my favorite people because I can be myself with them. With the Spencers I must put on the face of a maid. Yes, madam. No, madam. You are so much my superior madam that 'tis enough to bask in the aura of your greatness. With my husband and his family, I must pretend to all the refinements of a lady like Lady Spencer. Please, can you not see I am pretty like a lady? I speak nice like a lady. I will not lift a finger to lift my plate even though two years ago I scrubbed a hundred such plates a day. With my brother, the Tory, I must frown when he mentions the rebels, else he thinks I'm on the side of my other brothers. With the soldiers who leer at me, I must pretend not to notice. With my parents, I must say my life is wonderful, and soon Mr. Dalton is going to make us rich. Children speak their hearts, and I can speak mine. I don't believe Elizabeth and I would have ever become friends had I not met her when she was still a child."

"And with me?"

"You, Mr. Asher? How shall I say it? You are a man who hides his thoughts. I had a hard time imagining you having a mother, not to speak of such an entertaining mother as Madame Corinne. And you know this is the first time I seen you smile and laugh, although I'm sure you're not sparing of your smiles with Elizabeth. I fear in times of war nobody can be themselves. Yet you have the means. I dare say you have wealth. No one is going to show you the door and refuse to give you references. You make Elizabeth happy. If she makes you happy, I must end my speculation there."

"You seem very much yourself in my company as you said."

"You don't have any expectation of me to be this or that, so I'm myself. How am I in your opinion when I'm myself?"

"Entertaining. Maybe the children, Elizabeth, and I get the best of you."

"I hope Mr. Dalton does. And there are times when he would not disagree."

Millicent stayed with him until he had delivered the wine, flour, and sauerkraut to a Hessian major who paid for the rations for his men out of his pocket. No Captain Hoffman. The Jaeger's raids into Connecticut had given him minor fame and a recognizable name. Millicent accompanied Jonathan back to the city. He began to understand why her husband went against his family's wishes and married the maid. Mrs. Dalton was inventive and entertaining as well as becoming. And she had an unsettling penetration into the character of others.

When they started trundling along Broadway in the late afternoon, they came upon four guards marching eight prisoners down the crowded street—six in rags, two entirely naked. One of the guards was flogging those lagging with a ramrod. Joining the children and vagrants hurling rocks, clods of dirt, and insults were several well-dressed citizens.

"I can't bear this," Mrs. Dalton whispered.

"Let me assist you," Jonathan called out to the guards. "'Tis dirty business guarding vile rebels. My wagon is empty. You can all fit in and save your sore feet the last mile."

While three of the guards herded the prisoners onto the cart, the fourth, a very irregularly dressed fellow, turned toward them. Jonathan recognized the black scowling face of Richmond, Cunningham's servant and protector.

"Provost be in desperate way to see you, suh," Richmond said. "He jus' received big shipment of hard biscuit 'n less you buys it, he might be having to feed it to de rebel prisoners."

"I make my way home from here, Mr. Asher," Mrs. Dalton said, eyes now moss on steel, and her face, which a moment before had been full of smiles, ashen. She slipped down and ran off.

Two grinning guards took her place. "To the sugar house," one said.

Seeing Mrs. Dalton flee in horror brought home to Jonathan how he despised himself for engaging in this business of starving the Continental prisoners. He decided to cut ties with Castor and Cunningham, spying and profit be damned.

Although Jonathan yearned to be out of the range of the commissary's small piggish eyes that seemed to be perpetually calculating how to have him hanged, on further consideration, he realized he could not escape the devil just yet. He might persuade another officer or even Meredith James to sign the papers exempting him from requisition for a dozen bottles of claret. Washington not knowing how many barrels of pickles Lord Cornwallis had ordered or that a certain company of grenadiers in Queens had exchanged scenery with a company of light infantry in Harlem would win or lose the war. Yet, unless he had a reason to appear at the warehouse, he would have to cease his visits to Emma and Daniel. Jonathan climbed the ladder to their shelter on the roof, the casing of a tread-wheel crane, almost daily. Discovering the children could read, he added books to his gifts and later even paper and ink although such materials were in high demand. He was wondering whether one of the four abandoned kittens discovered by Elizabeth in her basement might provide them with a welcomed addition to their company.

Although Jonathan felt awkward talking to Emma and Daniel, he was like Mrs. Dalton in that he could be himself with them. The world of the children was far removed from the world of intelligencers and war profiteers, not to mention an avenger of the murder of an innocent girl. To abandon them would be to betray their innocence even more than their experiences had done already. Daniel explained in whispers so as not to upset Emma that their father had been a scrivener and their mother supplemented their income by baking rolls and loaves of bread. When the fire spread, their mother was trapped inside the house. Their father had rushed back to rescue her. He emerged with her in his arms, both on fire. Emma screamed for several long hours, then stopped speaking altogether.

Yet, they were still children. Jonathan occasionally engaged in the daydream of transporting the children to his mother, Madame Corinne. She would utter a Gallic imprecation about yet another imposition from heaven on her yielding nature and then take them into her heart unreservedly.

CHAPTER 5

April 1779

Aware he was gambling his entire enterprise dunning the officer who sat at the desk in front of him, Jonathan said, "I apologize, Lord Harold, for insisting on payment for my merchandise. You must realize I can make no exceptions if I am to pay my suppliers and maintain my business." Jonathan tried to keep his voice firm but suppliant. Earlier he had tried to lighten the tone by mentioning his acquaintance with Lord Edgar who was Lord Harold's nephew. Lord Harold asked coldly whether he was collecting on a debt of his nephew, and from there on the tenor of the conversation declined.

Unfortunately, nobody on the island of Manhattan was in a good mood. Over the course of a long war, the naval victory of John Paul Jones' *Bon Homme Richard* over the *HMS Serapis* was a minor event. Yet, defeats like that were simply not supposed to happen to the British Navy, and that put everybody out of humor. Hopes of easy victory had been disappointed two years ago, and now doubts that there was to be a victory at all were beginning to fester.

Of all the British and colonial leeches, vultures, and wolves that had descended on hapless New York City in search of fortunes, Lord Harold whom Jonathan was addressing, assistant to the Quartermaster General, Sir William Dalrymple, had become the greatest profiteer by the simple expedient of requisitioning horses from any private citizen that got within reach of his tentacles, then requesting from His Majesty's government compensation for the poor sods who lost their horses, afterward keeping the proceeds for himself, and renting out the teams to the army, again being paid. The dispossessed owners, if they were teamsters or carters and therefore had no other means of livelihood, were often obligated to drive the wagons that had once belonged to them. He had sixty teams, each earning him two hundred pounds a year. He also owned many of the river transport vessels the army required thereby contracting himself and paying himself from the Crown's purse. If Lord Harold considered Jonathan unworthy of payment because of his middling station, it would set a precedent. Other officers might follow suit. Meekly creeping away would confirm that opinion.

Lord Harold frowned as he digested this challenge. His powdered wig and elegant manners didn't hide commonplace features—eyes the washed-out yellow of beeswax in a blunt face reminding Jonathan of a blind ox his family once owned. "I understood our transaction as more in line of a gratuity for our good services in rendering protection of your enterprise than a mere vulgar tradesman's swap of a pinch for a penny."

"The stuff is wine of a quality few can provide, Lord Harold, and if the war lasts much longer, less will be able to acquire," Jonathan insisted, ignoring Harold's blatant assertion that he intended to never pay. "I cannot buy if my purchasers do not pay. Your valet has put me off for three weeks and gave me to understand I would be fortunate if you paid me before the Second Coming of Christ. I clearly stated the terms of the sale, and I expect the person to abide by those terms."

"Are you such an audacious rapscallion, sir, as to imply that I do not keep my word?" The jowls reddened and the eyes darkened, portending violence and ruin.

"You didn't personally give your word, however, your valet did so in your name, colonel." Jonathan verbally walked the tightrope while mentally strangling the man.

Lord Harold heaved a bored sigh indicating that the interview was over. "I will instruct him to be more cautious in the future, especially in the manner of men he makes contracts with. Now, sir, 'tis only my great forbearance that has kept me from teaching you a lesson on the dangers of presuming beyond your station. I suggest you leave."

Jonathan was not surprised. "Since you left me no choice, Colonel Harold, then consider the wine as a gratuity just as you said—a one-time gratuity. You can apprise the valet and your household of that fact and look elsewhere for your purchase of fine wines."

"Private Elmore!" Lord Harold bellowed, summoning a guard to escort him out.

To Jonathan's surprise, instead of the burly private with a pockmarked face, a beautiful lady in her middle years swept into the room. Tall in a gray sack-back dress that matched her gray eyes, she possessed a self-assured grace that the assistant quartermaster entirely lacked. Smiling at the colonel, she asked, "Won't you introduce me to your visitor, Harold dear?"

Lord Harold snorted. "I don't remember the blaggard's name. He is the tradesmen who provided us with wine and now has the temerity to come to me directly, me, while I am doing the king's business arranging the transport of twelve thousand bottles of porter to Knyphausen's brigade of thirsty Hessians, and demand payment for a few dozen bottles of his blackstrap and the German piss he calls hock. He'll be very unfortunate indeed if I do remember his name."

The woman bestowed her graceful smile on Jonathan. "I am Lady Beatrice, Mister Blaggard, or shall I say, Mr. Asher. Are you the merchant who supplied the excellent champagne?"

"Yes, Lady Beatrice," Jonathan replied, inclining his head. "I'm surprised you are familiar with my name."

Her smile now hinted at a private joke. "'Tis my business to know who supplies my household as 'tis my husband's business to know who transports goods to this or that regiment. How did you come into possession of such fine champagne and claret? We are not presently on the friendliest terms with France."

"I have sources," Jonathan said.

"Sources?" Lady Beatrice raised her eyebrows. "The harbor is full of ships, some waiting months to unload. The docks are crawling with customs officers, and any shipment of your kind would be instantly bruited throughout the officers' billets, yet you have sources no one else seems to possess. Harold, if we don't pay this man, I'm afraid he won't supply us with his excellent champagne from his mysterious sources."

"The only way he can obtain his champagne is to fraternize with the enemy, a treasonable offense, and additionally, he is breaking the law by avoiding the tariffs," Lord Harold grumbled.

"Mr. Asher, although my husband won't be reconciled at the present, I'd be most obliged if you come into my parlor to discuss your business." Lady Beatrice inclined her head as if making a slight show of respect. Jonathan followed her down a hallway and entered a small room that appeared to have been dipped in damask and gilt.

Lady Beatrice seated herself at an ivory inlaid desk with a heavy ledger book on it, which was even more out of place in the room than Jonathan. After inviting him to sit, she said in a matter-of-fact voice, "I will pay for the champagne now, and I will require two dozen more bottles which I will pay for when I receive them. This is to establish trust between us, Mr. Asher. I expect twenty days of credit in the future. I will give you a list of the merchants who supply me. They will swear as to my promptitude in canceling my debts."

"I am most grateful, Lady Beatrice," Jonathan said, wondering at the apparition of this angel of mercy, who seemed concerned with his business.

Lady Beatrice regarded him thoughtfully. "How many officers of the king owe you?"

"Four or five," Jonathan replied.

"How many officers have you provided with your merchandise?" She asked.

"I haven't counted. Several score."

"And only four or five owe you, including my husband?" Lady Beatrice inquired, her wrinkled brow communicating skepticism. "How do you avoid being run through with a sword like that poor miller who tried to collect a debt from a captain?"

"I first learn who honors his debts to tradesmen and who doesn't," Jonathan explained, somewhat unnerved by her directness and her interest in his business. "Those that don't won't receive credit. When an officer decides to casually rest his hand on the hilt of his sword, I casually rest mine on my tomahawk. Our conversation usually ends amicably."

Lady Beatrice rubbed her chin much like a banker considering a loan. "Yet you sell to my husband who doesn't pay tradesmen on a matter of principle and Major John André who has a poor reputation with your sort. Does the major owe?"

The blond Major John André, who always polished his impeccable courtesy toward Jonathan with a sneer, would only pay on receiving new merchandise. Recently, when Jonathan had demanded payment, André went off on a rant in French to a fellow officer about how unscrupulous and scurrilous these local leeches were, believing Jonathan wouldn't understand. This leech could suck all he wanted but would not get a drop of blood from him, even though the amount was trivial. He possessed treble the requested payment in his billfold. Then André continued in English, giving Jonathan a trembling smile, "I am temporarily short of funds, Mr. Asher. Be so kind as to come back next week, won't you?"

Jonathan noticed the billfold on the desk. Picking it

up, Jonathan extracted the amount owed and laid it on the table. André's face flushed beet red. "I couldn't help noticing there were sufficient funds on hand." Calculating the loss, Jonathan continued, "Perhaps you have other pressing creditors. I am under the belief that you will pay because you are a gentleman, and if I am mistaken in you, you are under no obligation to reimburse me for my error in judgment." The next day, he received payment from André along with a very large order. Of course, inevitably, the major fell behind again.

Jonathan replied to Lady Beatrice: "Lord Harold would take it amiss if I refused him on reputation alone and might find ways to hinder my business. Major John André is perhaps the least diligent of my clients, but he seems to fill the function of majordomo for the entire officer corps, so I must allow him a margin of credit to keep on good terms with the rest."

Lady Beatrice lowered her voice. "You are misinformed if you believe André is on good terms with you because he is indebted to you. I heard you cast aspersions on his honor the other day, and gentlemen like André never forget or forgive such a slight. Other men of influence and rank are aware of how you use their names on their orders to intimidate the customs agents, yet you always press for prompt payment. They and the Commissary Blanchard and several more officers unable to purchase your fine merchandise have persuaded Major James to apprehend you on the arrival of the next shipment, throw you in the Sugar House Prison, and seize your inventory. The reason my husband treated you mildly is that he believes in a few days you will be either another body floating down the

North River or a poor soul on the prison ship *Jersey* fighting with rebel prisoners over scraps of raw pork."

A captain to whom he had refused credit had recently gibed that so long as they were occupying New York they should also occupy his warehouse and all the inventory in it. Recently, before leaving on one of his secret enterprises Gabriel had warned Jonathan about Major James. "He old catamount. Turn your back on him 'n he tear you limb from limb." At their last meeting, James was overly solicitous—a bad sign in a man who loves to fool other men.

"I am taking precautions," Jonathan replied to Lady Beatrice.

"And what could those possibly be against Major James and the entire British officer corps? Yet…" Lady Beatrice smiled slowly. "I am paying you because I believe you have a future, Mr. Asher."

"I'm glad that you think so, Lady Beatrice," Jonathan said, truly glad.

"You see," Lady Beatrice explained. "Men like Major André and his friends do not plan beyond their next fete, ball, or campaign. They would ruin a source of fine champagne out of envy, greed, or to satisfy their overly delicate sense of honor. A woman must plan much further ahead. I, fortunately for you, have a proposal if my husband, Lord Harold, agrees. Entertaining is a very costly affair, and unlike most officers, my husband came into the army quite poor. He possessed his courtesy title as a son of an impoverished baron, a second lieutenant's commission, and little else, so we had to turn whatever we could to our advantage. I aim to do that with you, Mr. Asher. How many warrant officers have you in your acquaintance?"

"I can't recall very many," Jonathan remembered Pollux pointing out a very old ensign who was a warrant officer as if he were the phoenix itself.

"The talented poor soldier of the inferior station must singlehandedly storm and take a redoubt or save a brigadier general's life afore he is able to leap the chasm from sergeant to ensign in his regiment and thereby becoming a warrant officer. Although warrant officers are a rare breed, you find a surprising number of them on the payroll. Most of them never existed except on the paymaster's lists. Their pay goes to fill out the expenses of gentlemen officers or provide a stipend for an officer's widow. Harold has several assisting him to cover expenses. I think perhaps we could do with one more. 'Twould not be amiss if you were to become a warrant officer and give an actual face to a name on the paymaster's list. You will not need much of a kit, and I'm sure Harold can dig up a uniform out of his stores, and just think you have none of that endless marching about, practicing maneuvers, and going into battle. Of course, we receive your stipend."

"And how will that help me out of my dilemma?" Jonathan asked, bemused.

"First of all, murdering a miller or any provincial daring to collect a debt doesn't raise an eyebrow. On the other hand, if an officer is murdered, even an officer born in the colonies, even a fictitious warrant officer, well then 'tis truly murder, so being a warrant officer can allow you to pursue your business unmolested, don't you see? In working for my husband, you also have the freedom to visit any regiment, acquaint yourself with the officers nearly as an equal, find out what they like to quaff, and supply them, bypassing the sutlers and other such merchants."

Lady Beatrice spent a minute studying Jonathan. "You won't quite pass as a gentleman; you don't possess the gentlemanly knack that one born to his station acquires of presenting himself; yet you're no more offensively rustic than many of the loyalists from better families. Furthermore, because you represent my husband, the assistant quartermaster, and the officers of a regiment will desire to be on the good side of the individual who is essential to their comforts, you will be able to collect your debts without brandishing your tomahawk."

"And who will have ownership of the wine I am selling?" Jonathan asked.

"You will store the wine in the cellar of our house—there are few safer places in New York. I mean the quality vintages. You may keep your hogsheads of rum, blackstrap, and whatever other wretched stuff our soldiers and sailors drink to numb their lives. We receive thirty percent of everything sold. If I decide to take from your stock, I pay you the going rate, and of course, you give me thirty percent back. In other words, you own the wine. and we possess it."

"And do I have a choice, Lady Beatrice?"

"To my way of thinking, you have a very easy choice, Mr. Asher."

"Yes. Death or a partnership with you."

"Good. You are clear on the alternatives." Lady Beatrice clapped her hands together. "The commission of ensign won't quite do so we'll arrange one of a second lieutenant. I think since I just invented you, I have the right to give you your nom de guerre: Lieutenant Philemon Osborne. And, best of all, I will deal with Major John André who is a personal friend and is as ingratiating and obliging to those of his station as he is disdainful towards his inferiors."

"The man won't do. He won't be believed," Lord Harold protested shrilly when Lady Beatrice presented Lieutenant Philemon Osborne to him. "A provincial belongs in the militia, not in our army. He has none of the breeding of the British officer about him. He wouldn't even make a passable private."

"In spite of breeding, any fool or fop can become an ensign with five hundred pounds as we well know," Lady Beatrice replied coolly. "He will be believed because he will be one. Besides, I predict we'll develop a special fondness for Lieutenant Philemon who is paying us to make us money."

Lord Harold grimaced and directed his attention to a manifest on his desk, allowing his wife the last word.

Three hundred bottles of burgundy, champagne, and French brandy were transferred two days later under guard to the house of Lady Beatrice and Lord Harold. A place in the cellar was cordoned off and an inventory was carefully taken. After overseeing the placement in the cellar, Lady Beatrice officially rewarded Jonathan with the warrant commission of Lieutenant Philemon Osborne and handed him a uniform to be tailored. With this superior merchandise, his rank of second lieutenant, and the name of Assistant Quartermaster Colonel Harold supporting him,

Jonathan could rise from his station of mere tradesman to that of a friend and maybe an equal to many in the British officer corps. He would acquire valuable information for Hamilton and Washington and the cause of liberty. Jaeger Captain Hoffman, murderer of Amelia, if he was a lover of good wine might even seek him out.

CHAPTER 6

DURING THIS PERIOD, Jonathan acquired the habit of appearing at the millinery with a cup of coffee four or five mornings a week. He and Miss Elizabeth would stand at the door and converse about a variety of topics. They lingered as long as it took to finish the coffee—usually a quarter-hour. Jonathan couldn't predict where the conversation would go. The war, shop inventory, the best way to serve a goose, the beatitudes, the cost of flour, Thomas Paine's diabolical tract *Common Sense*. Elizabeth made up for her self-imposed confinement by reading widely and listening carefully to whoever entered her shop. She had many opinions and few people she could express them openly to. Jonathan loved the play across her features when she wrestled with a thought—as if her nose, lips, eyes, and forehead were doing a little dance. Her soft Irish brogue he found endearing. On leaving her presence, Jonathan often reproached himself for deceiving her. Elizabeth hated the rebels and hated deceit. He managed to combine both.

Elizabeth's view of her family was at odds with Millicent's. It was as if she had replaced her mother in managing her older siblings as well as the millinery.

"I know you must believe Percy terrible," Elizabeth said with forced conviction at the end of a conversation. "And sometimes I admit he truly is. Yet for the longest time, he has been as gentle as a lamb. And don't you know he was begging forgiveness every day for a week regarding his and Rudyard's behavior, and he was looking so sad and remorseful with his bruises and a great lump on his forehead you gave him. I told him he must make something of himself, and he agreed and said soon he'd do something that would make me proud of him."

A gentle lamb Percival was not. Elizabeth's brother often rode with the cowboys—loyalist partisans intent on plunder and revenge. Gentle lambs were not allowed into their company. Percy, however, desired the glory of true soldiering over mere rapine. He appeared one morning in the green uniform of the King's Guard, the same that Jonathan's brother had worn. Although the "Greens" were earning a murderous reputation, they actually engaged in real battles from time to time and performed reconnaissance for British regiments, which made them more respectable than the cowboys.

And there was one other thing. The animosity between Percy and Jonathan had intensified over an incident of a gambling debt. It had occurred during the first weeks of Jonathan's ripening relationship with Elizabeth.

Possessing the ability to make his presence felt several feet in advance of his actual self, the patrons stepped out of Gabriel's way as he approached Jonathan through the crowded tavern. Gabriel was brief as was his wont, "Git to the Queen's Court Gambling Hall, suh."

Jonathan did not ask questions. If more explanation was necessary, Gabriel would have told him. When he arrived at the hall—a favorite of officers—he noticed Castor's large carriage and elegantly attired footman out front. Curston sat next to the footman conversing, back turned. Jonathan should have been stopped at the door. He suspected the black manservant had been told to let him enter without a challenge.

Jonathan hesitated at the entrance of the hall. The room had fifteen tables—several devoted to vingt-et-un, and similar games in which odds could be stacked in the house's favor, and the rest for parties, where a small percentage of the winnings was contributed to the hall. The lighting was purposely poor in the corners of the room to facilitate cheating. This was a high-stakes establishment, and thousands of pounds could be won or lost in an evening. A frugal man might live comfortably for a lifetime on a thousand pounds.

Nothing appeared out of the ordinary except for two young militia officers cringing in the corner, clearly feeling out of place. Then Jonathan spotted Percy at a corner table, his face crimson, sitting across from Castor.

Before Jonathan reached the table, Percy rose to his feet, threw down the cards, and, struggling with his glove, blurted out, "You're a bloody cheater. I challenge you to a duel."

"You are not an officer very long, Lieutenant Littleton, are you?" Castor showed no sign of being offended.

"What the deuce has that to do with you cheating?"

Percy gave up on the glove and tried to straighten his posture and take on the disdainful pose that was the specialty of the English aristocrat.

"Tsk, tsk," Castor responded, amused. "It has to do with the fact that you obviously are ignorant of how to handle yourself as a gentleman. You should never insult another gentleman without proof. You are an ill-mannered poltroon, ill-bred, an empty boaster, a figment of a man, a prating pretense of a soldier, as stupid as a clubbed hog, deserving of as much respect as a poxed whore, so why would I duel with the likes of you even if I were disposed to duel. If you still insist on a meeting on the field of honor, I'll select one of the accomplished duelists among my acquaintances to stand in for me."

"Then I'll skewer you now." Percy began to unsheathe his sword. By this time, Jonathan was close enough to grab Percy's hand. A half dozen men had sprung to Castor's defense.

"Put the sword away, Percy," Jonathan said. "No good can come of this."

"You, after him. I swear it," Percy spluttered.

"You weren't cheated," Jonathan whispered.

"No man wins like he does without cheating," Percy insisted.

"Few match Mr. Blanchard's skill as a player. Could you not name the last fifty cards played, Mr. Blanchard?"

Castor nodded, unable to resist confirming the compliment, and rapidly named the cards in order. The foreheads of several officers wrinkled at this revelation.

"Don't you dare interfere in my affairs." Percy pushed Jonathan away.

"Did Mr. Blanchard offer you credit?" Jonathan asked.

"The cheater cost me one hundred and eighty-three pounds," Percy said.

"How much of that was ready money?"

"Four," Castor replied, smiling. "But he put up the merchandise of a nice little millinery as surety."

"I believe this is as much my affair as yours, Percy. Castor is after ruining me and believes by ruining the millinery, he can do me harm through Elizabeth."

"You are certainly surfeited with your own importance," Castor commented.

"You will receive the hundred and seventy-nine pounds in the morning, Mr. Blanchard," Jonathan assured.

Percy backed away and drew out his sword. "Elizabeth is not your affair and never will be your affair."

"I'll cancel my debt to you and add an extra hundred pounds if you run Mr. Asher through," Castor informed Percy.

"You ken that's murder, Mr. Blanchard," a kilted highlander captain exclaimed, hand on his claymore, easily the biggest sword in the room. At several other tables, bets were quickly made as to whether Percy would go through with the deed.

"'Tis only a jest," Castor said, laughing.

Percy stood there, sword in hand, quivering. "Running you through, Mr. Asher, would solve a host of problems."

Jonathan faced him unarmed. His only hope was to evade the shaky blade.

"You will be charged with murder of an officer of the King, sir, and I'll bear witness against you," the Scottish captain insisted. More rumbling as the odds were recalculated.

"Don't interfere with my bet," A purple-faced colonel whispered harshly to the Highlander captain.

"Killing a man isn't always a serious matter, Lieutenant Littleton," Castor went on. "To elaborate on the jest: all you need to do is convince the court you had sufficient provocation, and you get off with a slap on the wrist. The king needs able soldiers like you," he added. contradicting what he had been saying moments before.

Percy's two companions each grabbed hold of an arm and pulled him back.

"I'll pay you back, then I'll kill you, Mr. Asher!" Percy yelled as he was dragged out of the gambling hall.

Guineas now flowed into the hands of those who had wagered for a bloodless termination of the affair.

"Too bad," Jonathan said to the commissary. "If he had made a lunge at me, I believe I'd have sufficient provocation to kill you."

"Touché, if you will allow the play on words," Castor said, putting away the cards. "You are a worthy opponent, Mr. Asher, but you do realize, in the end, 'twill not be possible to win this game."

"Neither of us knows the end, Mr. Blanchard, yet I've heard you say a bad run can ruin the best player."

Standing before his sister and ignoring the presence of Jonathan, which he had done ever since the incident at the gambling hall, Percy asked, "Do I pass inspection? I have joined the Refugee Club and met the great William Franklin, much more a gentleman than his humbug father."

Elizabeth eyed him critically, adjusted his cap, and snipped off a thread with scissors she kept in her apron pocket.

"Really, do I have to have all the loose threads snipped to kill rebels?" Percy grinned.

"You are my brother. I am a milliner; therefore you must be the best-dressed soldier in the regiment," Elizabeth declared.

"Well, you may be right, dear sister," Percy said, bending down and kissing the top of her head. "Tarleton is always elegantly attired. He is a great soldier and a great gentleman. All the rebels know and fear his name. I would feel I achieved a worthy reputation if my name became half so famous and feared as his."

"I just want you coming back safely, Percy. Leave the bravery and the reputation to others," Elizabeth said, giving his uniform a final inspection, tugging here, straightening there.

"You do not believe what you're saying. I will make you proud, Liza. I've not made you proud of me as a brother. I been terrible at times. Do you forgive me?" A pleading note crept into his voice.

"Of course, Percy. Always, to be sure." Elizabeth gave his uniform a last look over.

"I don't believe you, Liza," His voice rose as if he were desperate for her to believe him. "I beg that you truly forgive me when I make our family name proud again."

"Just don't get yourself killed by any skulking rebel." She stood on her tiptoes and kissed him on the cheek.

"Me killed by a skulking rebel? I'll just have to out-skulk them." Percy took her hand and squeezed it perhaps a little too forcefully because Elizabeth winced.

"Forgive me again," he insisted.

"Don't get yourself killed." She shook off his clutching fingers.

"A guinea in case I do so I can have a good time before it happens." He opened his palm.

"A crown." She took the coin from her pocket and put it into the smooth receptacle.

The arrival of Stephanie, Elizabeth's beautiful older sister, in high spirits and great disarray from an all-night ball, occasionally interrupted their early morning coffee. Stephanie could not keep herself from flaunting a gift or making a boast about a compliment she had received from her special friend, Major Duckett. Once Stephanie seized the cup of coffee out of her sister's hand, sniffed it, and declared: "My major's coffee has such a richer odor."

"'Tis good to know the coffee powder I provide him meets with your approval," Jonathan remarked.

Stephanie gazed at Jonathan trying to piece out what he was saying. Elizabeth took her cup back. "Stephanie, don't be putting on airs when 'tisn't necessary."

Stephanie sniffed again as if she still held the cup, this time as a counterargument. "That is just the way I am, the way I always been. Don't worry, Liza, I apologize to your friend for I do what my dear little sister tells me to do."

"For I have your best interests in mind." Elizabeth tried to reset a curl that had fallen out of her sister's elaborate coif.

"You and my Major Duckett love me the most and the best." She spoke in the high syrupy voice of a woman convinced the whole world must love her. "Although I must say that if eyes were ravishers, I'd be the most sinned-against woman in New York."

Not quite, Jonathan thought. Before Jonathan had become aware that the circulating stories concerned Elizabeth's sister, he had heard a great deal about Stephanie. Although her beauty was generally acknowledged—'a damn fine looker' she was called—she was prone to gaffes and like Elizabeth nervous to the point of fidgetiness. Her gaffes amused the British officer corps and quickly made the rounds. Jonathan had heard an officer more than once deep in his cups in a tavern imitate her syrupy voice crying out, "Major Duckett." His fellow officers would inevitably dissolve into howls of laughter.

Unaware her sister was an object of mockery, Elizabeth would gently reprove Stephanie and say that it was as likely for a woman to regain her reputation as Satan to get his seat back beside the throne of God. Stephanie would laugh and say although a poor woman may lose her reputation, a lady by the virtue of being a lady can never lose hers, only make it more interesting. Her major told her so, and he knew of such things.

"Am I a foolish girl, Liza?" Stephanie asked in her little girl's voice.

"I think you are." Elizabeth eyed expertly her sister's dress for irregularities.

"But you love me anyway," Stephanie insisted.

"I do, to be sure," Elizabeth affirmed.

"You see, there I have you," Stephanie exclaimed delightedly. "People love me anyway even though I'm a foolish girl. My major loves me anyway and won't be able to do without his foolish girl."

After Stephanie left, Jonathan asked Elizabeth, "Don't you resent having to work so hard while your brother and sister go out into society?"

"This is my time and where I want to be," Elizabeth declared, holding up the cup of coffee. "My time with a friend. I truly do not need more, to be sure. I would hate living Stephanie's life with the ceaseless preening and prancing hither and yon to parties as much as she would hate mine of minding the shop. I know you're playing the gallant and I'm just a dalliance with you, Mr. Asher, but I don't care. That's what men do, don't they?"

"Miss Elizabeth, a friendship is never dalliance." Jonathan found himself annoyed, as he did frequently by her almost abject gratitude for the attention he paid to her. It was against nature. If the air had not been poisoned by her brother and sister and despite her occasional nervous tics which supported their contention that Elizabeth wasn't right in the head, she would likely already have been wooed and wedded. The process of becoming acquainted with her seemed to consist of scratching off dull paint and finding gold underneath. Jonathan was suddenly struck by the thought that what he felt for her was edging beyond friendship. Not the best state of affairs for a spy.

CHAPTER 7

UNDER THE PROTECTION of Lady Beatrice and in the guise of second lieutenant reporting to Colonel Harold, Jonathan's business trebled, and the conspirators, if they had existed, backed off. While not quite belonging to their club, Jonathan was lumped in with the other well-regarded loyalists so was tolerated enough to socialize with the British officer corps. Without a twinge of conscience, they would see a tradesman they owed money starve. A debt to a fellow gentleman, on the other hand, had to be honored at the risk of life, and an unpaid debt to Lord Harold, assistant to the quartermaster general, could have unfortunate consequences for the whole regiment. The sole exception to this restricted code of honor and fear of the assistant quartermaster was Major John André. Lady Beatrice was soon fed up dealing with him and passed on to Jonathan the role of collector of payment due. The major exercised on Jonathan his repertoire of snubs and slights, intending to demonstrate how hopeless it was for Lieutenant Philemon Osborne to pretend to be a British officer and gentleman.

Lady Beatrice kept her distance initially in their business relationship. When they went over the figures at the end of the second month, both were pleased with the profits. She invited him again into the parlor, produced a bottle of burgundy, and opened it, saying, "I already paid for this one." Jonathan sensed a slight impropriety about the situation, although could not quite put his finger on it. While the wine aired, she gave detailed instructions to the butler about a coming fete.

Suddenly, Lieutenant Edgar burst in. He was pale and his features displayed a gaunt anxious cast. He avoided looking at Jonathan.

"Is this the man you saw at the duel?" Lady Beatrice asked.

"Yes, aunt." He quickly bowed to Jonathan and averted his eyes again.

"That's all I require, nephew. You may leave," Lady Beatrice said.

Edgar seemed surprised and opened his mouth to speak.

"You may leave!" Lady Beatrice repeated.

Giving Jonathan inexplicably a murderous scowl, he left.

Lady Beatrice shrugged, frowned, swirled the wine around in her glass, and then said, "Lieutenant Osborne, I appreciate the confidence you have shown us. I will shortly return the favor. I understand that you questioned the merchants who dealt with me. I trust you have found me creditworthy."

"Admirably so, Lady Beatrice," Jonathan replied. "They all gave you the highest recommendation, saying you paid in a timely fashion. That's why I am pleased with our arrangement and am confident 'twill continue."

Lady Beatrice's expression showed pleasure and perhaps pride. "I do pay, Lieutenant, for I have uncommon respect for tradesmen. I was born the only child of a blacksmith and a milkmaid, as far away from a lady as an honest girl can get. I was also the prettiest and cleverest girl in my county, so I transcended my low station, although not without battle scars. My history is not the reason for our discussion. Your name frequently comes up in association with the name of the Commissary Castor Blanchard. As I understand, you even witnessed the duel between Major von Wurttemberg and Captain Gregory because Mr. Blanchard asked you to help settle a debt. So, to be direct with you, does the commissary cheat at the gaming table?"

"He doesn't need to cheat," Jonathan answered.

"What do you mean?" Lady Beatrice leaned forward interested.

"He is a keen reader of men and calculator of probabilities," Jonathan replied.

Lady Beatrice winced. "In other words, my nephew Edgar with a face like an open book and who has difficulty counting the coins in his pocket is completely overmatched."

"I dare say yes."

"Even in hazard, in which Lord Harold assures me, there is no skill in the throwing of the dice?"

"As I understand it, Mr. Blanchard bets high when he gains the advantage in that game and low when he is disadvantaged. I've heard him state he places more faith in probability than in the Holy Ghost."

"Then Edgar truly owes Mr. Blanchard eight hundred pounds."

"That is an immense sum, Lady Beatrice," Jonathan said, suppressing a premonition the news would get worse.

A slight nod expressed her agreement. "Edgar has a title and the money from his commission, but not access to that sort of wealth, nor does his baronetcy which charges rent on a half dozen poor smallholdings generate income worth mentioning. Is there any way Edgar can honorably avoid paying the debt?"

"I don't claim to be familiar with the nuances of honor," Jonathan confessed. "I think such a thing would be difficult. Yet Castor does rely on the goodwill of the army. Although he is careful not to embezzle more than the other assistant and regimental commissaries, he could be trapped. Misstate the quantity on an invoice of an irreplaceable item, then send him the corrected invoice two days later. Surely, he will have disposed of the difference between the first and second invoices. Then you can charge him with theft of His Majesty's property."

"No, no," Lady Beatrice responded and studied the wine in her glass. "Castor is not pressing for payment. Edgar claims they arrived at an agreement, which means Castor is extorting Edgar for other ends. We made our nephew our heir for 'twould be a shame for his title to have no emoluments except penury. However, 'twould be worse for our fortune to end up in the hands of the vile Mr. Blanchard. My husband claims he will take care of it. I must confess I'm not so certain."

"And these other ends have to do with me, I imagine?" Jonathan asked with a sinking heart for he knew the answer.

"I believe you are correct in that, Lieutenant Osborne."

"As you know, the commissary was in on the plot to arrest me and seize my business. That having failed and being now completely cut out of the wine trade thanks to our arrangement, and Major James being more cooperative in our venture than ever, Castor likely intends to use Edgar to spy out my sources. I believe he is after discovering the time and place of the deliveries, then seizing the whole shipment or at the very least confronting and interviewing Captain Rodrigo and bending him to his purposes."

Jonathan thought it unnecessary to add that Castor wanted his head on a platter as much as his wine in the warehouse. When the commissary saw Jonathan in his uniform, he appeared momentarily deprived of speech, then recovered saying, "Bravo again, Mr. Asher. As I said, you're a resourceful scoundrel. Bravo."

"I hope you're mistaken, Lieutenant Osborne. With Edgar's awkward lurking about and constant furtive expression, he does not make a fit spy. I'm not sure he has any abilities at all," Lady Beatrice said, shaking her head.

"He does have an amiable nature," Jonathan conceded.

"Yes, he is a sweet man." Lady Beatrice paused, then asked. "Given that my nephew is a poor intelligencer, Castor likely has other ideas. I believe the commissary is after trading his forgiveness of Edgar's debt for your place in the wine trade. Hints were made to Lord Harold to that effect. Major James, of course, is amenable to the biggest bribe. The problem is your Captain Rodrigo. It was suggested that Lord Harold seize his ship and not give it back until the captain agrees to use Castor as his agent instead of you. The only reason my husband is not agreed is that although he may dislike you, he detests utterly the commissary. Now, advise me, Mr. Asher, what shall we do?"

Jonathan pondered a moment—even if he could solve this, the commissary would find a dozen other ways to undermine him—then hesitantly replied, "Hold him off as long as you can. Meanwhile, I'll see if there is another solution to loosen the grip Mr. Blanchard has on your nephew."

Lady Beatrice put down the glass of wine without having taken a sip. "Just take care, Lieutenant Osborne, the other way must exclude harm to my nephew, who, although is a nincompoop, I love like a son."

Jonathan bowed. "I understand, Lady Beatrice."

LATE MAY 1779

A whirlwind in skirts rushed toward Jonathan as he exited the City Tavern. When it stopped, Lucretia Baldwin stood panting, completely undone by her distress. At the same time, he identified the acrid odor in the air as that of burning wood and paint, and glancing up he saw the darkening plume near the docks.

"Mr. Asher, the warehouse is on fire!" Lucretia said, shrill and breathless.

Rumors had been circulating that the rebels were contemplating a campaign of arson. Jonathan dismissed them because the Continentals had already lost much goodwill by being blamed for the Great Fire of 1776. Still, there were hotheads for whom the price of the cause of liberty could not be too high, especially when others pay it. Jonathan had a brief vision of Castor engulfed in flames—that image not entirely disturbing. It took a few seconds to comprehend the consequences for he had never considered Emma and Daniel's world as part of the warehouse. Lucretia cried, "Don't you understand! Pollux is screaming about saving his little mice!"

"Oh, God, no!" Jonathan spurred the horses forward, his heart in his throat.

When Jonathan arrived, flames were shooting hundreds of feet into the air and chaos engulfed the whole block of warehouses. Soldiers were firing on looters running from the burning structures carrying sacks of flour and rice. One man rolling a barrel suddenly jerked into a backward arch as he was shot. His place was immediately taken by two others without any loss in the momentum of the barrel. Seated on a piling, Pollux wept as the flames consumed an outer wall. Castor, red-faced and frothing, screamed orders, which nobody paid attention to. Several hundred soldiers and citizens had formed a line from the wharf to the flames passing buckets, which seemed as hopeless as spitting at the blazes of hell. Glancing up, Jonathan saw two faces barely outlined against the plume of smoke and a rope hanging down leaving a twelve-foot drop.

"Emma won't jump!" Daniel's yell seemed to be coming from the top of a mountain.

Covering his face with his cloak, Jonathan charged past the bucket brigade through the door into the cauldron of flames and smoke. His lungs and his eyes begged him to turn back. That avenue of flight was taken out of his hands when the doorway behind him collapsed. He forced his eyes open and saw the ladder in its usual place. Merely touching the ladder blistered his hands. Trying to curse away the pain, he moved the ladder and climbed up to the door in the wall. Choking, he wrenched it open. He experienced a moment of fresh air, then the smoke pursued him. Emma was now curled up clinging to a post of the treadwheel crane casing despite the roof being unbearably hot. Daniel was crying, trying to drag her away. Jonathan pulled the ladder up through the door and slid it down the side of the wall that was not yet on fire. The ladder crumbled into flaming splinters.

"Climb down the rope. I'll take her." He pushed Daniel towards the edge of the roof. "I can't take both of you. Climb down. I'll follow."

"You go first."

Jonathan heaved Daniel up and held him over the side so he had no choice but to grab the rope. The boy slid down. When he let go a dozen hands caught him. Jonathan pried Emma's fingers loose and picked her up. Fear had made her rigid. He saw no alternative other than to slide down the rope with one hand while holding Emma with the other. Perhaps desperation would give him the necessary strength. Carrying Emma towards the edge of the roof, he heard a clunk and then realized someone miraculously had found another ladder and laid it against the side of the warehouse.

"Hold on!" He shouted to Emma. *Hold on*, he prayed. Grasping the stiff girl to his chest he climbed onto the ladder and began the descent.

First rung.

Second rung.

The whole building seemed to wobble as flames towered above him. Heat seared his nostril and mouth as if a dragon was exhaling into him. Emma coughed pitifully.

Third rung.

Fourth rung.

The back wall of the warehouse had already collapsed and the other three were swaying about to give way, yet he could not move any faster.

Fifth rung.

Emma slipped and was caught by his knees. He pulled her up to his chest. She slipped again. He pulled her up again.

Sixth rung.

Then suddenly the ladder jerked down several feet, beginning to collapse as the walls of the warehouse fell inward. The warehouse dissolved in on itself with an explosion of smoke and flames, blistering his lips, and searing his eyebrows. Strangely the ladder didn't fall with the rest of the building. Jonathan didn't understand what was happening until he realized he and Emma were moving away from the burning remains of the warehouse. A dozen men had taken handholds on the ladder and were carrying it upright towards the cobblestone boardwalk. Slowly the ladder was lowered to the ground. Jonathan stood up and tried to croak out his thanks. A mug of hot ale was thrust into his hands as he backed away still clutching Emma. He gave her a drink, which she sucked in, then passed the mug to Daniel whose chest was heaving with sobs.

"Where will we go, sir?" Daniel asked as he hugged desperately his silent soot-covered sister.

Nancy attended to their burns, slathering an aromatic grease mixture on the blistered patches of skin while Emma and Daniel sat on a bench holding back tears. William was distinctly unhappy with this addition to his household. He paced around the room until he could no longer keep in what was on his mind: "I know we owe you a great deal, brother, but I made my payments regularly, and truly I can't live and do business here if you take in every ragamuffin that needs charity. And the girl doesn't even talk. She must be an idiot."

"I won't abuse your hospitality," Jonathan replied hoarsely, waiting for his turn to receive the salve. "Give us a week to mend here, then I promise to accommodate myself and the children at my warehouse."

"Why are they your responsibility?" William wiped his eyeglasses and gave Emma and Daniel a gimlet stare. "The children are too old to be yours."

"Well, they have become my responsibility, brother," Jonathan replied. "And I'll do my best by them."

"You have your week." William paused as Nancy gave him her version of a gimlet stare. "Or whatever time you require."

"Thank you, William," Jonathan said.

Jonathan had Emma and Daniel installed in his warehouse by the end of the week. It was a day's work for Josiah and his brothers to section off a separate room in the upstairs living quarters and carry up a stove and other pieces of furniture. They refused the two guineas saying that Gabriel had instructed them to ask for the much more valuable paper exempting from requisition whatever horse and wagon they drove. When Jonathan showed Daniel their room which was no more than fifteen feet square, the boy said, "What will we do with so much space?"

Rebels were blamed for the fire. Although he had no firm proof, Jonathan was certain of the real culprits. The people of Canvas Town had noted that the full warehouses that fed the army were well-guarded with strong locks. The plan was daring—light a fire on one side, break down the door and take food out the other. No matter if it failed—better be shot or burned than slowly die from starvation. Jonathan arrived at this deduction the next day when leaving his warehouse on the edge of Canvas Town, he did not hear any children crying and smelled the simmering food from hundreds of cooking fires.

CHAPTER 9

"If I am a gentleman, then 'tis unnecessary to aspire to other accomplishments. If I am not, then 'tisn't worthwhile to aspire to a lesser station." Elizabeth related this declaration of her brother Percy in an attempt to excuse him for what she called his airs. Her excuses for her brother and sister always stiffened the atmosphere when they shared a cup of coffee. Jonathan would assent in a half-hearted manner to whatever she said about Percival and Stephanie. There was no love lost between Jonathan and her brother. Percival usually expressed his disdain for Jonathan by the silent treatment, however, when Jonathan first appeared in the second lieutenant's uniform of the British Army not the Colonial Militia, greatly pleasing Elizabeth, his indignation could not be contained. "You've never lifted a finger in defense of the King."

"I am fortunate there are those who differ from you in their estimation of my efforts and so rewarded me with a commission," Jonathan replied mildly.

"Which you purchased. Any rascal with a pot of guineas can purchase a commission, sir, but you'll never have the blood and breeding to become a true officer, much less a gentleman."

Jonathan smiled and inclined his head in a rather good imitation of a gentleman's refusal to lower himself to answer an insult.

The real crisis came on another visit. Before Jonathan could wish Elizabeth "Good morning" and enjoy her shy smile of acknowledgment, Percy swept in, face glowing, and boasted, "'Tis a pleasure to see them beg. Last raid we kidnapped a Committeeman, a parson, and a rebel colonel's pretty young wife, burned their damn rebel houses, bayoneted a half dozen who protested. And I always make sure they know who I am. Percival Littleton—and let me tell you; the rebels have learned to despair when I announce myself." He glared at Jonathan as if daring him to match his boast.

Elizabeth nodded in hesitant agreement.

Looking down his nose at Jonathan in imitation of aristocratic disdain, he continued, "I expend sweat and blood upholding the family name and you, dear sister, elicit gossip and rumor by fraternizing with this villain beneath your station who steals from the poor to buy his commission so he can pretend to be what he can never be. He fools nobody. Remember our grandfather held a title. This worm's grandfather cleaned jakes."

"Mr. Asher wears a second lieutenant's uniform like you, which I'm sure he deserves," Elizabeth said, her eyes pleading with Jonathan not to respond.

"Nay, my grandfather was a French pirate," Jonathan answered, thinking of Danton, "and if he had ever met your grandfather, he would have made him bow to his sword, lick his feet, and plead for mercy."

Percy's lips curled into a wordless snarl. "Like the rebels, you are proud of your villainous heritage. Mark what I say Elizabeth: I will reclaim the title that belongs to our family by making my name the most feared name to the rebel mob, so you must also strive to improve our condition by avoiding association with the likes of this man who confesses to his low station and thereby causing all sorts of untoward gossip."

"You, dear brother," Elizabeth replied, her dander now up, "have associated with the worst riffraff the city offers. Don't you think that compromised the family name?"

"It may have," Percy replied not only with equanimity but also self-satisfaction. "A man of quality is forgiven the hot blood of youth. I'm being considered for promotion to captain now. With my rise, the family will also surely rise. You must follow by giving up your association with the maid Millicent who pretends to be a lady and this poor tradesman, no matter what uniform he masquerades in."

"And should I be asking the husband's rank or title of every lady who happens into my shop, and if they do not measure up to your standards, refuse to deal with them?" Elizabeth asked.

"In time, yes."

"And our sister Stephanie, how do you propose to resolve her situation?"

"If that major who seduced her don't marry her, he will have the unpleasant chore of meeting me on the field of honor." Percy noticed Jonathan's cane. "May I examine your stick?"

Jonathan handed it to him.

"'Tis weighted. I was once struck by a weighted cane." He batted it lightly on the palm of his hand.

"I'm sorry for it," Jonathan said.

Percival stared at the cane suspiciously as if looking for blood, then at Jonathan. "Makes sense," he muttered and handed the cane back, his hand trembling slightly. "I will one day return the favor to the scoundrel who did that."

"Are you both after causing me grief?" Elizabeth exclaimed, turning crimson.

"I come here to talk to you, not offend your brother," Jonathan responded. "That he takes offense is his own doing."

"Ruddy still can't use his hands," Percy said.

"Whoever Ruddy may be, I hope he doesn't miss them too much."

"Jonathan, don't rile Percy," Elizabeth said.

"I apologize, Mr. Littleton, for any offense I may have given," Jonathan said and turned to Elizabeth: "I bear your brother no ill will, and I'm only reacting to his insults which are undeserved."

"Do not, Liza, depend on this man to rescue you from your difficulties. If you make inquiries of him as I have, you'll find he has as many different faces as the people you ask."

Jonathan was about to reply when Elizabeth implored, "Johnny, don't persist in this senseless dispute. I can always depend on you and that is what matters to me. Go on your raid now, Percy, and take out your ill humor on the rebels who well deserve it."

After the fire, the British moved their warehouses into docked ships, so Jonathan no longer had information about the requisition of food supplies. Working out of Lord Harold and Lady Beatrice's house and spending much of the day consorting with British officers, Jonathan now had access to higher-quality information. Part of the code had to be changed to indicate the destination of shoes, bayonets, muskets, blankets et cetera, instead of sauerkraut, biscuit, salted pork, et cetera. Still, Jonathan felt his services were undervalued. In his role as the purveyor of fine wines to the officer class of the British army, he doubted there existed an intelligence agent who possessed greater insight into the morale of the British troops and the character of the officers. To convey that information a more flexible code was required. Washington being fully occupied trying to keep his starving army from mutiny, and Jonathan still distrusted because of his vendetta, none was proposed.

Meanwhile, Gabriel reported that Captain Hoffman had become separated from his company on a raid into Connecticut. It was feared that the brave Jaeger was either killed or captured. Before Jonathan could inquire through Hamilton about prisoners taken in Connecticut, Hoffman reappeared with seven other British soldiers who had been taken prisoner. The clever Jaeger had swallowed a short coil of wire. His father, being a locksmith, Jaeger Hoffman knew how to use the coil when he recovered it to unlock manacles and open doors. Nevertheless, Gabriel had narrowed the captain's whereabouts to three different camps. Jonathan began to stock up on hock and think hard on how to avoid Meredith James and Continental raiders such as those who had robbed him even of his belt and buckles on his last disastrous attempt.

Castor hated water so rarely went aboard the ship which had been turned into his warehouse. Jonathan almost believed the assistant commissary had lost interest in destroying him, although more likely Castor was lying in wait to catch him off guard. After speaking to Blanchard, Hogwood's brother, a lieutenant with formal manners and the permanent expression of injured feelings, visited Jonathan and asked him to swear on the Bible that he had not killed the captain, and if he lied, then for God to damn his eternal soul. Jonathan agreed, hoping to justify this falsehood before God when he arrived at the court of eternity. There being no Bible present, Hogwood's brother said the oath from a fellow officer was sufficient.

Meanwhile, the commissary had turned Lord Edgar into one of his puppets, requiring the poor pliable youth to attend him at the gaming table while he fleeced the officer corps or in the tavern while he consumed his ten pounds of meat and gallons of wine and ale. The commissary purposely treated Lord Edgar as a servant to pressure Lord Harold to settle the debt, preferably by usurping Jonathan's place in the wine trade. Lady Beatrice was working on her husband to pay off his nephew's debt and put an end to the affair. This was difficult because Lord Harold as a matter of principle did not pay debts to those beneath his station. Jonathan hoped Castor would be content with the intense personal satisfaction of making the infamous arrogant penny-pinching Lord pay up. What Jonathan never imagined was that Lord Harold would be foolish enough to match his wits against Castor at cards.

"Lord Harold is at the gaming table with Mr. Blanchard." Lady Beatrice had summoned Jonathan from what promised to be an enjoyable domestic evening with Emma and Daniel reading *Robinson Crusoe*. She had difficulty maintaining her composure and kept bringing her fingers to her mouth, seemingly having to exert willpower to not bite her nails. "He knows the commissary's reputation. He knows he will lose. Why did I marry such a pigheaded dunce?"

"Castor never presses for payment from a person of Lord Harold's station," Jonathan assured her.

"I know, I know. I would prefer losing everything. We can make that up. I dread Castor entangling us and using us for his ends. That is intolerable. And, as you are aware, your fortune is also at grave risk. I would charge in there myself and drag Harold out by his ear if I were allowed. I am not, so it's up to you to stop the play."

"Your husband finds me as distasteful as Castor. Nevertheless, I will make the effort," Jonathan said, at first without the slightest notion of what to do even if he could gain entrance into the club. Then an idea occurred.

CHAPTER 10

PRETENDING TO DELIVER a half dozen bottles of claret, Jonathan entered through the backdoor of the Queen's Court Gambling Hall and made his way into the gaming room.

The play indeed was going badly for Lord Harold who was hunched over the table with a reddened face. Harold was an intelligent man, and from the knitted brow and his eyes which appeared to be searching for an enemy hiding in the cards he was holding, one could see that he was fighting against the realization he was overmatched. Glancing at the piles of notes and guineas, Jonathan estimated the colonel's losses at two thousand pounds. Castor sat in his specially reinforced chair, his great bulk attired in a rich cream frock coat and emerald green waistcoat as solid and as unmoving as an immense gemstone. His plump hands manipulated the cards with a loving feminine dexterity, and his eyes glittered, alive and observant between the folds of fat.

"Lord Harold," Jonathan began. "Lady Beatrice desires me to remind you that you are to dine with General Clinton tonight." Lady Beatrice and Jonathan had agreed on that lie to pry her husband away from the table. Lady Beatrice at this moment was desperately trying to obtain the engagement with General Clinton.

"I am aware of no appointment with General Clinton. And why, sir, in the world did she send you instead of a footman."

"I was at hand and proceeding in this direction."

Castor displayed absolutely no emotion, although Jonathan could feel the simmering hostility when he spoke: "This indeed is unfortunate, Lord Harold. We barely begun and yet you're called away on an engagement about which you should have informed me at the commencement of our play."

"My apologies, Mr. Blanchard. I have no recall of such an appointment. We will resume tomorrow at this hour."

"I am looking forward to it, Lord Harold. We will cast up accounts at the end of the game tomorrow."

Lord Harold rose from his seat and, not deigning to acknowledge Jonathan, left the hall dragging what was left of his dignity.

"Stay a moment, Mr. Asher," Castor said as Jonathan turned to go.

"Yes, Mr. Blanchard."

"I hope you find it no great inconvenience that I speak to the proprietor and request you are forbidden from stepping inside this hall again."

"Mr. Allenby will be sorely disappointed that the quality of his spirits will markedly decline and likely, as a consequence, the reputation of the establishment," Jonathan responded.

"You understand I will take the severest measures to prevent you from interfering in my affairs," Castor said.

"I only interfere when your affairs touch on my business. In all your transactions with me, you have profited."

"You throw me a few guineas as a sop, while the real gains go into your purse. That is not profit. There is a place at the table that has just been vacated. Sit down and try your fortune at cards. You have bested me in other arenas, why not at the gaming table?"

"I'll play four hands of piquet with you, no more, Mr. Blanchard. Four hands I may win on account of luck. I have not your facility in remembering cards and calculating probabilities, no man in my acquaintance does."

At the end of six hands, Jonathan stood to go having lost four guineas, "If we continue Mr. Blanchard, by the end of the evening, you'll own me lock, stock, and barrel." This act of leaving the table was as difficult as parting from the arms of a woman he lusted after.

"You see, Mr. Asher, you present me another sop. Lord Harold is a man of honor, and he will return to my table even though he knows he will lose. God bless men of honor. As for you, we will cast up accounts soon enough. Remember, I can lose many times at our game without ill effect. If you lose once, then everything you possess is mine."

"As you are aware, I don't make it a habit to attend the gaming table, so I don't fear losing."

"You're being disingenuous, Mr. Asher. You are as much a player as I am except you don't utilize a deck of cards. Our reckoning shall not be long in coming." Castor also stood with a huge lumbering effort. "Your servant, sir."

"Your servant," Jonathan said.

The next day Lady Beatrice informed Jonathan that she could delay her husband's return to the game no more than three days. Castor had to be dealt with in the meantime. She could not see how her business relationship with Jonathan could survive unless he resolved their problem.

"I apologize for the ultimatum, Mr. Asher." She used Jonathan's real name when she wanted to emphasize the difference in station. "Mr. Blanchard has been scheming to put my husband in his thrall for two years, and since our joint venture into selling wine, he has redoubled his efforts. I won't stand for it. I saved your life whether you appreciate it or not. Now you must save both of us from the monstrosity. If Castor tempts my husband into finishing the game, then our business is done."

Aside from Jonathan, the only other person successful in resisting the machinations of Castor was the prostitute Davina who, slight as a girl of ten, had womanly endowments hinted at rather than defined. Castor was obsessed with gamine trull and returned time and time to the place of her trade with offers, but she was adamant in rejecting this lover five to six times her weight. Jonathan did not know whether Davina could be recruited to his cause or how he could employ her; nevertheless, she was the only chink in Castor's armor, so it made sense to try.

Jonathan arrived at the Cat and Mouse Brothel in time to see the climax of another confrontation between Castor and Davina. The commissary, his finely tailored twenty stones quivering with rage at the rejection and more than usually drunk, was roaring his displeasure in the parlor to the diminutive, determined whore standing arms akimbo. The hefty fellow entrusted with guarding the women and quelling threatening guests was trying to push Castor out, but when Castor wasn't disposed to budge, it took more than the efforts of one mere grenadier-sized individual to dislodge him. A few other patrons joined in the effort with threats and blandishments, yet Castor, the keen reader of men even when deep in his cups, could see their sound and fury was nothing more than that.

"I could say my guineas are as good as anybody's guineas, but, as you know, that's not true. My guineas are better for with my money comes my goodwill and with my goodwill comes favors and protection." Castor, red and panting, glanced at Jonathan and added a growl.

"There be not a drib nor drab of goodwill in your fifty stones," Davina countered.

"Then call it lack of bad will. Now, here are three guineas because I am six times the man you usually take up into your boudoir." Castor surged forward.

"And when you break the bed?" Davina did not retreat an inch.

"We fuck on the floor." He tried to stare Davina down.

"I doubt you can get your cock out from underneath your great belly," she sneered.

"Then you have nothing to worry about," Castor said and smacked his lips.

"Except being smothered in a sea of fat," she countered.

Castor guffawed. "True, I'm fat. He's skinny." Castor pointed to a marine who had been trying to assist the guard. "He's an idiot." Moving his accusing finger to the others in the room, Castor continued, "He buggers his valet. He hasn't touched his wife in eight years. He slit the belly of a whore in London." He stopped pointing before he got to Jonathan. "So, goddamn what?"

"And you sent me three scoundrels with the pox, requesting my services. Three scoundrels, so you will have the excuse to make a fire ship out of me, burn me alive," Davina said, her sharp poking finger sinking several times into his chest as she uttered these words.

Castor hesitated a moment, showing he was caught, then his face relaxed. "I'll send you ten more, and if you miss a little sore, just a tiny little sore, then I see you burn. And I'll see this place burn. And before that, I'll requisition every damn thing here, including all the cunts, and sell them to service the slaves in the Sugar Islands. And if you protest that you are free women and doubt I can do that, then just try me. Or you can accept my money—six times your usual rate." He pushed forward.

Jonathan took Castor's arm. "Tonight isn't the night for her to accept your generous offer, Mr. Blanchard."

"You presume too much if you believe I listen to you, Lieutenant Osborne or Mr. Asher or whoever you might be tonight?" Castor shook his arm off. "You're the worst of the bunch, the cold-hearted assassin of an upstanding British officer."

Jonathan moved around to face Castor. "'Tis to your advantage to heed me, Mr. Blanchard, for I am well aware you don't make idle threats. You can trust I don't want to lose my interests here on account of you not engaging a certain trull. Give me this evening to present your case to

Davina and the proprietress. I believe I can persuade them to the advantages of being amenable."

Castor eyed Jonathan trying to figure out his stake in protecting the whorehouse. He arrived at the inference that Jonathan wanted, which happened not to be correct. "Can it be you don't want to see your building burned, Mr. Asher? You were a landlord of another such establishment, I hear. Aha! Procure me this whore, Mr. Asher, and I promise after I seize everything else you possess to leave you this building and a half dozen poxed whores so you end your days as proprietor of a whorehouse."

Davina shook her head emphasizing the impossibility of convincing her.

"I take that under advisement," Jonathan replied coolly. "I will present your case, and if Davina cooperates, maybe we can reconcile to the extent of attempting a certain venture together."

"Nay, Mr. Asher. Why should I desire a venture with you when the business you have with Lady Beatrice and Lord Harold will drop into my hands anon? As I said I might be so generous if you bring the whore around to allow you to keep your whorehouse and a few whores."

"We move elsewhere if he burns this place down," Davina declared to Jonathan when he returned after guiding Castor out. "I don't care what you offer me, sir, or whether you own this building or not, I prefer to be fucked by every dirty rebel in Washington's army than allow that buffalo into my bed."

The proprietress, a lady of indeterminate age with large watery eyes, invited them both into her office, which unlike the rest of the establishment was Spartan in its furnishings. "Surely, Davina, Frank could stay in the room, and in case Mr. Blanchard tries to hurt you, he could interfere," The proprietress suggested.

"Like Frank was able to do this evening with those eight hundred pounds of blubber," Davina snapped. She was a high earner and therefore could speak her mind.

The proprietress turned to Jonathan. "Why did you imply to the commissary you were our landlord?"

"He'd have not listened otherwise," Jonathan replied. "And our goals happen to coincide."

"Nay, they do not," Davina spat back.

"The commissary will not be gainsaid. You have no choice in dealing with him, so we must figure out how to limit the damage he does," Jonathan explained.

"Nobody helps us out of charity, Mr. Asher. What is your interest in this?" The madam asked.

"The same as yours—survival. As he said, Mr. Blanchard has it in mind to take over my business of supplying French wine to British and Hessian officers. And he won't quit until he succeeds. He has been known to sit at a gaming table for three days to bankrupt a wealthy opponent."

"Why won't he go with Maria?" Davina asked petulantly, changing the subject. "He only has to pay a crown extra to have her."

"He doesn't want Maria," The proprietress replied.

Davina thumbed her small nose at the madam. "Maria owes me a favor and will take him even though she doesn't want to. She is disgusted by his greasy skin, and she could not work for a day after the last time. He is a cruel man. How long do you think it will take me to recover if I allow him into my bed?"

The madam shook her head helplessly, explaining that Castor was only permitted the hardiest girls with his twenty plus stones of bulk.

Davina added that she had told Castor he could have her if he lost ten stones, and she regretted even that concession. The robust whores, who accepted the surcharge to endure the smothering engulfment, told stories of his peculiarities that made them at times shy for their lives.

"He told Maria once that he was aware she despised him," Davina continued. "'All women despised him,' Mr. Blanchard said, which was fair because he despised all women and swived them accordingly."

"Mr. Blanchard isn't the sort of man who can be refused indefinitely," Jonathan rejoined. "He destroys what he can't have." Jonathan then related his plan. He had noticed Castor briefly clutching at his chest as he made his way toward his coach. He had seen Castor make that same gesture at the club when Lord Harold excused himself.

"If only that would kill the ox," Davina said after Jonathan finished speaking.

"I believe it will render him incapable of following through, which benefits you," Jonathan said. "Even rising from a table, he pants like a sow in heat. And after walking the forty paces to his carriage, he is more winded than a soldier who has double-marched fifteen miles on a summer afternoon. At worst, you can pleasure him—how should I say… pleasure him the way women do men while they're on their backs."

"He'll still have to pay three guineas if I do that," Davina asserted. "Nay, I believe you are too hopeful. Like you said he can sit three days at a gaming table until he gets his way."

"That is true," Jonathan agreed. "Castor drinks little and eats moderately while he is gaming and can go a full twelve hours without standing. This will be different. Your job is to make him over-exert himself after a full meal. I believe you possess the skill."

"And if I fail?" Davina asked.

Jonathan locked eyes with her. "Castor doesn't make idle threats. You might succeed. If you do nothing, you certainly will suffer this wrath."

Davina grimaced. "We'll slaughter a bullock and have a cask of rum, a barrel of ale, and a dozen bottles of claret at his table. I'll admire his prodigality and encourage him."

"Castor will catch on. Better to express disapproval and revulsion," Jonathan suggested. "That will spur him to greater indulgence."

"I prefer the activity of copulating to speculating on how to murder that hogshead of fat. I am going back to the sitting room." With a flip of her head, Davina signaled that she was about to leave.

"Let Castor disable himself in the effort to satisfy his lust," Jonathan summed up.

"Take it from a whore," Davina countered, standing eye to eye with Jonathan who was sitting. "The ones with the greatest lust are the last to fall."

"Stir his passion, excite him, make him run and gambol, and he will succumb. At worst, you'll have to pleasure him while he is drunk and helpless, which may be easier than pleasuring him in other ways at other times," Jonathan explained as Davina slammed the door shut.

"I have a brother with the king, I have a brother with Washington," The proprietress said, glancing at Jonathan.

"Castor steals from both, so for once perhaps I can do both my brothers a favor."

"And your business too. Castor does not forgive or forget."

CHAPTER 11

BY THE TIME Jonathan answered the summons to the Cat and Mouse brothel, Castor had already consumed three dozen oysters, a buttock of boiled beef, a hind quarter of roast venison, three bottles of claret, and an immense raisin suet pudding. Davina was nowhere in sight.

"Davina has lost heart," the proprietress explained with a note of panic in her voice. "She ran into her room, crying and terrified. Perhaps you could talk to her and coax her back down for this was your idea." With an air of desperation, the proprietress went on to explain that Davina had bravely tried to follow his instructions. She egged him on, teasing that the more a man eats the less he is able to perform. Castor had disagreed, claiming, "The more I eat, the faster my little baby Peter grows up into the big grenadier Peter." For an inexplicable reason, those words made Davina take fright and flee into her room.

Peeking through the door Jonathan observed a gallon tub of whipped syllabub being placed underneath Castor's flushed face.

"He has consumed more than all my girls do in a

week," the proprietress whispered in amazement. "I don't think we own a chamber pot that will take all his shit."

"Don't worry," Jonathan replied. "He has a special chamber pot fashioned from a barrel and dedicates two complete mornings a week to that activity. Can I talk to Davina?"

Jonathan was led up to Davina's room—the most spacious because she was the best earner for the Cat and Mouse. She lay face down on her bed, hitting her pillow, and crying like a little girl.

"There's no turning back," Jonathan said.

"He will kill me," she sobbed. "I see it in his eyes. Don't tell me I'm imagining things. I am a whore. I know more about what lies behind men's eyes than they do themselves."

"You can call for help. Your guard is quite capable..." Jonathan started to explain.

"No, he is not." Davina fought back her tears. "Castor whispered in my ear I shouldn't be alarmed because the only harm he has ever done to a whore was once breaking her back."

"Make him chase you," Jonathan suggested. "He'll tire out after a few steps."

"The lumbering buffalo won't. I just know he'll kill me." Tears began to stream again.

"If you refuse him now, he certainly will. If you follow through at least a little, I swear he won't harm you." This was as empty a promise as Jonathan ever made.

"Then you must be in my room to keep your word," Davina insisted, sitting up and wiping her eyes.

"Castor won't allow that," Jonathan said.

"Be nearby," Davina begged. "At least between you and Frank, both could pull him off me."

When she got up to wash her face, Jonathan said, "Don't. Let him see you've been crying. That will excite him more."

Davina gave him a murderous look, then went downstairs.

Jonathan observed the goings-on through a crack in the kitchen door. Davina entered the room sniffling. Castor was just finishing the syllabub. Another bottle of wine stood on the table.

"Come here, my little turtledove. Come, don't be shy, dearie." He wiped his greasy hands on a napkin, then hooking Davina, drew her closer. He kissed her hand. "I want to sample your flesh and see if it tastes better than the syllabub." He sucked the back of her hand. "Smooth skin. Suits my palate just fine. I must sample more."

The ensuing entanglement as his hand thrust into her bodice ended with the upper part of her attire yanked down over her shoulder and one small breast exposed. Davina stepped back when Castor raised himself from the table. He lunged and she scampered back further. He chased her around the table once panting heavily. "You can't escape me." His face had turned the angry red of a dying sun.

"I will not do it here, or anywhere," Davina declared, not bothering to cover herself. Castor lunged again, fell, crushed several chairs which he didn't seem to notice, and rose to his feet shaking. Davina ran up the stairs. Castor followed bellowing, snorting, and cursing. The door to Davina's room shut. Jonathan heard Castor heave himself up against it, making the whole upper story shake. The proprietress hurriedly climbed the stairs with the keys. After the door was closed behind Castor, there were a few minutes of eerie silence, then a gulping sound, perhaps of suffocation, perhaps of tears. Then slow footsteps shook the floor. Their pace quickened, followed by a crash and a long scream. Jonathan and Frank bounded upstairs and burst into the room.

They found Davina standing on her bed naked, screaming at the top of her lungs. Castor lay on his back on the floor, breeches missing, shirt askew revealing the massive belly, mouth gaping, eyes in a frozen stare. Initially, Jonathan thought Castor was dead. Then he heard the sepulchral breathing and felt the little eyes shift to him. Having predicted a heart seizure not an apoplectic fit, Jonathan was surprised. However, one seemed as good as the other. With witnesses present, finishing the commissary off was out of the question, even if Jonathan had the stomach for the coldblooded murder of a helpless enemy.

Jonathan enlisted aid from eight of the brothel's clients who had come out into the hallway to pick Castor up and put him into bed. Doctors were summoned. Pollux was sent for. Maids appeared. During all this activity, Jonathan felt Castor's steady gaze on him. The commissary had lost the ability to speak, but his eyes, small black stones carved from volcanic material, were eloquent in conveying undying hatred. The eyes were always on Jonathan. Those eyes burned with rage as Jonathan approached and said in one of the most purposefully cruel acts of his life, "Don't worry, Mr. Blanchard, I'll make sure you are well taken care of."

With the same sort of netting, block, and tackle used for transferring horses, the great bulk of Castor was hoisted into the hold of the warehouse ship the next day. He was gently lowered onto a broad bed and released from the net. Then eight marines carried the bed to a horse stall. The oppressive sky gave its salute to this procedure with thunder, lightning, and buckets of rain.

Pollux made sure that his brother was comfortable. He hired two servants, pretty. young women, to feed, massage, and bathe him. A rumor circulated that Castor, wanting to display he hadn't lost his acumen, insisted that a deck of cards be shown to him so he could slur out of the corner of his mouth their order. His mind was intact. As for his body, the physicians weren't optimistic.

Jonathan hoped the body's eventual decline would take the mind with it. Curston was no longer following him, so Castor for the time being had left off the project of destroying him by putting Lord Harold in his debt. Yet, a cautious man always doubts good fortune.

CHAPTER 12

November 1779

By the time he had downed his sixth tumbler of rum in the tavern named appropriately The Sour Grape, Jonathan was in a rare foul mood. With the apoplectic fit of Castor and his nearly total paralysis, Jonathan's world should have been in order, but it was not. Even though Meredith James had been wounded in a fracas on the sound and now was confined to his room above a Brooklyn tavern permanently drunk, the elements conspired to so muddy the roads on Long Island that Jaeger Hoffman remained beyond reach. There were also signs that the coming winter would be severe, putting off the reckoning with the Jaeger captain until spring. That morning Elizabeth barely gave the coffee a sip, screwed up her nose, and said she could not continue wasting time in such foolery. She had her moods, he had learned. She had been cooler since the scene with Percy. Then again, she often seemed disappointed at whatever he said. Here he was playing the swain, but for all she could tell, he was just wording her. Afterward, he passed Mrs. Dalton hurrying down the street on an errand with a bundle of candles under her arm. She pointedly ignored Jonathan as she had done in every encounter since Richmond had reminded him that he had to pick up the provisions meant for the starving prisoners of the Provost House. Daniel was upset with Emma for still not talking and so decided to do the same, which meant neither of them was saying a word to Jonathan.

Finally, later that afternoon, near the docks, the worst of all possible mortifications occurred. While conversing with a sea captain on a variety of issues, Jonathan suddenly felt a chill in his bones. Then he saw them—the Goodwins staring at him much like the odd old couple who were staring at him from the doorway of the tavern now, except the Goodwins' faces were ashen. Had the Goodwins been searching for him? Probably, for they would have had to obtain a pass from both sides to enter the city. Before he could figure out how to explain why he was wearing the uniform of the army that had murdered their daughter, they left.

Jonathan considered another tumbler. It was getting late. The regimental drummers had just played the tattoo summoning the soldiers in the public houses back to the barracks. Before Emma and Daniel arrived in his life, this hour would be the beginning of the evening. Now, not so much. He had asked Thomasina to see to the children, and likely she and four or five or her brood would be sprawled across Daniel and Emma's quarters asleep on rugs and quilts. Still, he felt an obligation to be near them.

As befits a man with dangerous secrets, Jonathan was usually a cautious drinker. This evening he had thrown out caution and was well on the way to getting roaring drunk and perhaps making an admission that would end the charade that was beginning to nauseate him. The proprietor shooed out the odd old couple, similar enough in their bent posture and drawn sober faces to be a matched pair of worn boots. Jonathan took a big gulp of rum and heaved a sigh of relief at seeing their backs. He was certain whatever business they contemplated with him entailed more bad news.

Bad news could only be put off for so long, so he was not surprised when after his seventh tumbler he stumbled through the door, and the old man and woman each grabbed an arm.

"Thankee," Jonathan said, trying to straighten and wondering whether he was about to vomit.

"Please, sir. Please, sir," They both whispered. "We beg you to listen to us."

"You each have an elbow, good sir and madam, so you each have an ear," Jonathan observed.

The old man tugged at his right elbow and spoke rapidly. "The provost at the prison said there was no hope for our son. The captain of his company who is a parolee says he can do nothing for him. Mr. Pintard, the commissary of our prisoners says he is powerless. We even tried to appeal to General Clinton. He was spending time at the house of the Spencers, loyalist friends. He said thank God he wasn't in charge of prisons for he didn't relish being judged by the Almighty for those sins, but on the way out, a nursemaid told us that if anybody could free our son it would be Lieutenant Osborne—she said shame might work where money don't. I know not what she meant by that. Are you Lieutenant Osborne? Our last hope is you."

"Be the maid a fetching girl with a lot of freckles."
Jonathan, quite drunk, adopted the language of a sailor
who had been telling him his life story for the last hour.

"That could be her. She spoke so finely that I thought
her a lady with fallen fortunes," the old woman said
admiringly, pulling at his left elbow.

"Aye, that be her." Jonathan succeeded in freeing his
arms, which they immediately clasped again. "She be
having a pretty speech for a lowborn wench. In any event,
finding hope be my specialty. The sort of hope I sell is by
the bottle, keg, case, or cask. How much hope do your son
and his friends require?"

"Oh, we don't drink spiritous liquors, sir," the old man
said anxiously. "Our son, our only child, Doctor Smith, is
a prisoner on the *Scorpion*. We hear terrible things about
those prison ships. We have not enough money to redeem
him, and he joined as a private so he cannot be paroled,
and we are fearful for his welfare."

"And what can I do?" Jonathan slurred.

"Find a way to remove him from the ship," they both
said as if they had practiced the phrase together.

"Pshaw!" Jonathan reeled this way and that, taking
his elbow supports with him. "Pshaw! Pshaw!" he said,
laughing at the word.

"In the name of God and His mercy," they both
admonished him.

Jonathan fell into a fit of hiccups. However, the invo-
cation of God added just enough sense of Christian duty
to his consciousness that he blurted out, "Well, certainly,
good folks. I'll go now and take your son off the *Scorpion*—just like that."

"Don't mock us," the old man cried furiously.

"Although 'tis true I be soused as a pickled pig, I'm not mocking you," Jonathan replied with anger that would have equaled the old man's if he had not been inebriated. "If I had more of my wits about me, I'd deny your petition and give the wench, Mrs. Millicent Dalton, a tongue-lashing she would ne'er forget. Unfortunately, my wits appeared to have deserted me presently, and so I will collect your son if he still breathes." At this moment Jonathan turned away and vomited. After he finished, he veered towards the wharves on the East River followed by the couple who were expressing doubts to each other about the enterprise.

"What choice do we have?" exclaimed the woman.

"That's right. What choice?" Jonathan hiccupped. He spotted a couple of boys huddled around a fire next to a dock roasting a fish. They scratched out a living by rowing in their bumboat goods and people from the docks to the ships moored in the harbor. He tossed them a handful of shillings and requested to be taken to the *Scorpion*. "Just like that, I promise," he said, waving his arms and stumbling into the boat.

Jonathan had no idea what he was going to do, and the sea air was adding an unwelcome measure of heavy headachy sobriety to his drunkenness during the long row to Wallabout Bay.

The mastless, rudderless black hulk was hailed, and after miraculously climbing aboard and landing on the spar deck without mishap, Jonathan made his way down a narrow passage between pig pens to the captain's cabin. The pigs were raised to feed the officers and marines and to sell on the side. Their existence added to the intolerable conditions of the prisoners, the pens taking up half the space allotted for their exercise. This being evening, the prisoners had been ushered below. The deck stank vilely—the odors of the pigs mixing with the effluvia of the unwashed and sick and dying men. Adding to the torment were the hordes of flies, gnats, and mosquitoes hovering as a semi-solid mass over their continual feast on the deck.

"What is the meaning of disturbing us at this godawful hour, Lieutenant Osborne!" The warden, a gaunt man who had lost a leg and an arm to cannonballs and had no pity for any soul except himself, hobbled to his feet. "The damn paymaster been late, and I can't purchase your merchandise."

"Dr. Reginald Smith," Jonathan said, trying not to slur. "I require Dr. Reginald Smith."

"Can't your requirement wait until morning?" The warden lifted and clacked down his peg to punctuate his question.

No, in the morning I would be sober, Jonathan thought. "Dr. Reginald Smith's presence is immediately requested."

"By who?" The warden asked, then added. "He also has an appointment soon with the Lord Mayor of Hell."

"By..." Jonathan's thoughts started to swim away, but he caught a small one, the name of another warrant officer whose fictitious purpose was to supply a stipend to a major's widow in Sussex and a captain's widow in Cornwall. "By Colonel Goshen. Yes, Colonel Goshen requires Dr. Reginald Smith."

"I'm not familiar with Colonel Goshen, and why

would he want the prisoner, Dr. Smith?" The warden wasn't making this easy.

"For the reason…" *Why do military men need doctors*—Jonathan's mind stumbled in search of the possibilities—*why?* "For the reason… for the reason… for… he has the clap!" Jonathan struck his hands together as emphasis and shouted this last declaration.

"The British army surgeons are quite skilled in treating all sorts of ailments including those of the venereal nature, so why would he want a rebel doctor?" The warden pursued logically.

"Because he has caught the American clap and American doctors, especially Doctor Reginald Smith, are experts at treating the American clap," Jonathan explained as if this were obvious.

The warden considered, his face contorting as skepticism fought with prudence. "As you are well aware, I must keep an inventory of the prisoners."

"An inventory or obituary?" Jonathan muttered and immediately regretted the statement.

The warden wasn't offended. "If Washington wanted them to live, he'd send more supplies."

Which would be fed to the pigs. Jonathan did not articulate this counterproductive argument and repeated in a calmer voice, "You can note down that I took Doctor Reginald Smith off your ship and that I'm responsible for him."

"American clap—I didn't think there was any other kind," the warden groused, then reluctantly gave the order to bring Dr. Reginald Smith up from the steerage.

Smith appeared, half carried by two guards. His sole

garment was a shirt that came to his mid-thigh. Dr. Smith trembled and seemed to be casting about with his hands to find support. He smelled of sweat and excrement, which was the common smell of the prisoners. Huge red weeping sores were visible on his naked legs. Jonathan estimated by the length of a ragged beard Smith had been a prisoner less than a fortnight, although he already possessed the staring unblinking eyes of a starved man.

"Can you find Doctor Smith's clothes?" Jonathan requested. "He mustn't arrive at Colonel Goshen's residence naked."

Some decent clothes confiscated from recent arrivals were produced, and Doctor Smith dressed. He had a narrow face, protuberant forehead, high-bridged thin nose, and dark eyes set deep in their sockets.

"How is clap got here different than clap got anywhere else?" The warden questioned Doctor Smith.

The doctor wrinkled his brow, momentarily confused, and then caught on that the question had something to do with the reason for his release. "'Tis not different… too much, except I suppose like us rebels 'tis more stubborn and unruly and resists all treatments except the severest."

Jonathan and the doctor did not speak to each other while they were rowed to shore. On docking, the old couple surrounded their son in an embrace. There were tears and kisses. Then all three, clasping each other tightly, started to walk away.

"You're not a free man, Doctor Smith," Jonathan protested.

They stopped. Doctor Smith's father turned and said coldly, "Our gratitude is immeasurable. We can pay over time whatever money you expended for the redemption of our Reginald."

"I didn't pay in guineas," Jonathan replied, now the opposite of drunk. "I signed my name. Abetting a rebel to escape is treason."

"We will not allow you to take him back." The old man lifted his chin in defiance. "Although I acknowledge our great debt to you, our love for our son is greater. See how thin he is! He could not have endured another week."

"See this uniform." Jonathan stepped in front of them. "I'm an officer in the British army. I can easily raise the alarm and have you all arrested and thrown back on the *Scorpion*. Your son is not a free man. If you cooperate, he will not have to return to the prison ship—at least, as a prisoner."

"What are you saying, sir?" Dr. Smith asked.

"I will arrange that you are paroled under the pretense you were misclassified as a private. Perhaps you can be exchanged later for a captured British officer. I will lodge you and your parents at the Sour Grape tonight if you give your word that you won't escape. Tomorrow, report to my warehouse. I believe I have a job that will enable you to support yourself while you are paroled."

"Supporting the British cause in any manner is treason in my book," Doctor Smith stated with pious conviction.

"That isn't what I have in mind," Jonathan replied. "I must have your word."

Doctor Smith hesitated. "I don't give my word lightly."

Then damn you and back to the Scorpion, Jonathan thought and was about to articulate this when Doctor Smith's father said, "I give the word for my son. He won't disobey his father and cause me dishonor."

"I obey unwillingly," Reginald Smith insisted.

"Tell Mr. Linkletter at the tavern that I will pay for your lodging, and he is to give your son plain food," Jonathan said.

"I repeat I am not in accord with this arrangement," Smith stubbornly declared.

"He will do as his father says," the old man whispered.

The next morning, despite a drumming headache, Jonathan laid out his plans for Doctor Smith to Lady Beatrice. When he had narrated the events of the previous evening and the vivification of Colonel Goshen, she had shown surprise, disapproval, and amusement by turns. When he explained how she could profit from his scheme, she gave hesitant authorization.

"It might save some poor devils. Lord Harold isn't diligent in these matters, so I will sit at his desk when he goes out for his morning ride and sign the paroles. I often do so to lighten his workload. How much did you say each signature was worth?"

Jonathan found the doctor and his parents waiting in his office.

"We kept our word," Doctor Smith said between gritted teeth.

"I see." Jonathan suspected few men would try his temper more than this churlish Yankee, nevertheless, he had a scheme. "You will return to the prison ship," Jonathan announced, pausing for a cruel minute trying to stare the basilisk Doctor Smith down. "However, not as a prisoner."

Jonathan explained that the doctor had become a parolee and would now abide by the regulations that applied to parolees. Because he had no means of providing for himself, Jonathan was giving him the job of gathering the names of those prisoners whose kith and kin might be able to pay the necessary bribes for them to also become parolees. Doctor Smith would bring pen and paper so the prisoners could write letters to their families and inform them where they were imprisoned. The reputation of the prison ships was such that the families would understand that the bribes were necessary to avert the death sentence of their loved ones.

Jonathan would manage the transference of funds and dispensation of bribes along the way. He would take nothing for himself. He saw this business of ransoming the condemned souls as penitence for his part in selling the starving prisoners' rations. For the sake of caution, Jonathan would give Smith the impression he was doing this solely as a lucrative business venture. "I gain my profit. You facilitate their freedom. The prisoners' supplies aren't filched for there's more money in redeeming a live prisoner than starving him of a pennyworth of bread."

"You reason like a slaver," Doctor Smith commented sourly.

"Quite the opposite if the captains agree to the transactions." Jonathan smiled as broadly as he could force his lips. On reflection, it was perhaps convenient that Doctor Smith was a prickly individual who said what he thought and held to his principles as if they were chiseled on stone tablets. "Yet, like a slaver, I'm a man of business. If you can accept my offer without sullying your principles over-much, then please do so without incrimination."

"I will accept it, sir, although I fear for my eternal salvation. Maybe, one or two out of a hundred may be saved. What about this diseased colonel?" Reginald asked although he must have known from his parents that it was a ruse.

"Colonel Goshen has experienced a sudden recovery. He does thank you for your efforts and regrets the inconvenience he has put you through," Jonathan replied.

"I will do your bidding, sir, if I am allowed also to practice my profession with the prisoners, although I fear 'twould be as futile as practicing the healing art in the dungeons of hell."

The following day, Dr. Smith accompanied the sailors who rowed the supplies out to the ships. Over the next weeks, he treated the prisoners he could and talked to those whose families might afford the bribes necessary for the parole. The dour Doctor Smith amused the tavern keeper, so he was allowed to sleep on a mattress in the corner of the kitchen and given food in return for chores, it being understood that his work with the prisoner ships always came first.

Still, there were problems. In the first week when he refused to deliver a necessary bribe, Jonathan threatened, "You have a clear choice: save lives or die with the men you could have saved."

Doctor Smith loaded hate into his stare as he took the money for the bribe.

Smith did take without protest Jonathan's suggestion

that when the family couldn't raise the required sum to satisfy the greedy officials but enough to fatten the pockets of a few guards to arrange that the living soul was included among the putrid corpses dumped in one of the mass graves, making sure that the covering of dirt was too thin to suffocate the man. Half of those released in this macabre way were so sick that they expired within days of their rescue. Half did survive. To keep up the pretense of this being a business venture, Jonathan kept part of the money, which was then recycled into more bribes. The doctor only showed suspicion once.

"You receive your lieutenant's pay and are very active in many profitable businesses, yet you don't reside in a large house with a score of servants bowing and scraping. Truthfully, I see no evidence you live like men of your station do."

Jonathan hesitated before he responded. Among his twelve properties were three grand houses where those who wanted to show off their wealth resided. He believed that although war might alter the value of real estate, it could not erase it.

"'Twould be unseemly for a mere second lieutenant to flaunt wealth and aspire to a higher station. The fortunes of war are notoriously fickle, the envy and greed of humanity a constant. I'd be taken down sooner or later for my presumption. I seen dozens of profiteers fall from great heights. I can point out two begging not three blocks from here. 'Tis better to keep in my place for the time being. When the war is over, and men's passions cool, I'll purchase my mansion and hire my servants."

"The children living in your warehouse, are they your bastards?" Reginald inquired.

"Nay. I suppose they are my accidental wards until I find a better place for them," Jonathan replied feeling defensive.

Doctor Smith frowned deeply. "I took the liberty of examining the girl. There is no reason she cannot talk."

"Her brother doesn't want her placed in a hospital."

"He isn't wrong," Dr. Smith agreed. "If they take her in as an idiot, her life would be an unending torment." Jonathan observed real sympathy and concern in his voice. "Tell me, Lieutenant Osborne, where in this city could two orphans find a better place than here?"

CHAPTER 13

SURPRISINGLY, THE WAREHOUSE ship Pollux and the paralyzed Castor occupied turned out to be one of Jonathan's best clients, purchasing such a great quantity of his merchandise that Jonathan imagined Castor bathing his prodigious body in a vat of expensive wine. It was also rumored that a calf and a hog were slaughtered every week just to feed the commissary's still gargantuan appetite. Jonathan dealt solely with Pollux who invariably treated him amicably, always inquiring after Emma and Daniel and seeming pleased they were well cared for. Castor was never mentioned; therefore, Jonathan was taken aback when Pollux suddenly announced, "My brother desires to speak to you."

Guided by a mute black giant, Jonathan descended into the hold amidships, a strange spectral world of weak lamps and large piles of crates and barrels. He followed the man through a narrow passage to a long low cabin two levels beneath the quarterdeck. There spread out on a chair that must have been specially widened and reinforced to support his bulk reclined the massive form of Castor. He had gained at least another five stones, and his shirt and breeches seemed to have been recently cut from the cheapest cloth. A young slave woman hovered next to him, holding a bowl and spoon. Castor weakly waved her away with his right hand. His left arm hung over the chair useless. A line of spittle mixed with food ran down the left side of his face.

"You look very well, Mr. Asher, or do you prefer the name of your fictitious identity, Lieutenant Osborne?" Although he spoke from the right side of his mouth, his enunciation was clear.

"Mr. Asher will do," Jonathan answered. "Although I owe my second lieutenancy to convenience, 'tis real enough."

"Yes. And you prosper." Castor cleared his throat, gasping and hawking for a long minute. "And I am not so fortunate as you can observe, which is entirely your doing."

"That is unjust, Mr. Blanchard." Jonathan struggled to not let revulsion show on his face.

Saliva bubbled at the corner of Castor's mouth. A fly buzzed around him, which the slave girl desperately tried to shoo away. Castor engaged in the long and difficult exercise of clearing his throat again. "Truth has no obligation to be just, Mr. Asher. The truth is also I was a fool. I wanted so badly to roger Davina that I fell into your trap. Did you poison me?"

"As far as I am aware, there was no poison in your meal," Jonathan replied.

The right side of his lips lifted in what might have been a smile. "I believe you for we are similar in that we gain our advantage by studying other men's habits and weaknesses. You anticipated I would eat too much, and the exertion afterward would result in apoplexy."

"How could I know that?" Jonathan asked.

The throat again took a very long time to clear at the end of which the girl wiped away the spittle and phlegm. "No use denying it. Frank the bruiser at the Cat and Mouse told me that was your intent with the cooperation of Davina. You saw I labored to catch my breath even seated. 'Twasn't too difficult to figure. When they brought me here, I could not speak, I couldn't lift my arms or bend my legs. I can speak now, I can lift my right arm and the doctor promises there is no reason why I will not gain command over the whole of my body eventually, although I will have to lose fifteen stone before I return to my old duties and habits."

"I am glad to hear that," Jonathan said.

Castor choked for a minute, then replied, "No, you are not, for I will murder you and Davina. Slowly, if I can. Swiftly, if the opportunity presents itself. As a gaming man, I like to play fair and give my opponents a warning. When I sit down at the gaming table, I make sure those sitting across from me know my reputation. You have done your worst to me, now I return the favor. You used proxies. I will use proxies. Do not love anybody overmuch for I will also make them suffer. I hear that you are now boarding Pollux's garret rats. Does the heat of your desires make you find pleasure in fondling those of tender years? And then there is a pretty milliner who you share a daily cup of coffee with. I advise you to keep to yourself so the only sufferer is you."

Jonathan studied Castor, then took out a handkerchief and wiped the new line of drool from the corner of his lip. "Mr. Blanchard, if you believe your present situation is due to my ill will, you are mistaken. I would have completed the job if I had decided to kill you. If you intend to kill me, do not make a mistake, Mr. Blanchard. As you know, my resources are equal to yours. If you set out to harm those dear to me, I'll have this ship burned to the waterline with you in it."

Castor's eyes glittered with pleasure despite the effort required to even take a breath. "Amelia was her name, wasn't it? That's why you killed Hogwood. That's why you made an attempt on von Wurttemberg's life. I put the puzzle together. You understand I can have you killed quickly; however, I prefer a slower method. I have you, Mr. Asher. Make no mistake about it. I have you in the palm of my hand—I can crush you now or I can crush you later."

"I believe you not, Mr. Blanchard," Jonathan contested. "For you would have already done so. In a court of law, it comes down to your word against mine. And as men of the world, we know that means who has the most friends and who the most enemies. I give myself superior odds to you in that regard."

"Nay, Mr. Asher. The one who inspires greater fear always wins, always, and you do not have the advantage there."

CHAPTER 14

WEARING AN ADMONISHING expression, Millicent Dalton accosted Jonathan just as he was entering the warehouse and announced, "We need to speak privately, if you please, Mr. Asher."

"Then follow me to my office, Mrs. Dalton," Jonathan said, wondering what additional misdeed he had committed to cause her to break the three months of silence.

Dr. Smith appeared before they could continue the conversation, harrumphing with his usual natural discourtesy when introduced. Pinching the cloth pocket with money for bribes between thumb and forefinger, the good doctor carried it out of the room with the air of carrying a dead rat by the tail. Emma and Daniel then peeked in expectantly. Jonathan shared with them at least one meal a day, and this morning he had promised to take them to the Bowling Green and purchase as many oysters and fish pies and sugared nuts as they could eat. Jonathan told them to go next door and play with Thomasina and Josiah's children for a bit because the lady needed privacy. Daniel frowned, and Emma blew him a kiss.

Momentarily disconcerted as the children disappeared, Mrs. Dalton's face soon recovered its severity. "Mr. Asher, I was unaware you were a British officer when you pretended to be a friend and I confided to you about my brother serving as a lieutenant in Washington's army."

"I do not pretend friendship, madam," Jonathan replied.

"Like you pretended not being another squinty-eyed profiteering spotted toad who sells the provision of starving prisoners. I trusted that what I revealed about my brothers you'd keep in confidence, which any gentleman should have respected. I suppose 'twas foolish of me to be surprised when you used my confidences to deprive my husband of his livelihood. Like men of your ilk commonly do when they glimpse an opportunity to steal a good man's investment and labor, you stole it for yourself."

"Why would being a British officer make a difference?" Jonathan replied, as put off by her dangerously reddening face as by the words. "I told not a soul about your brother. I have not even thought of him, and all I know about your husband is that he valiantly defended you from the Sons of Liberty. As for my wickedness, you might have a point there. I don't engross flour or grain, however, in this city, any morsel of food sold is taken from the mouths of the hungry."

It was clear from his visitor's fierce stare that she was believing none of his story. "Several times I seen you in the company of this detestable man who always wears a slouch hat, and I now know he is an associate of yours and your commissary friend. How else can it be explained that it was he who arrived and demanded payment of our debts?

When Terence said he couldn't start paying until the mill started milling, soldiers came, mind you, your British soldiers with bayonets, and seized the mill my husband had devoted his fortune and three years of his life to and threw him out. Terence said the corporal accused him of being an intimate of rebels. Terence's parents have never uttered a disloyal word against King or Parliament in their lives. Colonel Delancey is a dear friend of theirs. Mr. Dalton blamed not me—he is too high-minded for that—yet he always warned me that if word got out about my brother David fighting with Washington it would cause trouble. Few people know about my Continental brother, and the only person in my acquaintance untrustworthy enough to use this information to his advantage is you."

"I am ignorant of this affair and could derive no benefit from revealing your brother's allegiance to seize your husband's mill," Jonathan said in a voice too maddeningly cool even for his own liking. "The man you refer to is, I believe, Mr. Curston, who is certainly no friend of mine. He does hire himself out to collect on debts. I can investigate the situation. Offhand, having some familiarity with how these things come about, I'd say your husband probably offended the wrong person, or a competitor bribed the right person. Whether you choose to believe me or not, Mrs. Dalton, I would never conspire to deprive a man of his livelihood."

"Nay, you're just content to let us starve," she retorted, contempt hardening her features and her eyes. "And the king expects us to be loyal subjects when his red-coated vultures pick at our bones."

"Even though my iniquity seems beyond the pale to

you, Mrs. Dalton, I'm not at fault here," Jonathan replied, beginning to lose the battle with his temper.

She shook her head. "Could have only come from you, Mr. Asher, or whatever your name is at present. Only you and your friends."

"Since you already decided I'm the culprit and out of reach of redemption, what is the purpose of this interview?" Jonathan asked.

"To confront you with your vileness," she replied.

"Dear Mrs. Dalton …," Jonathan began, then shook his head, sensing behind the anger something fiercer. "Believe of me what you will. I promise this: I am aware how difficult it is for a good man to pursue an honest enterprise in this city so I will inquire into the cause of your husband's misfortune. Where do you live? I'll send a message if I find out who is behind the seizure of your husband's mill."

"As if I could read!" Her face now beet red, Millicent glanced at the books on his desk. Jonathan had never quite lived down the admonishment of the missionary Theobald and spent his few spare hours puzzling over the languages of the Bible. He made the acquaintance with a Jewish man who was for hire to teach Hebrew. He looked for a Greek speaker and was informed to his disappointment that the Greek of the New Testament was no longer spoken. "Mr. Dalton vowed to teach me as soon as the mill was operating so I could converse with other proper ladies. That, of course, is impossible now."

Despite her storm of vitriol, Jonathan felt a sudden pang of pity for this woman who seemed so ashamed by her illiteracy and who was hiding a greater shameful secret of having once been a prostitute. "I'm sorry Mrs. Dalton, you are so well-spoken that I thought you could read. When I find out who's behind the seizure I'll pay you and your husband a visit and pass on the information."

Millicent hesitated, the internal debate playing out on her flushed features before she continued: "I think if I were better educated as a lady, I might have seen you for the man you are, Mr. Asher. I hate to confess this: I deeply regret recommending you to Elizabeth. In my experience, a man who betrays one woman in a small thing will betray all women in anything when 'tis to their advantage."

"You requested I protect Miss Elizabeth. Are you asking me now to withdraw my protection?" Jonathan had no intention of doing that no matter what Mrs. Dalton's opinion was. Recently, Elizabeth had wistfully commented that she feared she wasn't as interesting as the people of the high rank and station that he rubbed shoulders with now. He had replied truthfully that these moments with her were by far the most pleasurable part of his day. She blushed when she admitted, "We are not too different there."

Mrs. Dalton mouthed a few words, then replied, "I'm saying what I'm saying."

Jonathan was tempted to throw in his visitor's face her familiarity with a brothel but decided on another tack. "Mrs. Dalton, I do regret your loss of confidence in me. I have not always failed you. Did you recognize the man to who I gave the pocket?"

"I never set eyes on that surly fellow before in my life."

"Pity. Dr. Smith owes you a great debt of gratitude. You recommended me to his parents as the sole personage able to effect his release from the *Scorpion* prison ship. I was so flattered by your faith in me that I could do no less than extract him. So, I have not let you down in everything."

She was quiet for a moment, apparently at loss at how to reply.

Jonathan continued. "You may be right to condemn me. I ask myself can a man deal with thieves and not be one himself, and I've not arrived at an answer. I no longer transact business with Provost Cunningham nor the Commissary Castor Blanchard, although that makes not a whit of difference in the welfare of the prisoners for better or worse. I will talk to Mr. Curston—if you desire—in your presence to find out who's behind your husband's misfortune."

"How will that restore the mill?" Mrs. Dalton shivered and gulped back a sob. "I just want us to have a chance for a living that is not blocked at every turn. I just want us to keep what we have instead of everything being whittled away! And I don't want to cause my Terence more problems than he already has, which I always seem to fail to do because I do not know how to be what he expects me to be."

"Again, I swear I haven't mentioned the allegiance of your brothers to a soul, so your confidences to me are not the source of your husband's misfortune." Her distress cut to Jonathan's heart. "I swear to you I will discover why your husband lost the mill. As certain as I am, it had nothing to do with me, I'm also certain it had nothing to do with you."

Mrs. Dalton hesitated, still wanting an enemy to

attack. "I apologize if I falsely accused you. You and your ilk feed on this war, Mr. Asher. I see it every day. I work at a house where Mr. Spencer and his three sons moan about their gout morning, noon, and night, then I walk home past Canvas Town and my heart breaks when I see children so thin that they seem merely paper cut-outs."

"I too see the same children, Mrs. Dalton. You just met two of them who live with me. My agent makes sure many more are fed. I perhaps could do more but not by impoverishing myself."

"You can't imagine how much I desire for Elizabeth's sake to believe you."

"Good day, Mrs. Dalton. I will root out what happened to your husband's business venture, not in the hope of changing your opinion of me, but because from your account of him, he is a good man who does not deserve his bad fortune."

"Forgive me, Mr. Asher, I believe I said things that will make me ashamed later. All I want…" she didn't finish the sentence.

"You speak your mind to me, Mrs. Dalton. That is fair. I regret the poor impression I made on you."

"Good day, Mr. Asher," Mrs. Dalton said, backing out the door. "Don't trouble yourself on our behalf. We truly don't need your help." A deep blush made the lie obvious.

His sole responsibility in the King's army being to make money for Lady Beatrice and Lord Harold, Jonathan had fewer restrictions than possibly any other man in uniform in New York. So long as he continued to enrich his patrons, they didn't care what he did with his time.

Curston, at that moment, was making himself scarce. Gabriel had disappeared somewhere into New Jersey, probably on a mission to guide more slaves to their freedom. This left Jonathan no choice but to broach the subject with Major André. Even though the seizure of the mill was a minor incident, no individual was better attuned to influence and gossip in the city as André, so naturally, he would know such things as who was bribing whom. It cost Jonathan a good bottle of claret and ten days more credit on an outstanding bill to persuade André to look into the matter. Jonathan expected a delay of a few days, but André on striking the deal exclaimed, "No need for delay, Lieutenant Osborne, for I witnessed the events myself."

"You seem quite happy to have gained so much for what cost you so little."

"I am. I am. Not everybody can boast of having bested Mr. Asher or Lieutenant Philemon Osborne in a transaction." He smiled happily, relishing the victory. "Several aspects of the affair are very curious, Lieutenant Osborne. This tall redheaded man, not quite of the right station, appears at the club in the company of Mr. Blanchard a few days before the commissary's unfortunate apoplectic fit. Apparently, this bumpkin had been playing cards with your former business associate and won a quantity of money. You know the ability of Castor at the gaming table, so this piqued our interest. Soon we realized that even if the individual hadn't overly imbibed a quantity of spirits, he would have been a complete nincompoop at cards. I doubt he had played a game of chance before in his life. He sat down at the table believing he had a special knack and fully expecting his winning streak to continue.

The inevitable happened. Castor cleaned him out. But the other inexplicable part was that Castor did not destroy him, which as you know he customarily takes so much pleasure in doing. After winning several hundred pounds, Castor refused to play, even though the man was begging him to continue so he could recover his losses. It was as if Castor was given a job to break the man, yet not utterly impoverish him."

"Castor got a mill."

"What would Castor do with a mill? Or for that matter anybody? Most of our flour is smuggled in already milled from Connecticut. Maybe he had information of a seizure of a large quantity of unmilled grain. There have been rumors that price controls on flour are to be lifted for a week and the windfall promises to be great."

Jonathan doubted that the reason that Castor had lured Millicent's husband to the gaming table was his wife's slight acquaintance with him. A visit to Pollux completed the story. Castor had acquired Mr. Dalton's loan from another creditor. Mr. Dalton needed an addition of a mere twenty-five pounds in his credit to finish the work. Castor said there was no difficulty in extending more credit to a gentleman but jokingly had added he would only loan the twenty-five pounds if Mr. Dalton would play a hand or two of cards with him. The man became so excited about his initial winnings. He said he was going to buy his wife a carriage, et cetera, et cetera. When the man wanted to quit, Castor said gentlemen allow other gentlemen to recoup their losses and took him to the club.

Jonathan now held a secret each of Mrs. Dalton and her husband. The shame of losing the mill at cards, the cowardice of blaming it on his wife's family versus the shame of having worked in a brothel. Yet what happened to Terence appeared the work of an enemy. And as for the brothel, half the women who labored there once held the opinion they would die before becoming a trull. Jonathan's heart went out to them—they were good people victimized by the circumstances war creates—and he felt obligated to help in some way.

The house where the Daltons lived lay on the margins of the city and had once been the comfortable residence of its dispossessed owners. Now it housed four or five families struggling to keep their heads above the rising tide of poverty. Activity surrounded the place: two women washed clothes in a tub of boiling water, a dozen children milled about, half doing chores like sweeping and gathering sticks, and half arguing about who would do the other chores. If the Daltons were lucky, only one family would be installed per room in the residence. Jonathan had purposely visited when Millicent Dalton was away.

"I am Mr. Terence Dalton," the exceptionally tall red-headed man responded to Jonathan's inquiry at the door of the establishment. "What is the nature of your visit?"

Jonathan explained he had learned of the loss of the mill and offered him the job of working in his employ as a teamster.

"Why are you taking such an interest in us, Lieutenant Osborne?" Terence Dalton asked in a vaguely threatening tone. Strangely, with the tension in the shoulders, the pride, and anger holding his head up, shame pushing it down, he reminded Jonathan of Mr. McDonald who had haunted him the early years of his preaching. He was fighting hard to not become a broken man. In Jonathan's experience, few things were as painful to observe as a moral man attempting to hide a large moral lapse.

"Your wife blamed me for this terrible affair. She believed I told the authorities about her rebel brother in Washington's army," Jonathan replied. "I value my good name."

"What is your connection with my wife? She never mentioned a Lieutenant Osborne as an acquaintance." Mr. Dalton peered suspiciously at Jonathan's uniform.

"I met her through a mutual friend, Miss Elizabeth," Jonathan explained. "She might have mentioned a Mr. Asher."

"Well, my dear wife who puts her nose into everybody's business and then chatters ceaselessly about it failed to mention either name, but I thank you for your offer, sir. Unfortunately, most here value their pocket more than their reputation." Mr. Dalton was suddenly racked by a coughing fit so loud that it seemed that an angry creature inside his hollow chest cavity was pounding to get out.

"I can find you other employment if driving a team of horses don't suit," Jonathan said.

"Thank you, sir, however, I do not need charity. I am starting work tomorrow with a dozen other laborers going out beyond Kingsbridge and chopping wood for your army. Not the sort of work I am accustomed to, albeit I'm as strong and willing as the next man, and felling trees fits with my humor at the moment. That will take care of immediate needs. I will then apply to my father. Perhaps he will allow me to assist in managing his estate on Long

Island." He coughed again, not so roughly. "This damn catarrh. Good day, sir. You cleared your name with me, and I will tell my wife you had no part in the seizure of the mill, which, unfortunately, to everybody except my wife and me, is of small consequence." He screwed his face into a frown before presenting the lie: "The power you represent don't consider it sufficient to be a loyal subject of the king and keep his laws to protect him from injustice."

CHAPTER 15

EVEN THOUGH THE extravagant Howe had been replaced by the parsimonious Clinton, Jonathan and Lady Beatrice's business in champagne and fine wines flourished as was natural in a city of thousands of thirsty soldiers and hundreds of officers with means. Not only were there horse races on Hempstead Plains, fox hunting in Queens County, cricket on the Bowling Green, and billiards at Kings Head Tavern, Major John André, who ruled the social life of the city, turned his engineering talents into organizing endless dances, fetes, plays, and possibly the grandest event New York had ever witnessed: the celebration of the birthday of Queen Charlotte with a parade of four thousand soldiers. Jonathan and Lady Beatrice's inventory was quite exhausted after the ball where Baroness von Reisdesel stood in for the queen.

The terrible winter of 1779 was the coldest in memory with sentries freezing at their posts, snowdrifts piling up to the eaves, the ice on the North River several yards thick, and a daily deadly toll in Canvas Town. Josiah claimed piss solidified in mid-stream. The cavalry exercised by stampeding across the frozen bay and river. After the raid by General Lord Stirling into Staten Island using the thick ice as a bridge, Governor Tryon drafted all males between 17 and 60 to help resist other incursions across the frozen waterways. Emma and Daniel adopted two more cats. On the worst days, the children of Josiah and his brothers played with Daniel because of the luxury of a room heated by two iron-grated coal stoves. Emma always sat off to the side—quiet with a pleasant smile. The sharing of the coffee now took place inside the millinery. Customers were rare. Elizabeth apologized for her frugality. Jonathan once tried to compensate for the lack by recruiting Lady Beatrice's pastry chef to make special rolls. That did not go well. "I grieve that you are dissatisfied with my poor fare," she accused him. Elizabeth was fiercely proud and wouldn't countenance the suggestion she couldn't contribute her part. Jonathan had to content himself with bringing the coffee while she provided plain rolls and butter. They did engage in the fiction of her accepting coal from him at one-fifth the market price, by claiming he had a special provider, so the millinery was always warm. Even though the pittance Jonathan received, he could do without, Elizabeth would freeze rather than not pay.

1780 March

Melanie delivered a note from Gabriel along with four hundred pounds from rent collection and various other enterprises: "Jaeger Hoffman Baiting Hollow Long Island." Jonathan knew that the company at Baiting

Hollow was a mix of British and Hessian troops. Although their short-bored rifled guns were not as accurate as the longer Pennsylvania rifles, the Jaegers were seen as balancing out the advantage the Pennsylvania riflemen gave the Continentals.

Gabriel had disappeared on undisclosed business, likely into Connecticut, hence the precise location of Hoffman. For once, the obstacles were minimal. The trip would take a week. Meredith James was still recovering. At the last unloading of Rodrigo's cargo, he could barely stand and gave orders in a whisper. The weather was clear, and Jonathan still had an assortment of wine and spiritous liquors highly valued by the Hessians. He hadn't seen Curston in months, and without considering the ramifications, he began to prepare for his venture into Long Island.

Daniel was furious at not being allowed to accompany him, and Emma expressed her disappointment with her maddeningly silent tears. Although Thomasina, Josiah's wife, fussed over Emma and Daniel more than over her children because she believed them fragile and vulnerable, nevertheless, Emma and Daniel were stubbornly loyal to him. The real source of their anger did not dawn on Jonathan until he started to cross on the Brooklyn ferry with his loaded cart: they were terrified he might perish like their parents. Furthermore, his assumption that somebody else, likely more capable, would take care of them in the event of his death was less than certain.

Jonathan had procured a letter of recommendation to Captain Oliver, the head of the British contingent of the company from Major André—the price of which was four puncheons of rum. When after three days of travel he arrived at the camp, which was a staging area for raids into Connecticut, Jonathan sold his whole cart at a profit to the officers. He had to admit these troops weren't a bad sort in part because Captain Oliver was a superb officer. The company rebuilt a loyalist's house that had been burned down by Continental raiders and hanged a grenadier who had raped a girl. The locals and the soldiers engaged in good-natured banter whenever they met.

Thirty Jaegers were stationed at Baiting Hollow. The greater range of their rifles made them invaluable in longboat battles. Hoffman was their captain and shared the general responsibilities of the company with Oliver. Twenty-nine Hessians were at the party where Jonathan's Rhenish wine was the main event and all twenty-nine got maudlin drunk and sang hymns and tavern songs in German. Captain Hoffman was nowhere to be found. Jonathan learned that Hoffman was also the commanding officer of another contingent of Jaegers eighteen miles up the coast, so was likely visiting there. His wagon empty, Jonathan couldn't justify his presence any longer, and in another day, they would begin to question why he was lingering. So, he set off, promising to return.

A quarter-mile from the camp Jonathan spotted Captain Hoffman walking toward a pond that was also a mineral hot spring, bare-chested and barefoot with a change of clothes under his arm. Jonathan stopped, tethered the horses, and followed. He carried his tomahawk and a long-barreled pistol, which was deadly accurate up to twenty yards. He acted automatically, feeling neither fear nor anger. This was a dirty job that had to be done. To kill the unarmed Hoffman would be an easy task; still, perversely Jonathan again wanted Amelia's killer to know why he was to die. It would make his act less like murder and more like judgment and punishment.

Hoffman waded into the pond. Jonathan was about to hail him as a preliminary to drawing closer when suddenly the Jaeger was attacked by three children, splashing, and yelling in German. Hoffman splashed back. Picking up a girl, Hoffman tickled her and threw her squealing into deeper water. He did the same to the two boys. Then he caught sight of Jonathan.

"You are the wine lieutenant," he called out in a thick accent.

"I am," Jonathan replied.

"I am Captain Hoffman. These my sons, my daughter—Hans, Klaus, and Christina." Hoffman's three children grinned hugely at Jonathan as he held up each one in turn.

"I'm just here to fill my canteen," Jonathan said, trying not to think of Emma and Daniel who were waiting for him to return.

"What?" Captain Hoffman laughed. "With all your wine and coffee, you save not a sip for yourself."

Jonathan wrestled with his conscience the rest of the afternoon, alternately accusing himself of cowardice and criminality. Finally, he asked, *what would Nate Cowan have done?* Unfortunately, he had no idea.

"Some judgments best left to God," Jonathan muttered as he accommodated himself in a bed he did not have to share at a roadside inn, and to his surprise fell soundly asleep.

CHAPTER 16

"I KNOW WHO you are, wine lieutenant, and I know you come to the camp to kill me." It was the afternoon of the next day. The neckless Jaeger Captain Hoffman stood in the middle of the road, leveling his rifle.

Jonathan stopped the horses. Keeping the rifle pointed at him, Hoffman walked around until he was standing next to Jonathan.

"Forgive, I am not so good with the English. Do not have the fear. I kill you already many times if that is my desire. Do not make the denial. Von Wurttemberg say you cry the name when you shoot him—Amelia, a name of a woman, is it not? A young woman. A Mr. Asher ask at Rhine Maiden Tavern for me. A Mr. Asher lose his wagon to rebel raiders. Why is Mr. Asher such the fool? You kill the British captain. A Lieutenant Philemon Osborne come to the camp, and I learn he is also the Mr. Asher."

Jonathan met the eyes, which were the blue of frozen lake ice. "I'd have killed you had it not been for your children."

Hoffman lowered the rifle. "I am a soldier. I saw the

death in your eyes. Was this Amelia the sister?" His voice was consoling.

"We were to be married," Jonathan said.

"Ah, such a pity! It wounds the heart." Hoffman shook his head that rested directly on his shoulders.

"Afore he died, Captain Hogwood said you violated her many times," Jonathan continued coldly and saw the Jaeger flinch as if slapped across the face.

"My first time to so ravish the innocent girl," Hoffman said and appeared to tear up. "Please to believe me. Please to believe I not strike her with the musket, I not run over her with cart. I am not so the cruel man. Yet I am her murderer for I ravish the innocent girl, and I, in my shame, fail to stop Captain Hogwood and Major von Wurttemberg from the bad things. I, a man with the good wife, make so ugly a deed. You understand I know who you are, wine lieutenant. I ask to myself what to do, and I answer to myself let God decide who to live, who to die. Alone we meet. No second. No witness. If God will you die, I bury you by the side of your Amelia. If God will I die, make so the body is found and never tell a soul how I ravish the beautiful innocent girl. Bury my shame and the crime and leave me to the judgment of God. Come, we must not put off this thing. I take you to the place where only the Almighty see and decide. My affairs are in order. The reason I let you live now is to see if God forgives me in this world or I beg mercy in the next."

"And your children?" Jonathan asked.

"I have two brothers in my regiment. My wife will marry one of them. She was the wife of my brother who died before she became my wife. That is how it is done in our family where the fathers die often," Hoffman explained.

"I would not go through with our duel for the sake of your children," Jonathan said.

"Please to let me insist, wine lieutenant. I love them, but I want not to be with them if God wants not the man who do the evil thing be with them."

Jonathan was beyond all bounds of reason relieved to find Emma and Daniel alive and well.

Unable to suppress the feeling that he was a vile betrayer, Jonathan begged Gabriel who had returned thinner but with an air of contentment to see that the children would fall into good hands if he did not return.

"Goodwins taking dem in," Gabriel said.

"They detest me," Jonathan exclaimed.

"I 'splain. Dey not hate you. Like Miss Amelia, dey no never turn away a poor child in need."

Jonathan was taken aback realizing the obvious truth that the Goodwins had raised their daughter to be kind. The next thing Gabriel said caught him off guard.

"I be murdering de Jaeger."

"No, Gabriel. 'Tis my job."

"Dese children your job."

"You have children," Jonathan argued.

"'N I puts my children afore my honor. De Jaeger be dead afore he know he dying. You for de sake of honor fight face to face, I for de sake of your poor children murder de bugger."

"Nay, Gabriel. I will not let you do this for me."

Gabriel shook his head.

Jonathan and Hoffman met early the next morning on a country lane that led to an abandoned homestead beyond the town of Gravesend in southern Long Island. To not attract attention to himself, Jonathan dressed drably as a teamster, carrying his uniform in a haversack. They proceeded south into a woody swampy region. On a rise, Jonathan glimpsed beneath a troubled gray sky the ocean in a cold boil and a small cutter threading the channel between Pine Island and Long Island. He and Hoffman faced off in a clearing. Both were armed with muskets and pistols. Jonathan had his tomahawk and a dirk. Hoffman carried a cutlass and a bayonet.

"You think to spare me for the children?" Hoffman asked. "Do not, for I spare not you. If God make it His will, I deserve the death for making death to your dear Amelia, my death for your grief. If not, then you, wine lieutenant, face His judgment first."

"With nobody else present we can't do a proper duel, so I propose we go our separate ways into the forest and then stalk each other," Jonathan said remembering the Hessian's physique when he bathed. Although muscled like a plow horse, he moved swiftly.

"I am a Jaeger, what you call chasseur, a man of the forest," Captain Hoffman explained with pride, allowing Jonathan to choose another venue.

"So am I," Jonathan said.

"We do what you say then," Hoffman agreed.

They placed themselves a dozen yards apart on the opposite side of the clearing. "We begin," the Hessian shouted.

They both plunged into the forest, Jonathan unsure

who was hunting whom. They worked their way closer to each other, the Jaeger making a lot of noise as if he didn't care whether Jonathan knew where he was or not. Jonathan began to see flashes of the Hessian's uniform and gray Scots' bonnet as both moved deeper into the brush and trees. *And he calls himself a man of the forest*, Jonathan thought. His strategy was simple. Find a secure spot, keep quiet, and ambush Hoffman when he shows himself.

Hoffman called out: "You know where I am, and I know not where you are, wine lieutenant. *Sehr Gut.* I think you are behind the tree."

What followed was a slight scuffling sound as the Hessian approached up the side of a shallow ravine not ten yards away. Suddenly the uniform jacket with the woolen cap popped up. Jonathan took the opportunity and fired. The jacket was blown away leaving the stub of a branch that Hoffman had dressed in his clothes. The Jaeger rose and fired, a hail of bark from the tree next to Jonathan sprayed into his face. Not having the precious seconds to reload, both threw down their muskets, crouched, drew out the pistols, and at a deadly ten paces discharged into each other's faces. Both missed, shooting high. Hoffman picked up his musket, pressed on his bayonet, and charged. Jonathan barely had time to throw the tomahawk before being impaled, which made the Hessian swerve.

Jonathan turned and ran—the instinct for self-preservation not giving him time to think. Hoffman discarded his musket a second time so he could pursue unencumbered and drew out his cutlass. Hoffman's strides more than matched Jonathan's as he fled deeper into the woods crashing through the underbrush. They reached several hundred yards of salt marsh that sucked down their boots. Jonathan was fortunate that Hoffman fell twice because as a chasseur—a hunter—Hoffman was a tireless runner. He was a few paces behind Jonathan when they arrived at a rocky beach. With no time to consider that the ocean might be an impassable barrier, Jonathan hurled himself into a huge sucking breaker. Hoffman was almost within a cutlass's reach, so the same wave knocked them both on their rears. Before either could get his feet, the next wave engulfed them, the water swirling over their heads. Recovering first, Jonathan scrambled back to the rocky shore just as Hoffman tore himself free from the angry foam.

"No good, wine lieutenant, to run away. You either die here and now or die on the gibbet." Hoffman shouted as he strode through the surf cutlass in hand.

"God has not rendered judgment yet," Jonathan replied, his voice as hoarse as the cawing gulls.

The dirk being useless in such a contest, Jonathan picked up a soggy piece of wood that may have once been an oar. The spongy wood being no weapon, Jonathan flung it at the Jaeger who batted it away and continued approaching

The only other object at hand was a large round stone. Jonathan crouched, found a slippery hold, lifted it above his head, and heaved it at Hoffman who was now taking the last long step forward with raised sword. The stone struck Hoffman square in the chest a split second before he would have cleaved Jonathan's skull in half with the heavy blade, making the Jaeger stagger back, the wind coming out of him with an oomph, then stumble to his knees.

Jonathan bent down, quickly hefted another stone of similar size, and with an underhand swinging motion hurled it at the chasseur who rolled out of the way, clutching the cutlass to his chest. Jonathan recovered the first stone, and screaming, raised it above his head and began an unbalanced charge. For an uncertain moment, the stone seemed to be slipping backward. He tottered, managed to direct the stone in front of him, and it fell on the chasseur's sword hand just as he was using the sword to prop himself up.

"*Ach! Mein Gott! Mein Gott!*" Hoffman transferred the sword to his left hand and rose to his feet. Jonathan fingered the dirk and again decided that it would not do. Retrieving the oar, Jonathan hurled it without effect. Hoffman lurched forward, gasping to regain his wind.

Jonathan squatted to pick up a rock the size and shape of a small cannon. His grip failed—the stone was too heavy—and he collapsed to his knees. He threw two rocks which bounced harmlessly off the Jaeger, then desperately flung handfuls of sand into the Hessian's face and dodged as the sword sliced the air next to his ear. Jonathan grasped and twisted Hoffman's injured wrist eliciting a howl of pain but failed to get a grip on the hand with the deadly cutlass. Cursing and panting, the chasseur thrust the cutlass upward attempting to penetrate underneath the ribcage into Jonathan's lungs and heart. The tip of the cutlass struck a brass button diverting the blade and making it slide upward, cutting the leather of his coat, barely slicing the skin of his chest.

Jonathan shoved Hoffman away. The chasseur stumbled backward and skidded on the wet sand. A wave engulfed him. Jonathan attempted again to pick up the heavy oblong stone thrusting his arms underneath it. Closing his eyes and gritting his teeth, he succeeded and ran forward, doubled up. He dumped the stone on the chasseur's chest as the water withdrew. He heard the crack of a breaking rib and an expletive in German. A second wave swamped the chasseur and ran up to Jonathan's armpits.

It receded, revealing, less than two yards away, the Jaeger who had fixed himself in the spot by driving the cutlass its full length into the sand and clinging to it with his good hand. The stone lay between them. As Hoffman drew out the sword, Jonathan crouched, thrust his forearms into the wet sand beneath the stone, raised it to his thighs as he stood, and let it roll off his hands onto the crown of Hoffman's head. The moment froze. Blood running down his temple, Hoffman sat with the sword free and raised to strike. Jonathan, now fallen on hands and knees next to him, was defenseless. The Jaeger gurgled as he lost consciousness and fell face down. Jonathan pulled out his dirk and with a trembling hand slit Hoffman's throat. As the foam reddened around them, he shouted wildly "Are you watching God? Is this your will? Is it?" Then he heard a voice.

"Dis your doin'?"

Jonathan turned to see Gabriel picking his way over the beach toward him.

"My doing, May God have mercy on my soul."

Gabriel nudged the body with his boot. "'Rived too late. Dis man I plan to kill 'fore you getting here."

"I told you 'twas my business."

"Damn inconvenient my partner getting himself

gutted, which damn near happen. Den where our business be, where Emmy 'n Danny be?"

"We will leave his body so it can be found," Jonathan declared.

"No, suh. I want nothing connectin' you with dis damn dead clodhopper."

"I gave my word I would so his family learns he is dead."

"I say, no suh. Nobody find dis body. I cut off de hand with de ring. I send de bloody ding to his company wid note saying account evened now for de burning of Gis town Connecticut. Dat what dey see 'n dat what dey bury. Now get you gone. Emmy 'n Danny waiting for you."

Jonathan changed into his uniform, making himself as neat as possible, returned to the clearing, and then threaded the lanes which eventually led to Jamaica Road and the Brooklyn ferry. He felt nothing. His presence of mind was barely adequate for the simple task of taking the ferry to New York. He still felt numb when Emma hugged him in welcome and he answered Daniel's inquiries with halfhearted lies. Jonathan was ashamed of betraying them by putting his life at risk. He resisted thinking about the Jaeger's children. It was not until the night when he tried to sleep did the enormity of the day's events hit him. Then he relived the duel hundreds of times, sometimes prevailing, sometimes not.

He prayed that morning to never have to take a life again.

CHAPTER 17

May 1780

LADY BEATRICE'S ENTERTAINMENTS were famous and numerous. These fetes of a chosen few or balls with hundreds of guests allowed Jonathan to observe her business instincts and acumen closely. As well as saving money on claret and champagne, she ingratiated herself with her guests, working the colonels and brigadiers of the upper station much like Jonathan worked the lieutenants and majors of the not-so-exalted in the camps and taverns—engaging them in conversations and steering the topics toward what might make her profit. Her charm disguised her intent, and most would have been surprised to discover their gracious hostess early in the morning, wrapped in her hooded cloak, pouring over ledger books as diligently as any penny-pinching caster of accounts.

Major Duckett and Elizabeth's sister Stephanie were occasionally invitees to these fetes. Jonathan never presumed to participate because although as a well-off Tory and British officer he wasn't objectionable to the English officer class, they made it clear he should never consider himself their equal. Still, occasionally, Jonathan was present when the parties took place.

At one of these events celebrating the fall of Charleston to Cornwallis, while enduring a very bland colonel describe in detail the testicular ailment of his foxhound, Jonathan heard a cry that had a ludicrous resemblance to a quack, and then overheard Major John André whisper to a young lieutenant, "It appears Miss Littleton has hopelessly fuddled herself again."

There followed a moment of silence. Then the strange quacking wail of despair restarted and increased in volume until it arrested all conversation.

"She is in her cups," Jonathan's colonel explained. "This is going to be a trying evening. We can't just make our excuses to Lady Beatrice, but I'm damned if I am going to hear that drunken slut caterwauling for the next three hours."

Lady Beatrice approached Major Duckett, who of all the people present appeared not to hear the wail, and with her eyes and a nod communicated, "Tell your consort to get a hold of herself." They both directed themselves toward the door with a look of grim resolution on their faces.

Passing by Jonathan, Lady Beatrice whispered, "I'd be grateful for assistance."

Jonathan followed. In a small side room, Stephanie sat slumped in a chair, mucus and tears flowing copiously, hair half undone, dress askew showing more of the bosom than was fashionable. On seeing Major Duckett, she cried, "Oh, pity me, pity me, I am lost. I am so lost," and hurled her empty champagne glass at him.

"Really, Stephanie, you are making more of an ass of yourself than usual," Major Duckett said coldly after dodging the flying glassware.

"I asked you to calm her, Major Duckett, not provoke her," Lady Beatrice remarked icily.

"I don't see how I can accomplish that task since, obviously, she believes I'm the source of her woes." Major Duckett backed toward the door.

"Pity me. I am lost. I am so lost." More mucus, more tears, more desperate sobbing quacks.

"I am acquainted with her sister," Jonathan whispered to Lady Beatrice. "Let me see what I can do." He approached Stephanie who had buried her head in her hands. "Miss Stephanie, you remember me, don't you?"

Elizabeth's sister raised her thoroughly moist face wildly surmising, and then nodded in dim recognition.

"I'm going to bring Elizabeth to collect you."

"Oh, please do. I am so lost. Do you know she branded me?" Stephanie lifted her arm showing the white scar.

Jonathan commandeered the cart he used for small deliveries and drove to the millinery. After hearing his voice, Elizabeth, holding a flickering Betty lamp, answered the door in a rumpled dress and petticoat hastily put on. When Jonathan apologized and explained the situation, she sighed and said, "Nay, I'm glad you roused me. I must go to her."

Twenty minutes later, they arrived back at Lady Beatrice's residence. Crossing the drawing room towards the feeble quacks, Elizabeth, with her fine complexion of dark roses and cream, ringlets of black hair escaping her bonnet, and shining deep blue eyes drew many admiring glances. Jonathan led her to the side room that now only contained Stephanie.

On seeing her sister, Stephanie exclaimed, "Oh, dear Liza, I am so lost! So lost!"

Elizabeth embraced her sister, earning a wet shoulder, then sat beside her and held her hand. "We must go, Stephie."

"He is married. My major is married. I threw my reputation away on a married man!" Stephanie began to howl.

Elizabeth quietly whispered as she petted Stephanie's hand, "I am sorry for it, dear, but something lost can always be found again."

At this point, Major Duckett reentered the room, wobbling a little from drink, but in full possession of his arrogance. "I promised the guests to make sure her confounded bawling stops. Truly, Stephanie, you are demonstrating a scandalous lack of dignity."

"Yes, we are leaving, Major." Elizabeth's murderous glare met his eyes.

"You…" Stephanie exclaimed, rising, and pointing a trembling finger. "You deceived me, you scoundrel." The quacking sobs resumed.

"Madam…" Major Duckett swayed and surged forward. "Madam, just because I lay siege to a city and capture it, that doesn't mean I intend to spend the rest of my life residing there."

"You were already married," Stephanie howled.

"Marriage is a Divine Institution, not a crime," Major Duckett replied. Lady Beatrice now entered the room, her accusing gaze searching out Jonathan for worsening the situation.

"You said you would marry me." Stephanie began panting in preparation for another round of quacking howls.

"Yes, I did. I don't believe I said to who I would marry you. My valet is a fine young man…" Duckett said making a special effort to overcome his slurred pronunciation.

Elizabeth interrupted, "I always believed British officers took pride in comporting themselves as gentlemen. You, sir, prove I am gravely mistaken."

Duckett's mouth formed into a sneer. "The fact you claim kinship to this slut means you also are familiar with catering to the bawdy needs of the officer class."

"That is enough, Major," Jonathan said. "We are leaving, so you can put your mind at ease."

Elizabeth's Irish ire was up. "You are fortunate I am not having such an officer as a friend for he would challenge you to a duel for that gross insult."

"Maybe this lackey could stand in for you." Major Duckett nodded dismissively at Jonathan. Lady Beatrice stared daggers at Jonathan. Stirring this boiling pot by taking offense at Major Duckett's insult would endanger their business arrangement.

Jonathan wasn't certain he cared when he opened his mouth. Good sense prevailed barely, and he replied in a seething whisper, "I do not accept challenges from men too drunk to stand, nor do I challenge them."

"I could outfight you after quaffing ten more glasses of champagne." Major Duckett peeled off his glove, however before he could slap Jonathan, fumbled, and dropped it. When he bent to retrieve the glove, Lady Beatrice firmly put her foot on it.

"I'll duel you, to be sure," Elizabeth exclaimed, "with pistol, or sword, or nails, or teeth."

The major laughed. "Teeth, that's what I would want to duel with. Teeth."

"There will be no duels coming out of my fetes." Lady Beatrice was livid

"Teeth. That would be just the thing," the major repeated.

"Sir," Jonathan took his arm. "You are making a spectacle of yourself that you'll regret if you have any shred of decency sober. You have grossly insulted both Miss Littletons and Lady Beatrice."

"I say I challenge you to a duel." Major Duckett shook his arm free and began to peel off his other glove.

"With pleasure, I duel you if you can prove that you are in possession of your wits. Stand on one foot and salute the wall."

"As easy as eating pie," Major Duckett exclaimed, too drunk to question the silliness of the suggestion, and lifted a foot and stumbled forward. Elizabeth could not keep herself from a scornful laugh. He tried three more times.

Finally, Jonathan declared, "Since you are too cockeyed to know what you are about, Major Duckett, I will not pay heed to your challenge. Tomorrow, when you have recovered your wits, you may renew your challenge, and then I will consider it."

"My husband will visit you tomorrow, Major Duckett," Lady Beatrice added. "I suggest you spend the rest of the evening preparing your apologies."

"I can't duel Lord Harold." Major Duckett's thin wall of confidence was beginning to crumble.

"Fine brave soldier you are. You duel a young woman, but not a man," Elizabeth said derisively, her beautiful features momentarily distorted by contempt.

"You can't help putting yourself into further difficulties, Major Duckett, by continuing in this vein," Lady Beatrice lifted her foot off the glove.

Lord Harold who had been listening at the door then flung it open and walked in: "Major Duckett, I give you two choices. You can either depart now and we forget this unfortunate incident, believing that no soul is to be held accountable for his drunken babbling. Or you can stay, in which case, I report to our guests that you challenged a young woman to a duel. I vow you won't be able to live down the iniquity of this evening. You'll be the infamous Major Duckett, the coward who challenges women to duels."

Duckett tried to mouth, "'Twas in jest," but he could see Lord Harold was having none of it. The vestige of sobriety in Major Duckett slowly asserted itself, and he turned and tottered out of the room without a further word.

Stephanie could not sit upright so Jonathan and Elizabeth laid her down as comfortably as they could in the back of the cart. Her muttering and sobbing as they drove down the dark streets were interrupted by occasional spells of clear speech.

"Did I tell you, sir, my sister branded me?" Stephanie announced, sitting up.

Jonathan didn't respond.

She continued: "Liza, I'm so thankful you take care of

me. Where would I be without my little sister? Where…" a spell of rapid hiccups prevented her from finishing the sentence.

"At the party inebriated and making a fool of yourself, Steph," Elizabeth replied wearily.

"That don't matter for I was the prettiest girl in the room. My major said so. The eyes of all the men said so. I was so pretty, and I was feeling so happy…"

"Then you were having too much to drink," Elizabeth interjected.

"No, then a new lieutenant from London complimented Major Duckett on the riding habit of his wife in Hyde Park, which matched the colors of his regiment. Did I do anything then? No, I just smiled and let other men's eyes devour me. How I love being devoured by eyes. Then my major became jealous. Still, I was a good girl. I acted the part of the lady, and then I had too much champagne, and I'd say something, and I couldn't remember what I said. I knew I was saying foolish things, but I couldn't remember them, so I couldn't cover them up, and then I was in this room crying my eyes out, and the major was yelling at me, then you came, dear sister, who I don't deserve even though you branded me. Why did you brand me, Liza?" Stephanie finished this speech panting.

"So, you could tell everybody that you were branded by your sister, sure," Elizabeth replied.

"That couldn't have been the reason, could it?" Stephanie seemed bewildered by the idea. "I was the prettiest girl in the room, and the prettiest girl not in the room even with my mucky face until you came Elizabeth, then I no longer was, and that made me sad even though I was glad to see you."

"I am not gifted with great beauty like you, Steph," Elizabeth commented.

"Bosh! Just on account you never been kissed, may never be kissed because you're so... What's the word? So..." A spell of hiccups interrupted Stephanie at this point. When they passed, she went on, "So serious. And so... What's the other word? Contrary. And you are strange—you must admit that, Liza. Men don't like serious, contrary, strange ladies. So, you may have the good fortune of never being kissed. And you know, Percival and me, we can't get along without you. We go off and do these silly things, and you take care of us and father too."

There was a gasp followed by the sound of shifting. Jonathan glanced back and saw Elizabeth's sister hanging her head over the side of the cart and throwing up.

Jonathan and Elizabeth supported Stephanie up the stairs into her bedroom. Not wanting to return to the party, Jonathan next drove the cart to the boarding stable, unhooked it, and attended to the horse. He was surprised to see Elizabeth when he came out.

"I will thank you personally this time," she said softly.

Jonathan thought he could discern a smile in the weak lamplight. "I am glad to be of service. Is your sister alright?"

Elizabeth sighed and laughed. "Stephie is singing to herself. She will sing herself to sleep and wake up tomorrow without a care. I am so worried about her. I believe she is too much of a dunderhead to realize how she is damaging her reputation."

"Forgive me for speaking thus, but your sister seems

the sort of woman that doesn't feel she is alive without masculine attention," Jonathan ventured to say.

"Unlike me, who is perfectly happy to live being contrary and strange," Elizabeth stated with unexpected bitterness. "Except you don't seem to think so. At least, you wouldn't be bringing coffee to a contrary strange woman."

"Nay, I wouldn't, and allow me to disprove one other contention of your sister. Please, stop and face me."

"Is that a command, Mr. Asher?" She asked.

Jonathan hesitated then nodded. He wasn't sure of the propriety.

Elizabeth turned and obeyed.

He gently clasped her shoulders and slowly pulled her towards him giving her plenty of time to protest. He kissed her surprisingly soft lips. She momentarily surrendered herself to him, then stepped back.

"I think as with coffee, I need to be trying it again just to make sure." She giggled.

Jonathan obliged.

"Oh, one more time, Mr. Asher. I haven't decided yet," Elizabeth whispered.

He kissed her again.

"I am very much in your debt now, for I, the contrary strange woman, can claim to have been kissed before I die. I think kissing is preferable to coffee, at least in the evenings, and I wouldn't mind if you are coming around every so often to give me one—I mean like you do with your coffee."

"I don't find you at all contrary."

"But I'm serious and strange, to be sure."

Jonathan laughed. "Perhaps, and warm and witty and brave."

"Still maybe that isn't sufficient to balance out my flaws." Elizabeth stared at Jonathan, then intently gazed upward. "I'm not so accustomed to seeing the stars," she remarked wistfully. "I think I may come to enjoy looking at them."

Jonathan held her hands. The words that they both desired wouldn't come out. Later that night Jonathan told himself that enough was enough. He wanted no more of the war. He would give up spying. He would surrender his commission. He would marry Elizabeth and spend the rest of his life with her Irish sweetness and her Irish temper. He began to plan another meeting with Hamilton.

CHAPTER 18

THE CRISIS IN the Littleton household occurred a few days later. Percival challenged Major Duckett to a duel. Instead of accepting, the major declared he didn't duel snot-nosed colonials. That evening, several men Percival believed were British officers jumped him and beat him severely with cudgels, mocked his pretensions, poured yellow paint over him, then dumped him on the doorstep of the millinery.

The colonel of his regiment visited and assured Percy that he would find the culprits and make the rascals suffer. Stephanie's major appeared next and apologized for his insulting manner and explained he was sorry about Miss Stephanie, however, he refused to duel over a woman who misunderstood his words. Stephanie then arrived and explained that the major had not deceived her, such a good man could never deceive. She just hadn't under-stood—he knows how sometimes she doesn't understand very well. Besides, another major, an honorable man, who she was more than certain was not married was courting her, and if Percy persisted perhaps that honorable major may take it amiss.

Jonathan met Percival coming down the stairs, bruised and stiff. He carried a knapsack and was dressed in his uniform. A furrowed brow and dark circles under his eyes marred his usually smooth and clean face. Elizabeth, who normally would be fussing over his appearance, seemed afraid to approach him.

Glaring at Jonathan, Percival declared: "Tell your friends in New Jersey we will lay waste to the property of whoever has ever harbored a rebel. They will sleep in caves and ditches and gnaw bark this winter." Percival avoided looking at Elizabeth until she caught his hand. "I'll prove my blood with my sword," he swore, not meeting her eye. "And anyone who doubts can meet me on the field of honor."

Jonathan discerned fear on his beloved's face.

Percival's colonel spent a good part of the following weeks denying the reports of the viciousness of the raids conducted by the loyalist troops led by Governor Tryon, a newly minted brigadier general, who accompanied the Hessian General Knyphausen into New Jersey. The King's forces were driven back into New York leaving behind not only death and ruination but irreconcilable hostility to the King's cause.

Insisting on the meeting, Jonathan rode half the night in the bitter cold to talk to Hamilton at a crossroad in New Jersey. Hamilton, always eventually good to his word, was waiting. Jonathan explained that he was giving up the spying business. He was perfectly honest as to his reasons. He had become attached to people, meaning the children and Elizabeth, and they returned his affection, therefore his life was no longer completely his to give to the cause of liberty.

Seemingly sympathetic, Hamilton inquired: "And the Hessians involved in Amelia's murder?"

"One has disappeared," Jonathan replied, avoiding Hamilton's stare. "And I doubt we'll see the other on this side of the ocean again. Rest assured, I will not pursue Major von Wurttemberg into the Palatine."

"But if he returns, will you not challenge him?"

"I'd certainly lose in a duel. I leave his punishment to the Lord who after all has claimed the right more than once in his book."

"I wish you joy and success, Mr. Asher. You have been instrumental to our cause. I do feel obliged to mention a further consideration. If you marry Miss Littleton and in the least way contribute to her business, and afterward are discovered to be a spy, her millinery would be subject to confiscation."

"The millinery is in the name of her father." Jonathan's protest sounded hollow.

"You better than most know how these things work. Your wife's family might win in court when civil courts are reinstated, but in the meantime, they starve. The purpose of the confiscations is to dissuade others from acting as you have acted. No matter what, the revelation of their connection to you would ruin their business. Spies more than soldiers shouldn't marry. I am saying that as a friend. I shall no longer expect your valuable communications. I do advise you to wait until the war ends, Mr. Asher, then marry your lady, and may you receive all the blessings you well deserve."

Jonathan would not wait until the war ended, however, he decided to delay a few months, giving him time to shift assets to a safer harbor. If he scrimped and bought no more properties, he could accumulate two thousand gold guineas. In the event of being discovered as a spy, he wanted to make sure Elizabeth, Emma, and Daniel were provided for. He would tell Gabriel his plans. He thought it odd that he trusted that dour black man more than any other soul. Gabriel rarely gave his word, never broke it, and consequently could call on hundreds of different people to facilitate this or that enterprise.

Millicent Dalton's frown portended another tempest when she entered the warehouse. Although his name was clear at least with her husband, Jonathan had looked forward to having as little conversation with Elizabeth's intimate friend as possible. Jonathan was uncomfortable knowing the secrets that would damn husband and wife each in the other's eyes. The keeping of such secrets acted like a slow poison. Their revelation could break hearts and lives. In his opinion, neither good soul deserved the hurt.

Jonathan felt a stab of pity at her appearance. Poverty was nibbling away at the edges of her dress—a patch, a rip, a stain on her shoe. She wore a chastened air, that is until her green eyes—the moss in them catching fire—met his eyes. Emma and Daniel scurried away. Jonathan girded himself for battle.

"I find myself forced to appeal to your goodness, Mr. Asher," she announced with great effort. "Since the situation doesn't directly concern me, I have hope for your cooperation."

"Why do you think I would exclude you from a favor, Mrs. Dalton?"

"After the words that have passed between us, Mr. Asher, I doubt you view me with sympathy."

"A few good words have also passed between us, Mrs. Dalton," Jonathan remarked, remembering when she was a passenger in his wagon. "Did your husband clear my name with you?"

His visitor reddened and nodded, suggesting to Jonathan that she had discovered the truth. Then she glared at him with close to unquenchable hostility and shook her head as if trying to shake it off. The result was a total fluster.

"What is this favor that doesn't concern you directly?" Jonathan asked.

Mrs. Dalton shook her head again as if getting rid of a gnat, and said, "What a goose I am. I have this little speech prepared, and then I say all these other things I don't mean to say. Mr. Dalton speaks true when he criticizes my peevish manners, saying they make me unladylike."

Jonathan's expression must have shown puzzlement. Most people never guessed her low station, and he had observed that in whatever company, Mrs. Dalton made an effort to be pleasant to all. He was the exception, and only then at times. "Well, I'm waiting for your speech, Mrs. Dalton."

She straightened her shoulders. "I heard it said that once you save a person, you're obligated to do so for the rest of your life. The matter concerns Elizabeth."

"I just returned from a trip last night. The last time Miss Elizabeth and I last shared a dish of coffee was four days ago, and she appeared in fine spirits then. She was only worried about Percival and Stephanie, which is her wont," Jonathan said. "I plan to visit her tomorrow and introduce my wards. If she were in trouble, she could have told my brother—he knew where to find me—and there is no reason for her to doubt I wouldn't respond immediately."

"But she was in doubt," Millicent challenged him.

"I don't understand why. When have I failed her?" Jonathan had a clue. Elizabeth was displaying an increasing impatience with him playing the young swain courting a love, yet not articulating a proposal.

"Well, she does," Millicent insisted. "I believe she believes you find her lacking."

"I will disabuse her of that notion very soon."

"She feels confused and ashamed and is afraid to ask, although she had done nothing shameful," Millicent asserted.

"Tell me plainly: what needs to be done?"

"This might not be so simple as just clubbing a few ruffians. Liza came to us in the middle of last night in tears. You see now that General Howe has gone back to London to explain himself, Mrs. Loring can no longer dispense favors such as keeping Elizabeth's millinery free from military lodgers. In other words, the people who decide such things have decided to quarter three officers in her house. I believe Percy may be at the bottom of it. The officers belong to Delancey's loyalist regiment, and I think are friends of his. They flatter him by calling him Lord Percy, and he is putty in their hands. They joke about who is going to marry Elizabeth and have a bedfellow that night although they've not attempted to compromise her yet. They joke that if she refuses their offers, they will persuade Percy to make the millinery into a dram shop because that would be more accommodating to their needs.

"Liza escaped when in the spirit of a jest they tried to perform a wedding ceremony. She ran outside and spent half the night wandering the streets until she found our place. Luckily, it was Saturday night, and I was at home with Mr. Dalton. She obviously cannot remain with us. We have only a single room, and giving over her shop, which is her world, even for a week to those lodgers, puts her business at great risk. A resolution to this problem is beyond our ability and means given that those in power, especially under martial law, receive complaints like hers unsympathetically. I believe Percy's friends possess a higher rank than you, yet you seem to exert influence beyond your station. I am remembering how you got Doctor Smith off the *Scorpion*. Maybe you could figure out a similar ploy."

"What is needed," Jonathan said, thinking out loud, "is a light touch in the right place or the right two places.

Millicent's face darkened at the word "light."

"Don't despair. Elizabeth will be taken care of." Jonathan glimpsed a solution that solved two problems and wouldn't require more than three bottles of claret as bribes.

"Do I have a promise?" She pleaded.

Jonathan observed her slowly redden before replying, "Nay, because I'd move heaven and earth to help Elizabeth, and a promise would mean I might consider doing otherwise. I do not doubt your love for Elizabeth, which you have shown in a hundred ways. Do not doubt mine. Good day, Mrs. Dalton."

CHAPTER 19

THE DILEMMA OF Emma and Daniel who were snug but isolated in their room above his warehouse suggested a solution to the problem. Jonathan had been worried about his two garret mice. Winter was coming. Sometimes he was gone for days, and there always existed the possibility of his arrest. Canvas Town was a dangerous place, although Gabriel assured him that on account of the goodwill built up and because people were aware of their history, Emma and Daniel could wander the whole of it and be safer than the children of Governor Tryon in their bedchambers. Jonathan was unaware of a specific threat, yet he had seen how quickly fortunes turned in the city and how unconcerned fate was with the lives of husbands and fathers who had families depending on them. Although Josiah and his brothers, now occupying the two houses on either side of the warehouse, would protect Emma and Daniel in an upheaval, sacred property or lives did not exist in a food riot. Adding to his worry were Emma and Daniel's attachment to him. In his opinion, they could have chosen a better object of loyalty and affection.

He once asked the children, "Are you not lonely in this cold, lonely place?"

They both shook their heads and Daniel said, "Who else would guard your merchandise?"

Jonathan had come up with a neat solution. He decided to try out his idea on Lady Beatrice, certain she would be delighted with the ruse.

As an excellent reader of men, Lady Beatrice never quite accepted Jonathan at face value. On hearing his proposal, she challenged him: "What is the use of the wealth you gained by cornering the market on French champagne if you play the miser and don't cut a figure in the world."

"As you know very well, one needs a title and manners to cut a figure, and I doubt I can acquire either," Jonathan replied, parrying her comment.

"There's another game you're playing at, Lieutenant Osborne, and I'll nose it out, anon. I always do. Now, you're telling me you want to give Colonel Goshen a son and daughter?"

"Yes, that is my intention." He was beginning to worry because Lady Beatrice hadn't immediately seized on his clever idea.

"And for them to be quartered at Miss Elizabeth's millinery?" Lady Beatrice's smile was rather on the temperate to cool side.

"That is what I'm proposing, Lady Beatrice," Jonathan said, unable to avoid sounding smug. "I'm certain with your influence on Lord Harold, it can be done."

"Clever, I admit, yet I must refuse," Lady Beatrice replied.

"I know 'tis unusual..." Jonathan began to protest. Lady Beatrice thrived on unorthodox ideas, including her business relationship with him.

"That isn't it, Mr. Asher," Lady Beatrice interrupted hotly. "The problem is you. You have cared for the children for ten or eleven months?"

"That is true."

"You once recounted how you and your sister were found on the banks of the River of the Cherokee by the good people who raised you." Lady Beatrice drew herself up to her intimidating height.

"That is also true," Jonathan confirmed.

"What will happen to Colonel Goshen's children after the war?" Lady Beatrice asked, her mouth rigid, her color high, her eyes emitting flares.

"I will take care of them, of course. What are you suggesting?" He asked.

She drew in a deep breath. "I am suggesting, Mr. Asher or Lieutenant Osborne or whatever other name fits you at the moment, they become your children."

"I don't see how they can become my children." Jonathan felt himself flushing.

Lady Beatrice now smiled wickedly, and Jonathan sensed that her anger had been merely an act. "True, adoption is not allowed under the Common Law, and I understand 'tis rare here because estates must flow with the blood, yet with the British military bureaucracy, and in this case a quartermaster's signature, all things are possible. If we can create a colonel out of thin air, we can certainly make adjustments to the patrimony of a second lieutenant.

"I believe that for the purposes of quartering, I can persuade Lord Harold to declare your garret mice the children of Lieutenant Osborne, in other words as your children. In fact, I will do it with or without your consent. Congratulations, Mr. Asher and Lieutenant Osborne, you now possess a son and daughter. I calculate just from our little business you must be a man of substantial means. If you die, you need somebody to leave your riches to. Tell the troubled young lady to visit me. When she came to collect her horrible sister the other night, the sudden apparition of this beauty startled many of my guests, and she was a topic of conversation for a good hour afterward. She puts the more common beauty of her poor confused sibling to shame. I'll entertain her while you make the arrangements."

"She is only a proprietress of a dress shop," Jonathan said.

"Young man, as you know, I'm the daughter of a milkmaid and blacksmith, a woman of no station, until I married an old, impoverished baronet, so I'm not put off by people of low degree. Why wouldn't I become a lady? I was the most beautiful woman in the county, and I was cleverer by half than any man. Lord Harold only had to be keen enough to realize that if he married me, a widow of the old foolish baronet, after the scandal and the shunning died away, he would have a companion who would ably manage his career. Ladies that had refused to occupy the same room as me because they considered me a trollop who seduced a doddering old fool, over the course of a few years, came to consider it a social disgrace not to be invited to my fetes, even though they were still snickering behind my back. Bring this Elizabeth to me so I can look her over. I sense she has brains along with her beauty. She might help me figure you out. At least, she is a new diversion. I might even make a project of her since my nephew Edgar appears to be a futile ungrateful object of my attention."

The next day, he and Daniel spent an hour coaxing Emma outside. They did not like the idea of moving and were initially afraid it was a pretext to abandon them. When Jonathan informed the children that they were now his son and daughter, and therefore they would see him often, Emma and Daniel appeared confused but were somewhat mollified by the idea of having a real father again. The hint that the woman they stayed with might become their mother and the assurance they could bring the cats sealed the deal. Three cats, Jonathan decided, would be less of a bane to Elizabeth than three lubricious militia officers.

They first took a coach to Dalton's residence. With some pride, Jonathan noticed how much better dressed Emma and Daniel were than the children they passed on the street. They climbed the narrow stairway that led to the narrow room that Millicent and her husband shared. Elizabeth answered the door, her eyes red, her nose red, her lips turned down in utter despondency. Coughing came from behind the door. Millicent was apparently at the Spencers' residence working.

"Miss Elizabeth, I'd like to introduce you to the new people who will be quartering at your house. This is Emma. Although she does not talk, she is very well behaved, and this is Daniel, who will help you with your chores. I told you about them. They have become thanks to the wisdom and omnipotence of the British bureaucracy my son and daughter," Jonathan said in a formal voice, then waited a moment for the surprise to register on her face, which it did.

He continued: "The powers in the British command decided I needed a family and thus ordained it, at least as far as quartering is concerned. We are to be quartered in your house. I prefer for myself the warehouse or my brother's hospitality because of my late hours. I will provide for Emma and Daniel food and upkeep. The gentlemen who are staying with you presently are to be escorted to another residence tomorrow, I hear a small cottage with three unmarried daughters, all over six feet tall. Lady Beatrice has been essential in arranging this and desires to make your acquaintance. You may stay at her house along with Daniel and Emma, who she also desires to meet until the officers are situated in their new quarters. Tomorrow, you may attend a ball that she is hosting."

Elizabeth stood mouth agape and then shook her head. "I can't possibly be going to her like this…"

"You can't possibly refuse," Jonathan said.

Elizabeth's eyes widened. "I will at least have the words this time to thank you, Mr. Asher."

"I would miss our dish of coffee together and I would grieve a grogshop. And my two garret mice," Jonathan nodded at Emma and Daniel. "They need a warmer place and womanly care this winter."

Elizabeth recovered her composure on the way to Lady Beatrice's house, complimenting Emma on her hair and telling Daniel that if he worked hard, she would give him a shilling for pocket money every month. When Jonathan introduced the three to Lady Beatrice, Elizabeth's lips trembled, and her right eye blinked a dozen times before she was able to control her eyelid.

Lady Beatrice took her by the hand. "Dear Miss Elizabeth, please, do not be frightened. I am not a crocodile, and once, years ago, I was the same as you. The main thing to remember is that you're truly a lady. I suspected it when you came to collect your sister, and I can see that clearly now. There are ladies born to the station and then there are those of us who must find the way to become what it is in our nature to become. As soon as Mr. Jonathan leaves on his gallant mission, I will tell you how. Be careful of Mr. Jonathan…" Without finishing the sentence, she then called Emma and Daniel to her and hugged them. "You're partly mine since I made your fortune." She then presented Jonathan with the order to remove the soldiers from the millinery to be replaced by his new family.

Jonathan collected Elizabeth and the children two days later after escorting the three disgruntled officers to their new quarters. It seemed to Jonathan that the stay at Lady Beatrice's had changed Elizabeth. By turns, she was dreamy and immersed in her thoughts and then very solicitous of him, calling him her savior, yet she seemed to be overplaying her gratitude somehow.

Finally, Elizabeth said in a whisper, "Lady Beatrice was so gracious. And the ball was more delightful than I ever imagined. Adjutant General John André taught me the steps of a minuet, which I had seen so many times from the stairway with the servant girls, and I only made two mistakes, which nobody cared about. And after that,

Lady Beatrice's nephew, Lord Edgar, was staying by my side the whole night. Such a kind attentive man."

"He is indeed attentive, yet I'd say that he is a few years short of manhood," Jonathan grumbled.

"Then I must be just a girl to you for we're the same age," Elizabeth asserted.

"I meant in his manner of comporting himself," Jonathan explained.

"You're just not accustomed to polite company." Elizabeth lifted her chin; a gesture Lady Beatrice did when she wanted to demonstrate unbridgeable superiority.

"Given that polite company is the mainstay of my business, I am perhaps suffering from a surfeit of that type of company and am not so overawed by them," Jonathan said.

"Then you are jealous," she accused.

"Yes," he admitted.

"I am sorry for it, Mr. Asher. There is no need for you to be jealous of a boy, especially you, no matter how high his station. And I feel so keenly my indebtedness to you now." She closed her lips, determined to say no more.

Jonathan was certain of the difference between indebtedness and love. Two days later when he visited Elizabeth and Emma and Daniel, she let the children take up the time. They were excited about their new lodgings, and he enjoyed their excitement. Fair enough, but she pushed the children on him during his following visits, eliminating their intimate conversations over cups of coffee.

Lord Edgar, a man Jonathan considered a fool, was winning the heart of the woman he loved. Obviously, he had been mistaken as to the identity of the true fool.

CHAPTER 20

1780 August

JONATHAN PULLED ALONGSIDE Rodrigo's boat just as the customs agents were leaving. They failed to find contraband that had been unloaded last midnight in the cove on Long Island under the jealous gaze of Major James, who had finally recovered enough from his wounds to resume his raids. As Jonathan stepped on the deck and held out his hand to Rodrigo, he felt a whoosh by his cheek and a soft blow on his shoulder. Timothy had landed.

"Well, you're the chosen one now," Rodrigo said, shaking his hand vigorously. "Saladin fell ill of yellow jack and died a month past. Since then, old Tim has been in the rigging, mourning the loss of his master. This is the first time he has descended. He's yours, and you're welcome to him. I don't like the idea of a grouchy monkey that might tear off my face swinging through the rigging."

"Timothy has never viewed me with favor," Jonathan protested. Even now, the monkey was regarding him with jaundiced eyes.

"Take up your differences with him," Rodrigo said.

"Saladin always claimed he was a most reasonable beastie. These are the commands. One chirp: prepare to attack. Two chirps: attack, but don't go for the eyes. Three chirps: go for the eyes. A whistle: desist. Otherwise, the beastie does what he pleases."

The champagne had already been inventoried by Lady Beatrice and half of it sold so Jonathan spent the night delivering and collecting payment. Timothy sat in the wagon with admirable self-possession through all these transactions. The next day, Jonathan visited the commissary ship to deliver sixteen bottles of burgundy to Pollux. He arrived just in time to see Castor winched up for his daily dose of sunshine and fresh air. Castor did not acknowledge Jonathan.

On climbing aboard, Timothy, who had accompanied him, immediately took off and settled himself on top of the stump of the cutoff mast. Jonathan descended into the hold to examine the barrels of sauerkraut. Doctor Smith insisted that Jonathan acquire sauerkraut to dole out to the prisoners to combat scurvy, and Jonathan wanted to make sure that the barrels weren't spoiled. When he returned to the office, which in other days had been the captain's cabin, to settle accounts, he saw Timothy and Pollux sitting across from each other. Timothy's muzzle was smeared purple from the paper of a sugar loaf. They seemed quite companionable. To his relief, when Jonathan left, Timothy remained aboard.

CHAPTER 21

1780 September

FOR THE SECOND time that week, the seventh time that month, and the forty-fifth time since he made John André's acquaintance, Jonathan stood in front of that blond smug face with its ever-present secret smile and watched the man shuffle through papers, pointedly ignoring his presence. Jonathan knew the game well. He did not expect to be acknowledged for another twenty minutes. Adjutant General John André, that tireless organizer of fetes, theater productions, and festivals, keeper of General Clinton's wine cellar, and, in his spare time, head of General Clinton's intelligence operations, was perhaps Beatrice and Jonathan's best client. Major André, lamentably, thought it beneath a gentleman to consider the cost of anything so it was an unending battle to make him pay.

Beatrice had tired of dealing with him. She explained: "He smiles his sweet smile and says with the voice of a swain flirting with a shepherdess that, of course, he will pay me on the morrow. Unfortunately, the morrow is always the morrow, never the day. He challenges my good humor more than my husband, my nephew, the gnats, and the whole Hessian officer corps combined"—so she gave the job of collecting from André back to Jonathan.

Jonathan was not feeling too charitable either. Elizabeth admitted that she had attended Major André's last party escorted by Edgar and would soon attend another on the arm of the young lord. "Lady Beatrice told Edgar I was a fine young lady. I had blood and breeding, she said. Blood and breeding. I told my father about the compliment, and he claimed that 'twas him who gave me the blood and breeding."

Although fuming at the memory, Jonathan persevered in André's game. The next move with Adjutant General John André was to engage in banter. If the banter resulted in him producing a bon mot that tickled his fancy, then he would pay. If André wasn't amused, and such items as a stain on Jonathan's waistcoat or a smudge marring the polished boots could put him out of humor, then payment would be delayed. At this moment, Jonathan was content to observe and, out of habit, try to memorize upside down a list of names on his desk. Were the names Tory spies, suspected Patriot spies, or invitees to a birthday party? Jonathan didn't recognize a single one.

Suddenly, André sprang up, paced around the office, and, on pretending to suddenly notice Jonathan, exclaimed, "I'm on the verge of winning this whole bloody war, and you are going to pester me for a past due account."

Considering that the major was prone to theatrics and an inflated sense of self-importance, Jonathan almost passed off this comment as a typical exaggeration. Next to the list, however, Jonathan recognized what could only be a sloppily written cipher letter lying open. That letter kept on attracting his eye as if he could gain an idea of the information the cipher conveyed. And André's manner was different—not a hint of foppishness or playing to the audience of the world—rather a combination of excitement and desperation. Mere information on troop movements wouldn't have sufficed for this change. Even when such intelligence was accurate, the troops themselves were never punctual as to timing. Washington was also unreliable in following his own plans. Jonathan reminded and congratulated himself that he was out of the business of intelligencer.

Then André muttered sotto voce, "'Tis a matter of placing trust in the most untrustworthy knaves who ever plagued the earth." The adjutant general shot Jonathan a dark look. "That is you and your kind, or should I say kine." This almost constituted a bon mot. Suddenly André exclaimed, "Damn you!" and threw Jonathan a small pocket. He strode out of the room and said to his secretary, "If General Clinton asks, inform him I have an urgent appointment with Mr. Moore."

Jonathan left convinced that a great event was in the offing. He tried to calm himself with the thought that this was war, and in the nature of war, there was always a major event in the offing. Still, the ciphered letter annoyed him. Even if he revived his mode of conveying information, he couldn't hope to figure out what it said. He'd have to steal the letter to have a go. And that still was impossible unless he acquired the book used to code and decode. Words and numbers that referred to pages and the position of words on those pages. It was a long book—one of the page numbers was 1290. Not many books with so many pages. Futile, nevertheless.

Then suddenly Jonathan broke into a cold sweat. He knew the hand that wrote the coded message—almost beyond doubt. That hand could change the course of the war. Jonathan furiously tried to summon back the image of the letter. He could not be certain, yet the more he considered, the less he doubted. The hand that wrote that ciphered letter was Arnold's hand—left not right. He had witnessed his friend compose an anonymous threat to a customs agent on Saint Martinique with his left hand, and on at least two other occasions he had seen that left-handed scrawl.

Arnold, trusted patriot, celebrated general, who was now the commander of West Point, was communicating with Major John André, head of British intelligence. Arnold was incapable of conceiving a small enterprise, even if the enterprise was a betrayal. In his mind's eye, Jonathan saw a gate left open at the West Point Fort, a wall unguarded, the company half muddled by a triple ration of rum. Arnold would surrender the fort, the two thousand men, and the supplies for the entire army. Jonathan considered returning to steal the letter to make sure. Then he realized that events were already in motion and the information could not be delayed. The reason for shifting the bivouacs to the North River side of Manhattan became clear now. The trap was ready to be sprung.

Given the urgency of this message, Jonathan had to ask himself how fervently did he believe in the cause of liberty? His father thought the rebels ungrateful. Elizabeth believed them to harbor a defect in character. His brother

William hated them with a passion. And now, not even Arnold believed in the cause he had suffered wounds and privation for. There were good men and bad men on each side. "Give me liberty or give me death" was a foolish phrase—the majority of men would choose less or no liberty and life.

But love was not love unless it went beyond reason. Jonathan had discovered that after years of pro forma, half-hearted devotion to the cause, he had fallen in love with it. Liberty was an inconvenient notion to fall in love with. It permitted a man to make of himself what he could and so own his failures as well as successes. It was a fearful thing. It quickened the pulse. It engendered dreams beyond people's means and abilities. The devil used liberty to tempt us. Yet, without liberty to act, we were like cut flowers in a vase—decorative, ultimately inconsequential, and soon dead. With it, what we did mattered. His father and mother loading the wagon with goods that were blood payment to the Seneca for his life; Nate Cowan giving Leadwell a child instead of killing him; Jane's father sitting down with her in the field and taking her hand; The *Danton* docking at his pier; Amelia's kiss, and the story he told her on her deathbed; Elizabeth's beautiful hesitant smile; Emma and Daniel's hands in each of his. Jonathan shook his head. He did not understand why he considered those moments as arguments for the cause of liberty, but he did and made his choice.

As Jonathan drove to the warehouse, he reviewed the various ways he could deliver the warning expediently. His code, even if Hamilton was still perusing the gazettes, did not have the flexibility to communicate such a momentous event. Coded letters might take a week to arrive at their intended destination. The only reliable way would be a courier, but who? The inescapable conclusion was Jonathan would have to deliver the message personally.

He found a roadblock to this plan in the form of Daniel standing shyly at the door of the warehouse, Emma hiding behind him.

"We come back to live here," Daniel said.

"Why in the world do you want to return to a drafty cold warehouse?" It wasn't only cold and drafty, a food riot, thankfully small, had broken out in Canvas Town a few days before.

Daniel was silent.

"Does Miss Elizabeth treat you well?" Jonathan asked, incredulous that such a question would be necessary.

"Oh yes, very well. She treats us very well." Daniel began to stutter. "But… but… her brother…"

"Did he hurt you?" Jonathan felt the anger surge in him. He had forgotten about Percy's cruelty when he moved the children in.

"He pinched Emma twice," Daniel hurriedly explained. "He said he knew how to make her talk. He said he would not stop unless she told him to. He did stop when she started to bleed."

"I swear he will not touch Emma again," Jonathan said.

"How can you do that? He said no matter what I told you, he could do it again and again for he was the master of the house, and he was going to become a captain and you were only a lieutenant." The brave boy was near tears.

"I shall make him stop." Jonathan reached for his weighted cane. "You will see."

Another idea occurred to Jonathan as he drove Daniel and Emma towards the millinery. He turned around and drove to the wharf where the Commissary ship was docked. Pollux greeted him in a friendly manner and gave a huge, distorted smile to the children who seemed pleased to see him.

"I need to borrow Timothy for the afternoon, if he will accompany me," Jonathan said.

Timothy, curious about the new visitors, had come down from the mast. "Is that agreeable to you Timothy?" Pollux asked.

Timothy vaulted onto Jonathan's shoulder and started chattering to Emma and Daniel. On their way to the millinery, Timothy sat between the children holding their hands.

On arriving there, Elizabeth rushed out, "Emma and Daniel, I been frantic with worry. Why did you leave without telling me?"

"Just a minor problem, Miss Elizabeth," Jonathan said. "Take Emma. Daniel, you come with me so you can tell your sister that my word will be kept. Do you know about Timothy's reputation?"

"How can a monkey have a reputation?" Daniel asked.

"Timothy does," Jonathan assured him.

"What's happening?" Elizabeth exclaimed.

"No violence will be done, Liza," Jonathan explained to the aghast Elizabeth, who was hugging Emma, and walked upstairs followed by Timothy and Daniel. He unhesitatingly entered the room of Percival, who had just put on his uniform and was adjusting his powdered wig.

"How dare you invade my privacy," Percival turned angrily toward them.

"'Twill only take a moment, Lieutenant Littleton Have you met Timothy?" Jonathan knew that Percival was familiar with Timothy because two weeks before he had commented on the hundreds of teeth wounds on the face of the carter who had tried to cudgel Pollux as punishment for requisitioning his wagon. "Timothy this man hurt Emma, the nice little girl you were talking to," Jonathan said then gave one chirp.

"I don't have any monkeys in my acquaintance." Percy nervously stood and measured the distance to his scabbard, which was in the corner while Timothy turned his jaundiced eyes on Percy and hissed, showing his teeth.

"Timothy will rip off your face if you touch Emma again," Jonathan said.

Timothy gave a screech for emphasis and ran his nails down his cheeks. Jonathan turned away from Percy as Timothy hopped on his shoulder and left followed by Daniel.

Elizabeth glared at him. "How dare you…"

"Dare what? Emma show Miss Elizabeth your arm," Jonathan said.

Emma shyly revealed two deep red circles on her forearm. Elizabeth gasped.

"That won't happen again," Jonathan said.

"Is Percival…?" Confused and conflicted, Elizabeth couldn't finish the question.

"Not a hair has been harmed on his gorgeous head albeit I think he might be a little shaken," Jonathan replied.

"I'm so sorry." Tears rolled down Elizabeth's eyes. "So sorry," she repeated, afraid to look at him.

Emma and Daniel wanted to ride with their new friend back to the commissary ship. Jonathan agreed thinking that it would calm them further and only add a few minutes to his departure. While Timothy sat between the children in the wagon again, holding their hands and chattering away, Jonathan plotted the best way to contact the Continental forces. He needed to pick up proper clothing and supplies at the warehouse and then, at the livery stable, hire the best horse available. He could reach West Point sooner if he crossed at Paulus Hook ferry, then followed a road paralleling the Hudson. Jonathan hoped he wouldn't regret the time intimidating Percy.

On returning to the warehouse, he was surprised and dismayed to discover Doctor Reginald Smith pacing his empty office, the expression on the doctor's thin face as disapproving as ever, his eyes tiny boiling cauldrons, his lips tight. Jonathan had ceased to expect a scintilla of gratitude from the doctor. It wasn't in his nature. Nevertheless, the man was good in the sense that he hated suffering and would walk through the fires of hell to keep his word. He tirelessly searched out the family of prisoners, shamed them into paying redemption and had even been known to shame officers into misstating a private soldier's rank so he could be paroled as an officer. He harangued the brutal guards until they agreed to anticipate a prisoner's death by throwing him overboard at night in a loose shroud. A boat oared by friends or family would coincidentally be nearby. Jonathan was certain that Dr. Smith could shame the Archbishop of Canterbury into stooping and washing the filth off a leper's feet.

Jonathan was about to brush Dr. Smith off and prepare to leave when the doctor stated tersely, "I won't turn you in."

"Why on earth would you turn me in?" Jonathan fought his sense of foreboding from the heavy flat tone of Smith's voice.

"I was offered money to find out everything about you, and I refused," Dr. Smith declared proudly.

"Castor Blanchard I presume was the one who offered payment," Jonathan said.

"He summoned me to his boat. I refused him directly, although I decided to keep my eyes and my ears open. I know who you are, and I won't turn you in," he insisted.

"If you know who I am, why would you turn me in?" Jonathan could see that the plainspoken Reginald had now become adept at this verbal cat-and-mouse game.

"Another man might in my circumstances, but I will not turn you in," he stubbornly repeated.

"Well, why won't you?" Jonathan inquired, exasperated.

"More to the point, why would I?" He fumbled a moment for words. "You passed me in the street the other day in the company of a young lady, Miss Lucretia Baldwin."

Jonathan encountered Lucretia with the doctor a week ago. They had paused to talk. Jonathan had little doubt that Lucretia was using the doctor as a means to spy on him. On being introduced by Doctor Smith, Lucretia said, "Mr. Asher and I met before. We have a mutual acquaintance, Castor Blanchard, in common, who was so kind as to give me some small employment when I fell on hard times."

"Yes, we are acquainted," Jonathan had replied, wondering how Castor planned to use her this time. Only an informant? Poisoner? Or a diversion from another plot to harm him?

While they walked away, Jonathan observed Lucretia suddenly clasp the doctor's arm, showing pride of possession. Reginald stiffened and she released it. Maybe he was mistaken. He wondered at this—Doctor Smith, being of severe morals, would only welcome the temptation to boast about rejecting it. Yet the next assertion by the doctor came as a shock.

"I am ashamed to say Lucretia is with child. My child, I suspect. Nay, I can't say I suspect for that would cast aspersions on her character that she doesn't in the least deserve. I have no doubt the child is mine." He said this so forcefully that Jonathan immediately suspected that the child wasn't his.

"Well, are you going to marry her and give your child a father, a name, and a home?" Jonathan asked.

"I am not a man women find appealing." The tip of Reginald's nose reddened, which was as close as the doctor came to a blush. "Lucretia came to me and asked if I could help redeem her betrothed imprisoned on the *Scorpion*. He was already dead so there was nothing to be done. Learning I was a doctor she later visited me concerning a consultation about a sore throat. Her throat was indeed inflamed, and I gave her a soothing balm. She then came the next week and said she had a strange wart on…"

"Ahem. You don't have to give me the details," Jonathan said, considering the surprising possibility that a lie may have passed through the Doctor's lips.

"And then there are my parents." The doctor added to the natural frown of his face a real frown. "They were instrumental in my rescue, you understand. Unfortunately, my father can no longer work as a wainwright, and 'tis my responsibility they are fed and cared for. And then there is my cousin…"

"Your cousin?" Jonathan inquired.

"A young man who is a stranger to the Patriot cause, or to any cause save that of his vices." The fact of just admitting to fornication hadn't lessened the Doctor's moral authority. "He visited a gambling den and lost eighteen guineas that he didn't possess nor have the least hope of obtaining, and when the bruisers came for him, I offered surety for his debt."

"Which you didn't have?" Jonathan completed the thought.

"You would have done the same," Smith insisted.

"Your opinion of me has improved." Jonathan gazed longingly at the door and saw in his mind's eye the British soldiers who were to deliver the telling blow to the cause of liberty mustering to sail up the Hudson.

"I could not turn you in for you are a good man doing a dangerous job. You are a spy. You also do not make a penny off the men you ransom. I kept track of how much is paid to this man and to that man. I seen what you pay to Lady and Lord Bloodsucker. Thirty-seven men I redeemed from that hellhole including twelve not-quite-dead buried in the pits where they bury the dead and then collected later and six thrown overboard. I could not turn you in." There was a disconcerting note of regret in the Doctor's voice.

"Yet, you appear threatening to do so," Jonathan commented.

"I'm just saying what a man might do, but I won't do. A man might ask quite a sum to preserve your life. I don't want money—I want remunerative employment so I can take care of Lucretia, my child, and my parents."

"And to pay off your cousin's debts?"

"Yes, that too."

"Is Lucretia aware of your suspicions? As you know she is also acquainted with Mr. Blanchard," Jonathan said.

"Lucretia's connection with Mr. Blanchard is accidental," Smith explained. "When he first arrived in New York, he needed a suitable place to reside. Lucretia was taking care of a sea captain's house. She offered rooms to Castor who promised to protect the house from the depredations of the British army, which he did. Even though he sleeps there no more than once a fortnight, he still protects the house. Lucretia is no threat to you. I've breathed not a word of what you are in her presence, and I won't ever. I said what I meant when I vowed I'd not tell anyone."

"Even if I refuse to help you?" Jonathan was envisioning the whole American enterprise crushed by Arnold's treachery, but he couldn't leave this conversation, which was like quicksand, the more he tried to extricate himself, the deeper he sunk.

"I haven't forsaken our cause despite the desperate

straits the Continental Army is in. I understand Lucretia's acquaintance with Mr. Blanchard might create unease. Lucretia herself mentioned you might have the wrong impression about her and could be against our project, although she hasn't talked to Mr. Blanchard in months."

"What is this project you have in mind?" Jonathan asked, not believing for an instant that Lucretia was truthful, not even to a man, or perhaps, especially to a man, who was going to be her husband.

Reginald Smith appeared shifty for a moment, then said, "You don't fully use this warehouse. If I could set up a consulting office here and have a space for examinations, I believe I could earn a sufficiency for my needs."

"I am not such a good fellow that I won't ask what benefit I derive from this arrangement." Jonathan did see a marginal benefit. It would not be a bad thing to have Lucretia indebted to him. He never ate at the warehouse so there was no chance of her poisoning him. As for Reginald inadvertently letting slip that he was an intelligence agent, the project neither increased nor decreased the odds.

"And once my practice is running, you may charge me rent," Dr. Smith said.

This was a problem that Jonathan had no time for. The fastest way through the conversation was to agree in principle and object to the details later, so he did. The doctor smiled, the unaccustomed expression straining his face. They shook hands at the same time Jonathan was certain transportation barges for the British forces were docking at the embarkation points.

CHAPTER 22

FINALLY RID OF the good doctor, Jonathan copied out three letters, not bothering to take the time to code them, conveying his suspicions, then collected twenty guineas and started for the ferry.

It was near midnight when Jonathan was finally able to take the crowded Paulus Hook ferry across the North River. He sensed restlessness and excitement in the encampments on both sides of the river. They could not possibly be aware of Arnold's betrayal, yet he imagined the soldiers felt in the air an impending action. After dropping one of the letters in a hollow tree trunk that would be collected sooner or later, Jonathan intended to ride along the Hudson as fast as he could, braving the most treacherous country in the Americas, given that neither the British nor the Continentals had control of the area. That left it free for the marauders of every description to treat every lone traveler as an enemy, thereby meriting a stripping and a beating if they were in a merciful mood, a hanging if they were not.

Nothing occurred during the first hours of brisk galloping down dark lanes under a moonless sky, generally heading north. Jonathan covered fifteen miles, slowing the last leagues as his horse tired. The few times he sighted the river he did not see as he feared the silhouettes of barges filled with soldiers silently rowing toward West Point but an empty flat blackness. In truth, as Jonathan rode through the darkness it was easy to imagine that he was traveling through a world devoid of humanity. That illusion changed when an orange glow broke the murky darkness ahead of him. Wondering at the existence of any structures left to burn in this blighted region, Jonathan halted and started backtracking to find a way around the fire. Suddenly, three small flames punctured the darkness in front of him. Before he could realize that these were horsemen carrying torches, he was surrounded by a small troop.

Behind him, he heard a familiar giggle and a voice, "So what are you about in the middle of the night in the middle of nowhere without your monkey, Mr. Asher?"

"Personal business," Jonathan replied.

Percy, who was holding a torch, positioned himself facing Jonathan, "Personal business? Out here? Out of uniform, Mr. Asher?"

"You may do me the favor of addressing me as Lieutenant Osborne. We are, after all, fighting on the same side," Jonathan responded angrily.

"That don't answer my question." Percy raised his high voice in probably what he imagined was a commanding tone.

Jonathan lowered his. "I'm not obliged to answer your question; however, since you insist, my business, of course, brings me here. I can say no more than I'm meeting a captain of a cutter and would like to continue on my way."

"I'd say you are intending to deprive King George of his duties with your smuggled merchandise. We might as well do the king a favor by collecting them ourselves," Percy said. There was a grumble of assent among the other men.

"You may rest assured that the agents of the king, specifically Assistant-quartermaster Lord Harold and Lady Beatrice, know what I'm about and thoroughly approve my mission," Jonathan countered.

"We can't allow our betters to go without their wines and spiritous liquors." A shadow in a saddle, whose tone of command and sarcasm left no doubt he was in charge, disengaged himself from a dark clump of men and rode forward. "Now, can we?"

"You can impede me in any way you see fit, captain. But in that event, trust you those present to keep their mouths shut? The majority of your party appear barely sober enough to know which is the right end of their musket to point at the enemy, and I wouldn't rely over-much on their discretion." Jonathan persisted in his bluff.

Percy's torch illuminated the captain's lean face with a mouth set naturally in a mocking smile. "I know who you are, Lieutenant Osborne. You insisted I pay immediately for your expensive libations, and when you discovered I was short of funds, you took your business elsewhere. Humor me for a bit. The cutter captain will wait. 'Tis my opinion a man is not a real officer until he is blooded. We are visiting the Edwards who live a few miles down this road. His brother and brother-in-law are with Nathaniel Greene in the south, so we intend to teach the rebels the lesson of keeping near hearth and home, lest their families fall into the wrong hands."

"I've no taste for marauding,"

"We are not marauders, Lieutenant Osborne," the captain replied coldly. "And as your superior I insist you accompany us—for your safety, you understand. It would grieve me if you fell into the clutches of the rebels, and those who could afford your expensive wine were forced to do without."

"Nor have I an appetite for mayhem, but since you command me, captain, I ride with you."

Since the raiders were heading in a northerly direction, traveling with them would bring Jonathan closer to West Point. He anticipated disappearing in the chaos of the next raid.

The small farmhouse appeared deserted when the soldiers surrounded it. They shouted for the rebel scoundrels to appear and then blew out the windows with musket fire. Behind Jonathan, a rider whispered, "Percy promised the Edwards had three daughters as ripe for the picking as late summer plums. That's the only reason I am missing a night of sleep and wandering about this hellish wilderness on this damned expedition. Percy better deliver what he promises."

The captain overheard the comment. "We are fighting for the King and Country, not for your cock, Ensign Phillips. Remember that and you and your cock may survive the war."

Six men dismounted and went into the house. There

was a sound of breaking plates and splintering wood. The men returned with a feather bed and a dresser.

"Fools, how in the blazes are you to carry those things all night?" the captain shouted at the men.

"I'll come back for the mattress in the morning," Ensign Philips protested shrilly. They all laughed. The house was set on fire. In the flames, an outbuilding became visible at the edge of a field. Jonathan who was starting to back off into the darkness spotted a dead dog at the door of the outbuilding and felt a sudden chill.

"Bloody damn," he muttered, then borrowed a torch and rode over to the small barn. He dismounted and walked through the door which was ajar. The family was there, huddled in the corner, not attempting to hide, the husband holding a flintlock pistol which was in danger of going off in his quaking hand, his wife and young daughters crouching behind him. Jonathan stared at the family and then gave a slight nod to his head and a shift of his eyes indicating that they should come forward and stand at the wall next to the door.

"Nothing is here!" Jonathan yelled, flinging the door wide open and waving the torch showing the vacant space. "The horses and cattle would be in the forest."

"I want to look for myself." Ensign Phillips came forward.

"Mr. Phillips," Jonathan said, stepping in front of him. "Don't you think we should take care of their next month's harvest?" He threw the torch lighting the field on fire. Distracted, the ensign turned to admire the flames.

The next farm lay five miles down the lane. Percy and

the captain assured Jonathan that a notorious rebel spy lived there.

"No daughters, just an old wife," Ensign Phillip muttered disappointedly under his breath.

When they arrived, they found the old wife in front of a tree where her old husband hung too high for her to reach. Around his neck was draped a sign, "Thus die Traitors to the Cause of Liberty." The men milled around for a few minutes unsure what to do until one of them remarked, "If ever a soul were fated to meet his end this night, 'twas this poor devil."

"I'm moving on, captain," Jonathan said. "You possess no clear idea who you're persecuting,"

Percy blocked his retreat. "I have an item of honor to settle with you."

The captain irritated by the situation seemed disinclined to restrain Percy.

Jonathan decided that the quickest way out was to make amends. "Let it be, Lieutenant Littleton. I was protecting my children the same as you protect your sister. Elizabeth is safe from me now that a lord is courting her. I apologize for the offense I gave in my overzealous concern for Emma and Daniel. I'm certain you'd act no differently than I. If you so insist, I will duel you, here and now, but 'tis under protest."

"Come on, Percy. We have no time for this fiddle-faddle, and it don't reflect well on your petition for a captaincy," The captain said angrily. "The next farm belongs to Theodore Logan, and he is supposed to be the wealthiest man in these parts."

"Do not cross me again, Mr. Asher," Percy threatened.

"I'll endeavor not to as long as Emma and Daniel are unmolested." Jonathan could not quite contain the anger in his voice.

"Are you accusing me…?"

"Come on, Lieutenant Percy." The captain grabbed his reins. "We're after rebels, not purveyors of wines and spiritous liquors, no matter how deserving the scoundrel is to be hanged for not giving credit."

"I withdraw the accusation now that you understand my concern," Jonathan declared.

"If you want to advance in rank, Percy, you need to attend to your quarrels on your own time," the captain advised.

Percy hesitated, snarled, then galloped off to the Logan farm followed by the rest of the raiders.

Jonathan weighed his choices. He couldn't risk going along the same road. His horse was too exhausted to make the remaining forty miles even if he eluded the cowboys, the skinners, and other marauders. Sailing up the Hudson was equally problematic. That would be the route that the British used to transport their troops to West Point, and they had certainly placed lookouts and interceptors along the river. That left one other option. Clark claimed Washington had salted New York with spies. Jonathan believed he could find one of them.

Jonathan had observed the wealthy Tory merchant railing against the rebels too loudly for the pot and a half of ale he had just consumed. His loquaciousness disappeared and he paid close attention whenever an officer began to speak about military matters. His store on Broad Street was a favorite with British officers. Jonathan had seen the same man at the docks at least a dozen times in good weather and bad observing the arrival and unloading of ships. It took a spy to recognize a spy. The question remained: how fast could this man convey information out of the city?

The last person Mr. Townsend wanted standing on his door stoop was a British lieutenant. He gaped at Jonathan at a loss for words. Jonathan, of course, could not announce on the street that he had an urgent message for General Washington. He tried whispering it. Mr. Townsend shook his head as if hard of hearing. Jonathan grabbed him by the collar and put his mouth next to his ear and repeated the words. "I have a message for General Washington." Townsend went limp. Seeing a marine saunter by, Jonathan slapped him. There was nothing unusual in a British officer abusing a colonial. After staggering back, Townsend regained some stiffness.

Jonathan pushed himself inside and closed the door. "The message is urgent. If you cannot post it to Washington within the hour, tell me your contacts and how I can persuade them to trust me."

"What is the problem?" Said a man coming down the stairs. Bald, with dark curious eyes, and a wrinkled forehead, he was more self-possessed than Townsend.

"He knows, cousin," Townsend muttered hopelessly

"Knows what?" The cousin asked.

"I have an urgent message for Washington." It took all of Jonathan's will not to yell and pound the table.

The cousin frowned. "Why do you come to us, sir?"

"Dammit, don't pretend you're not spies," Jonathan

exclaimed and censured a half dozen other expletives that came to his lips.

This put the cousin into a huff. "We are definitely not. Spy is a low term for those who have no allegiance except to money. Our business is quite different."

"Whatever you are, your business is passing information to Washington, and this is the most important information you ever will pass to him."

"How do we know you're not trying to uncover our contacts?" The cousin asked petulantly.

"I believe Benedict Arnold is going to betray West Point. You must get that message to Washington as soon as possible." Jonathan himself began to feel panic.

"How did you find out our identity?" The cousin asked with calm coolness.

"I can recognize my kind," Jonathan replied. "I saw Mr. Townsend many times on the wharves looking with too keen an interest at the ships sailing in. I heard him in the coffeehouses leading the conversations around to the sort of information I like to acquire. He has even conversed with me about the commissary's warehouse."

"And now you met me, his contact." The cousin's forehead wrinkled more.

"Yes," Jonathan said. "Now, I've met you."

"You must have a means of conveying your information," Mr. Townsend observed.

"Most of my information is passed via code in advertisements for coffee in the Royal Gazette or Rivington's Loyalist Gazette, so it arrives quickly courtesy of the British although I haven't advertised recently."

The two men appeared impressed. "Then you must

be Mr. Asher, purveyor of fine coffees. I always wanted to purchase your coffees. I had no idea that you were also a British officer and in our business. Quite a busy fellow."

"Yes, I am also Lieutenant Osborne, under Colonel Harold, the assistant to the quartermaster general, and I am the purveyor of fine wines of which Colonel Harold earns the third part. The fact that I have two names and two identities bothers nobody in this city."

"Three identities, at least, Mr. Asher—I'll call you by that name. I will take your letter to Washington with as much dispatch as possible. It should reach him in four or five days. Do not try to do so yourself. If you are captured, then it will put our efforts at greater risk. And please do not contact Mr. Townsend again, nor me. I am sure you understand the liability we pose to each other."

CHAPTER 23

HAVING TAKEN EVERY measure possible to prevent Arnold's betrayal of Washington, Jonathan thought the best course was to sleep the next forty-eight hours and then wake when hopefully the crisis was resolved, one way or another. The feather mattress in the room upstairs beckoned to him as seductively as a beautiful mistress. On entering his warehouse, however, he had the unpleasant surprise of finding Miss Lucretia Baldwin waiting for him. She put a lot of effort into her brittle smile and bowed prettily at his arrival. Her large eyes seemed to be floating in an excess of moisture.

"I am exceedingly conscious of the great service you are rendering Reginald despite your doubts about my character and my connection with Mr. Blanchard, and I thank you with all my heart." She coated each word with treacle.

"Reginald is a good man, a man of his word," Jonathan replied. "You must be aware that Castor is trying to destroy me, and your acquaintance with him leads me to suspect you participate in his plan."

"A woman has not as many options as a man in this world, Mr. Asher. In return for a favor, he urged me to become your friend. He assured me he wasn't asking for anything contrary to propriety, just friendship. When I told him that I was certain my friendship wouldn't interest you, he laughed, saying, 'What man would want you?'" She lowered her head and blushed. "What man would? My Reginald would. It is my hope you do not judge me too harshly for my condition. I am only a weak feminine creature, and I hope you will not hold me in less esteem once Reginald and I are joined in holy union."

"I do not judge you harshly, madam. I congratulate you and Reginald on your coming marriage." Jonathan wanted with all his heart and soul for the conversation to end.

"May I impose on you one tiny condition, one little thing to you, yet ever so important to me. I could almost beg…" She began to flex her knees.

"Please…"

"Discretion—that's the word I want to say. Perhaps the word can serve both of us well. Reginald can only say what he thinks is true, and in my situation…. You understand 'tis better some things are left unsaid. You know how people talk, and my fortunate and unfortunate condition, well, what might they think of me? I'm a poor girl with only my reputation…"

"I will not breathe a word of your condition to a soul," Jonathan said at the same time the thought occurred to him that he might use her indiscretion to find out what Castor was planning—the commissary swore to destroy him after all—but not now, not here.

"I am in your debt, exceedingly." She drew out the last word as if making an offer of herself as payment for discretion. "One day I may do a deed in return which will cancel the debt." She took his hand with both of hers and gave extra brittleness to her smile, then released it caressingly. "Discretion," she whispered. Her blue eyes were as large as a child's and as empty as an idiot's, yet behind the eyes, he sensed a universe of calculations.

Jonathan was certain sweet oblivion was a blink away, but he was mistaken. He could only drift so far toward unconsciousness before the bitterness of Arnold's betrayal took over his thoughts. He had always believed every time he coded information into an advertisement for coffee he was helping his friend promote the cause of liberty. He imagined sitting down with Arnold after the war and sharing a bottle of the best brandy and trading stories—Benedict's about battles and strategy, Jonathan's about operating in the camp of the enemy. Now, although his belief in the cause of liberty had strengthened over the past years, it seemed this friendless and dangerous endeavor was also futile.

The low spirits stuck to him over the following week. His business suffered. Although not the sort who could while away a day in a tavern and normally averse to imbibing his profit, Jonathan drank more. He made efforts to be in a good mood and sober when he was with Emma and Daniel, and in truth, they raised his spirits. For the rest of the day, Jonathan felt as if he were slowly losing control of himself. One night after two hours in a nearly derelict out-of-the-way tavern, Jonathan visited his favorite whorehouse. Having quaffed so much beforehand that it was touch and go whether he could perform, so to self-commiserate he finished the job of getting thoroughly drunk afterward. He then staggered home. It was near dawn.

Jonathan hardly felt the blow on the back of the head, though he half believed Arnold was delivering it. He was vaguely aware of his pockets being rifled as he ineffectually waved his arms in an effort to stop the thieves. They kicked him several more times. In the dense mental fog, he heard one comment after a kick: "Better to beat him to death instead of running him through and make it look like just an unfortunate encounter with footpads."

Jonathan was trying to find the words to protest when he heard a command and a gunshot. For a moment he wondered whether he was dead or merely wounded. Then he heard the sound of running footsteps. The next thing he remembered was a female voice he almost recognized. Several arms hefted him up and flung him into a wheelbarrow. There followed a jarring ride to his warehouse. Again, the female voice directing the several arms to carry him in. Jonathan lost consciousness as he was laid on his cot and his clothes were stripped off. He came to a few minutes later.

CHAPTER 24

"BENUMBED, BESMEARED, ROBBED, and most likely be-whored. A fine example you make as an officer of the King's Army." Millicent Dalton had taken a sponge to him. Jonathan winced as she passed over the bruises. "You were most fortunate that I knew 'twas you the men were stomping to death for I often had visions of doing the same, so I shot at them hoping to scare them and said in my best brigadier general's voice, 'Come on, fellows, let's rescue the poor chap.' I dare say I frightened them away. I'll leave here, poorer in time and richer with an anecdote to recount to Elizabeth."

Jonathan muttered an inarticulate curse. "Don't tell her or at least not in the presence of Emma and Daniel, please."

"You even proposed marriage to me," Millicent said, enjoying her superiority and his gasps and flinches when she ran the rag over a bruise, "which was flattering, by the way. It would have been more flattering if you had used my correct name. Anyway, I am already married. Be careful, if you are not murdered by one of your numerous enemies, you might wake up someday married to somebody you don't have the slightest acquaintance with."

Jonathan groaned. "What does it matter? I believe Lord Edgar has taken Elizabeth's heart."

"Perhaps the reason is that Elizabeth discovered the truth about you. Don't stare at me like that. If anything, Mr. Asher, I have been more complimentary on your behalf than you merit and have kept mum about my reservations."

"Enlighten me as to the truth, Mrs. Dalton." Jonathan groaned again.

The smile disappeared from her face. "This is the common opinion of you, Mr. Asher. Although you have some admirable attributes, you are, by and large, a disappointment as a man. Not that you drink, you whore, you get yourself robbed, and almost get yourself killed. Not that you keep only your particular secrets and are careless with the secrets of others. I am certain Terence was being kind when he cleared your name mentioning a minor financial embarrassment. Not even that you engage in criminal activity to earn your guineas. Most men scrape to survive in this city. I realize that now. 'Tis that you sold the food of starving prisoners. You claim you are no worse than others who took your place. Perhaps so, but you did it. A murderer no worse than other murderers is still that." Mrs. Dalton turned to leave, then looked back and added bitterly, "If I were a just person, I would have left you to the footpads. Yet, you have acted as a friend more than once, so I could not abandon you."

Jonathan was suddenly sober and sitting bolt upright despite a stab of pain in his side. "As I already admitted, for a time, Major Provost Cunningham and Assistant Commissary Blanchard hired me to dispose of what they had stolen from the prisoners as well as what they were stealing from the forces of the King. I deeply regretted my role and stopped. Now the foodstuff goes to speculators, and you know the misery they are causing. I am not engaged in that activity for six months. I swear for every penny I made off the prisoners' stores, I gave back a shilling to feed the poor. Still, you may be correct in that I am beyond redemption: I may never get over the revulsion at the part I played in that evil business."

"If you were so beneficent in the matter of taking food out of the mouths of starving prisoners, why did you stop?" Millicent asked.

"Perhaps I shouldn't have," Jonathan responded. "In the end, I was too good to dirty my hands in that trade, too afraid to hazard my soul, so the speculators, not so good or fearful, have taken my place and instead of one misery, we have two. God can decide whether I am a good or bad man."

"You drawn too fine a line between good and bad for a poor silly girl like me to understand."

"As I stated, I'm out of that business altogether. Look in my account books. Oh, I forgot, you can't read." Jonathan realized this cruelty came straight from his angry heart.

"Then how did you become so wealthy?" Millicent seemed eager for a fight.

"Do I appear to you a wealthy man?"

"You do not flaunt your wealth, Mr. Asher," Millicent said. "Yet I am aware of you owning at least a dozen properties including a house of prostitution."

"Three of which are in Canvas Town with a dozen wretches occupying their charred foundations. No whorehouse. The wealth and property I possess are because of French brandy, French burgundy, French champagne, and coffee—not hard biscuit, spoiled salt pork, and barrels of sauerkraut from the last war. Go ahead and tell Elizabeth you found me drunk in the street. Assure her of the good choice she made in encouraging Lord Edgar to court her. I'd not have you hide from her one jot or tittle of the truth, as you call it. You can tell her I visit whores. You may personally understand that necessity." Jonathan wanted to take back these words as soon as they left his lips. Still, he pursued, "But if you say I made a profit from starving the prisoners, know that you are telling a bloody damn lie."

"What do you mean I may understand the necessity of visiting whores?" Murder had darkened the moss in Millicent's eyes to almost black.

"I observed you at the backdoor of one such establishment. They seemed well enough acquainted with you to call you 'Millie,'" Jonathan said, unaccountably ashamed he was causing distress to this woman that had been savaging his character.

Jonathan had seen many women angry—his diminutive mother, who would stand snorting for a full minute before bursting into a stream of Gallic imprecations, had been particularly daunting—but he never had felt in imminent physical danger from a woman before. "You did not tell anyone?" She asked in a low voice.

"Not a soul. Nor would I. In my experience, most women are reduced to that profession by misfortune, and I don't pretend superiority to another's misfortune."

Millicent hesitated, her expressive features passing successively through hate, anger, shame, then back to hate and anger before softening. She suddenly asked, "Liza informed me you were a preacher. I found that incredible and told her you had not a thimbleful of the man of God about you. She insisted, saying that you knew much of the Bible by heart. Is that true?"

"I left home to evangelize the world at the age of sixteen. In my fervor, I digested whole books of the Bible without guidance and therefore without the depth of understanding. My flesh was weaker than my spirit was willing, as you no doubt can imagine, and I could not preach what I had no intention practicing," Jonathan explained.

"I have a question that even an unchaste preacher of poor understanding may answer." Millicent bit her forefinger nervously. "Does going to the theater mean I'm going to hell?"

Jonathan was taken aback. "You accuse me of starving helpless prisoners to death, a sin that must be infinitely more deserving of God's wrath than attending a theatrical production, yet you want me to render a theological opinion on the evil of seeing a play?"

"Please, 'tis a topic that particularly distresses me," Millicent persevered.

"Well, that was a subject I never addressed in my sermonizing at the age of seventeen, likely due to a lack of theatrical productions in the backcountry." Jonathan studied the flush on her features. "Do you attend the theater?"

"My husband, Terence, said that it was so, and the closing of theaters before the British invaded was the one measure imposed by the Committee of Safety with which he agreed." She sensed his incredulity and hurried to explain. "Terence said that if I couldn't understand the sinfulness of theaters, he would have Pastor Jenkins explain it to me. That is my great vice my husband tells me. Then he says he doesn't worry for with so many British officers attending plays 'tis near impossible for someone of my station to visit the theater, and since I was a married woman and he would never take me, I was safe.

"My poor husband is mistaken. General Clinton also loves the theater, and last year Major John André organized Clinton's Thespians to put on productions, which I am allowed to watch from behind the stage in part because I assist the ladies—wives, mistresses, daughters, and yes, even a trull or two, properly dressed as ladies—in the necessary room. I don't show myself, you understand, and I use the actors' tricks of makeup to appear different from what I am. I am sometimes given the task of escorting one of those decorative creatures back to her place, so I am not an unfamiliar face there. Do I need to assure you I haven't stepped beyond the threshold of those establishments? My brothers would have unmanned my guests, burned the building, and then strangled me."

"'Tis dangerous to be wandering about in that neighborhood so late," Jonathan said.

"I have a pistol, which saved your life." Millicent smiled. "In any event, 'tis worth it. I used to save my extra pennies, and if I could, I'd go to John Street Theater on Saturday evening to watch the plays. The plays would give me something to think about all week while I was mending my lady's clothing or polishing her shoes. My husband said I should have been contemplating higher things. I told him I was sure he didn't contemplate higher things when he was milling his wheat. My husband is a good man and persisted not in the argument, yet I could see how disappointed he was in me. I agreed with him that when we had children, I'm sure I'd not have the time."

Jonathan groped for words of wisdom. "I've known some preachers to take a stand against the theater. Theater-going had never seemed a sin God was overly preoccupied with. I even attended twice and found the experience pleasing, although you must consider that I'm a lapsed man of God."

"When I was nine, Gregory, the son of the owner of the theater, charged me a kiss to get in." Millicent blushed deeply. "I'm sure you preachers think what I did was sinful. I only paid that way four times. I've been virtuous since, and 'twas no easy matter to maintain your virtue in houses with young gentlemen who promise you the world for just that one time. I used to dress as a boy to not be bothered. Later the owner caught on and gave me free admittance if I helped the ladies in the necessary room—the proper and the improper ones. Mr. Dalton would despair if he were aware that I was acquainted with those unfortunate creatures. I kept my distance from their section, of course. They understood, and they still liked me. If a gentleman or a bully boy tried to compromise my honor they'd immediately jump to my defense."

Millicent laughed. "No man, no matter how brave on the battlefield, wants to fend off four or five angry molls. Now, I sometimes help one or another of the poor creatures who haven't found an assignation make their way back. The bruiser must guard the girls who are plying their trade in the nearby rooms. It's simply not safe for any woman, virtuous or not, to return unaccompanied."

"And your honor is not compromised?"

"I put on a cloak and wait around the corner. When a man approaches, I begin to loudly discuss my pox sores, and, of course, I have my pistol." She gave a small helpless laugh. "I shouldn't help the poor girls, but they are such sad people for all their brave pretense of gaiety. Mr. Dalton would throw me out on my ear, and no house would employ me if they knew. But the doormen at the brothels give me tips, so like you, I make a profit from this immoral world."

Jonathan felt a pang when he realized his first mother—a shadow in his memory more imagined than real—used a similar stratagem of pretending to be diseased to protect herself. "How many plays have you attended?" Jonathan asked.

Millicent considered. "About half my Saturdays for the last ten years, less the time the theaters were closed by the Committee of Safety, I found a way to attend, so I must be beyond redemption. But is it so sinful to watch the players suffer adversity much worse than you suffered and then vanquish their enemies or die tragically, or in the comedies to allow yourself to laugh at the follies that by the grace of God you have been spared?"

"Over two hundred plays?" Jonathan asked, surprised.

"Those I've seen three or four times I can repeat many of the lines by heart," Millicent said not without pride. "Having all those lines in my head is why I think people often mistake my station."

"I'm certainly not the man to preach to you about denial of worldly pleasure," Jonathan said. "There is plenty of feasting, drinking, dancing, and singing in the Bible. So long as you're not doing it in the presence of a golden calf or another idol, I think God may smile on it too."

"Thank you," Millicent whispered meekly.

"But don't escort the prostitutes back to their residences. 'Tis not safe for you, no matter how well armed you are, and, sooner or later, someone will find out and your reputation will be damaged beyond repair," Jonathan reprimanded. "Every Saturday, there will be a cart with a black driver near the theater who will take the women home." Jonathan was certain this would be good work for a refugee slave. "Make it clear the driver is to receive your tip."

"I'll have to tell my dear molls," Millicent said.

"Yes, you will."

"Oh, well, I'm sure 'tis for the best. I feel terrible putting Mr. Dalton's reputation at risk by consorting with fallen women, and I told myself a dozen times to stop, but then I see the poor girl, alone, unwanted, crying, and I can't help myself." Millicent gazed at the books. "You know, I read a little. I spent three weeks as a maid to this lady, learning how to read. I can make out half the words if I speak them. One day, I'll surprise Mr. Dalton by reading Rivington's Gazette to him, so that was unfair of you."

"I thank you for picking me up off the street. Here…" He stood still draped in a blanket and went to his desk.

"I don't want to be paid," Millicent protested.

"Not even with a book—a primer that teaches you

how to read better, which I got for Emma before I discovered she already knew how," Jonathan explained.

Millicent took the book. "I won't be too uncomplimentary when I speak to Elizabeth, although you cannot expect me to keep from her completely how entertaining you were in your state.

Jonathan shrugged. "It hardly matters now. As I said, Lord Edgar possesses all the virtues I lack plus he has a title."

Millicent gave him a warm smile. "Elizabeth is a sensible girl, and I think the novelty of playing the lady will wear off, and then she'll choose the better of the two. Although I cannot choose for her, despite my ill temper in your presence, I'm not against you." Her eyes softened. "Take care of yourself, Mr. Asher. I want Elizabeth to have a choice to make."

CHAPTER 25

ARNOLD'S INGENIOUS PLOT had come up against General Washington's astonishing luck, and the latter, as usual, won. Caught ununiformed behind the lines by a band of soldiers turned highwaymen with incriminating papers in the soles of his boots, Major André was hanged as a spy. The whole city of New York raged at the injustice. Although he had hanged André in his imagination dozens of times, Jonathan still felt the execution was not quite right. When Jonathan visited Lady Beatrice to give her the news that André in a pique had inadvertently paid them off, she at first didn't want to take the money.

"I would prefer losing a thousand pounds over losing the annoyance of his company," she stated angrily.

Jonathan agreed. Arnold's betrayal and André's death had clarified for him the stakes involved in the rebellion. New York under the domination of the British was dirty, filled with refuse, and populated with soldiers able to act as they pleased toward the people whom they were supposed to protect. Only men like him with an eye to profit and a nose for the corrupt official thrived. Liberty would not correct the crime and corruption, the flawed nature of humankind, but it would give the better sort the chance to fight it. Jonathan had returned to the spying business and had started coding his coffee advertisements again.

Two weeks after the death of André, Lady Beatrice summoned Jonathan. He imagined it was to settle their biweekly account early, so was surprised that Lady Beatrice did not have the ledger book open when he entered her office.

"I was under the impression that you avoided affairs of honor, Lieutenant Osborne," Lady Beatrice remarked coldly, always using his warrant officer's name when the subject concerned the army.

"I do," Jonathan confirmed. "Affairs of honor are bad for business and an unreliable way of achieving justice, and if I unintentionally offend somebody, I make amends as quickly as I am able."

"There is a certain Hessian major recently returned from his homeland, Christoph von Wurttemberg, an acquaintance of ours, in the next room who desires to talk to you about an affair of honor. He chose this venue for he believed you might not agree to an interview otherwise. He asks I not be present because the discussion, although unlikely to turn violent, will be unpleasant."

"Then I believe I must speak to this von Wurttemberg," Jonathan replied, feeling his blood run cold.

The major was gazing out the window when Jonathan entered the room.

"Please, to take a seat and not speak until I am finished," von Wurttemberg said, then turned his narrow face toward Jonathan and regarded him with his cool blue eyes.

"I prefer to stand," Jonathan said.

"As you wish." There was a pause as von Wurttemberg seemed to be marshaling his words. "The fat man tell me you are to marry the young woman by the name of Amelia, and three men—the Hessian major, the British captain, and the Jaeger captain—violate and murder this Amelia."

"And you were that major," Jonathan interrupted.

Von Wurttemberg waved his hand as if that wasn't of great concern. "The British captain is murdered, and when I look for the Jaeger captain, I discover he also is the dead man, of which the fat man has no knowledge. Near the dead British captain is his sword, which makes me to think he die in the duel. The Jaeger captain disappear after you visit his camp with your wine. Three days later Captain Oliver receive the hand of Hoffman holding the cutlass. I, therefore, conclude he also die in the duel. Before you shoot at me, you cry the name Amelia, so I know the reason you to kill me. And you have the revenge but not the murder because I cannot raise the arm over the head." Von Wurttemberg lifted his left arm shoulder high and winced.

"The fat man promise to give to me five hundred pounds to kill you or to make you the terrible hurt. I am not the man to duel for the sake of money. To avenge the murder of the woman I love I do no less than you. To kill in the duel two men who know how to make the death is the admirable thing. I, therefore, present to you a gift—

the gift of life. You cannot prevail over me in the duel. So please to accept my gift of life."

"Do you feel remorse for raping and murdering an innocent young woman?" Jonathan asked, barely hearing his voice over the pounding of his heart.

"Remorse?" Von Wurttemberg chuckled. "A strange word, remorse. She is nothing to me—the peasant girl who knows not the best way to survive the ordeal is not to scratch at the eye. When I learn that she is the beloved—you are the lover—then I confess to the weakness of a little remorse. And so, I decide to spare your life. You may ask for the duel, and I do you the honor of acceptance, and then you die with the honor. Eighteen lives I take to only suffer two wounds, and some I kill have the fame of never losing a duel."

Jonathan stood trembling. Acceptance of what the major called his "gift" seemed an admission of cowardice and a betrayal of Amelia and himself. The manly reaction would be to insist on a duel and be resigned to death. Yet, he did want to live, and he had already taken two lives to avenge Amelia. That was not enough. If he killed a hundred for her sake, he doubted that would be enough for the justice his heart demanded.

"I will think on your offer, Major. I gave Jaeger Hoffman the chance to back out for I didn't want to take from his children their father. But Hoffman desired God to decide his fate so we fought. God wasn't merciful. If I refuse what you call your gift of life, I will challenge you, and we will duel. I will not ambush you. I will make you pay for your crime on the field of honor or die."

"In my religion, purgatory is where we make the payment," von Wurttemberg said with a smile that verged on laughter. "What is the payment, Lieutenant Osborne? Tell me, for my curious mind—how to pay for Amelia's death?"

"You cannot, except on the scaffold. I ask you to give me your word not to violate or hurt any other woman like you did to Amelia," Jonathan responded, not certain this concession would be sufficient.

"Ach, you are making the condition for me?" Von Wurttemberg shook his head and a look of disdain mixed with pity came over his sharp features. "No, I do not make the promise I will not fulfill. When my blood runs hot, then the wives, the sisters, and the daughters of the enemy I take as spoil of war. They should resist just so much to say they have no choice in the matter but no more."

"If you are unable to show mercy to those innocents, then I will find a way to make you pay for your crime. I will not ambush you. I will do it face to face, and God willing my luck will exceed the others who have met you on the field of honor," Jonathan insisted.

"Then you will die, brave man," von Wurttemberg said.

"Your servant, sir," Jonathan bowed.

"Your servant." The major clicked his heels together.

Jonathan left the room. He tried to visit the camp of von Wurttemberg a week later, wanting again to persuade him to respect the wives, sisters, and daughters of his enemy. Jonathan despised himself for considering this concession. He was not more afraid to die than the next man. A spy learns to live with the expectation that death waits around the corner. It was that throwing away his life betrayed Emma and Daniel. Yet a gentleman must put friends and family out of his mind to stand on his honor and duel. Von Wurttemberg's gift depended on Jonathan not acting as a gentleman would act. He couldn't decide whether it was fortune or misfortune that the major was away on a raid into Connecticut.

CHAPTER 26

Oct-Dec. 1780

For a fortnight after his flight into the city, Arnold seemed to have just left every place Jonathan visited. His friend had thrown himself into the organization of his loyalist regiment, boldly calling his former comrades to mutiny, promising honor, and glory to those who joined him, and finally offering three guineas to all recruits. Despite the execution of André, the news of Arnold's defection and near betrayal of West Point and Washington had lifted the spirits of the city. Even though Arnold had failed to deliver the Continental Army's largest supply depot into British hands, there was a feeling that the rebel's best general had defected, and surely more men of sense and talent would follow. That along with the rebel setbacks in the Southern colonies made the final victory seem just a matter of one more campaign season. Loyalist New York was jubilant. Many claimed that with such an accomplished aggressive general the war was already won.

The army was not as enthusiastic. The sacrifice of Major John André who had ineptly tried to assist Arnold grieved his many friends. Sure, Arnold was perhaps a brilliant soldier, but André was a good fellow, loved by many. With the new optimism, sales of wine and champagne increased. Jonathan spent long days and nights filling orders. Much to his surprise, Jonathan also grieved the absence of André. He had been one of those aggravating souls that still gained a small hold in the heart.

Jonathan was leaving the Merchant Coffee house when he finally encountered Arnold alighting from a carriage on the arm of a diminutive sweetly beautiful blond woman, the famous Peggy Shippen Arnold. Jonathan stared momentarily stunned. Thinking about that ardent patriot reneging on all that he swore sacred made Jonathan doubt the fidelity of the human heart.

Arnold also appeared surprised—as if meeting an acquaintance ten thousand miles away in the waiting room of the palace of the great Khan. They were both in uniform, Arnold wearing a general's epaulet and armed with a brace of pistols as if he momentarily expected an assault. They both groped for words.

"I had heard you anticipated me in shifting your allegiance," Arnold said after introducing his wife and forcing a smile.

Jonathan imagined his smile was equally forced. "In a fit of enthusiasm, thanks to your reasoning, I almost joined the Continentals, as you know. After experiencing Washington's ire in the form of a cat-o-nine-tails on my back, I discovered I lacked the philosophy you accused me of possessing. I became a Tory. The King and Parliament pay better. Besides, as a smuggler, I learned their foibles, so 'twas like going back to a family whose faults you know but who you love despite those faults."

Arnold never looked just at you—he either looked into you as he was doing at the moment with Jonathan or through you. "I heard men express the same opinions, and I saw the same men hanged in Philadelphia by the Revolutionary Council, and I witnessed the men who hanged them throw the loyalist widow and children out into the street to starve and divide up the spoils."

Jonathan shook his head and continued: "When I swore allegiance to the King, I spoke true. If you inquire about me, you find that people believe my uniform is a commercial convenience, which is also true. We can't war without eating and drinking."

Benedict's features darkened as he went on with his reflections: "I paid for an army out of my pocket. Nary a man under me can claim they weren't fully compensated, which not a soul in Washington's rabble can say. Yet I was censured for trying to replenish a portion of what I lost. And so, I am accused of greed."

"That would also be a fair accusation directed at me," Jonathan admitted. He then explained his business relationship with Lady Beatrice. "I will send around in the way of advertisement a bottle of champagne to your lodging."

Arnold's cool demeanor showed that he wasn't disposed to renew their old friendship. Jonathan did not fail to note that by the firmness with which Mrs. Arnold clasped her husband's arm and her expression of feminine loving possessiveness that she had as much to say about Arnold's affairs as he himself.

"We are very obliged to you, Mr. Asher," she said in a

civil enough tone. "We will depend on you to supply the wine and champagne for our get-togethers and dos."

The balding cousin of Mr. Townsend must have been observing the warehouse for several hours because he walked into Jonathan's office just after the newly married Lucretia and Dr. Smith had left to attend a dinner given by Smith's parents.

"I have an urgent message from Colonel Hamilton to you," Townsend's cousin announced without as much as a "Good day, sir."

Jonathan had anticipated that Hamilton would try to contact him because the changing circumstances necessitated an updated key to the code. He was shocked at the boldness and the rashness of sending another spy to consult with him openly at his warehouse.

"What is this urgent message that puts both of us at a risk we can ill afford," Jonathan asked.

"A young man may approach you and request your assistance," the cousin said. "You shall do everything in your power to promote this young man's enterprise. He will identify himself as John Champe."

"What does this John Champe require? 'Twould be helpful to know so I'm prepared."

"I am not privy to the nature of what he may require," the cousin went on. "Only that 'tis of the highest importance."

"And if Mr. Champe is captured, my position is compromised." Jonathan imagined himself already swinging on the gallows.

"Hamilton values you too highly to put you at risk

except for the most compelling reasons," the cousin declared.

"I thank you for your message. I hope Mr. Champe needs not too much help for I will likely refuse him. Now, I request that you never visit me here again for I prefer my services to the cause of liberty remain hidden."

"I understand, Mr. Asher." Townshend's cousin stood and bowed. As he was leaving, he stopped at the door. "I thank you, Mr. Asher. I am aware of the risks you run, perhaps more than any other man in the city, and I thank you for helping our cause from the depths of my heart."

Jonathan nodded, feeling pleasure at the novelty of being thanked.

Two days later, a tall young man wearing a crisp new loyalist uniform accosted Jonathan near the wharves.

"You are Lieutenant Osborne, are you not? I am John Champe," the young man declared breathlessly. "I believe you have been charged to aid me in a matter of great urgency."

"What is the nature of this urgency, sir?" Jonathan asked in a low voice, glancing around to make sure of their privacy. Dozens of people including British officers and most disturbingly Curston happened to be in the vicinity. This was the second time Jonathan had spotted Castor's slouching, spitting, snake-eyed agent in the last week, which meant the commissary was intensifying his campaign to undo him. Fortunately, no one was near enough to overhear the young man's incautious words.

John Champe's height, very broad shoulders, and nervousness made him stand out like a scarecrow in a mown stubbly field. From his manner, the young man appeared ignorant of the meaning of discretion.

"They did not tell you of the task I am to perform? Oh, then, I must explain." He clasped Jonathan's arm as if in fear of falling to his knees.

"Let us walk down the way and you can tell me about your task, Mr. Champe," Jonathan said, dreading what he was about to hear.

He led the overly earnest young man beyond the wharves and the shipyards on the East River to a small pebbly beach where the sound of the waves could mask the conversation. Curston followed at a distance. They stopped near a ship that had been hauled up on the beach to be refurbished, then subsequently abandoned. Jonathan wondered that Gabriel had not claimed it for firewood yet.

"You are on familiar terms with the traitorous Benedict Arnold," Champe said, his whisper as loud as any man's normal voice.

"General Arnold is an acquaintance of mine," Jonathan confirmed.

"And you are an intelligencer for the Continental Army?" The young man again had gripped his arm.

Jonathan drew in a deep breath. If he had possessed a pistol at the moment, he would have been sorely tempted to shoot Champe in the mouth.

"If I am mistaken in you, I have signed my death warrant, but I'm not mistaken in you. I have volunteered to kidnap the traitor or, failing so, assassinate him, which I will do at the cost of my life," Champ proclaimed earnestly. "As you see, I even joined his regiment to place myself closer to him."

"A dangerous assignment, Mr. Champe." Although Jonathan found Arnold's betrayal repugnant, he could not hate his old friend. There were too many shared bottles of wine, too many conversations, and too great a debt of gratitude. And Arnold remained in many respects a good man. He insisted that his old companions who had fallen prisoner were well treated, no matter what their rank. Arnold even forced Provost Cunningham to parole several former comrades-in-arms kept in the sugar warehouse, thus saving their lives. Jonathan once mentioned to Peggy Arnold these efforts to help his former comrades. "They still hate Benedict," she had replied bitterly, giving Jonathan an interrogating look, signifying she did not trust him.

Champe continued: "He changed residences that very night I had planned to abduct him. It was midnight. The boat was waiting. Three friends were stationed behind his house. I sneaked in through the back door, at first not believing my luck on how easy it was to enter. Then the realization struck me that the house was empty. Now I must beseech your assistance in this matter." The earnest young man searched Jonathan's face. "I was informed you had business connections with the traitor before the war. You are able to draw near him. Bring me along when you visit his new residence?"

"I am just a mere tradesman who delivers wine to his household. I rarely encounter General Arnold, rather I usually deal with his sister, Hannah. Arnold hasn't shown interest in reviving our old ties of friendship." Curston slouched against a post possibly within hearing distance.

Jonathan exclaimed loudly, "I can't lend you any more money, cousin!"

"If you could just take me along, and then I'd sneak away and look for Arnold," Champe said almost as loudly and grabbed Jonathan's sleeve again.

Jonathan pulled his arm free, tired of having to do that. "Impossible. His residence will be crawling with servants. And you must realize whether you succeed or fail, I am compromised and hanged."

Champe shrugged his shoulders. "Isn't the cause of our liberty more important than our lives? I apologize, sir, but the scoundrel Arnold isn't simply a traitor, he is the best general they have as he was the best general we had, second to Washington, of course, and once he takes to the field, we will face difficult times indeed."

Jonathan shook his head. "The British won't give him the same opportunities as Washington. They might allow an apothecary to raise a regiment of loyalist militia, but never a command in the regular British army, no matter how brilliant a soldier he may be, even less take his advice as to strategy. Breeding and blood are what count in the British army. Ability is not much valued."

"With a militia regiment he will do great damage," Champe insisted.

"So, what do you want of me?" Jonathan asked.

"If you cannot facilitate my entry into his household, then I require you do the job yourself," Champe said in his loudest voice yet.

"Kidnap Arnold alone?" Jonathan reluctantly arrived at the conclusion that Champe was truly mad. "You'd need fifty men to do the job."

"We wait outside. Four of us." Champe announced as if four were equivalent to fifty.

"I repeat such an attempt won't succeed." Jonathan's protest washed up against the deaf ears of Champe.

"If there is some way you can lure him out of his house alone and then we can net him."

"That's a better plan." Any plan was better than the proposed madness.

"Then when can you do it?"

"I didn't say I could. If the opportunity appears, I will contact you, that is if I believe you can carry it out in such a way that my identity is not compromised," Jonathan replied.

Champe's blank expression showed resistance to the idea. "The thing, the main thing, the only thing, is to get Arnold."

"My main thing is to survive the war, Mr. Champe. I don't have the luxury of sacrificing my life in the cause of liberty for I have people dependent on me," Jonathan said, thinking of Daniel and Emma. "I can help you no further than what I'm proposing, and only then if the opportunity arises."

"Get the traitor." Champe pounded his fist into an open palm.

"If the opportunity arises, I shall contact you, so long as you don't plan to compromise my safety."

Champe's face did not hide his disappointment. "I'm disillusioned at your lack of patriotic fervor." Jonathan could see that Champe wanted to say cowardice. "Visit me at the regiment. You just need to whisper to me the place and time. My friends are hiding on Long Island, and they can be here within the day. Before I am shipped out, we must bring off this thing. For our cause, for everything we hold dear."

Jonathan mentally cursed Washington and Hamilton for recruiting such a clueless oaf for that impossible task. Curston had disappeared as if he had important information to relay.

A week later, a pounding at the door of the warehouse woke Jonathan out of a dead sleep. When he stumbled downstairs and opened the door, John Champe burst in, discomposed, flustered, and full of excuses. Champe related breathlessly that he had obtained an interview with Benedict Arnold. He had even found an old comrade of Arnold's from the Quebec campaign in one of the church prisons for whom he was going to lodge an appeal. His three co-conspirators had been waiting in the back alley. What had disrupted his plan utterly was Peggy Arnold. She was seated by her husband. Diminutive, beautiful, contemplating the raw nervous young man with appreciative intelligent eyes.

"I couldn't do violence to him in front of her. I just couldn't. Curse me! I couldn't. I swear I will carry out my assignment when I can discover him away from her company. Do you know how beautiful she is and how kindly she regarded me? I could have fallen in love with her ten times over. Now my regiment will go off and I shall be fighting against the cause of liberty. What a fool I was to take this on."

"Mrs. Arnold saved your life by preventing the attempt," Jonathan remarked dryly.

"Well, 'tis up to you now to bring him out so we can capture him. I tried twice."

"Betray the betrayer, so to speak. I will do no more than what I already stated. That shouldn't prevent you from trying again. There's a rumor about the third time being the charm."

"I don't see how charm will help me bring the traitor to justice," Champe declared. "'Tis your patriotic duty to assist me."

"Don't dare tell me my duty. You fight your war, and I fight mine."

Champe turned in disgust and stormed out of the warehouse.

Jonathan stared regretfully at his bed, sleep now impossible.

CHAPTER 27

BEING IN HER words a prominent loyalist and an acquaintance of the man in question, Lady Beatrice insisted that Jonathan attend a reception welcoming Benedict and Peggy Arnold to New York. Jonathan didn't particularly desire to attend the gathering and therefore have the opportunity to set up a betrayal of Arnold to the fool Champe, but no excuse would pass Lady Beatrice's scrutiny.

Jonathan had barely graced the door of the hall when von Wurttemberg made his entrance—the major's gleaming presence and fear-inspiring reputation momentarily riveting all eyes—his attendance representing the Hessian appreciation for the new brigadier general. Other notable loyalist friends of the King and Parliament soon followed.

After greeting Benedict who looked gray and Peggy who also appeared ill, bowing to Elizabeth on the arm of Lord Edgar and having the slight satisfaction of seeing her blush, frown, and blink, and then pursuing the civility with Percival who had a nervous black-haired girl hanging on his arm like a drowning person clinging to a log, Jonathan took care to position himself facing a curtained window and start a conversation with a florid loyalist colonel who also seemed out of place. While nodding in reply to a compliment on the quality of champagne Lady Beatrice supplied, von Wurttemberg's loud high voice interrupted the conversations in the room.

"We lose Adjutant General John André, a most cultivated and amiable gentleman," von Wurttemberg exclaimed to Arnold. "And what do we gain in exchange? An apothecary."

"I hope to be of greater service to the king than as merely an apothecary," Arnold replied, his face turning an unnatural purplish red. Peggy went crimson.

"No doubt you will be. You are a good soldier but forgive me for not yet forgiving you. You kill my fellow countrymen by the score, and I feel I must speak for them."

Arnold's purplish hue deepened. "I was just being obedient to my duty. Unfortunately, my talents were not appreciated."

"Ach, that is the complaint of a spoiled maiden," von Wurttemberg said, openly sneering. "A maiden who cannot understand why everybody think her not the most beautiful in the room."

Arnold's smile was rigid as if held in place by tacks. "You are mistaken, Herr Christoph. A maiden moans and faints. A soldier acts as I have acted, formerly to your detriment, and now I hope to your great advantage."

A warm smile spread across von Wurttemberg's face. "*Sehr Gut*, General Arnold. I \no longer be the unpleasant person to you. A man must say what he thinks, especially if other men think the same thing and have the fear to speak. Now that I speak the bad parts, we are free to welcome you. I agree with those who say your invasion of Quebec make you the American Hannibal, and I furthermore declare that your battle on Valcour Island is most the brilliant soldiering in the war."

"I was defeated on the lake," Arnold said, the purple gradually fading from his face.

Von Wurttemberg shook his head. "You are the small dog that so hurt the great British lion that the lion had to make retreat and lick the wounds."

"I thank you for your gracious compliments," Arnold said, still not quite recovering his temper. "As for Major John André, Peggy and I grieve his loss as much as the loss of a brother. Washington's execution of him was a crime of the deepest dye and shows the man for what he truly is. I will have my revenge. I'll search out every damn spy in this city and hang them as Major André's memorial."

"Very good, General Arnold," von Wurttemberg said, then made his excuses and moved away. He paused before Jonathan, seeming to consider whether to address him or not.

"I hope you are enjoying this evening, Herr Christoph," Jonathan said.

Von Wurttemberg eyed him keenly. "You are too much the liar. You hope I choke on the biscuit."

"Yes, I do, but for the sake of civility and our hostess, I will be courteous," Jonathan replied.

"Courtesy is proper between honorable enemies," von Wurttemberg continued in a lower voice. "Courtesy until you make the cut across the throat. The fat man is unhappy with me. He has the desire I challenge you to a duel in the manner you cannot make the refusal. I am a man of my word and will not offer you the offense. If you are still of the disposition to avenge Amelia, then I am to be pleased to honor the challenge."

Jonathan stared, trying to articulate his reply.

Von Wurttemberg went on, "But you do not make me the worry." He pointed to Edgar who, aware that Elizabeth was the prettiest girl in the room, had taken to showing her off to as many of his fellow officers as possible. "He is like the very little mouse that has the belief he is the cat."

"Lord Edgar is not a bad fellow," Jonathan commented.

"No, not bad fellow in the least," von Wurttemberg affirmed. "But it is in his head to think I love him so much that I to lick his boot for the pleasure of licking. I do not. For the Lady Beatrice, I do this favor of saving his life. Now, he shows me off to his friends and then makes the threat like he is making the joke if they do not do what he desires—I understand this is to jest—he says I make the challenge them to the duel and kill them. He assumes intimacy that never to exist between us. He has no talent except the cheerful idiocy."

At this point, Edgar, who was well into his cups, made a beckoning gesture to von Wurttemberg as if he were summoning a servant. Von Wurttemberg clicked his heels, smiled maliciously, then strode toward Edgar. Elizabeth appeared distressed, and Jonathan followed the major to rescue her from what certainly was going to be a scene.

"Vut iz your heart's desire, my most gracious lord," von Wurttemberg said with loud sarcasm, exaggerating his accent.

Edgar was put off. He seemed to realize he had done something wrong, and the panic swimming in his eyes showed that he was searching for a way out. "Oh, I apologize, Herr Christoph. I did not mean to be so…" The right word was not to be found.

"Imperious?" Von Wurttemberg suggested, emitting a harsh cawing laugh. "No need to vorry, Lord Edgar, I live to be your most humble servant and am always happy to please you vith zee favor." The Hessian major's tone was anything but that of a servant. The conversation in the room began to subside.

"As I said I apologize for my gesture. I do not believe it was apt."

Von Wurttemberg drew himself up, communicating danger like a snake ready to strike. "You, a lord, to lack zee courage to not apologize? If I remember vith correctness, the last time you required zee courage, you borrowed mine."

"I know not what you mean…" Edgar fumbled for words.

Lady Beatrice sailed into the confrontation. "Major Christoph, this is a party to welcome our brilliant adversary who has now become our brilliant friend."

"Your nephew is the most foolish boy, Lady Beatrice," von Wurttemberg said, staring icily at the hostess. "I do not to press the point now, but I will not endure insults from this child who still needs his mother to wipe the boogers from his nose."

Elizabeth gave a small gasp and shot Jonathan an imploring look as Edgar started to unpeel his glove. Jonathan stepped forward, grasped Edgar's wrist stopping the action, and said loudly, "Lady Beatrice forbids duels, and we shall adhere to her wishes."

"How can I not…" Edgar possessed fewer words than usual.

"You insulted him, Lord Edgar. He insulted you. You are now even," Jonathan reasoned to the flustered young lord.

"And what if I do not agree we are even," von Wurttemberg said, smirking.

"He apologized. There is no point of honor in a duel that would simply be murder," Jonathan asserted.

"And you might have the acquaintance with the act of making the murder?" The tone of his voice could be taken as questioning or stating a fact.

Jonathan bowed and escorted Edgar towards the table with the punch bowl. Elizabeth followed and stared frightened at Edgar who was ashen and who had to set the cup of punch down because he wanted to conceal his trembling hand.

"'Tis over, isn't it, Mr. Asher?" Elizabeth asked.

"Just a minor contretemps," Jonathan whispered. "Too much to drink, Lord Edgar. I suggest you escort Miss Littleton home now."

"How dare he…" Edgar mumbled.

"If you could be so kind, Lord Edgar," Elizabeth said in her sweetest brogue and pulled on his arm. "I am having a headache, sure. This has been a treat for me, and I am so grateful. Now, please, escort me back to the millinery so I can rest."

"As you wish Miss Elizabeth." Edgar attempted to lift the quivering glass and put it down quickly.

Jonathan watched Edgar and Elizabeth leave. They both looked so young. They were a handsome couple.

A half-hour later when the party had regained the normal tenor of laughter and clinking glasses, Lady Beatrice came up to Jonathan and seeming to read his thoughts said, "You believe Elizabeth no longer loves you."

He shrugged he hoped with persuasive indifference. "She never loved me in the first place."

"Such a bitter sentiment," Lady Beatrice commented. "Of course, she loved you and may still, but she was always after a man of higher station. I, for one, cannot fault her ambition. She is a handsome woman and harbors no malice in her heart. She is a little mad—nothing that should keep a suitor away, but enough so to make life entertaining."

"Lord Edgar is courting Elizabeth with your encouragement," Jonathan accused, not hiding his anger.

"Yes, my nephew has fallen for her." Lady Beatrice touched his arm in sympathy. "I am not discouraging him. He is a sweet man, although regretfully too prone to act foolishly. As you know his estate is meager. He will inherit a sufficiency from us, so he needs a certain type of lady. Elizabeth is a good match in that regard. She lacks not pedigree, which would make her acceptable to his family, and she has sense enough for both of them. Lord Edgar needs to be led gently, lovingly, but firmly, in a companionate union, and Elizabeth has the character to do so. You are the only possible impediment."

"How could that be?" Jonathan shook his head. "You just said she was looking for a lord."

"And she found one," Lady Beatrice affirmed. "Yet she was looking to you to fix Edgar's quandary, and she glowed when you triumphed. I want to thank you for disarming the combatants. I heard Major Christoph will not be reasoned with when he's after a duel."

"Tell your nephew to avoid the man, for the good von Wurttemberg will provoke a duel that Edgar can't win."

"I'll tell Harold, and he'll persuade Clinton to have them posted as far apart as the colonies allow. You seem to have settled your differences with the Hessian."

"We established a truce of sorts," Jonathan said. "Over a personal matter."

"You might be the first person to have persuaded that bloody-minded Hessian to a truce. Please do not break the truce. I would not know how to replace the income your merchandise provides."

Given the intimate drift of the conversation, Jonathan asked, "Was the debt to Castor Blanchard settled to the satisfaction of both parties?"

"Lord Harold offered to give him three teams of four horses, which Mr. Blanchard can rent back to the army for 54 pounds a month. The commissary said he was studying the offer."

"Von Wurttemberg said Mr. Blanchard requested that he provoke an incident with me."

A dark cloud scudded across Lady Beatrice's features, then she smiled. "But he did not. I believe, personal matter or no, he might be your friend."

Jonathan felt all the muscles in his face stiffen in the effort to not contradict her. "With the good Lord Edgar courting Miss Elizabeth, I am not very much wanted in this city."

"Self-pity doesn't become you, Mr. Asher. And to tell

the truth, I am more certain of Elizabeth's affection toward you, than your affection toward her."

That's because I'm a damned spy, Jonathan thought. He then made his way to Arnold to congratulate him on his command and begin his plot against the traitor

CHAPTER 28

DESPITE THE COOLNESS of their recent interactions, Jonathan and Elizabeth still shared the bond of Emma and Daniel. Jonathan's "son" and "daughter" always greeted him when he took coffee with Elizabeth, which was appropriate because the children had become the sole topic of conversation. Elizabeth was teaching Emma how to tat, and she was actively looking for a tutor for Daniel. Jonathan made a point of having at least three meals a week with Emma and Daniel, and for their moral and religious education, he seldom failed to take them to church on Sundays. After herding them to services, Anglican because it was easier for the children to sit through the shorter sermons, they usually went to the Bowling Green where they would buy rolls and butter, then walk to the Battery and eat sitting on a low wall by the promenade and watch the ships.

Jonathan sometimes persuaded the captains he did business with to allow the children on board. They might even take the ferry to Long Island. He taught Daniel how to fish, how to paddle a canoe, and was disputing with

Elizabeth whether he should show his "son" how to throw a tomahawk. Emma seemed happy to just be outside. She still refused to speak, although her eyes always shone with gratitude when Jonathan presented her a sweetmeat or a trinket. Elizabeth made sure that Emma was as well-dressed as the most pampered daughters of the city. Daniel often pleaded with Elizabeth to come on the outing and share the fun with them, but the milliner always refused. On the chilly Sunday after the party welcoming Arnold, however, Elizabeth acceded to Daniel's pleas to accompany them. She seemed anxious, even afraid, and Jonathan sensed that she found comfort in his presence.

On the way to the park, Daniel suddenly cried out, "Look there's Mrs. Dalton!"

Millicent Dalton was pushing an apple cart down the street. She turned away red-faced and probably would have fled had it not meant abandoning her merchandise. Jonathan approached, unaccountably angry. "Why did you not appeal to me for better employment?" He threw the cart on the ground, spilling the produce. "Here is money for the apples I destroyed."

"A penny earned is better than a pound given in charity," Millicent muttered, ignoring the proffered note, righting the cart, and beginning to pick up the apples. She held up one. "Like most bullies and brutes, you over-estimate your strength, Mr. Asher. Your fury could do no more than give this poor fruit a slight bruise."

"Come with us, Millie," Elizabeth urged. "We have buttered rolls, and oysters, and tarts. Just for an hour. We have not talked in so long. Gather up the apples, and we'll be making apple pies you can sell tomorrow. Jonathan is going to show Daniel how to shoot a fowling piece, and Emma and I will be quite forsaken."

Millicent glared at Jonathan and seemed unwilling to take the money. Finally, she conceded, "For your sake Liza. Just for an hour. Mr. Dalton will be pleased I got back early and am not breaking the Sabbath."

After they consumed the rolls and oysters, Millicent said, "Liza, if you please, let me take Emma on a walk alone. The men can keep you company for another quarter-hour." She took Emma by the hand and led her away.

Daniel soon went off to play with the other boys. Remaining seated on the low wall, Elizabeth and Jonathan began an awkward conversation about the weather, then about Lady Beatrice, and then the conversation took a surprising turn.

"Why have you never mentioned Amelia?" Elizabeth asked.

"How did you hear about Amelia?" The name sounded strange coming from Elizabeth's lips.

Elizabeth tossed her head triumphantly. "You thought you could be keeping her a secret. Nancy, your sister-in-law, told me her husband made a pair of glasses for her because she was so nearsighted. Don't worry, she gave nothing else away. Nancy just came in for some ribbon. I said I was having trouble seeing, and she said that."

"Amelia is dead." Jonathan felt a small incurable ache on pronouncing the words.

"I'm so sorry," Elizabeth cried, surprised. "I didn't want to open old wounds."

"Not so old," Jonathan whispered.

"If I had only known…" She gazed intently at

Jonathan. "I thought you might be the sort of man who trifled…"

'With a woman's heart?" Jonathan asked.

"Many do," she responded defensively.

"Well, among my surfeit of flaws, Miss Littleton, that is not one of them," Jonathan said.

"You are so difficult to know, Mr. Asher." Tears shone in Elizabeth's eyes. "That's the problem, to be sure. I am wishing you had spoken of Amelia sooner."

Jonathan could have asked what difference that would have made, yet he knew the difference. She might not have encouraged Lady Beatrice's nephew. Still, there remained hope for them. Not quite wanting to explore the hope yet, he changed the subject which went nowhere. They then continued in uneasy silence until Millicent returned with Emma, both talking. Daniel forgot his fury at not being taught to shoot, rushed in from his game, and waved his arms excitedly. Emma blushed deeply and said shyly, "I love you all."

Emma only spoke a few more words during the rest of the outing, mostly in reply to Daniel's rush of questions— "What did you think of our hiding place?"

"Wasn't Mr. Blanchard a funny man"—but seemed happy that she was doing so.

It became apparent that Millicent wasn't in a hurry to return to her husband. She finally confessed, "We ran out of money. The Spencers told me they no longer required my services even though their grandchildren were crying for me to stay, nor did anyone else want to hire me, although I am certain I did nothing that bears reproach. Terence's parents took him back. They say I'm the reason he's ailing. I can visit him once a week, although 'tis so hard with them living halfway up Long Island. I think his parents are beginning to see I am not the calculating seductress they supposed me to be. Now I live with eight other girls in a room. We're given apples to sell. I sometimes take one to my husband and tell him I bought it."

"What about your family?" Jonathan asked.

"My brother always warned that I'd pay for marrying above my station. He is a good man otherwise and supplies the wants of our parents." Millicent's face softened into a smile. "I eat at his house two or three times a week so, you see, I am not so skinny."

Elizabeth pleaded illness the following Sunday. Jonathan and the children again came across Mrs. Dalton and her apple cart. She appeared very tired. She couldn't resist Emma's teary entreaty and allowed Jonathan to buy all the apples for the children to give to the people strolling along the Battery walkway. While Emma and Daniel handed out the apples, Jonathan and Millicent sat and conversed. Millicent was subdued, unsure of herself. All animosity seemed to have left her.

Millicent explained how she induced Emma to talk. She intuited that the reason Emma hadn't yet started speaking was that the child was afraid she would sound strange, so while they walked, Millicent persuaded Emma to practice.

The conversation went around to his business. Millicent made a face when Jonathan mentioned that Dr. Reginald Smith had married Lucretia Baldwin, and they were now paying rent on a portion of the warehouse that Josiah had made into two rooms for the doctoring practice. Jonathan asked whether Millicent was acquainted with Lucretia.

Millicent nodded emphatically. "Lucretia Baldwin then has caught the good doctor in her web. Truly, I do not know whether to laugh or cry. I wondered how she was going to extricate herself from her predicament this time. Don't take it from me that Lucretia is a bad woman. I'd not even call her loose. Lucretia managed better than most of our sex who find themselves in her circumstances. Her parents died when she was young. She was given over to a wealthy aunt. Lucretia devoted fifteen years of her life solely to caring for her aunt, a resentful bitter demanding woman if there ever was one. No outings, no balls, no friends, much less gentlemen callers. The aunt wouldn't stand for that sort of tomfoolery. Lucretia endured all with the understanding she would be the beneficiary of her aunt's fortune. Well, she was deceived. She got a pittance that couldn't pay a fortnight at an inn, not a shilling more.

"The poor girl was thrown out into the world at the age of twenty-four with no family, no skills, no connections in society, and few social graces. Yet for several years now, Miss Baldwin has fed and dressed herself decently. 'Tis amazing she hasn't become a fallen woman. She lives by her wits, a commodity most people think she lacks. She persuaded a sea captain to let her take care of his household while he was away and then rented out his rooms. I believe the captain is dead, but she claims she gets correspondence from him, so the property isn't confiscated. She goes out into society. Ladies used to snub her, yet she endured the snubs, and now they are afraid of her because of her connections. She is never invited to receptions or parties, yet always appears on one pretext or another and is never asked to leave."

"Do you believe she deceived the good doctor?" Jonathan asked.

"When I said Miss Baldwin was not a bad woman, I meant she never purposely harmed those who did no harm to her. Although the doctor is deceived, I doubt she intends to cause him difficulty. About her condition, which you were discrete enough not to mention, there are three things I know to be true: Miss Baldwin was visited several times at night by a certain dragoon lieutenant. She had herself rowed across to Wallabout Bay two months ago. Her dragoon died of smallpox.

"So, Mr. Asher, let me string these actions together for you as we gossiping servants do. That lieutenant is the father of the child in her belly. He likely laughed in her face when Miss Baldwin confronted him at his quarters and demanded to know whether his protestations of love had been truthful. 'Alas, dearie, 'twas all in fun,' he probably said, as such men usually say. Our Miss Baldwin did not cry, she did not complain—that is not her way. No, she had herself rowed across the East River and visited the swampy burying pit of the prison ships. When the work party from a prison ship dumped their load of fresh corpses there, she joined the women who scavenge the rags off the skeletons. But she wasn't there to scavenge, instead, she looked for the bodies of those that had recently died of the pox. She was unafraid, having been inoculated. She took the lieutenant's handkerchief and wiped it across the faces and mouths of several corpses. Did I tell you her dragoon was a sweaty man?

"She procured another amorous meeting with him—in the spirit of fun you understand—and tenderly wiped his sweating face after he had had his fun. That is what I believe. You might call her a murderer. I'd not do so. I know of no incident where Miss Baldwin was cruel for the pleasure of cruelty. She has displayed nothing of the harpy or harridan in her character, nor does she pretend to an exalted station. She treats servants kindly. I believe Miss Baldwin truly only wants a protected place in this world, and your Doctor Reginald provides that."

"And her relationship with Castor Blanchard?"

"I am not familiar with that name. Oh, yes, he was the fat gentleman who stole from the prisoners. He must be the connection that causes everybody to fear her."

Emma returned, snuggled in Millicent's lap, and closed her eyes as her hair was stroked. "If it weren't for Emma and Daniel, who love their benefactor, I would pity you, Mr. Asher. With all your fortune they are the only treasures you have."

"I wish there were less truth in what you're saying. And what are your treasures?"

Millicent stopped stroking and gave him a hard stare. "A husband, two brothers, and friends that still love me."

"Emma and Daniel will have to do for me, then."

"On second thought, love is not strong enough a word, Mr. Asher," Millicent smiled as if she were remembering a private joke. "Your children adore you."

"My children? Strange to hear somebody else say those

words, yet that is the way I think of them, and I cannot imagine loving any child more than these children."

"Is the rest of it worth it for you, Mr. Asher?"

"What do you mean?"

"Your wealth, which you do not spend. Your station, which you have carved out for yourself, I dare say at the expense of others, yet do not flaunt."

"As you know, the French woman who became my mother taught me to look into the heart. As for my wealth, there is no middle ground there. I can either be poor and hungry or what I am."

"I still pity you."

Over the following days, Elizabeth avoided him completely, even suggesting he should only come for coffee once a week. Percy had the pleasure of informing him that Lord Edgar disapproved of his presence, and if that meant getting rid of his brats, then, well, so much the better. Jonathan was puzzled by Elizabeth's reaction to Lord Edgar's courtship. Her passion seemed lukewarm. Yet her defense of criticism of him was fierce. She still turned to Jonathan when frightened, usually making the excuse of the danger to Emma and Daniel as a pretext. This was the case when what she termed a man of mean aspect started haunting their street, taking a particular interest in the millinery.

With the help of Josiah and his brothers, the man was apprehended and brought into Jonathan's office in the warehouse. He was a little man, not much beyond boyhood, with a humped shoulder, a grimy face, and given to sudden theatrical sighs. He first cowered when pushed before Jonathan and on seeing the second lieutenant's uniform seemed to melt with fear, then controlled himself and stood as straight as his humped shoulder allowed.

"I am Lieutenant Osborne. What is your business with the millinery?" Jonathan demanded.

"I done nothing wrong," the man asserted in a squeaky voice, making continual efforts to square his unsquare-able shoulders. "So, there is no need to threaten to cut off my privates, hang me upside down, and use me for lance practice."

"I have no intention of injuring you, sir, if you intend no harm," Jonathan replied. "I only want to know what business you have on that street."

"What business? No business, of course." He erupted into a bout of high squeaks which Jonathan interpreted as laughter. "I thought I had. After I saw what he did to my father and brothers, I thought... Oh, what did I think? I thought I was a brave man. I thought nothing could get in the way of my righteous anger. Surely, my sis-ter's ghost would prick my conscience. He announced his name: Percival Littleton. Littleton Percival Littleton. So, I find his house. His sisters and brother. Perfect revenge on Lieutenant Percival Littleton, but they are innocent, so I wait for him. Littleton Lieutenant Percival Littleton appears. Still, I cannot... Do you know what it takes to murder a man, even one who has done you a great wrong? Am I a coward or merciful? Kill me because I no longer can endure myself, but do not take so long as he took with my family."

"Those children are my charges and no relation to Lieutenant Littleton," Jonathan said, feeling great pity for the poor soul whose doubts and self-questioning he knew only too well. "They have suffered as much as you, seeing their parents burn to death in the Great Fire. Leave here, or I'll arrest you, throw you in the Sugar House where you will get your slow death."

"Give me until tomorrow," the young humpback begged. "I have one more errand to do if I possess the courage. I swear nobody is harmed. Just a few hours and I leave never to return."

"Is the errand worth your life? Leave, my good man. I will protect my charges, and I am neither a coward nor merciful where they are concerned. Do not step foot in this city again."

Josiah was given the job of escorting the poor boy to the Paulus Hook ferry. Josiah confessed that the boy escaped by going into the jakes behind a tavern, then sneaking out when his back was turned. After two hours he found him skulking along the docks. Josiah made sure to escort him onto the ferry.

After thinking it over and talking to Gabriel, Jonathan decided to post an unofficial guard on Jacob Street. Gabriel suggested paying two vendors—of sweet corn and fried fish on each corner. During the night, an unofficial night watchman would walk down the street every half hour.

Gabriel went a step further. Jonathan returned one evening to his office to find Percy squirming on a chair as if he were nailed to it. Gabriel and the threatening presence of two huge refugee slaves kept him in his place.

"What is happening here?" Jonathan asked.

"Waiting for you, suh, to show you dis," Gabriel said, his dark face grave.

"So, you're behind this African kidnapping and holding me against my will? You have a lot to answer for, Mr. Asher. I swear I'll unmake you," Percy snarled and squirmed.

Gabriel suddenly backhanded Percy's face, the sound of the contact as loud as a gunshot. "I your savior in dis world. As for de next world, doubt you getting one."

Blood began to seep out the corner of Percy's mouth. His chest heaved. His eyes showed fear.

"See, it like dis," Gabriel continued. "Dis piece of dung make everybody so mad 'cross de river dat de fellow killing dis piece of dung earning bounty two hundred pounds. De damn fool announce his name every time he burn farm, kill husband, father, or brother, or swive der wives, daughters, 'n sisters. Everybody know de name of Percival Littleton." Gabriel raised his hand to strike again, and Percival cringed.

"I returned the favor of what they did to us," Percy spluttered and averted his cheek, screwing his eyes and contorting his mouth waiting for the blow.

"No, suh, you be boasting in every tavern you done ten times worse what dey do. I harbor no love for de slave-masters, but I 'ways pity de innocents. You see, Mr. Asher, it come to dis. Not safe for de children 'n him living under de same roof. Too many after his blood. So, Mr. Asher, do I slash his gullet 'n collect two hundred pound for us, or no?"

"Is there another remedy?" Jonathan asked. He was tempted to say, "Do with him what you will." He did not doubt Percy deserved harsh justice for his crimes. Still. he couldn't quite stomach causing Elizabeth grief.

"'Nother remedy?" Gabriel thought a moment then addressed Percy. "You free go anywhere 'cept de house on Jacob Street. Den I collecting de reward for your pretty head. Truth be, little shit, de camp wid your fellow scoundrels only safe place for you. I advise you never go out of sight of 'nother soldier even to piss, 'n when you go visiting 'cross de river, stay in de middle of de company—no leading your fellow rascals, no lagging behind."

"I will report you and have you drawn and quartered."

Gabriel shook his head. "Fine ding to say to man who just save your worthless hide. Go ahead, dung-hole. Leave now 'n report me. Come back wid your friends. Come 'n find me in Canvas Town. Go ahead, leave."

Percy hesitated.

"Wise man. You last not ten steps outside de door."

"How am I to go?" He looked around wildly. Panic was beginning to get the better of him.

"I walk wid you 'til you safe in your camp. Den you can report me, which be guaranteeing you dead man 'fore de end of day."

CHAPTER 29

AT THE PARTY at Lady Beatrice's, Jonathan had mentioned to Arnold the profits in whaleboat privateering and the existence of a new specially modified boat, ten feet longer than the usual whaleboat and made with the stoutest hardwood to mount heavier cannon. Meredith James had commissioned the boat, which he, of course, was unable to finish paying, so the builder was looking for an investor or buyer.

"I'd like to see such a craft," was Arnold's immediate reply, his eyes glittering with the possibilities of adventuring and making money. Jonathan arranged a meeting with the builder around twilight at the wharf which conveniently was isolated from other wharves by at least a hundred yards.

There were so many reasons not to follow through. Could he abandon Emma and Daniel? Broken hearts aside, the hard answer was yes. Jonathan had told Gabriel about his interview with von Wurttemberg and his decision not to pursue the Hessian. Gabriel, whose opinions were usually rendered immediately and absolutely, took a long time to reply. Finally, he asked, "Want me kill de Hessian bugger for you?"

Jonathan after an equally long pause responded, "No. 'Tis my job to do or not do."

"'Tis de children, suh?"

"Yes. 'Tis them."

"Know me as man of word, suh?"

"I certainly do."

"Den understands, suh, de children be not lacking for care if you gone."

"I thank you."

"Dat's what Miss Amelia would be wantin'. Doin' it for her."

Gabriel would be true to his word. Furthermore, Jonathan, judging himself from Millicent's point of view—whoremonger and profiteer who steals provisions from starving prisoners—often thought Emma and Daniel would be better off without him. Additionally, he was a spy, which meant betrayer of those who placed trust in him. Was the cause of liberty worth this betrayal of a friend? Ever since saving Arnold's life in the Sugar Islands, he felt in part he owned Arnold's victories. Now that Arnold had betrayed the cause, Jonathan couldn't shake his responsibility for the betrayal either.

Despite misgivings, Jonathan informed Champe who would play the part of the whaleboat owner. His three stout fearless comrades would hide nearby to carry off the kidnapping. Jonathan asked to be taken with Arnold and treated as if he were also a prisoner.

Jonathan called on Arnold at home and was led to the parlor where he found the brigadier general sitting with his wife Peggy. As always, Jonathan had to fight against being unnerved by her interrogating gaze.

"'Tis good to see you again, Jonathan. May I still call you by your Christian name?" Arnold said, rising from his chair to shake his hand.

"Yes. I will still call you General Arnold if that doesn't displease you for I don't want to forget rank." This was a weak excuse, however, calling his old friend by his Christian name seemed to use their former friendship as a means of betrayal.

"Before we go off to examine this naval marvel, I want to make sure we are not in arrears with you." Arnold was now studying him closely.

"Your sister Hannah is quite diligent, general," Jonathan said, suppressing a shudder when he observed Arnold wore a brace of pistols even in his home. The only way to carry out the plan, Jonathan realized, was to put everything out of his mind but the task at hand.

"She always been the better person. I compliment you on your fine claret or should I say Captain Rodrigo's fine claret." Arnold threw his head back and laughed. "You think I'd not recognize the provenance of your wine? How I wish for the simple life of evading revenue cutters and smuggling a hundred casks of the finest Madeira past customs agents. I flatter myself that some of your present prosperity is due to my tutelage."

Jonathan nodded and earnestly wished also for the same simple life. "You would be correct, General Arnold."

Arnold put on his bonhomie face. "Maybe one day

after we put down this traitorous rebellion, we join forces together in commercial ventures, and you can tutor me. I will need the help of friends to recuperate my fortune."

"Perhaps this venture can be a beginning, at least in recovering your fortune." Jonathan was aware that Arnold had received a payment of ten thousand pounds for his treason, which for most men would have been sufficient to last several lifetimes. He doubted it would see Arnold through two years. His friend always possessed absolute confidence he could make more than he spent.

"After devoting my wealth and health to the cause that not only bankrupted me but allowed the knave Mr. Reed of the Revolutionary Council, a man whose malice is only exceeded by his cowardice, to persecute me, the sole thing I had left to sell was my talent at arms."

Arnold took in a deep breath and waited for Jonathan to speak and when he didn't, went on: "Some would have it that I sold my soul, others say I never had a soul to sell. Despite my many adversaries, I would have continued to suffer poverty and opprobrium for the cause of liberty. Because you are a friend, Jonathan, I am explaining myself to you. You cannot be faithful to men and principles. Sooner or later, they diverge, and then you must choose which to betray. The new offers from King George and Parliament give us all the liberty we ever desired. That satisfied, how could we pursue this damn spilling of blood? I chose to betray Washington for the cause of peace."

"I wear the same uniform as you although I don't have so high-minded an explanation. The uniform protects me and facilitates sales," Jonathan said to Arnold. *Mind on task*, he whispered in his head.

"I also must apologize, Jonathan, for my coolness and distance. I confess I did not want to test our friendship. The fact of the matter is I suspected you were a spy. You had already done the work of a spy in fetching that miserable whining French dunce from his prison here."

"Washington can be very persuasive," Jonathan replied. *Mind on task*, he repeated in his head. "That is my sole contribution to the Patriot cause. Afterward, to please the Marquis, I was whipped for my efforts."

"I wished I had suffered such a whipping early on instead of enduring the venom of a thousand envious tongues so I could have chosen the King's side ere I spilled so much blood to advance the rebel cause. Looking at you now, you being a spy don't make any sense. But, as you know, I swore to avenge the shameful criminal murder of André by searching out every rebel spy I could find in this city and hanging them all. And since I learned of your defection to the Parliament's cause, I harbored a grain of suspicion. Later, I learned that Hamilton was running spies in New York. I know that he talked to you before your punishment…"

"Hamilton wanted to apologize for what he believed an injustice," Jonathan interrupted. "I accepted the apology and three days later accepted and signed the oath of allegiance to the King."

"I'm not certain whether you are aware of the incident in the fall of 78 of the lad who shot himself on being exposed as a courier for a spy in Washington's camp. The boy stated afore he blew his brains out that a merchant from New York who had killed a British captain was watching him. And in the distance, I believed I spotted you. The distance was great, although my eyesight is keen. Why would you be there? I encounter you here and discover you could fairly be described as a merchant from New York. Why are you here wearing a uniform? I spent too many evenings with you, Jonathan, sharing a pot of ale or a glass of Madeira I treasure in my memory, so I desired not to see you grace the halter. I even had you followed with the idea of warning you to flee if my fears turned out to be true. Although you have access to information, I found no evidence of you conveying that information to the rebels."

"I thank you for your frankness. You can rest easy. I am not a spy. As you know from our many discussions, I hold no strong political opinions. I make more from my legitimate commerce than Washington could ever compensate me for risking my life. My family were always loyalists, and now that you have joined the King's cause I have no deep ties of affection with the rebels." Jonathan felt he was overly explaining his allegiance. "I do not take umbrage at your suspicion. You are the most wanted man in America, and you cannot be too careful." The pressure on the dam holding back his doubts about this enterprise increased. *Mind on task*, Jonathan repeated to himself, then said aloud, "Now, shall we see the boat?"

"Still, forgive me, for distrusting you, Jonathan. Deceit is in the nature of war, and you could have only improved in that regard. Nevertheless, for the sake of our old friendship, we shall visit this naval wonder," Arnold declared and clapped him on his shoulder

They drove in Arnold's carriage to the wharf. The streets were muddy with melting snow. Would the rivers freeze with four feet of ice this winter like the last, Jonathan wondered? A chilling wind had arrived with the twilight, and few people were seen on the streets. A skiff, most like the kidnapper's boat, was pulled up onto a stretch of pebbly beach. The shipwright, as was his custom, was treating himself to a tumbler of rum at a nearby tavern before continuing home. The kidnappers were nearby, watching them, waiting for their opportunity. Champe was in the cabin. The trap was set.

"Well, if you were to do me harm, Jonathan, this is the place," Arnold said in a cheery voice as he checked his brace of pistols.

"What do you think of her?" Jonathan did not see a light in the cabin. *Mind on task*, he screamed inside his head, his nerves on fire.

Arnold walked down the wharf, running his hand along the railing of the boat. His eye missed little when examining a boat or a horse. "What a joy 'twould be to captain such a vessel. Sixteen oarsmen, a sail, a twelve-pounder mounted on a swiveling platform which I would design myself. I could out sail and out maneuver any larger ship and play havoc with all the smaller ones. I'd resign my commission for the chance. Alas, I cannot do so for bigger things are expected of me."

"You could invest in the boat. The shipwright, Mr. Southwell, must be sleeping in the cabin. I'll wake him before we completely lose the light. Ahoy there!" *Mind on task, so help me God, mind on task.* Jonathan stepped onto the deck and crouching down entered the low cabin, involuntarily grimacing as he expected a blow. Nothing happened. It was as dark as sin. He listened for the breathing of the kidnappers, momentarily believing all four were crowding in the small space.

Soon Arnold called to him from above. "Have you also fallen asleep down there, Jonathan?"

"The shipwright isn't here," Jonathan said. "I'm looking for a lantern." The pressure was so high that he barely heard himself speak. *Mind on task.*

"Don't bother, Jonathan," Arnold said. "I can examine the craft better in the morning."

Jonathan emerged. "Mr. Southwell should be along shortly." Desperately, Jonathan scanned the shore in both directions looking for his conspirators in the kidnapping.

"When I have time, I'll communicate with this Mr. Southwell at an earlier hour. I need to bring along a crew and see how the boat handles myself. I already found the name for her. *Peggy,* of course. Small, beautiful, quite the clever thing for dangerous waters."

"I'd not name a thing that might be blown to bits after a person I loved," Jonathan opined, still searching the now dark wharves and empty streets for signs of life. He wasn't about to kidnap Arnold by himself. Jonathan felt betrayed at the deepest level. Did Champe realize what toll it took on his soul to lead a dear friend into a trap? He'd rather die than relive the last half-hour.

Then he spotted them. Three large men stumbling out of a shabby tavern two hundred yards down the road. They hallooed and weaved toward Jonathan and Arnold. They neared, the reek of rum on their breath preceding them by twenty feet. It would be a miracle if they were able to row themselves across the East River. Again, vainly Jonathan looked for Champe. *Mind on task?* The young fool was nowhere in sight, and, at least, two sober men were needed to kidnap Arnold.

"Are you the traitor Arnold?" The tallest of the trio asked.

"What's it to you?" Arnold drew out his pistols.

"Twenty guineas," The speaker leaned forward and blearily tried to focus.

"He is Arnold," Jonathan said angrily. "And you are drunken sods." He laid vigorously into the biggest with his weighted cane. The man staggered back cursing. They had just enough presence of mind to flee.

"I thought I was worth more than twenty guineas," Arnold said as he watched them disappear around the corner. "I heard Washington was offering a thousand for my head. I would have liked to converse with those gentlemen further."

"You don't converse with the vagabonds in this city," Jonathan asserted, trying to control his panicked breathing.

"They were too well dressed to be vagabonds, and no vagabond could afford the quantity of liquor they had just quaffed. Also, I had a sense they were expecting me. Did you tell the owner of the boat my name?" Arnold asked.

"No, I didn't directly speak to him."

"Well, somebody knew I would be here. Either an informant on your side or my side let the cat out of the bag." Jonathan was glad for the darkness that made his features difficult to read.

"You cannot be too cautious," Jonathan said. "Especially since you've been feted and celebrated in this city for the past month so any vagrant, footpad, or bruiser might recognize you."

Arnold took a long time to digest this, then said, "That in mind, a plan has been stewing in my head ever since Washington paid me the compliment of a bounty, and this happens to be the evening I put it into play. I will visit my former friends over in New Jersey. Since I'm such valuable merchandise, I make tempting bait. I will land with a small party of ten horse and ride a few miles inland. I'll inform whoever I come across that I'm on a vendetta after Mr. Partridge, a member of the Continental Congress, who deviled me, along with Mr. Reed. The rebels will believe I am such a fool for they are fools. The countryside will be roused, and soon a passel of the scoundrels will come after the hated traitor Benedict Arnold. I'll lead my pursuers on a merry chase into a neat trap sprung by the rest of my company. That will teach them a chastening lesson." Arnold chuckled, imagining the scene. "Why don't you accompany us, Jonathan, on this romp? My blood is up, my troops need exercise, and 'twill indeed be quite diverting."

"Is it wise to place yourself in such danger?"

"Bosh. Soldiers are only dangerous when they're well led, and the officers of the New Jersey militia are to a man incompetent ruffians. I chosen the place well, and we'll vanish like a puff of smoke if they muster more than we can handle."

Jonathan, mindful of Arnold's suspicion, accepted. "'Twould be a change from fighting off footpads, bruisers, and drunk soldiers."

"Good! We will be departing three hours hence when the tide is rising through Sandy Hook. I canceled the leave of my best company. The captain of a sloop *Andromeda* is standing by. We will be towing a flat bottom landing barge that General Clinton has been so kind to lend me."

Two hours later Jonathan made his way to the wharf where *Andromeda* was docked. The shifting shadows of a hundred plus men crowded the deck. Nothing was said. Jonathan was shown a place on the bow next to the hooded Arnold who knew the Jersey coastline as well as any pilot.

Fourteen hours of cold mist and spray later, Arnold whispered as they approached the Jersey coastline in the gray morning, "I am certain you recognize our old haunts."

"Yes, my farm lies twenty miles south," Jonathan confirmed.

"And the road that leads off that point there, what do you think of it?"

"Too many places where ambushers can lie in wait."

"My men, not rebels, will be lying in wait. However, the terrain don't quite suit my purpose. You might be familiar with a trail a mile inland running down a narrow wash that feeds into the Metedeconk River. That's where we'll divert ourselves with the merry chase. My company will take positions on both sides of the wash, and where the trail meets the river, we'll plug up with cannon loaded with grapeshot. When our pursuers commit themselves, we'll cork up the other end and make them prance and caper like they're stricken with Saint Anthony's fire. If we outnumber them, we finish the rabble off with a bayonet charge. If the odds turn against us, we slip away like a fox who has just raided a chicken coop and taken the fattest hen, leaving all her sisters cackling."

"You seem certain they'll pursue you."

"As certain as one can be of anything in war. With

Washington flattering me with a bounty of a thousand pounds on my person, those who don't pursue out of hate will pursue out of greed. Merely showing my face will inspire every rebel to leave his wife abed, his roast on the spit, or his plow still hitched to his horse in the field. By the way, how's your marksmanship?"

"Middling," Jonathan said.

"Well, then, just fix the bayonet on the musket. You can hurry the wounded who aren't surrendered on to the next world."

"Shoot I will. If I am to murder wounded men, then you might as well string me up for refusing an order now."

Arnold laughed. "There's no murder in war, and the more merciless we are, the sooner the war is over, and the more mercy we achieve in the end."

"I cannot imagine you bayoneting a helpless wounded man," Jonathan said.

"You are right," Arnold agreed. "I'm as sad a hypocrite as are you who will shoot a healthy man, yet fail to put out of misery a man that is sure to die."

A pilot rowed out to meet them and guide the barge and the boats to the intended landing spot. It was too dark to see him although Jonathan recognized his voice— a respected Son of Liberty. After disembarking, the bait, that is Arnold, Jonathan, and eight others rode inland. The terrain was heartbreakingly familiar to Jonathan. He seemed to be choking on his breath, as they rode into the yard of the Goodwin family. Did Arnold know? Or was this a coincidence?

CHAPTER 30

"THIS APPEARS A convenient place to take our ease and let the news of my arrival spread. I imagine friends of yours reside in this county?" Arnold inquired. He had announced his presence at two other farms and soon the countryside would be simmering with the news.

"I once courted the daughter of the man who owned this land," Jonathan replied, dully staring at the oak half seared by lightning.

"I heard rumors that if I desired to see a pretty girl, a farm hereabouts had the prettiest. I can't imagine she found you lacking?"

"She died... of a fever."

"I apologize for evoking a painful memory," Arnold said with genuine sympathy. "Where incline the sympathies of her family?"

"With the King and Parliament," Jonathan flatly lied. The Goodwins had no sympathy for either side.

"That is good, although I imagine the few who still maintain favorable opinions toward their mother country keep their mouths shut with so many rebels in the vicinity. Your neighborhood prospered greatly in the business of privateering. We have two hours before my company is in position. Do you think this family might serve us breakfast for a few shillings while the countryside rises in arms to snare me?"

"I'm sure they are heartily sick of soldiers, but they might grant you hospitality," Jonathan answered, having no idea how to deal with this predicament.

"I don't fault them. Most people prefer to keep their heads down and get on with their lives—just what I desire to do with all my heart, especially now with a sympathetic wife and a new son. Alas, I fear my beloved country needs a savior to extract it from this mess." Arnold's voice took on a dreamy quality. No doubt Arnold viewed himself as that savior.

Arnold posted a guard on top of the hill with a view to the west and north and another covering the road leading in from the south. Meanwhile, Jonathan knocked on the front door. The shock on the face of Mr. Goodwin gave Jonathan time to momentarily brush his lip with his forefinger. Mr. Goodwin hesitated, speechless.

"Pray, Mr. Goodwin," Jonathan said hurriedly. "I know you are a true and loyal friend of the King. Some British officers would like to breakfast at your table. They will pay. Please be so kind to tell others inside not to be alarmed."

Mr. Goodwin's hostile stare met Jonathan's hard stare. Uncertainty flickered in his eyes. He had caught the signal although he seemed at a loss to know what it meant. Jonathan went on: "I am aware my presence grieves you as I am grieved beyond words to be standing here in front of you. We shouldn't let that get in the way of our sympathies and the furtherance of the cause your family is so devoted to—defeating those who brought this unnecessary war into our hearths and homes."A light glimmered in the gaunt hating face.

"Truly, for the sake of Amelia's memory," Jonathan pleaded, "welcome us."

"I will inform the others," Mr. Goodwin muttered.

Arnold walked up. smiling. "I am General Arnold. We are indebted to you, sir."

Jonathan turned to Arnold. "I would like to visit Amelia's grave." Arnold nodded and directed his attention at Goodwin, "Tell me about your allegiance to the king."

Mr. Goodwin replied haltingly: "I'm not a man of strong political opinions, still I'm wise enough to know that when you have it good, you don't improve your situation by turning everything upside down. I signed the oath of allegiance. I rendered no aid nor comfort to the king's enemies although they took my cattle and hogs and paid me with currency that loses half its value every time I look at it. If a loyal subject is one who does his duty and minds his business, then I am him."

"Yes, visit the grave, Jonathan," Arnold said. "I like this man of good sense so I will spend more time conversing with him. I wonder if he knows of his neighbor, Mr. Partridge, who is the damnedest of the damn rebels." Jonathan walked up to the knoll where he had buried a girl so emaciated that she had lain as light as a feather in his arms, and with her, his heart. He stared, tried to pray, tried to think of a way to warn the gathering militia of the ambush. His mind drew blanks. Mrs. Goodwin walked up with an armful of flowers, knelt, and handed them to Jonathan.

"Arnold is bait. Lead militia into trap. Company waiting along wash to ambush. Cannot pursue. Must warn," he whispered. "You must do so."

Mrs. Goodwin's small sparrow face crinkled into a smile. "Men have no cunning," she replied.

Jonathan returned to the house and joined the table where Arnold and the other officers were sitting. The breakfast was huge with plentiful ale as if to purposely weigh them down. Midway through the meal, a blood-curdling scream came from the upper floor.

"Well, finally, the lying-in is ending. Theresa been nothing but miserable the last fortnight," Mrs. Goodwin said as she went upstairs. Two screams later, she came down and confirmed, "Yep, it's Theresa's time. I'm to fetch the midwife. Appears to be a breach. Lety will remain with her and give what help she can."

"I forbid you to leave this residence!" Arnold insisted.

"My residence, sir. My daughter's life is in danger. You may bayonet me on the way out, but I'm going through that door," Mrs. Goodwin argued.

"Madam, I'm quite aware of the tricks women play to distract men." Infamously, Arnold's wife Peggy had given her husband time to escape when his treason was discovered by pretending to be mad and tearing off her clothes.

"Short of tying me up or knocking me on the head General Arnold, you will not stop me." A scream rose to a bloodcurdling pitch holding all in hearing hostage.

"I'll send a soldier, no two soldiers with you," Arnold said in a pause between screams, not quite hiding his satisfaction that her ruse would play into his and alert the neighborhood to his presence.

"Don't you think their uniforms will draw unwelcome attention?" Mrs. Goodwin asked.

"Out of uniform, they are spies, and spies are looked upon with particular disfavor these days," Arnold said.

Another scream interrupted them.

"Send whatever ragtag soldier you want with me. I leave now."

Arnold directed a young ensign to accompany Mrs. Goodwin who because of his size, his bright red hair, and large ears perpendicular to his head was sure to attract attention. Off they went at breakneck speed, several more screams pursuing them. Jonathan hoped that Amelia's mother understood. Rousing the local militia was exactly what Arnold wanted.

"I would like to visit your daughter," Arnold told Mr. Goodwin.

"That's highly improper sir," Goodwin protested.

"I learned to never trust but my own eyes, sir, and I'll not intrude more than the necessary propriety allows," Arnold said.

Arnold hobbled upstairs and opened the door to the bedroom. A scream was followed by a chamber pot aimed straight at his head—luckily empty. He closed the door, rubbing his head but not suppressing a satisfied smile. "Give my apologies to your daughter. A soldier cannot be too careful. I suppose this is the first time I've been wounded in the service of the King and Parliament." From his contented expression, Arnold believed the hook well baited.

An hour passed. The screams had died down into whimpers. Amelia's sister occasionally appeared at the top of the stairs to request water or more linen. Mrs. Goodwin finally returned with a small hunchback who introduced himself as Doctor Glub. Her disheveled guard returned fifteen minutes later, offering an unpersuasive explanation that he was forced to stop because of the flux. Jonathan and Arnold played an inconclusive game of chess. Arnold was a superior strategist, yet Jonathan won half the games simply by waiting for the mistake in Arnold's predictably bold attack. Arnold had just made the losing move when the sound of firing came from the distance, then the unmistakable boom of a cannon. This wasn't supposed to happen yet.

A lieutenant burst through with barely enough breath to inform Arnold, "General, they are attacking the boats, and the company is being pushed back. You are in extreme danger of being cut off."

"Bloody damn. Why aren't they come for me?" Arnold momentarily glared at Jonathan.

A minute later, Arnold, Jonathan, and the others of the party were riding at full gallop down the wash toward the river. Because of his stiff leg as the result of a wound at Saratoga, Arnold was no longer the superb horseman he once had been and lagged a hundred yards behind. Jonathan kept him company. When two musket balls whizzed past his ear, Jonathan realized the pursuit was on. Ahead of them, several militiamen scrambled down into the wash and positioned themselves behind rocks. Arnold spurred his horse on, blood flying back from a wound in the horse's neck splattering him. They charged past the rocks as the militiamen fumbled their reloading. A second hail of bullets whizzed over their heads. Arnold's horse stumbled then collapsed perhaps two hundred yards beyond the militiamen.

Jonathan pulled up and stopped. Here was Arnold, the most wanted man in the colonies, struggling to extricate himself from underneath the horse. Jonathan could make the difference between defeat and victory. Over the last months, he had thrown himself into the American cause, yet he owed a greater debt to Arnold than any person living except Julian Asher and Madame Corinne. Anger and frustration were registering on his friend's face, and unusually as he stared up at Jonathan, there was fear. Jonathan expected Arnold to order or implore him to help. His foolhardy friend just continued to stare as if he were daring Jonathan to betray him. Arnold was depending solely on the ties of friendship to save him. He would not command, he would not beg. That is unnecessary with a friend.

A few soldiers from Arnold's company provided covering fire from the ridge, and the Patriot militia's advance stalled. Cursing himself and perversely aware that less than eighteen hours before this was exactly the fate he had designed for his friend, Jonathan dismounted, disentangled Arnold's foot from a stirrup, lifted the stout general onto his horse, remounted himself, and rode away.

The situation on the river was dire. A dozen different boats—whaleboats, bateaux, gondolas, armed with swivel guns and muskets—were attacking the cutter's bow and stern where only the smaller swivel guns could come into play.

Arnold jumped off the horse, fell flat, picked himself up, and directed the gunners to load the three cannons they had landed. One after another, the cannons were charged and Arnold sighted the target. His aim was deadly, sinking a bateau and a gondola within five minutes and putting the rest to flight. The troops were ferried in the barge to the sloop while Arnold and his cannons kept guard—two loaded with grapeshot pointing down the wash, the other commanding the river. He scored another hit on a whaleboat trying to come at the *Andromeda* from an angle where the body of the sloop should have protected it from cannon shot. After the barge was unloaded, Arnold directed the men to dismantle two of the cannons and put them into the largest pinnace, leaving barely enough room for the rowers. The third gun was muscled into a second jolly-boat, the wheels of the carriage wedged between blocks, and tied with a dozen lines. The four oarsmen awkwardly propelled the craft that rode so low that water lapped at the gunwales.

Three whaleboats quickly challenged them. Arnold sighted a target in the choppy water. The recoil of the cannon almost capsized the boat, loosened two planks in the bottom, and broke an oarsman's knee. By then the sloop had pulled up its anchors and was slowly turning to present its broadside to the whaleboats which retreated. Arnold and the crew of the jolly-boat came aboard, the man with the broken knee on the back of Jonathan, while the boat itself with its cannon was left to sink. They were harassed by small arms fire as they sailed off. Arnold kept his distance from Jonathan, only approaching and asking the question once: "Was it that difficult to make the decision to save me?"

"Yes, 'twas a difficult decision to risk my skin to help you keep possession of yours," Jonathan acknowledged.

"Nay, I know you too well to believe of you the poltroon," Arnold said.

"I did save you. I know not what else matters."

Arnold grunted and nodded. They talked no further on the trip back to Manhattan.

Champe was waiting in his warehouse, his eyes lighted, his smile broad. "I thought I'd never forgive myself for waiting at the wrong boat. But I heard you went off with the traitor. Did you get him?"

"If you mean did I murder Arnold? No, Mr. Champe. I rescued him from capture. You can tell that to Hamilton or to whoever you desire so now I can be a traitor to both causes."

Champe showed no sign of believing Jonathan.

Two days later, Jonathan coded information about the rumored expedition of Arnold's loyalist regiment into Virginia that he had picked up from a conversation between his friend and another officer.

CHAPTER 31

After returning on a chilly December morning from a late-night round delivering wine, Jonathan discovered Millicent Dalton huddled in a chair in the corner of his office, sleeping fitfully. Reginald had stayed the night to explain why he had let her in. Lucretia, eyes narrowed by her suspicion, had also stayed. "The woman seemed in a desperate way," Smith said apologetically. "If I hadn't let her in, she'd have froze to death."

"Thank you, Dr. Smith. I'll take care of her now."

The doctor and his very pregnant grumbling wife left.

"Wake up, Mrs. Dalton." Jonathan gently touched her shoulder.

Millicent jerked upright clutching her dress. Once Jonathan lit a second lantern, he saw her bruised face, a bloodied lip, and a black eye.

She started to talk rapidly, keeping her head down in embarrassment. "The landlord, Peter Harmony, took advantage of me. He and his brother. They said that was the only thing I was good for, then they... they... pushed me out. I cannot go anywhere else like this. Terence's parents will say things, and my brother, yes, my brother, he'll come to harm trying to protect the poor remains of my honor. I'm so ashamed. I thought you might help me collect my clothing and things and keep this secret. They refused to let me take anything, and it was so cold, not even my cloak. They said they were holding it for back rent because I sold not enough apples. I am so stupid. I knew what they were after all the time."

Jonathan found her a cloak of fox fur out of the stores a loyalist privateer had sold to him. "You can go into Emma and Daniel's room. I'll bring you a basin with water and light the stoves. I'll fetch your things, and then we can go to the millinery. Emma is always glad to see you."

"Just keep this secret, I beg you. I don't think Terence would touch me ever again if he knew." She rubbed her arms trying to control her shivering.

He took her hands into his. She flinched, and he almost let go, but then her shivering stopped. "I return in a few hours with your belongings. Don't worry. Clean yourself and rest. I'll not tell a soul, and if I ask Dr. Smith to give his word, he won't either."

Jonathan had no idea of how he could go about collecting Millicent's possessions until he had walked several blocks in the icy morning air. In the city where martial law had eliminated magistrates, such men as the Harmony brothers relied on protectors—officers who would shield them in the event of a complaint. The uniform of a mere lieutenant would not intimidate them, for they could produce a major or even a colonel in support of their cause. However, it dawned on Jonathan that they couldn't produce a brigadier general, which he could. He would call in a favor. Jonathan's feet led him to the house of Benedict Arnold, hoping his regiment had not departed yet.

Arnold didn't need persuading. That he was a chivalrous man was one of his deepest held conceits. "If they refuse, I'll make them run a gauntlet all the way to the East River."

A half-hour later, Jonathan knocked on the door of a narrow three-story brick house. A gruff muffled voice asked, "What do you want?"

"Mrs. Dalton's belongings," Jonathan shouted.

"Go to hell," was the answer followed by deep-throated laughter.

Jonathan nodded to Arnold who summoned two of the twelve largest men of his regiment that he had chosen for this purpose. Lifting the butts of their muskets they smashed through the door. Screams came from the upper rooms. On seeing Arnold's dark angry visage leading a half dozen bayoneted muskets, the Harmony brothers fled upstairs. Jonathan followed. At the end of the hallway on the second story, an open window indicated where the brothers had jumped to make their escape. From the yelps, squeals, and curses, the soldiers that Arnold had posted at the rear of the house were entertaining themselves, pricking the brothers with their bayonets.

In his fury, Arnold pounded open the doors of the bedrooms, discovering in each, eleven or twelve frightened girls seated in their undergarments or covering themselves with blankets. The thin hopeless faces gazed numbly at Jonathan and Arnold. A minute later, the Harmony brothers appeared whining and crying as they were prodded upstairs by soldiers who seemed to be enjoying their task. The plump triple-chinned brothers were listing the names of their powerful friends and protectors and promising to all involved a court-martial and a hanging.

"As I requested, I want Mrs. Dalton's possessions," Jonathan said, noting with satisfaction the splotches of blood on the Harmony brothers' breeches and shirts.

"Major..." the elder Harmony goggled at the brigadier general's laces on Arnold's sleeve.

"I wouldn't mention his name or any other in connection with you for I'm certain they will deny it," Arnold warned.

"I suppose the little cunt told you we mistreated her. Well, let me tell you, she was asking..." the curling lips promised more venom.

Unsheathing his dress sword, Jonathan struck the brother in the chin with the hilt, knocking him to the ground. He was about to drive the blade through the cowering man's fat belly when Arnold's hand stayed him. The gulping red-faced reprobate struggled to his feet and stood cringing by his brother who had peed his pants.

"If you want to avoid considerable discomfort over the next hour," Arnold said, "I advise you to refrain from casting aspersions on that lady. As the gentleman stated, we require the lady's possessions and seventeen guineas to compensate her for injuries, although if she is of a mind to bring you to court for rape so you get the hanging you well deserve, I'll make certain that the witnesses you plan to call on your side will find it not convenient for their careers to testify. Pray that she doesn't pursue you in court."

After handing over the guineas and Millicent's small trunk, Jonathan said, "The other women, I hope you treat with respect."

"Some can only pay rent by…" A look of terror came into the younger Harmony brother's eyes.

"I will introduce myself to them," Arnold stated, "and tell them that if you mistreat nary a one, throw her out, then she is to come to me, and since you suffer from a surfeit of blood and flesh, I'll arrange for you a thinning diet at the Sugar House, or on a prison ship."

As they were walking away, a soldier toting Millicent's trunk, Arnold said, "I owed you no favor that needed to be repaid. 'Twas your duty to rescue me, as 'tis my duty to protect the likes of your Mrs. Dalton. I still question why you hesitated those moments before lending me your horse."

"I'm not so good a friend as you deserve. I was afraid for my life and judged whether our friendship was worth the risk. I was even tempted by Washington's bounty when I saw you trapped underneath your horse. I had much to think about, Benedict, in those seconds so forgive the delay."

"I may choose to believe you. Ah, but let's not dwell on bounties and loyalties. This was a glorious start to the day. 'Twill give me something entertaining to recount to Peggy at breakfast. By the way, you said this Mrs. Dalton worked as a lady's maid."

"Yes, she served in several respectable houses."

"Send her to us when she recuperates. Peggy wants such a maid."

On returning to the warehouse with the small trunk, Jonathan found that Millicent had fallen asleep on Daniel's bed underneath a cloak and several blankets. She had washed her face. Jonathan quietly laid her trunk by the bed, deciding to let her sleep a few hours before taking her to Elizabeth and then to the Arnolds. Jonathan allowed himself a moment to study her. Her lips formed a childish pout he never saw on her when she was awake. Her lashes were long and reddish. Her blond hair spread out like a fan across the pillow. She was indeed lovely. Jonathan wondered whether he could make a difference if he visited her husband's parents and explained to them what an excellent daughter-in-law they had. If they were involved in trade at all, he might find ways of pressuring or rewarding them to give Millicent a chance.

When he turned around, he discovered Gabriel standing behind him. Not one to waste words, Gabriel asked, "Dat de lady who take de molls back to der place?"

"Yes. She is the one."

"She fine lady, suh."

Three days later, Jonathan introduced Millicent to the Arnolds. Her eye was still bruised. Her smile was uncharacteristically unsteady. She blushed on being introduced. Earlier, Millicent had almost refused because the Arnolds were aware that she had been violated. "I feel so ashamed."

"There's no reason—you did nothing wrong, nothing," Jonathan responded vehemently, questioning why

Millicent should feel disgraced while the Harmony brothers displayed not an iota of shame.

"I don't suppose I did, although I cleaned myself more times than Pontius Pilate washed his hands." Millicent unexpectedly laughed. "I was confident you would collect my belongings, Mr. Asher, but I had no idea you'd enlist a brigadier general and a regiment to accomplish it."

On being introduced, Peggy Arnold took Millicent by the hand. "You have nothing to worry about now, dear. You are under the protection of me and my Benedict. Nobody can hurt you."

Millicent wiped her eyes. "I know ma'am. I can see you are the kindest sort of people."

CHAPTER 32

AFTER ARNOLD LEFT to plunder and burn rebel farms and towns in Virginia, Jonathan felt the pressure ease. His private war of vengeance was over. Even if he decided otherwise, von Wurttemberg was beyond reach in northern Long Island. The major spent half his time conducting raids into Connecticut and New York where he was as likely to be killed as the next man. According to rumor, Castor had suffered another stroke which left him completely immobile. As for the big war, there was a sense on both sides that it could not last another year. Washington and Clinton eyed each other warily across the North River. The French army had settled down in Rhode Island. Cornwallis was wreaking havoc in the Carolinas. Although Jonathan had resumed conveying enemy troop movements, the arrival of ships, and quartermaster's manifests via the Royal Gazette and Rivington Loyalist Gazette, he became reconciled to a future under British domination. Despite avoiding the outward trappings of wealth, he was gaining a reputation as a rich man. Gabriel warned him that the wrong people were beginning to take notice. "Ever take off dat uniform, de wolves tear you, limb from limb."

"I can't be a British lieutenant forever. When the war is over, they will have no need of me,"

"Make dem need you," Gabriel said. "Make dem."

This state of serene disappointment, which seemed permanent, lasted less than a month. The first fly in the bittersweet ointment was Lucretia who was not sufficiently distracted by motherhood.

Lucretia would ask Jonathan questions unceasingly about every conceivable aspect of his life, always seeming to offer something intangible in return until Doctor Smith would angrily call her away. What was disconcerting was that her memory rivaled Gabriel's. This talent served the doctor well because she kept track of his patient's complaints and the prescribed remedies. She couldn't count worth a bean, but if Jonathan mentioned he had twenty-four sacks of coffee beans, she wouldn't forget that until her dying day.

Lucretia, of course, had seen the maps on his desk and had noticed Jonathan glancing at the maps as he prepared the advertisements. Fortunately, by now, he did not require a ruler to find the coordinates.

"You seem quite enthralled with maps, Mr. Asher. What do you find so fascinating about them?" After asking this question, her usually vacant eyes were suddenly filled with her calculating intelligence. She was studying his reaction.

"I always been fascinated by maps, Mrs. Smith. One of my innocuous vices," he replied.

Lucretia smiled her sweetly insincere smile. "I see. You men are always thinking about property lines and battles and who has what and who does what."

A few days later before he went out to consult Lady Beatrice about what to order from Rodrigo Jonathan left the maps on the table sprinkled with ash. Lucretia and Reginald were busy with their patients below. When Jonathan returned, the maps were in exactly the same position. The ash, however, was gone. Jonathan began to doubt whether Castor was as incapacitated as reported. Equally disturbing: he was encountering Curston frequently. But Castor was not the first to penetrate his cover.

CHAPTER 33

JONATHAN, EMMA, AND Daniel arrived late at the shop after spending the day sailing around New York Harbor, Emma in Jonathan's arms fast asleep, Daniel staggering from fatigue like a drunken man. Elizabeth was waiting for them at the door. While the children ate a late-night snack, she talked in a desultory manner about the virtues of Edgar—the outstanding ones seeming to be his cheerfulness, his title, and his lack of prejudice. Jonathan was too tired to care. He did not have a title, was less than cheerful, and with the few exceptions of close acquaintances was overflowing with prejudice against the entire British aristocracy and most of humanity.

After the children were bedded, Elizabeth turned to him. "I don't know what to do with you, Mr. Asher."

"I thought I no longer posed a problem," Jonathan replied dryly. He didn't want a repeat of their last argument.

"You are a problem, John." She hadn't called him John since Lord Edgar appeared on the scene. "The most distressing problem of my life."

"You talked for the last quarter-hour about the virtues

and accomplishments of Lord Edgar. Again, how could I cause you any distress?" Jonathan made no effort to hide his exasperation.

She smiled. "He is a dear. He is also very jealous of you."

"As I am of him. He is the winner of your heart, so that is that. There's nothing more to be said. Excuse me, Miss Littleton, I must be gone." Jonathan headed for the door.

"How did Amelia die?" Elizabeth suddenly asked.

Jonathan stopped and turned around. "Of a fever," he said slowly. "Why do you want to know?"

Unaccountably, intense anger registered on Elizabeth's face. "Bits and crumbs of gossip fall into my shop. There was an Amelia in New Jersey who suffered at the hands of soldiers. She was left for dead but survived despite her brutal injuries. She was lingering for a month nursed by her betrothed. I am believing you were that man."

"Yes, I was that man," Jonathan admitted.

"Was she a victim of Washington's rabble?" Elizabeth's face was sharp and predatory like that of a fox after prey.

Jonathan was silent.

"Or were they Hessians? If they were Hessians, why are you fighting on their side? Why are you wearing a British uniform?" Her voice was ragged with tears. "And then there is Gwen."

"I have not exchanged over two dozen polite words with Percival's fiancée. She can have no bearing on what you're suspecting."

"Gwen put me on to you although she had no clue what she was doing. She visited me three days ago. That horrible hunchback who had been loitering on our street broke into her home and told her terrible things about Percy. She had tried to forget them, but she couldn't get them out of her head so asked me if Percy were capable of such monstrosities. God help me, I hesitated too long afore I denied them. She did not believe me. That hunchback criminal also told her that he'd been brought to you, and you let him go if he promised to leave the city. No loyal king's subject would allow a man who wants to kill an officer in the loyalist militia to go free. Whose side are you on?"

"I decided the boy was harmless after conversing with him," Jonathan replied, ignoring her question, and gazing longingly at the door through which he could escape.

"Whose side are you on?" She repeated.

"I have no side," Jonathan insisted, although he knew it was futile.

"Oh, you do, you do. Edgar told me that a man tried to kill Major Christoph and before he fired, he yelled out the name Amelia. Amelia? Edgar has been looking for this Amelia. I almost told him where to find her. Then I thought about everything else you were doing. How you are so close to the army of the king, yet you do not seem to celebrate our victories nor are downcast at our defeats. How you say so little about yourself. How you have privileged knowledge that is quite useful to the rebels. You are after more than the murderers of Amelia. You are taking your revenge on the whole British Army. You are a spy, dear Mr. Asher, a damn rebel spy, to be sure." The word "damn" came out of her mouth coated with venom. "And what am I to do with you? Turn you in? You are the world to Emma and Daniel. They talk about you all the time. They ask me every other day when I am to marry you. They are even proud of your uniform."

"You are mistaken," Jonathan protested weakly.

"I am making no mistake, Mr. Asher. I am not. Like many a woman who loses her heart to a man, that man becomes the object of close study. I am recovering my heart mostly. Thank God or I would have scratched out my eyes in despair. Still, do I become a traitor too by not turning you in? So, Mr. Asher, what do you propose?"

"I do love you," he said as if that declaration was a solution.

"You were unsuccessful in killing Major von Wurttemberg, but I believe you were successful in killing other men involved in Amelia's death. Is that not true?"

Jonathan was silent.

"And if I asked you to forgive Major von Wurttemberg, give up spying, you'd agree out of love for me." She searched his face anxiously.

At that moment, Jonathan felt his insides go cold. "Von Wurttemberg broke Amelia's jaw after raping her with the two other officers. I saw her starve to death. I cannot forgive him even though my campaign for vengeance is done. I do not plan to take his life."

"You might have been able to love me enough, Mr. Asher, if you hadn't been so set on vengeance," Elizabeth said with vehemence. "In any event, I no longer love you. The fever has passed, to be sure. Edgar, simple good-natured Edgar is what I need—no dark corners there."

"Then I can only rely on your forbearance," Jonathan said.

"Not even I know how long that forbearance will be lasting, nor how little of it is left."

"Whatever you decide, I want Emma and Daniel taken care of. Tomorrow, I will leave you five hundred pounds for those ends."

"You don't have to ask for that, Mr. Asher, and I don't need your money. How I hate you." She blew out a long breath between her teeth.

Jonathan could tell by his increasingly cool receptions and falling orders for his merchandise that Elizabeth was not alone in her suspicion of him. He began to lay plans for leaving the city. Therefore Peggy Arnold's order of several dozen bottles of the best claret to celebrate with a fete her husband's return from his successful campaign in Virginia surprised him. When Jonathan delivered the order, he paid Arnold a brief visit for friendship's sake and to congratulate him on his successes. Arnold offered him a chair, and as they sat conversing, the sound of two girls giggling came from another part of the house. Jonathan judged the girls to be twelvish.

Arnold, noticing his distraction, explained, "'Tis the maid, you brought us. When Peggy and Millie are not ogling over Neddy and seeing to his needs as if he were the emperor of the China, they are giggling together—over God knows what. I believe Peggy can more easily do without her Benedict than without her Millie."

"I'm happy Mrs. Dalton worked out so well for you."

"Truth is so am I. This business has been so hard on Peggy who is such a good person and who harbors no ill will towards a soul, yet half of her acquaintants detest her, besmirch her reputation. I seen her crying over a letter too many times. But since Millie has come into our service, she has reverted into a happy girl again. When I talk to her about this, Peggy says she was always considered a serious young lady and sometimes a girl who gives herself too many airs. In truth, she was too timid to be anything else. Millie makes her laugh, and she makes Millie laugh. And I must confess my dearest's joyful gaiety delights me."

"Mrs. Dalton has had a rough time of it, especially with her estrangement from her husband. I wonder if your influence might be of help," Jonathan said.

"Yes. We love our Millie so much we will even sacrifice our happiness in her company for her happiness. It seems her husband is open to a reconciliation, especially now that I am looking into the question of the loans and the mills. Peggy even has plans to polish Millie's manners so she can shine as fine a lady as any gentleman could hope for." Arnold then gave Jonathan a direct hard stare. "I heard rumors about your loyalty. The whisperers say you're a spy. But a spy would have let me be captured, so I tell them, and they have nothing to say in return, or they assure me that their opinion changed. Then the next day, they accuse you of being a spy again."

"As you are no doubt aware, no man can achieve success without engendering considerable envy. Castor Blanchard is behind these rumors and wants to destroy me."

"That may be. But it occurred to me that the reason you saved my life was that the bond of friendship was stronger than your loyalty to the rebel cause. You are sentimental that way, Jonathan. You would choose friendship over principle."

The following Sunday, while Jonathan was delivering Emma and Daniel back to the millinery after their outing, Edgar entered the shop with Major von Wurttemberg. Seeing Elizabeth behind the counter, Edgar announced in his boyish contralto, "Do not be alarmed, dear. All is forgiven. Herr Christoph has been so kind not to hold me to account for my drunken behavior. He is a great soul."

Elizabeth turned white, then ashen, and sat down.

Von Wurttemberg glanced at Jonathan and gave a slight nod indicating that he deduced Elizabeth was aware of his role in Amelia's death. Not at all put off, he smiled insinuatingly at Elizabeth, recalling to Jonathan's mind the phrase, "the daughters and sisters of my enemy." As Edgar glowed in the aura of the renewed friendship with the famous duelist, von Wurttemberg remarked in a tone that would appear sarcastic to any other than Lord Edgar. "Yes, we are the greatest of friends now. Come with me on the next campaign. I show you the joys of defeating the enemy. Ach, I believe your beautiful girl is ill. Do not worry, Miss Littleton. I look after him like the mother hen. I to never let him not out of the sight. We to leave now, Lord Edgar, eh."

Edgar kissed Elizabeth's hand and said, "I return tomorrow. dearest."

"No more make the love, Lord Edgar," von Wurttemberg said in a proprietary voice. "A soldier must forget the wife and the betrothed. To kill the rebel you to have all your wits."

Jonathan could see that von Wurttemberg was toying with Edgar. The major had no affection for the boy.

"Von Wurttemberg is jesting about that," Edgar explained.

Elizabeth shook her head.

After the pair left, Elizabeth said in a snarling whisper to Jonathan, "Don't say a word."

"Tell Edgar to be careful."

"If von Wurttemberg is valuing his life…" Elizabeth did not know how to finish the sentence.

Jonathan tried to tell himself that their life was their life and no affair of his. He was certain that Elizabeth would extract a pledge from Edgar to behave in a campaign as a gentleman should toward the vulnerable and unarmed. Edgar likely would. As dominating as von Wurttemberg was, he believed Elizabeth exercised greater influence. Furthermore, Edgar had become aware that he was unable to hide his feelings on his face. Elizabeth would know if he broke his pledge merely by the expression on his face.

CHAPTER 34

JONATHAN ENTERED THE office just a few minutes or seconds after Lucretia had left. Her scent still lingered. A glance told him that his maps were missing. Earlier he had spotted Dr. Smith's parents on the Bowling Green with their grandson, meaning she was unencumbered. Even more worrying was the absence of the recent editions of the Rivington Gazette. He rushed outside to intercept her. He found Lucretia hurrying down the darkening streets two blocks away from the docks with a bundle under her arm. He managed to block her just as she arrived at the wharves.

"Give me my maps and the papers."

"And if I refuse, Mr. Asher?" She hugged the bundle to her chest.

"Then I will take them from you."

"What is the problem, sister?" Curston stepped out of the shadows holding a pistol.

"Mr. Asher wants to rob me."

"I simply want my papers back."

"You will return to the warehouse, Mr. Asher, but I

would not advise you to remain there long. I'm not the only one who has you in his sights."

Over the following days, Jonathan was puzzled why he wasn't picked up and questioned. It seemed everyone was in on the secret that he was an intelligencer. Acquaintances avoided him or engaged in strained conversation which they broke off as soon as possible. Nobody would buy his coffee. Lady Beatrice insisted that she had purchasers for the entire inventory of wine.

Suspecting he was watched, to test the surveillance, Jonathan tried taking the Paulus Hook ferry. While he was waiting, a man sidled up to him and commented that it wasn't a good idea to leave the city. Before Jonathan could ask why, the man joined two others stationed by the ferry gate. When he attempted to leave the city on the Post Road, he discovered a carriage and eight soldiers blocking his way. Still. he wasn't scooped up. It was as if they were waiting for a contact to approach him and net them both. To keep up the frayed appearances, Jonathan put on the uniform even though wearing it condemned him to be hanged. Only Emma and Daniel displayed delight on seeing him. He felt desperate about them. Elizabeth was icy in her interactions. When he explained the situation, she immediately responded, "I told no one. I know not whether that condemns me as a traitor."

"My concern is for Emma and Daniel."

"Do not doubt Mr. Asher that I will care for them as I always have—as if they were my own."

"Gabriel will deliver 600 guineas for their upkeep.

Obviously, on the way to the gallows, I won't be needing such a sum."

Elizabeth sighed. "If you had only chosen the side of the king. I understand you couldn't because of Amelia. Still, I believe things would be so different."

"Yes. You might not be looking at marrying a man with a title."

"As if I cared about that. I just cared about proving my father and sister and brother wrong. I never expected dear Edgar to own a part of my heart, but he does, to be sure." Then Jonathan saw the old tic of the quivering eyelid appear. "This is hard to ask, John. If they capture you, they will hang you. Make it so that when they take you, they must kill you. I can explain that better to Emma and Daniel than the spectacle of you being hanged. Oh God, why did you ever make the children love you."

The guards at Lord Harold's residence, who usually gave him a friendly salute and occasionally a wink, appeared unsure whether to let him enter although Lady Beatrice had summoned him. They seemed surprised and somewhat shocked that she wanted them to admit the pariah. When Jonathan was shown into her parlor, she displayed none of her imperturbable demeanor, that gracious cynicism that she carried about her person. She was furious, surprisingly not with him, and she was afraid. Nailing him with her stare, she said, "Edgar challenged Major Christoph."

"They appeared reconciled when I ran into them a week ago," Jonathan said, not quite hiding his sarcasm.

Lady Beatrice laughed hollowly. "Herr Christoph explained to Edgar as a jest *le droit de seigneur* and said it applied to Elizabeth on the account of him being his overlord since the duel, and Edgar took offense, and von Wurttemberg took offense at his offense. Edgar half believes the major was testing his mettle and that he will apologize for the ill-natured jest on the field of honor as a gentleman would naturally do with such an insult to a lady. Lord Harold agrees and thinks the duel would help Edgar regain the face he lost when von Wurttemberg stood in for him. I am not so sanguine about the Hessian beast. I think he means to murder Edgar."

"Von Wurttemberg despises the playacting of apologies and satisfied honor," Jonathan confirmed her suspicion.

Lady Beatrice showed her exasperation in a short outburst of breath. "When the monster's blood runs high, he cares not for the consequences. He'd be a major-general commanding a brigade or at least a colonel if he was not so bloody-minded. Lord Harold contrived to get his regiment into New Jersey leading raids. Still, that is much too close. I fear Major Christoph will take up the challenge when he returns."

"And what do you want me to do?" Jonathan asked.

"You're the only person in my acquaintance that von Wurttemberg ever seen fit to agree to a truce. Prevail on your friend to withdraw his acceptance of the challenge," Lady Beatrice demanded.

"I am nobody's friend now as you are well aware, least of all, von Wurttemberg's."

Lady Beatrice was silent for a moment while she rearmed her argument. "I kept you from being arrested this last fortnight in the fear this might occur and you might help resolve it. In two weeks, Edgar will be transferred to the Caribbean."

"You solved your problem, don't you see? Arrest your nephew, keep him in jail in the meantime until he leaves, and in that way the duel is avoided."

Lady Beatrice's shoulders slumped. "Well, my best hope is that a rebel has a superior aim to the poor men von Wurttemberg faced in his affairs of honor."

"It appears our partnership is coming to an end, Lady Beatrice. Not my doing. I thank you for your protection, and I regret any loss of regard you suffered as a result of your association with me. There is my portion of the inventory. After taking thirty percent off would you use the remainder to provide for Emma and Daniel? I believe there is to be a union between Elizabeth and Lord Edgar. That makes it convenient for you to look after their welfare."

She laughed. "So, you became their father."

"I already was when you forced me to recognize the fact. Whether I can continue to fulfill that role is doubtful."

"Answer me this, Mr. Asher: are you a spy?" Lady Beatrice asked.

"That seems the consensus so admitting it is irrelevant," Jonathan dodged the answer. "You must exercise great influence, Lady Beatrice, to prevent me from being arrested. Was it solely for Lord Edgar's sake that you did this?"

"We were friends," Lady Beatrice said. "Also, as I said, I thought you still might be useful."

"And so, I will, Lady Beatrice, in return for you keeping an eye out for Emma and Daniel in case Elizabeth is unable. I've gone too long allowing von Wurttemberg to destroy lives like Amelia, the woman I was to marry."

Lady Beatrice opened her mouth as if to say "Ah," but no sound came out.

"Emma and Daniel—will you give your word?" He needed her promise. She was as punctilious about honoring her word as the honor-bound men in his acquaintance.

"They will not lack," Lady Beatrice said.

Curston caught up with Jonathan as he left.

"Mr. Blanchard desires an interview with you," he said as he hooked Jonathan's arm.

"Do I have a choice?"

"You have a choice whether to resist or not," Curston replied.

"I can't imagine what he wants."

Curston laughed, a disturbing hacking sound. "To cast up accounts. The game is over, Mr. Asher, and he has it in his mind to gloat."

The hour was twilight. Pollux greeted him with a warm handshake and led him down to the second deck which reeked with the sickening overripe odor of Castor. Two young girls who resembled Davina and were as thin as his arms were thick hovered on either side of the commissary. A guard stood in the corner, head touching the low ceiling. Nearby was a table with Jonathan's maps, a stack of gazettes, and a pile of papers.

Castor smiled on seeing him. "I must thank you, Mr. Asher, for the hours of pleasure your code has given me." The commissary had grown so large that the features of his face seemed to be floating in a tub of fat. His clothes were newly cut from cheap fabric to keep up with the weight gain. The left side was still paralyzed, and the corner of the lip had a thin line of drool, yet he seemed no worse than the last time Jonathan visited him.

Jonathan measured the distance between him and Blanchard. Doubtful he could kill the guard and wring the commissary's neck, but worth a thought.

"The greatest regret of my present condition is I no longer attend the gaming table. That made my life tedious beyond measure. But then I discover that you are a spy and that you have an interesting way of conveying information where words are numbers and numbers words—perfect for advertisements. I have collected the issues of the Royal and Rivington Gazettes for the past four years and paid special attention to your advertisements. What joy it was when I figured out that when the price of coffee has six pence following the word shillings in the Rivington Gazette, that 6 has to do with Hessian dragoons. The number of letters in the first four words are the coordinates on your maps, of course. There is so much more to decipher, so many more hours of pleasure. Just today, after reviewing old inventories I realized that the four pence in the Royal Gazette referred to hard biscuit and the words were quantity. I think I shall become a puzzler of codes. It surprises me you are still wandering free. I told them to lock you up, and if I got stuck for a clue to apply a hot poker to your privates so you could give one."

"You failed to persuade the officer corps with your outlandish theory."

"Have I not? Ah, the code breakers are just jealous because I won't share my insights, although they do agree you are a traitor and a spy. Your time is coming to an end, Mr. Asher. I will soon have the pleasure of seeing you hanged. I'll request they set up the gibbet on the dock. If that isn't possible, then I'll have myself winched out of the hold and carted to your place of execution."

"If they had proof, I would already be in prison." Jonathan decided to resist giving Castor satisfaction.

"Bah, Mr. Asher. It seems not to fit into their plans to arrest you just quite yet. You are the wriggling bait on a hook that the authorities want to dangle for a bit and see what else they catch."

"Is this what Curston meant by saying you wanted to cast up accounts?" Jonathan asked.

A smile floated to the surface of the vat of fat. "Yes, and in your case, the utter ruin does not consist of loss of guineas, but the loss of life."

"You believe the game is over?"

After clearing the phlegm and having his chin wiped by one of the girls, Castor responded: "Ah, when a poor man plays against a much wealthier man in a game of pure chance, no matter how fortune smiles on him, he will lose because fortune does not smile forever. You lost, Mr. Asher, for you no longer have the assets to continue the game. 'Tis my pleasure to inform you that tomorrow your suffering begins. Good night, sir."

Jonathan inclined his head.

CHAPTER 35

WHEN HE ARRIVED at the warehouse, now nearly empty except for a dozen bags of coffee, he found Gabriel sitting at his desk as if he were trying it out for himself.

"Being bloody damn rebel spy bad for business," Gabriel said dryly.

"Sorry for making life difficult for you," Jonathan replied, not bothering to deny the accusation.

"Got to be getting you out of here, suh."

"There are three men across the street, and I wager two at the back entrance. I would love to depart this city. Unfortunately, they are partial to my company."

"I count seven. Put dis on." Gabriel threw Jonathan a cloak. "Hurry now. The boat be waitin'."

Jonathan put on the cloak.

Gabriel eyed him and placed a large slouch hat on his head and handed him a roll of pound notes. "Now you go outside 'n walks into Canvas Town towards Trinity. When you hearin' de voice of my daughter Melanie, follow it."

In the twilight, Jonathan walked toward the ruins of Trinity Church. Canvass Town was quiet as if its denizens had fled to a better world, yet a hundred campfires indicated otherwise. Seven men were following him. Jonathan was certain he could not shake them. Just beyond the ruins of Trinity, he heard Melanie whisper, "This way."

He stepped into a charred alcove. Suddenly he heard a dozen whistles.

"Don't make a peep," she whispered. "Give me your cloak and hat."

Jonathan discerned the silhouettes of six men with cloaks and large hats like his standing up, starting to walk in a weaving pattern. Then they fanned out in six different directions. His pursuers started shouting to each other in confusion, arguing over which one to follow. Other men emerged from their hovels to block their pursuit. Melanie tugged at his sleeve, gave him a shawl, and after a minute led him back to the docks.

Jonathan rowed the two hours through calm waters to the Jersey shore and climbed a narrow path up the face of the cliff. He stood still for a moment and inhaled deeply. He could sense New Jersey, wounded, and scarred by its three hundred battlefields, spreading out before him in the pitch-blackness. He had no intention of saving himself yet. Somewhere out there was his quarry: Major Christoph von Wurttemberg. He doubted he could keep his word to the major and challenge him openly. Those points of honor mattered little with the welfare of Emma and Daniel in the balance. Still, the greater likelihood was he'd lose his life before he had a chance to break his promise. The area was crawling with cowboys and skinners.

After walking most of the night, exhaustion finally got the better of Jonathan, and he made a cold camp a little off the road. Hard ground, chill in the air, danger lurking in every sound and shadow made no difference. Jonathan slept soundly until a kick in his side woke him.

He sat bolt upright and discovered Curston standing over him leveling two pistols at his head. "Should I finish my job?"

"If that is to kill me, I fail to see how I can prevent you," Jonathan grumbled, more annoyed at being woken than at his impending extinction.

"True. You must give me credit, Mr. Asher. Being tasked with following you off and on for three years, I learned to navigate these country lanes and anticipate your moves. I must admit your snores were a helpful guide." Curston sat down, quite at home with his role as executioner.

"Consider the credit given," Jonathan replied.

"As you are aware Lucretia is my half-sister. 'Twas through her importunity I was released from the Provost House and obtained employment with Castor," Curston said.

"And you were cared for by an aunt."

"Nay. Although I was older than Lucretia, I was a scrawny brat from the wrong side of the family, and the aunt refused to have my likes around, so I lived however I could. Lucretia always helped when she was able, even persuading Castor to spring me from the Provost House, and since then I returned as many favors to her as I received."

"Must I listen to your family history before you execute me?"

"My family history bears strongly on our present dilemma, Mr. Asher. Castor offered me a thousand guineas for murdering three people. That is enough to last a careful man a lifetime. I am a careful man, sir. You are well worth the price—half the sum or a quarter of the sum or a tenth of the sum would have sufficed—but he also desired the children murdered. I am to kill them and then inform you. Preferably, Castor told me, I should display their heads to you. That is the completest revenge, he said. He would have pressed for your arrest, had he not wanted you to see their heads. The fool Blanchard overreached himself. If he had just desired your head, well, he would have had it. I asked him what if I just killed Mr. Asher. He said I'd be paid only when the brats were dead. I do not murder children, especially children thrown out into the world with no parents as Lucretia and I were thrown out. Unfortunately, other people Castor employs lack my qualms regarding children. So, Mr. Asher, you must go back, figure out how to take the brats with you, and escape again."

"I can return the favor. A thousand guineas to kill Castor."

"A thousand guineas are no good to a dead man."

"I have Lady Beatrice's promises that the children are protected."

Curston laughed. "She cannot possibly keep her word."

"How do you mean?" Jonathan demanded.

"As you know their nephew fell into debt with the commissary. Lord Harold tried to win the debt back at the gaming tables from Castor, which you stopped."

"Lord Harold paid Castor with four teams of horses that he rented to the army."

"Lord Harold is a clever man, and one only has to

wait a while before a clever man overreaches himself. Lord Harold could not resist an invitation to finish the game on board the commissary ship. The greatest thief in New York could not believe someone was cleverer than him at the gaming table. Five thousand pounds, he lost. Castor owns the Lord and Lady. Are your orphans worth five thousand pounds?"

"Five thousand pounds." The number was like a blow to his gut.

Jonathan realized he now had three options of how to die—hanging, dueling, or dispatching Castor while Castor's guards dispatched him. "And what does your sister think about the children?"

"Lucretia is of like mind. She pressed me to bring you back. She has her hard spots as a result of disappointments in life, but she'd never countenance the murder of children. Nay, she told me she could not look into the face of her little Amory knowing she let this happen."

Although Jonathan started back before the first morning light, he didn't get far. At the turn of the road, Jonathan came upon four men at the bottom of a hill struggling with a cannon mired in mud.

"You there," a harsh voice called out behind him. "You there, lend us a hand."

Jonathan turned and caught a glimpse of a mounted captain before a lash stung his cheek to emphasize the order. Seeing little choice, he lent his shoulder to the effort. The wheels of the gun carriage sank and then slowly rose out of the mud. The soldiers cheered. Jonathan turned to go.

"Nay, you must prove whether you are either with us or against us," the captain insisted.

Jonathan lent his shoulder again and pushed the cannon another thirty yards up the slope into the position that had already been leveled with split rods. He found himself in the middle of a company of light infantry fixing their bayonets. Below, spread a valley with several farms. A dozen or so Continentals were putting up a spirited defense from a brick house against several dozen loyalist militiamen. On the other side of the valley, a company of Hessian soldiers was also gathering on a hill. The cannons and the two companies sealed the doom of the Continentals.

A horseman galloped up the slope sent by the Hessians across the way. Von Wurttemberg and Jonathan both grimaced on recognizing each other.

"What are you to do here out of uniform, Lieutenant Osborne?" von Wurttemberg asked.

"Visiting family," Jonathan said.

"The lie is not worthy of you, lieutenant. The question is whether to kill you or let you to hang. I make the decision after this little entertainment." Addressing the man who stood next to Jonathan, he continued, "Sergeant, shoot or run this man through if he to leave. Now, to teach the peasants what war is." Von Wurttemberg rode on to confer with the captain who was surveying the valley with an eyeglass.

"They know what war is," the sergeant muttered. "We taught them while he was away, and now they instruct us."

The cannons were loaded. Jonathan was given the job of carrying the cannonballs.

The battle began. The first round of shells fell short.

Before he returned von Wurttemberg stopped by Jonathan and, smiling, observed, "Now, you are the traitor to the cause of liberty as well as the cause of the King George."

"You need not so many soldiers to kill so few rebels, Major von Wurttemberg," Jonathan commented.

"Ach, my friend, look at the farms. They are not touched. They are like the only virgins in the sinful world until this glorious day." He grinned. "You understand. To ravish the valley is the pleasure for these fine men."

The soldiers started marching down the slope. The artillerymen waited for the smoke to clear before firing again. On the second round, their aim was still low.

"The rebel peasants inside the house are the dead men but I think not so much the women," von Wurttemberg added, broadening his smile at Jonathan, and galloped off to join in the attack

The huzzah was too close to be coming from the marching soldiers. A hundred men in fringed hunting shirts with tomahawks swarmed out of a copse that had seemed too small to hide so many and overran the artillery position. Jonathan raised his hands and stood there while the carnage took place around him. On the heels of the assault, a group of Continental artillerymen rushed in, loaded the cannon with grapeshot, and then lowered the guns, and these were followed by more soldiers, each holding two rifles. The first salvo of grapeshot and rifle lead cut through the men advancing toward the trapped Continental detachment below them. The British soldiers were confused at first, and by the time they turned, the riflemen and the artillery men had reloaded and let loose another salvo. A few started a halfhearted charge uphill, but most were scattering.

Jonathan observed von Wurttemberg on his horse, turning this way and that, shouting orders in his imperfect English to little effect. The group was routed, and the cannoneers directed the guns toward the Hessians on the other side of the valley. These remained in good order, and von Wurttemberg galloped over to the Hessian company to lead them in a charge. A bayonet charge over a short-range was nearly unstoppable; however, when the distance was great enough that riflemen could get off two rounds, the casualty rate of the attackers rose to frightening proportions. That was what happened. Yet on seeing the advance of Hessian, many of the fleeing men regrouped with their comrades and, ignoring the trapped Continentals, began trotting up the steep slope with lowered bayonets and grim expressions portending vengeance.

"They want their guns back, lads. I regret we must oblige them. Retreat!" the Continental major, a short man with a square face and bristling mustache yelled. They ran, Jonathan included. They were fresher than the charging soldiers and therefore faster. Retreating across the road behind the hill, they stopped at a prepared position in the woods on the edge of a meadow. Having gained the hill, the Hessians and the British infantry did not seem inclined to pursue them. Turning the guns around, they started to fire, but all they could see were trees so stopped after a few rounds. Von Wurttemberg's enraged voice echoed through both valleys. The Hessians and the remnants of the English company stood and started to advance. The

Continental major nodded to a man standing apart as if he expected a job. The marksman calmly loaded his rifle and took aim from three hundred yards. His shot at first appeared to have no effect. Then suddenly the captain's horse collapsed.

"*Schiesse!*" echoed clearly across the distance. Taking his time, the same man reloaded and fired. A second later a Hessian grenadier gripped his thigh. "Hand a little shaky," was the marksman's comment. The Hessians and the British soldiers decided it was wiser to crouch or lay down in the grass.

"They are likely scheming to go around to bite us in the rear. That will occupy them the rest of the day," the Continental major commented with satisfaction, then turning to Jonathan, he asked, "Who the hell are you?"

"Jonathan Asher, sir."

"I don't care about your name. What were you doing hobnobbing with those damn bloody-backs and Waldeckers?" he asked threateningly.

"I was on my way to visit the family of my betrothed. They happened upon me and forced me to help them push the cannon up the hill," Jonathan replied.

"And fire it, too?" the sharp-eyed major had probably seen him carrying the cannonballs.

"They wouldn't allow me to get away," Jonathan explained, not liking the drift of the questions.

"I may believe you, I may not." The major scratched his chin. "For the time being, consider yourself a prisoner until we can check out your story. Where do you live?"

"New York," Jonathan said, immediately realizing his foolish mistake.

"You're a loyalist traitor then," The major countered.

"No. I'm a merchant. That's where I conduct my business."

One of the riflemen had unfortunately opened his knapsack, which contained his Second lieutenant's uni form. Jonathan thought it might be useful to filter through the lines. The rifleman held it out for all to observe.

"Your prospects for living out this day look poorly, sir. What does your side do to spies?" The major shook his head with an expression of exaggerated pity.

"I have no side," Jonathan insisted hopelessly.

"They hang them." The major spat out the words

"Not without a trial," Jonathan pleaded, feeling an itch encircling his neck.

"Agreed," the major said and turned to his men. "Raise your hand all those here who think this man be guilty of spying."

A hundred hands were raised.

"There's your trial, a jury of a hundred."

"I didn't raise my hand, Brother Mark." A short stubby man came forward. From the rolling eyes of more than a few, this man filled the role of the company's contrarian.

"You're only one, Brother Matthew. One against one hundred and six."

"I only want to say a word," Matthews drawled, "and then you can hang the poor fellow."

"You always have to get in your word, Brother Matthew."

"If he be a spy, then he has information of utmost importance to General Washington, so we should take him back and let him be questioned," Matthew explained.

"We were told by the General to hang Arnold if we

found him. Well, we found another traitor, so we hang him in Arnold's stead."

"There be plenty of time to hang him afterward," Matthew contended.

"But then we have not the satisfaction of doing it ourselves," Mark retorted.

"Do you. sir," Brother Matthew addressed Jonathan, "have information that makes your life worth saving until tomorrow or the next day?"

"Absolutely. I am a spy—a spy for Washington."

"Expect us to believe that addle-headed yarn?" Brother Mark asked.

"Nay, not until you convey to Colonel Hamilton that you have Mr. Asher in your custody. I promise you his reaction will be more agreeable than if you report you executed Mr. Asher. If he is unfamiliar with my name, I'm certain he'll give you the pleasure of hanging me."

"And who would convey your name to Captain Hamilton?"

Brother Matthew cleared his throat.

The Continental Army was readying itself to receive the French forces that were within a day or two of arriving. The hotly debated question in all three armies was what Washington's next move would be. Was he going to help Greene and Lafayette fight Cornwallis with a united force in the south or lay siege to New York? General Heath threatened Clinton forces in New York from the north and Washington was collecting boats and pontoons along the New Jersey coast for a crossing.

When Jonathan was marched into camp between the bickering brothers, Matthew and Mark, Hamilton was too busy for an interview. To the disgust of the brothers, Jonathan was thrown into a small brick house that served as a prison and informed that the Continental Army would get around to him when it got around to him. At least, he wasn't to be hanged. It was two-thirty in the morning before a weary Hamilton entered the stifling enclosure and set down a loaf of bread, a bottle of wine, and a wedge of cheese.

"I'm tired of meeting you in improvised prisons or rundown shacks," Jonathan said. He needed to contrive a reason to return to New York to make sure Emma and Daniel were safe. That meant, of course, killing Castor. Once accomplished, he believed he could render a final service to the cause of liberty, which he thought of as an ailing mistress he had belatedly discovered he loved.

Hamilton smiled wearily. "I could release you immediately. 'Twill be better for your reputation to release you in the morning and commend you for your services in front of the whole army. You can come with us, although accustomed to the fat living of a profiteer in New York, you might not take well to the fatigue of an army on the move. On the other hand, you can retire to Pennsylvania and wait out the war. I suppose you forfeit what I hear is a fortune in New York. You might take comfort from the fact most of the officers who possessed fortunes before the war lost them over the course of the conflict."

"Thank you, colonel. I have another proposal that might render the cause one last service. You are planning to join with the French and either lay siege to the city or march to the Chesapeake. Clinton will be afraid to move until he's certain of Washington's intentions. The thing is to keep him in a state of high uncertainty. I can help with that. I am suspected of being a spy. I am watched. My mail is opened, the papers on my desk perused when not stolen. If Washington plans to go south to the Chesapeake, send me back with coded communications instructing the Patriots inside the city to rise up and cause havoc when you make the feint towards the south, wheel around with the army, and attack the city. The code should be challenging although breakable. If Washington plans to lay siege to New York, code that you want gangs of Patriots in the night to ram small boats filled with barrels of pitch into the transports, light them, and set the fleet on fire, so Clinton believes you mean to prevent him from reenforcing Cornwallis."

"How will you escape the fate of spies and doubly in your case traitors?" Hamilton asked.

"Well, no matter. Urgent business calls me back to the city, and I must return as soon as possible."

"What is more urgent than your life? Surely not the cause of liberty?" There was both a note of sarcasm and admiration in Hamilton's voice.

Jonathan considered. "No, I'm not returning for the cause of liberty, although if the surrendering of my life was what stood between liberty and no liberty, then I would regretfully surrender it."

"So, Mr. Asher, you will die to make a difference like so many young men."

"Yes, like so many I die for those I love."

Hamilton returned an hour later with a coded letter.

"Don't ask. Not even I know our next move, and over the last three years I have written two-thirds of Washington's correspondence." His face was suddenly lighted by an expression of childhood delight. "Thank God, no more. I've just been given a field command."

Better than dealing with the likes of me."

"Better than writing a hundred dispatches a day." Hamilton then gave Jonathan a wooden wine flask. "In between the inner and out sheaves of wood is a pass from Washington that will help you avoid unnecessary trouble like what brought you here. God be with you, Jonathan. God be with you."

CHAPTER 36

WHEN JONATHAN VISITED the millinery three nights later, he had not expected to encounter von Wurttemberg in the parlor with Elizabeth. The major was flushed and had lost his savage cheerful air. Elizabeth was white and trembling. An argument had been in process.

"Are Emma and Daniel safe?" Jonathan asked.

"Yes, of course, they are as safe as all children in their beds," Elizabeth lashed out angrily.

"No surprise your rebel friends make the release to you, but why does the spy come back to die?" Von Wurttemberg asked.

"Major Christoph was explaining to me a droll custom they have in his country," Elizabeth said.

"*Le droit de seigneur.*" Both seemed surprised at the fluidity of Jonathan's French. "Which makes every bride a duke's whore."

Von Wurttemberg stared sourly at Jonathan. "A small price for a milliner to pay to raise her station. Lord Edgar make me the challenge to the duel, and I give him the honor of accepting. If I kill him, she is not to be the lady.

I duel to kill, always, as you have the awareness of. For her, I promise to make the exception one time and let the silly lord live. Miss Elizabeth understands not the small sacrifice I make the requirement of her. Lady Beatrice has the understanding. Miss Elizabeth's sister has the understanding and is the splendid whore. Hundreds of women have the understanding, but she has not. I duel Lord Edgar tomorrow."

"I thought Lord Edgar left for Jamaica," Jonathan said.

"His ship to make the delay, so we are the fortunate to not put off his little affair of honor. He die or live according to my pleasure. I save him from the Captain Gregory. Yet, the pretty girl saves not the simpering dunce. Thus Lord Edgar to be the dead man. You understand, Lieutenant Philemon, you come at the wrong moment, so please to make the leave."

"Elizabeth is not the daughter or sister of your enemy," Jonathan argued.

"Lord Edgar make the challenge to me. I make not the challenge to him. So I ask the question, 'What is the price for his life?' I answer the price is the small moment of the pleasure with Miss Elizabeth. Now I discover she has not the love for Lord Edgar to believe his life worth the small moment of pleasure I ask of her."

"Duel me first," Jonathan said. "I challenge you."

"Little honor to duel the man doomed to die, Lieutenant Osborne. But I agree to your request after I kill Lord Edgar. The time is set for tomorrow, and I do not break the appointment," von Wurttemberg declared.

"Here and now, we duel. Let us step outside," Jonathan insisted.

"We have not the pistols to duel, only the sword, which you have not the knowledge to handle." von Wurttemberg sneered.

"I can use this." Jonathan showed his tomahawk.

"The understanding of that weapon I lack. I am not the rash man, so I duel you with the pistol the morning after I make Lord Edgar the dead man." Von Wurttemberg's eyes clouded, then cleared, and he addressed Elizabeth. "I molest no longer, Miss Elizabeth. Lord Edgar is my enemy. Any man who make the insult to me, even the man who make the insult from the stupidity, is the enemy. Tomorrow, I to present you the body of your beloved Lord Edgar." He then directed his gaze to Jonathan. "I touch her not. She face the consequence of the denial of one small moment of pleasure to me. If she is the last woman on earth, I touch her not."

Von Wurttemberg left.

"What are you wanting?" Elizabeth asked in a surly voice.

"You weren't considering…"

"This damn war," Elizabeth said trembling. "Lord Edgar told me Major Christoph would come here to test my virtue, but he would not mean what he said. Afterward, Edgar assured me the Hessian beast will congratulate him on my chastity. Edgar assured me that Major Christoph will shoot wide for he does not want to make Lord Harold an enemy. It would all be in play, Edgar said. I cannot conceive he is right."

"Von Wurttemberg duels to kill."

"I must tell Edgar to not appear. Let the world call him a coward. I will not." Elizabeth gazed fiercely at Jonathan.

"Do you love Lord Edgar?" Jonathan asked.

"Edgar is needing me. I can only love a man I can be part of. You do not need a soul, Mr. Asher. You probably were not even needing your dear Amelia," Elizabeth said bitterly.

"The part of me that loved her is buried with her," Jonathan replied coldly. "Edgar is also Lord Edgar."

"I am flattered that he considers me worthy of him," Elizabeth asserted.

"Well, this is an old and tired dispute, as you know."

"I think the reason you gave up so early on me is on the account of I could never measure up to your Amelia."

"You can't love and measure at the same time, but that has little importance now. I'd like to see Daniel and Emma. I would prefer to live for them than die for Amelia. Please, may I wake them? I would like to see the children…" Jonathan could see that Elizabeth was fighting back tears.

"They are with Lady Beatrice." She flushed an angry red.

"Why?" A nauseous lump of panic rose and stuck in his throat.

"She said she had a special treat for them. It was so kind of her to show interest in your little garret mice."

"Did Gabriel bring you the six hundred pounds?" Jonathan asked.

"Oh, yes, I don't need your money. I must return it to you."

"Castor means to punish me by hurting the children. If I am unable to kill Castor, please use the money to take Emma and Daniel to safety," Jonathan pleaded.

"I suppose you mean rebel territory," Elizabeth replied scornfully. "That isn't 'safety.'"

"Pray I succeed in killing the commissary. Do not speak poorly of me in front of the children. Tell them I loved them as much as children of my blood. If I am dead, tell them directly so they won't have to guess. If I happen to survive by some miracle and am forced to flee, assure them that at the first opportunity I will return for them."

Lady Beatrice had left instructions to refuse Jonathan's entry. An elderly servant backed by a stiff young guard informed him of the fact. He gave the elderly servant an envelope and said, "I will wait here for the reply."

"I insist you leave," the servant said.

"Are my children, Emma and Daniel, here?" Jonathan asked for the fifth time.

"I wouldn't know," the servant replied, and his face gave the blank defiant appearance of a shut door.

"If you value your life…" The guard began to lower his bayoneted musket.

Lady Beatrice came into the hallway behind them. "They are here, Mr. Asher, and they are safe. Come into my parlor."

Once seated, Lady Beatrice said, "Emma and Daniel are sleeping."

"Lord Harold owes Castor five thousand pounds. How can you protect the children from a man who holds over you such a debt?"

"I see Emma and Daniel are truly the children of your heart. I am aware of Castor's intentions. That's why this house is the safest place for them."

"I have deeds to property worth over five thousand pounds with me that I can…."

"Dare you suggest I would allow harm to Emma and Daniel?" In her fury, she seemed as equally capable of hurling thunderbolts as any Jove.

"You don't know what Castor is capable of," Jonathan said.

"Don't I? The commissary has no idea what I am capable of. I keep my word even to men who I deplore. If Castor makes a move, I will personally relieve him of his fat miserable life, and nobody will regret the deed. Just to simplify the situation I should have you arrested as a spy. However, the crisis with Edgar and Major Christoph is coming to a head."

"They are to duel tomorrow," Jonathan confirmed.

"My poor fool Edgar is intent on seeing the business of the duel to its end, believing that way, somehow, he'll recover his honor. You failed me in preventing the challenge. I am keeping Emma and Daniel from harm here, so it is incumbent on you to stop von Wurttemberg from murdering my dolt of a nephew. If you can't prevent the duel, at least perform the duty of a friend to the ungrateful dunderhead and advise him. He is surrounded by people who have no care whether he lives or dies. I know you to be a resourceful man, Your Elizabeth will not find a kinder soul than Edgar. Within a fortnight you will be hanged as a spy. Think of her as well as the children."

Jonathan next paid a visit to Edgar at his quarters, a dismal house on Wall Street. Edgar was alone, pacing back and forth and talking to himself. On seeing Jonathan enter, he said, "Come to gloat, Mr. Asher?"

"No, I come to dissuade you," Jonathan replied. "You

don't stand a chance against such an accomplished duelist as Major von Wurttemberg."

"A dozen fellow officers advised the same, yet he carries dueling scars. He is not invulnerable. I been practicing and am as good as the next man with a pistol." The weariness in his eyes and the hard set of his mouth and jaw made Edgar appear for once his age.

"But not nearly so good as the major." Jonathan sat down without an invitation. "Apologize, and if he insists on the duel, walk away, and let him call you coward."

"They all expect me to shy away. Even men with fame as duelists make apologies to Major Christoph. But I'll not do it. I swear I'll not." He waved his arm as if swatting away a fly. "He's out for my blood, and he'll find ways to humiliate me again and again. Even if I chose to endure his humiliations, which I might, the coward that I am, I am not to let Elizabeth be insulted. No, he will not insult her with impunity. I am played for a fool for in truth I am one, but Elizabeth, no, her honor is worth my foolish life, is worth a dozen of my foolish lives, a hundred of my… I am speaking sense, I think."

"In that Elizabeth is a fine lady, you are," Jonathan said, uncomfortable with the grudging respect he was beginning to feel for Edgar. "She cares deeply for you, and your death would grieve her more than any insult. I have also challenged Major von Wurttemberg, and my reason is greater than yours. Put off your duel for a few days. Let me avenge the death of Amelia."

"Amelia?" Momentarily, Edgar was distracted from his thoughts. "You mean…"

"Let me avenge her death, then if I fail, you have your chance."

"Nay." Edgar shook his head. "I am aware my aunt sent you to stop the duel. Although you have reasons to kill von Wurttemberg, better reasons than I have, allow me this. Your Amelia is dead. Elizabeth is alive. Allow me to fight for her honor. I want to do at least one brave thing in this damn war."

"Nobody benefits from your bravery," Jonathan stated as a last futile effort.

Edgar did not seem to hear. "My second won't appear. I believe he wants not to incur the wrath of my aunt and uncle. Will you be my second? I believe I can trust you. Be my second. Witness my defense of Elizabeth's honor. Tell her that I defended it courageously. Be the one to tell her. She will believe you. Be the one to console her. You are the only person who can. Speak well of me."

Jonathan nodded. Witnessing the duel would give him another opportunity to stop it. "I am afraid I won't be much of a consolation to Elizabeth. I am a dead man anyway. I will act as your second if I can finish an errand first, and maybe between the two of us, we can figure out why Christoph's opponents always suffer such poor luck."

Jonathan returned to the warehouse planning to spend the rest of the night putting his affairs in order. Although he tried to console himself with the belief that he'd see Amelia soon, he had never felt so isolated and hopeless. A few hours into this black mood he heard the door open.

"Damn ungrateful coming back here to your death after I save your life," Gabriel said.

"Curston informed me Mr. Blanchard wants to murder Emma and Daniel to avenge me. I had to make sure they were safe. I can't be certain until he is dead."

"You believe him, suh."

"Curston was holding a gun to my head. He could have done it himself."

"Bad business killing British officers."

"Sorry, Gabriel. I've another request. I am settling my affairs. I'm giving you a copy of my will."

"A traitor got no property."

"Well, there's my farm in New Jersey, which I will to my brother."

"When dey confiscate his house 'cause it belong to a traitor?"

"Yes, when they do that. I've provided for Emma and Daniel. As for my other property, I'd like to sell it to you. If you buy it, and there is a bill of sale, they can't confiscate it."

"Maybe dey can, maybe not."

"One pound is the price. I made out the bills of sale for more but consider the difference a gift. Quickly as possible sell to Tories of unimpeachable reputation— preferably those who have influence and power and on account of that exercise the confiscatory power. They won't be afraid of the provenance of the properties. Keep half of the proceeds for yourself and half for Emma and Daniel."

Gabriel nodded. "What else you wantin'."

"I'd say kill Castor if I fail. If you can't do that, make the necessary provisions to keep Emma and Daniel safe and that my will gets into the right hands."

"My whole dang life keeping folks from killing oder

folks. You got two children. I got two hundred." He made a gesture indicating Canvas Town that surrounded them on three sides. "Hundreds needing feedin', needing doctoring, needing jobs. Dey at me day 'n night. And what I doin'—I going out 'n getting me more. I tell you dis. Dem children, der hearts break when you hang. To be sure, my men keeping eye on dem. I do my best, but only fool guarantee what not in his power."

"Thank you, Gabriel."

"Your servant, Jonathan." This was the first time Gabriel uttered those words.

Von Wurttemberg, contrary to custom, always scheduled his duels two or three hours after sunrise. Jonathan decided to take advantage of his last day on earth. He spent the early morning hours at Lady Beatrice's mansion visiting with the teary Emma and the bravely tearless Daniel after telling them he needed to go away for a time. He wanted to condense years of future fatherhood into those moments. He wanted to tell them a story of their future lives like he had told Amelia—one that would be true. That, of course, was impossible. He'd likely die today—in the act of murdering Castor—or tomorrow as another victim of a duel with von Wurttemberg. And if he by miracle survived, he would certainly be picked up as a spy and hanged. All Jonathan could do for the children was listen to them—Emma wanted to talk about her sewing lessons with Elizabeth; Daniel wanted to know who was winning the war. In the end, Jonathan gave way to cowardice and promised that he would be back in a few weeks.

Then he called at the backdoor of Arnold's house hoping to talk to Millicent.

Millicent had spied him through the window and answered the door. She gazed at him sleepily while he practically begged her to make sure Emma did not withdraw into herself.

"I know Elizabeth will do her best, but you have a special way with Emma. The poor girl took it hard that I was leaving," Jonathan explained.

"Why are you going?" Millicent, now awake, demanded angrily.

"I cannot help it," he replied, avoiding her eyes, dark moss on a dark stone, which seemed to demand his gaze meet hers.

"Mr. Asher, you can help it. Simply remain where you are. If you find yourself walking in the wrong direction, turn around and walk back." She appeared to be ordering him.

"A spy can't do that."

Millicent stared wonderingly at Jonathan. "No, I suppose he can't. Who knows?"

"Too many now," Jonathan shrugged. "I have business to conclude with two men." He handed her forty pounds. "This is for them. In case you see a need of Emma or Daniel that Elizabeth misses, I would appreciate it if you made up the lack as a gift to not ruffle Elizabeth's pride."

"Oh, Mr. Asher," Millicent cried. "Fly away from here. God give you wings. Fly away and come back when the war is over. Don't worry about the children. They will be cared for. I promise. Elizabeth doesn't know how to be false to her word—always."

CHAPTER 37

JONATHAN'S FIRST BUSINESS was to eliminate entirely the
threat of Castor, and that meant eliminating the man. He
armed himself with a brace of pistols, his tomahawk, and
a dirk. He figured he could talk himself into getting as far
as the hold without using weapons and then murder his
way to Castor. If by some miracle, he survived, he would
fulfill his appointment as Edgar's second at the duel. On
arriving at the docked ship, Jonathan found the gangplank
pulled up. He woke the sleeping guard and asked him to
hail the ship and request to lower the gangplank. At that
moment six wagons arrived with several dozen teamsters
and soldiers. Cursing his luck, Jonathan hurried on to the
site of the duel.

Jonathan arrived at three hours past dawn, the
appointed time for the affair of honor. The other par-
ticipants were already present. Edgar, his gray pallor
anticipating perhaps his color fifteen minutes hence,
barely nodded to him. Major von Wurttemberg, fresh
and perfectly groomed, bowed. His second, the Hessian

lieutenant with the pallor of old ivory and wearing his silver gorget, followed suit. There was no doctor present.

"Are you expecting to console the poor woman when you bring her this fool's corpse?" von Wurttemberg said grinning. "I beg you to wait a day so I to bring her two corpses."

"I ask you, Major von Wurttemberg, whether you are open to a reconciliation," Jonathan stated in a loud voice.

"You must ask that question, Lieutenant Osborne, to the boy who make the challenge," von Wurttemberg replied.

"I do not withdraw," Lord Edgar cried.

"You to be the twenty-eighth I vanquish, Lord Edgar."

"Save your boasts, major, until the outcome is decided," Jonathan said.

Von Wurttemberg chose the ground, strangely placing himself so he faced the sun. Jonathan guessed that with his deep-set eyes, the sun wouldn't make a difference. Jonathan and Lieutenant Gross loaded the guns, fired, then reloaded and handed them to the duelists.

Von Wurttemberg and Lord Edgar paced and turned. Jonathan was briefly distracted. He noticed a glint on the trees behind Edgar. Gross stood a few feet to von Wurttemberg's left side, motionless as a statue, one hand underneath the gorget. What a strange pose Jonathan thought. Then the gorget flashed in his eye, directly catching the sun.

"Dammit to hell," Jonathan exclaimed, suddenly realizing that von Wurttemberg's second was manipulating the gorget. He moved in front of Gross. "Give me that," Jonathan demanded.

"Lieutenant Gross only understands German," von Wurttemberg explained.

Jonathan seized the gorget and tried to tear it off Gross's neck. Gross drew his sword. Jonathan fell back as Gross slashed the air in front of him.

"*Sehr gut.* The fools to amuse us," von Wurttemberg exclaimed, laughing.

Just then Jonathan let loose his tomahawk which struck Gross squarely in the chest. The lieutenant sat down and stared amazed at the weapon stuck in his sternum.

"What's the meaning of this?" Edgar asked, enraged.

"The lieutenant was using the gorget to reflect the sun into your eyes when you were about to fire. That is why the major duels at a later hour and chooses to face the sun."

"I have not the need for such tricks, Mr. Asher," von Wurttemberg said, although his assertion lacked his usual overweening confidence.

"Major, let us proceed. I am waiting," Edgar declared, having raised his pistol.

Von Wurttemberg grinned, "Impatient to meet your maker. Ach, the boy to become the man. Enjoy being the man for the small moment. You are soon to be the dead man." He aimed. There was no dropped handkerchief. They both fired.

Edgar fell to his knees with a wound underneath his arm. Von Wurttemberg stood with a small red spot on the corner of his mouth and a larger spreading patch of blood where the bullet had exited the jawbone underneath his ear. Spitting out blood and teeth, von Wurttemberg slurred, "I finish you off, boy." He stuffed a handkerchief partly into his mouth, drew out his sword, and spat more blood. Edgar did not carry a sword.

Jonathan picked up Gross's sword and interposed himself.

Von Wurttemberg shook his head and said in a muffled voice, "The fat man tell me death is too much good for you. He say to put out the eyes, to cut off the nose, to rip out the tongue, and then to take your manhood. He say to leave the ears so you to hear the mockery and pity. I refuse him. Now for the sake of Gross, I to do the bidding he ask."

Jonathan struck a pose and realized he had never used a sword.

"Impossible for you to kill me. Here, come. I raise not my sword to you," von Wurttemberg slurred through the handkerchief stuffed in his mouth.

Jonathan rushed and von Wurttemberg stepped to the side and tripped him.

"Try again." The dribbling blood stained his chin and white waistcoat.

This time Jonathan swung the blade in wide arcs. Still the major was able to pound him on the back of the head with the pommel of his sword, knocking him down. "What fast to you is slow to me. Come, I not to make you the dead man, I to make you the man too ugly and pitiful for eyes to see."

Jonathan charged. Von Wurttemberg sidestepped and tripped him. Jonathan flinched expecting the worst as the major loomed over him, blood still seeping from his mouth and the wound in his cheek.

Edgar yelled, "Me first!" as he fumbled reloading

the pistol. He had finally succeeded, and bleeding profusely, raised it with his left arm. "Load your weapon," he demanded von Wurttemberg.

"You, I to take my time carving your face," von Wurttemberg addressed Jonathan, spitting out the bright red handkerchief and sheathing his sword. He picked up the pistol with incredible coolness. The blood from the exit wound now covered the top half of his uniform. He inserted the packet with the lead shot, rammed it down, and then put a pinch of primer into the firing pan. Raising the pistol, he started to cough blood. He and Edgar fired at the same time. An angry red dot appeared on von Wurttemberg's forehead. "Imposs…" the major began to say as the back of his skull exploded and he fell forward.

Jonathan stared at the fallen man. He heard Amelia's voice: *'Are you satisfied now, dearest?'*

'Yes, he will no longer murder and ravish.'

'That is good, but what of you?'

'I have saved two children.'

'And will you be able to take care of them when you are hanged?'

'Elizabeth will take care of them.'

'She cannot replace you.'

'My heart breaks for them. At least, I'll be with you.'

Her voice in his head was quiet.

Although Edgar's wound was not necessarily life-threatening—the ball had exited beneath the scapula—it required immediate attention. With his arrest imminent, Jonathan needed to visit Castor and add one more crime that merited hanging. This dilemma, however, was taken out of his hands. He had been followed. After stopping the blood and binding up Edgar's wound, a dozen soldiers entered the clearing, ten minutes too late to stop the duel but in time to arrest him as a spy. He hardly heard the lieutenant braying at him about the reasons for the arrest because he was praying hard that Lady Beatrice would keep her word and protect Emma and Daniel.

CHAPTER 38

IT WAS ON the third day of the interrogation that Arnold visited Jonathan. They had not treated him badly yet. Jonathan believed they were waiting for the coded letters to be deciphered to better direct their questioning. Castor's success at deciphering the gazettes was not mentioned, probably due to professional envy. His interrogator was a captain who managed to be unctuous and comically menacing at the same time. The sessions were long and were as trying for them as for him. Jonathan did his best to sow confusion, implicating most of the wealthy Tory families in a plot to overthrow Clinton and, more accurately, delineating the shortcomings and vices of high-ranking British officers. Having tippled with them, Jonathan was privy to more personal secrets of the British officer corps than perhaps any spy in Washington's employ. How his interrogator loved the gossip and asked for further details while scribbling notes which could only be for his own use. Jonathan was not entirely believed, but they needed as many details as possible to diligently confirm their disbelief.

His interrogator seemed to be finally losing patience, when Arnold swept in, still swarthy from his campaign in Virginia, exuding command and confidence. He invited the interrogator to leave, then set down a bottle of wine, a wedge of cheese, and a warm loaf of bread on the table.

"The same you offered me on our first meeting." Arnold made himself comfortable in the chair.

"I believe 'twas rum, General Arnold," Jonathan replied.

"No, 'twas a bottle of very mediocre Madeira. That was a lifetime ago, my friend." Arnold paused, pressed his lips together, and then went on, "You might recall, Jonathan, that when I wanted to kill as many of those damned islander slaves as I could and didn't care whether I lost my life in the effort, you pulled me back into my boat. I am returning the favor now. You are a friend and a gentleman I much respect. I value friendship…"

"General Washington was your friend and patron, yet you betrayed him," Jonathan said in the same conversational tone of voice that he used to challenge Arnold during their long discussions.

Arnold reddened either in anger or embarrassment. "He was a man who refused me protection when I was the most vulnerable to my enemies and, more importantly, who stood in the way of a peaceful resolution to the rebellion. If he were captured, then we'd no longer have this wasteful spillage of blood. How many lives of good men have been lost since? 'Twas a tragedy I failed."

"Washington was still a friend and benefactor and would have likely promoted you to a position second only to himself," Jonathan insisted.

"What separates civilized men from savages, Jonathan, is the holding of principles higher than themselves. I won't deny Washington possesses noble qualities. The fact that people admire those virtues overmuch makes his flaws of greater consequence. What I did, I did for the good of the whole. Grant me the concession—however, you consider my actions—I was acting with rectitude of conscience and with foremost consideration of what I thought best for the people. Whether I was mistaken in my course of action, I leave history to decide." He laid a hand on Jonathan's arm. "But I am not come here to debate politics. I come to save your life. For the sake of our old friendship, I petitioned Clinton to let you live, and he agreed under certain conditions."

"What is the price of my life?" Jonathan asked, slicing off a wedge of cheese. He was remarkably hungry despite the topic of conversation. He had been only fed foul soup over the last three days.

Arnold also cut himself a wedge of cheese. "Not ten thousand pounds could obtain for you what I obtained. The first condition is that you must renounce the rebel cause."

"Easily done." Jonathan no longer had any value to the cause. He had inflicted whatever damage he could on the British, so the renunciation in return for his life caused no qualms. By any fair assessment, Arnold had done more damage to the loyalist cause and the British army, and here he was a brigadier general. The British were a forgiving people, after all.

Arnold grimaced, perhaps thinking the same. "And easily undone. Second condition is that you must surrender your contacts to us. Now, I comprehend that as a matter of honor you will not betray a compatriot if he is to be led to the gibbet. I give you my word that none of the people you reveal as your contacts will be executed."

"My contact with the Continental Army began with Colonel Hamilton. I have no contacts here for the information I passed on I did by means of coffee advertisements in the Royal Gazette and the Rivington Gazette. Mr. Blanchard, the commissary, is amusing himself deciphering my code and he would be more than pleased to relate to you his progress. The British army, who was eager to get the newspapers' boasts of their victories and our defeats into our hands, was my agent. Oh, yes, when I was visiting John André, the poor young fop let on that he personally was on the verge of winning the war with an intelligence coup. I passed this directly on in an uncoded letter in invisible ink that I left in the hollow of a tree behind King George Tavern in Perth Amboy. The letter still may be there. I didn't suspect you," Jonathan lied unpersuasively.

"I do not agree with your characterization of John André. Adjutant-General John André was the highest class of civilized man. There was not a scintilla of dishonor in his character and his wanton murder will forever stain the character of Washington." Arnold frowned then continued: "The third condition is that you assist us in an enterprise. We want you to pass on certain information that might tempt Washington into a rash adventure. If your information succeeds, then you'll be amply rewarded."

"Even in the unlikely event that Washington is affected by my information, wouldn't this be a matter of honor?" Jonathan sipped the wine slowly. It was a French burgundy he had sold to Arnold. He had developed a real taste for wine, and he hoped the pleasures of heaven, if he were allowed in, were not entirely spiritual.

"And a matter of peace and prosperity," Arnold replied, subjecting Jonathan to that stare that seemed to burn through him. "Which are of infinitely greater consequence than just mere personal honor. You need to make your decision now. The forbearance I gained for you is only temporary."

More wine, more cheese. Jonathan ate slowly as he mulled over the offer. The authorities might not hang him, but they weren't about to allow him to go free. They would transport him if he were lucky. They might shut him up in a prison and let starvation do what they would not. He would not be able to protect Emma and Daniel. Gabriel, Lady Beatrice, and Elizabeth would try to shield the children; however, he doubted they would be a match for Castor who had nothing to do with his long hours but like a grotesque spider weave a vast web to catch them. No, he needed more from the deal than his life to betray the cause of liberty.

"If I agree, will I be able to walk out of here?" Jonathan asked.

Arnold's hesitation followed by, "I'll see what can be done," clearly indicated the answer Jonathan didn't want to hear.

"I have a question—a point of curiosity. While you were betraying Washington, how did it feel?"

"I often felt that my chest was being crushed by an immense weight," Arnold answered in a low voice. "Even the last time, while we crossed the Hudson together, I could not help thinking how much I loved Washington. He is a good man at the head of a bad cause."

"That is the way I see you now, and in the service of that cause, you done what you would have once considered unthinkable. The Arnold of the battles of Valcour Island and Saratoga would hang the Arnold I see before me now."

"You had an opportunity to betray me, Jonathan—you could have abandoned me to the rebel militia at the wash near Toms River and nobody would be the wiser, yet you did not. Maybe my old self whose mind you have the conceit to read would do the same. You were never a political person and pretending to be one don't suit you. I was curious why you joined the rebel cause until I learned how your Amelia perished. I am truly sorry, and I regret not making her acquaintance. You took your revenge. The men who violated her are dead. There are evil men in both armies. For every crime you cite on the British side, I can cite two on the American. I believe 'tis now time to give up the cause, do what is necessary to shorten this damn war, and return to our domestic ways."

"And what about liberty? You dilated for long hours on that topic. That was your highest principle, you claimed." Jonathan sipped wine and ate another wedge of cheese.

"We have more liberty than any people on the face of the earth, and with the recent offers of the North government, we will be so deluged in liberty that we will be drunk on it. We will possess greater liberty than a people can ever possibly want or use."

"I come to another understanding." Jonathan broke

off a large chunk of bread to save and eat at his leisure. "Although 'tis true I am not a political man, I read Locke on your recommendation and Sydney and many other thoughtful men with ideas about the social compact and liberty. I admire them, yet I believe they don't quite understand the issue as well as Moses did. Forgive the preacher in me. I haven't sermonized in quite a while, but 'tis to the point of liberty, which can be called earthly salvation. The Jews did not have it bad in Egypt. They owned their own homes. They ate well. They wore jewelry so they must have worn other finery. They were such good friends with the so-called oppressors that their gentile neighbors trusted them with their gold. They left anyway to suffer forty years of privation in the desert. Why? Because they were not their own masters. That is what liberty means—being your own master, for better or worse. The Lord called them stiff-necked, which is what the British could fairly call us. Nothing else but being our own masters will do."

"I take it you're refusing my offer." Arnold stood, seeming much sadder and older than when he entered, and turned to go.

"Benedict," Jonathan suddenly blurted out when his friend was at the door. Arnold stopped. "I will do the unthinkable and betray the cause I came to value above my own life if you comply with one condition."

Arnold turned. "The offer is over generous already."

"I will do my best to sow the seeds of confusion if you kill Castor Blanchard." Jonathan regretted saying the words, but he could not take them back.

"Out of revenge?" Arnold asked.

"No, out of love," Jonathan replied.

Arnold shook his head. "I am sorry. I will not commit murder for you, Jonathan. Your new jailer who collects you anon has shown keen interest in you ever since you were detained. I do not believe he is inclined to mercy. I wished it could be different, Jonathan."

"So do I, Arnold."

Jonathan heard a carriage pull up outside. The carriage door opened. A large man got out. The door to the building where he was kept imprisoned opened, and the unmistakable piercing voice of Provost Major Cunningham announced himself.

CHAPTER 39

MILLICENT LEARNED ABOUT Jonathan's arrest six days after it had occurred while Arnold was ranting to his wife in a high rage about Clinton's late departure to capture Washington. "I told him that Asher isn't to be believed, nor his correspondence. I don't care how much Provost Cunningham poked, beat, and whipped him; he isn't to be trusted. No, the whole affair stinks to the heavens. I know the man. In fact, I taught the man. He could tie a snake in a knot."

"Surely General Clinton is not only relying on the information Cunningham has extracted from Mr. Asher," Peggy asserted.

"There were other indications—but everything is too damn convenient, too damn easy." Arnold slammed his fist on the table. Their little son began to cry.

"Mr. Asher will hang like poor André?" Peggy asked between efforts trying to soothe little Neddy.

"Jonathan won't last that long, poor soul. If only he had accepted my offer," Arnold continued in a softer voice. "Cunningham will only keep him alive if he thinks more information is to be gotten. Asher realizes this—so holds on although in the end, he must talk."

Millicent entered carrying a tray with two goblets of champagne—the last of the stock purchased through Jonathan. She laid the tray down just in time to avoid dropping it, turned, and left the parlor so they could not see her face. She went into her room—a closet as near as propriety allowed to the bedroom of Peggy.

There was no person she was closer to in this world than Peggy Shippen Arnold. Millicent had discerned immediately that although Peggy outwardly mastered the forms and addresses of a lady, inwardly she was as scared and vulnerable as a small child who finds herself in the wrong place amidst frightening people. Peggy played her part perfectly, putting a good face on the fact that her husband was nearly as disliked by the loyalists as by the patriots, hiding her grief at the separation from her family, doting with a desperate love over her new son, irredeemably in love with her husband, worried about his famous or infamous disregard of danger.

On the first day of service, they had made the connection when Peggy, after reading a letter, quoted half mockingly, half in tears the Merchant of Venice: *"Though justice be thy plea, consider this,*

That, in the course of justice, none of us should see salvation: we do pray for mercy."

Millicent replied with the next line: *"And that same prayer doth teach us all to render the deeds of mercy. I have spoke thus much to mitigate the justice of thy plea…"*

They naturally fell into a conversation about plays.

Peggy was incredulous that Millicent couldn't read and said, "You're cleverer by half than any lady I know." A few days after that conversation, Peggy declared, "I am separated from my sisters, and you never had one. I believe we can each supply the lack in the other."

"But you are such a fine lady," Millicent replied.

Peggy laughed. "Fine doesn't mean good. I ask myself, am I good? I don't know, although when I'm talking to you, who is fine and good, I feel that I might be."

Once, when her husband was away, they reversed roles—giggling, Peggy acting as the maid, and Millicent, the lady. Three months later, Peggy seemed to have cooled in their friendship. That only lasted a day. She confronted Millicent. "You have a brother in the Continental Army fighting against my husband in Virginia."

Millicent came out with a half-choked, "Yes."

"What would you do to my husband if he killed him?" Peggy asked.

"I could not harm in any way the man you love, Peggy." Millicent used her given name for the first time. "I'd leave your service and grieve for the rest of my life the loss of my brother, David, and my dear friend, Peggy."

"I will tell Benedict that if he happens to capture your David to treat him as if he were a general." Her brother was not killed or captured—and Millicent had cried from relief.

Millicent could happily spend the rest of her life as a lady's maid to the good Peggy Shippen Arnold, her dearest friend. She clutched her chest, allowed herself a few tears, then went up to her closet and collected her coat.

Ten minutes later Millicent was hurrying through the darkening streets. The air was so cold and moist that it seemed you could create snow by rubbing your fingers together. She needed help. She knocked on the door of the warehouse. Doctor Smith answered. She was afraid he might not invite her in—so dauntingly priggish he was.

"You been crying," he observed.

"They took Jonathan and are beating him until he betrays his secrets," she said, wondering why she had used Mr. Asher's given name.

"I regret his predicament. I felt it my duty to pray for him. No one escapes the Provost House Prison except in a canvas sack."

"No, that definitely will not do for Mr. Asher," Millicent stated firmly. "It would deny me the opportunity of telling him how utterly stupid he is. Do you not have in your acquaintance anybody with influence?"

"If Arnold can't help, then I fear there's no hope. As for me, I am a parolee. Even if a British officer offered friendship, I would not accept it on principle." Smith's wife entered, smiling the smile of a bad actress. Was she jealous? Dr. Smith stiffened. "Lucretia, I believe I hear little Amory crying."

"Little Amory is asleep, dearest."

"This is a confidential consultation," Doctor Smith said irritably.

"There should be no secrets between husband and wife," Lucretia snapped back.

"Except where a patient is concerned." Anger rose in his voice.

"Does she have a complaint that requires your special expertise?" Lucretia ladled on the sarcasm sweetly.

"I promise not like your complaints, dear. Now you can leave."

She sniffed, frowned, gave her bad actress smile, and left.

"There must be someone else with influence we can petition…" Millicent pursued.

"What do you mean by influence? A spy has no friends." The natural frown on Doctor Smith's face deepened, then, suddenly, his expression changed. "On second thought, there is a person who perhaps can exert a special influence. He, after all, required my expertise. I do not see how it can work. No, no, too many difficulties."

"Tell me who this person is, and I make him do it, even if I have to stick my pistol into his back," Millicent declared.

"I don't see how we surmount the obstacles."

"Surmount what obstacle?" Gabriel stood at the door.

"What are you doing here?" Dr. Smith asked.

"Collecting my property which be dis warehouse 'fore they decide 'tisn't mine. I say what be de problem?"

Dr. Smith explained to Gabriel his idea, enumerating the two impossible things he lacked.

"I 'gree. Only damn fool try dat."

"What damn fools, these mortals be," Millicent remarked. "General Arnold signs a dozen papers a day and hardly glances at them. I'll get the signature if Doctor Smith writes the order."

"I'll write the order. Still, the other thing I can't do."

"Nor I," Gabriel said.

"Is there not a soul in your acquaintance who can help us?" Millicent asked.

Doctor Smith shook his head. Gabriel added, "'N be making dem traitor?"

"I must do it then," Millicent said.

Gabriel smiled and even indulged in a laugh. "Den, we must do dis ding, Miss. After 'tis done, good riddance to you 'n your kind which bring naught but trouble."

CHAPTER 40

CUNNINGHAM LEANED BACK and hummed a little ditty, well satisfied with himself. After three hours of questioning yesterday, Asher had revealed a trove of valuable information, although it was now hard to get him to speak clearly. When Cunningham realized Mr. Asher was the man who had forced him to let that French count go free, he struck him across the face six times with a truncheon. Hampering Asher's ability to speak was a mistake, of course. He put Asher's leg in a vice and had Richmond jump on the exposed part until the broken bone pierced the surface. The slightest touch there elicited wild screams of agony. Cunningham had been so tempted to mutilate—slit a nostril, resize an ear. Regretfully, some officers took exception to such tactics, and he preferred to stay in their good graces. The injuries Mr. Asher had sustained thus far could be explained as resulting from a fall from a horse, or maybe two or three falls from a very tall horse. He did not think that Mr. Asher could hide his remaining secrets much longer. The provost had come back from an interview with his friend Castor Blanchard who told him exactly what to say to scrape the last secrets out of his prisoner down to the last dirty detail. The wretch resisted, at first, however, the advice seemed to be producing the desired effect.

A knock on the door interrupted these thoughts. His guard announced, "An officer is here to see you, sir, a Colonel Andrew Goshen."

"Colonel Goshen?" The name sounded familiar, yet he was certain he had never met a Colonel Goshen. "Let him in."

Lieutenant Colonel Goshen entered with a martial swagger. He was a slender young man, therefore must have come from a family with sufficient wealth to buy the 3500-pound colonel's commission. He stared disdainfully down at Provost Marshal Cunningham. Despite his youthful, freckled face, Goshen emanated a definite air of command, an air that only is acquired by a long custom of being obeyed. Having once made a living breaking horses and confident he possessed the character that could break any man or beast, Cunningham decided to teach this young swag a lesson. Richmond shifted in his chair and opened his half-closed eyes fully as if interested in the visitor. Good. Richmond added the right measure of intimidation.

Colonel Goshen handed Cunningham a paper and announced, "Provost Marshall Cunningham, this is the order to release Lieutenant Osborne also known as Jonathan Asher into my custody."

Provost Cunningham shook his head. "I made great progress with my questioning, Colonel, and I believe I found the right screw to turn to force him to reveal his final secrets."

"Your progress has impressed us, Provost Cunningham, and I am sure you are to be duly commended, but it is also best to verify the results with different interrogators." The high sharp voice was hard on the ears.

"Clinton did not sign these orders." Cunningham handed back the paper.

"As you can see, General Benedict Arnold signed them." Impatience made the voice higher and sharper and, annoyingly, he tapped his finger on Cunningham's desk.

"I do not recognize General Arnold's jurisdiction, and I am not familiar with his signature. In my book, a loyalist general ranks slightly higher than a true British private and slightly lower than an ensign." Cunningham leaned forward pretending to occupy himself with a list of supplies. Richmond was now standing, his fists clenched. Almost a giant, he was strong enough to break the slender colonel in two. That might be going too far, although roughly shoving this young peacock out would be just the thing. Worth the apologies and bum kissing that would have to follow later. Cunningham caught Richmond's eye. That intelligent servant was an excellent reader of his face and understood the nod as permission to proceed.

The paper was thrust between Cunningham's eyes and the list. "I don't give a damn about what you recognize or not recognize or your novel theories on rank. I insist you surrender Osborne today, here and now. You may complain to the proper authorities if you believe your jurisdiction has been violated. I would welcome the opportunity to inform the same authorities concerning your lack of cooperation and insubordination."

"As I clearly stated, I don't recognize your jurisdiction." Cunningham saw that Richmond had taken another step forward and strangely enough appeared intent on circling the desk to get a better view of Colonel Goshen. Grabbing him by the collar and pulling him out would be more appropriate.

Colonel Goshen bent over the desk and, holding the trembling paper so it was hovering a fraction of an inch from Cunningham's mouth, declared, "I'm not in the habit of entreating an officer of inferior rank. Now I will either ram this order down your throat and make you eat it and shit it and then obey your shit or you will do as it requires you to do." Colonel Goshen, now aware of Richmond's threatening demeanor, addressed him, "What do you want, man?"

Richmond reached out as if to caress the thin mustache on Goshen's face. The colonel flinched. *Why is Richmond engaging in such an intimate personal affront with this young peacock?* Cunningham asked himself. *This will be hard to explain.*

"Colonel," a middle-aged black servant with a well-trimmed beard stood at the door. "You ask me to 'member you 'bout de appointment wid General Clinton."

Cunningham observed Richmond withdrawing his hand. He seemed to lose interest in Goshen and returned to his chair where he slumped.

"Thank you, Gabriel," Colonel Goshen said, not moving the paper which was now tickling Cunningham's upper lip. "'Tis necessary to settle this matter first."

Cunningham wavered. The colonel seemed about to ram the paper down his throat, and the punishment for striking a superior officer if he resisted was five hundred lashes. This horse would not be broken today. He resigned himself to letting the arrogant asshole have his way. "I would like you to write a letter of explanation."

"The order is all the explanation the circumstances require." Colonel Goshen implied it was beneath his dignity.

Cunningham gathered his anger and what remained of his pride for one last attempt at defiance and then thought it better to put off the protest. "I will write the letter explaining the circumstances of the release, which you will sign and date. Your signature signifies you take responsibility and accept the consequences. Our superiors can then determine who is the more effective interrogator."

This simple request put Colonel Goshen into worse humor. "Scribble your damn lines and I will sign."

Provost Cunningham spoke as he wrote: "I am surrendering the prisoner Mr. Jonathan Asher also known as Lieutenant Philemon Osborne by order of General Benedict Arnold to Colonel Andrew Goshen. Colonel Goshen's signature verifies the transfer."

Colonel Goshen took up the quill and bent over the entry book, his hand trembling slightly. Like many wealthy young officers, he likely spent last night's late hours drinking, whoring, and gaming. Straightening, still holding the unused quill, he said, "I want to see the prisoner before I sign for him."

"Follow me," Cunningham said.

"No, Provost, bring him here," Goshen demanded.

Orders were given. Cunningham experienced several long uncomfortable minutes while the damned young swag colonel, regarded him with an expression of utter disdain, like dirt underneath his fingernails. Finally,

Osborne was delivered on a stretcher, groaning, near delirious with pain. The colonel frowned and said coldly, "I could have gotten twice the amount of information with half the damage. You are a very clumsy interrogator, provost marshal."

"The traitor fooled other interrogators with such lies that Washington was plotting to cross the North River," Cunningham protested. "I studied the fellow. I recognize when he lies for he can't hide his fear that I will hurt him more. I have extracted fifty pages of confessions. Hah! Which I believe are of great significance to General Clinton. All that remains for Lieutenant Osborne to reveal are his contacts, which I can get from him today. What else is there?"

Colonel Goshen turned a hard look on Cunningham, the green eyes darkening dangerously into hard black beads. The impression recurred to Cunningham that this young peacock was entirely capable of inflicting physical harm on his person. "Many things beyond your understanding in this world." Colonel Goshen turned to the guards carrying the stretcher and ordered, "Take him to the carriage waiting outside. Lay him gently in. I did not expect he couldn't sit."

"I can sit," came a voice miles deep in the chest of a man on the stretcher.

Cunningham started to mouth the word "gently" in disbelief, but the cold murderous scowl of Colonel Andrew Goshen like a knife tip at his throat stopped him.

CHAPTER 41

EACH TIME THE carriage jolted over a pothole, Jonathan's mind went white with pain. He wondered to what new hell this personage was transporting him. He thought he recognized the name, Goshen. He vaguely remembered a Goshen on a list somewhere, nothing more. He opened his eyes to a slit to view this new tormentor. The face seemed familiar, but his thoughts were so scrambled that he could not place it. Had he been a client once who had purchased wine from him? Jonathan vaguely sensed that the colonel was related to Arnold—a friend or family member.

Then the colonel performed an inexplicable gesture. He brushed back Jonathan's hair affectionately and murmured, "This is a fine mess you've gotten yourself into, Mr. Jonathan Asher. We need both the luck of the devil and the grace of the Lord to whisk you away. I take you to Elizabeth's house—her brother is out persecuting Whigs and hasn't returned in months, her sister is ruining the rest of her reputation with another new major, and her father never descends from his dreams downstairs. Since you saved Edgar at the risk of your own life, she will not refuse you safe harbor. She wouldn't refuse you in any event, for, when it comes down to it, I believe she loves only you, although you don't presently appear an ideal object of affection, and then there's the minor objection to you being a rebel spy."

The colonel seemed to be smiling. Jonathan, noticing the moss in the green eyes as soft as velvet, shook his head disbelievingly, "Mrs. Dalton?" Then he remembered that terrible thing or rather that there was a terrible thing. "I…"

"You must try to be quiet. Our next trick is to smuggle you out of the city."

What was it that he needed to tell her? It was so terrible and so important. The only words he could think of were, *Have mercy…*

Elizabeth did welcome him. They made a stretcher out of two of Percy's coats, the sleeves threaded through a mop and a broom, then they, with help of Dr. Smith who had driven the carriage, carried him down to the cellar. Dr. Smith who hated any appearance of deceit quickly replaced his private's uniform with regular clothes and examined Jonathan while grumbling about the immorality of spying, all wars being a waste of men's lives and dishonest, all soldiers being wolves and cannibals in uniform, all British being compromised by the evil deeds of their mercenaries. Daniel and Emma peeked into the room and were allowed to gently hug him. Emma cried large silent tears. Jonathan smiled and was strong for them until the ugly thought landed in his consciousness like a vulture with a gory beak and talons. It was them. He needed to talk.

Dr. Smith hemmed and hawed, then said, "I fear he'll scream when I set his leg. I can tell by his face he is a screamer."

"How long will it take to set the leg?" Millicent asked.

"A few minutes if we're fortunate, an hour if we're not."

"Please…" Jonathan pleaded but then stopped. The vulture had lifted and only the dread remained. *Lord, have mercy…* he thought.

Millicent and Elizabeth stared at each other, then Millicent said, "Elizabeth, remember when I taught you a most amusing song that my sailor uncle taught me when he was in his cups. We giggled about it for days. Do you recall it? Maybe we could have a contest of who can sing the loudest."

Elizabeth nodded. "I'm half Irish. Why wouldn't I be having the loudest voice? I believe I can sing as loud as any woman alive, sure," Elizabeth answered.

"I'm full Scottish, which means my lungs are bagpipes, so I do not believe you will prevail, dear. This is how it goes. 'Tis slightly improper…"

"If Sorrow, the tyrant, invade the breast, Haul out the foul fiend by the lug, the lug!"

Millicent sang in a throaty contralto and Elizabeth repeated the phrase in a voice that was like an out-of-tune flute. Jonathan made the observation in-between the spasms of pain that you would be hard put to find a prettier duo or a more discordant one.

Reginald did a jerk and a twist when Elizabeth repeated after Millicent the second verse.

"Let no thought of the morrow disturb your rest, But banish despair in a mug, a mug!

"Or if business, unluckily, goes not well, Let the fond fools their affections hug;

"To show our allegiance we'll go to 'The Bell,' And banish despair in a mug, a mug!

"Or if thy wife prove none of the best, Or admits no time but to think, to think,

"Or the weight of the horns bow down thy crest, Divert the dull Demon with drink, with drink!

"Or if thy mistress proves unworthy to thee, Ne'er pine, ne'er pine at the wanton pug;

They sang as Dr. Smith wrenched and twisted the leg back into place. There was no mercy in the man, which was beneficial for mercy impeded setting a limb.

Later that day, as Jonathan returned to consciousness, he became aware of an argument. Elizabeth's brother was drunk and demanding money for a horse to go with his friends to plunder the house of a secret Whig. "You're gone for six score days, not even a note of what you're up to, and the first thing you request on coming here is money? Take the damn purse and be taking your unruly comrades out of my shop," Elizabeth cried, and he heard the coins spill. Jonathan sunk back into delirium again. An indeterminate while later, he became aware of Millicent and Elizabeth hovering over him. Were they looking down into his casket? Again, the blur of semi-conscious pain took over his thoughts.

Jonathan dreamed he was a bloody snake with all its bones broken trying to pass over the hot sands of a desert. The vulture with the gory beak landed again and stared at him, its face transmogrifying into that of Cunningham's. Mockingly, it said, *I'm told you have a special fondness for two children by the names of Emma and Daniel. Shall I bring them here? I would wager that if they asked you to tell the truth, you would tell the truth. Do you believe they are protected? I promise you this: if one soldier loses his life on account of your intransigence, their welfare is the price you pay. You can't die to save them? I swear an oath that is what I'll do, and, as you know, I am a stickler when it comes to oaths.*

More voices. He thought he heard Amelia's breathy whisper. Dr. Smith's screwed-up worried face came into and out of focus.

They then all became aware of rapping on the door which must have been going on for a long time. He heard Lucretia's high insistent wheedling, "I would like to speak to my husband."

"He's…" Elizabeth began to stutter.

"Don't dare tell me he's not here. I want to speak to him now!" There was a brief struggle and Lucretia burst through the entrance of the cellar.

Doctor Smith gazed unsurprised at his wife and in a voice of annoyance and tenderness said, "Yes, Lucretia dear."

"You cannot remain here any longer." Lucretia glanced around. "I told her. She asked me, and I told her everything, so you must leave. Let the rest suffer the penalty for treason. You must leave."

"And if I refuse?" Doctor Smith asked.

"I refuse to let you refuse." Millicent blocked Lucretia from approaching the table, the uniform adding the bit of authority that made Lucretia hesitate.

Smith continued in a soft, reasonable voice. "You know who I am. You know I always were a Patriot."

"For that reason, you make me protect you from other patriots and loyalists and that big fat commissary Castor Blanchard," Lucretia continued in a voice that could cut glass. "Do you think that is easy to do? I spend half my life trying to stop little Amory who's breaking a tooth from crying and the other half protecting you from yourself."

"I don't need protection, Lucretia," Dr. Smith assured her.

"You're a dear fool, husband. This lady visited me, Lady Beatrice, and asked why my husband was helping Jonathan Asher escape. Did I know? Did I? I lied. I told her no. Then I went to him. Maybe I thought to tell, my telling for your life, dear husband. He sent his guard and his slave away for he wanted a nasty thing with me. That fat ogre said he would hang you along with Mr. Asher if I didn't do what he demanded. So, I did what he asked, and whatever I did was never enough. I could see that. At times I believe I'm the only person with sense left in the world. Never enough. Never enough. He threatened and threatened. He could not even control the spittle down his face. Still, he threatened. I could cry and scream at him. Never enough. I could beg and even offer myself again to his gross touch. Never enough." Panicked or out of breath, she panted heavily.

"You understand he promised. He promised he'd save your life if I would, then after he said he wouldn't. He laughed at me when I accused him of lying and said, 'My good lady, you are no longer useful, so you are fortunate I not exert myself against you. As for your rebel doctor, he hangs.' So, I take this small knife from the table and go around to the side where he can't move, and I stab him in his neck. A dozen times, a hundred times, I stab, and I stab until I got the vein I wanted." Lucretia looked around as if daring anyone to admonish her.

"At least, you'd not die, my good foolish husband who I do not deserve, who I deceived, and who I love as much as any woman loves a man. I thought I am dead, knife in hand, blood everywhere. Then his brother comes in.

"'I heard everything,' he says. 'And you won't suffer for this, Miss.'

"'How can you say that when I have the knife in my hand and blood everywhere. I killed him!' I scream at him.

"'Nay, lass, he killed himself,' the brother says, then takes out a pistol, places it in Mr. Blanchard's hand, puts the barrel in his mouth, and pulls the trigger. 'Go, lass,' he says. 'I discover him anon and say that he killed himself out of despair at no longer being able to attend the gaming halls.'

"'Why?' I ask.

"'I cannot see clear what good your death would do,' he tells me. 'Nor that of your Dr. Smith. 'Tis all a great pity. Don't stand there gawking. True, he was my brother, yet he knew not the meaning of kindness or mercy. He destroyed more men than von Wurttemberg in his duels. Two lives I save now. That's something a man like me can take pride in.'

"Then I went to her to beg her to take pity on us and told her everything. I didn't mean to but I told her everything. Everything. And she only said one word: 'Hurry.'"

There was a moment of astonished silence.

"Go," Millicent then said to Dr. Smith. "You must not sacrifice yourself for our sake. Go after you help me load Jonathan back into the coach so Elizabeth and her family aren't implicated. She is as good a Tory as Governor Tryon, and 'tis an injustice for her to be linked to what we're doing. I am implicated, sure. That is my due for being a poor actress."

"I see through to the end what I start," Smith insisted.

"There's no help for it. Doctor Smith," Millicent argued. "Please, if you could do us this service. I'll take the coach around to the backyard."

Millicent had never driven a coach and sensed this enterprise would end miserably. While Lucretia stood at the door fuming, she climbed into the seat, feeling absurd and vulnerable in her uniform. The horses were unconvinced, but finally her Colonel Goshen's voice stung them into action, and she drove the carriage around to the yard. Doctor Smith, dressed again in his borrowed uniform, and the sagging Elizabeth transferred Jonathan from the stretcher to the seat in the carriage. Jonathan appeared to possess just enough consciousness to feel the pain.

"Return to me," Elizabeth whispered in his ear. "I wait for you."

There followed an argument between Dr. Reginald Smith and his wife, he, insisting on driving the coach, she, protesting.

"I will see this through, woman," Doctor Smith exclaimed, trying to terminate the conversation.

It ended with him swearing never to support any cause again that put his life at risk, and Lucretia entering the carriage and taking a seat across from Millicent and the slumping Jonathan and giving them the evil eye with arms crossed. They set out at a fast pace. The jolting was such agony that Jonathan did not see how he could survive the journey. He started to say, "I'm to die..."

Lucretia snarled, "Well, hurry up, and do it."

Millicent responded: "If you die after all my effort, Mr. Asher, then I'll spit on your grave and pray you go to hell."

"Emma and Daniel and..."

Suddenly, with a particularly painful jolt, the carriage stopped. Another argument took place outside.

"And Cunningham..."

"I am transporting Colonel Goshen on an important mission," Doctor Smith was heard saying.

"I'm a particular friend of Colonel Goshen," the feminine voice replied.

Lucretia began to rock back and forth in panic. "Don't let her see us. Don't. She's the one."

"That is impossible," Dr. Smith shouted in his piercing voice.

"I insist you show him to me. He will not deny our long acquaintance."

Millicent squared her shoulders and stepped out. There was a peal of laughter, followed by, "Such an attractive colonel I must say does credit to the British army. You must put Lieutenant Osborne into my carriage. Arnold is on the warpath about the disappearance of a rebel spy. You, Miss, must change into your proper attire and go to my residence where I will provide you with an alibi. Nay, do not come with me for I do not think the brigadier general will be fooled by his maid." Lady Beatrice opened the door. "There you are, Mr. Asher. 'Twill be much more comfortable in my carriage. Don't gape like a stuffed owl. Put him in here."

"I must go back. Please," Jonathan groaned. "Lord, have mercy on them."

"You, Mr. Asher, have no choice. I said I would return the favor if Edgar lived, and I'm keeping my word whether you are in accord or not." She turned to Millicent. "You must tell me where to take my charge. No guard will presume to challenge me."

Millicent seemed unsure how to respond.

Lady Beatrice continued: "Dr. Smith, I suggest that you drive Mrs. Dalton back to the millinery where she can quickly change into a more suitable costume and rub that thing off her upper lip. Provost Cunningham must have sand in his eyes! Mrs. Dalton should then go to my residence. Meanwhile, I'll think up a pretty story to give the Arnolds when I return her to their establishment. 'Tis in our favor that Cunningham would die afore admitting he was intimidated by a lady. Now, where do I need to take this gentleman?"

"How can we trust you?" Millicent asked.

"How can you not? We must not dally," Lady Beatrice exclaimed. "Or we are all compromised."

Jonathan was lifted and put into the soft bench of the carriage, then covered with a blanket. Somewhere on the streets, they were challenged. The young sentinel was no match for Lady Beatrice's high dudgeon, and they were allowed to proceed. Again, gently, he was transferred into a boat. He shivered violently as three or four blankets were laid over him.

Jonathan heard Gabriel's deep voice. "You white folk always causing me problems. Dis last favor I doin', Mr. Asher." He felt the cool fog on his face. Gabriel's rowers were strong. Jonathan doubted he'd survive the night. And if his prayer were not answered, Lord, have mercy on Emma and Daniel for Provost Marshal Cunningham would not.

CHAPTER 42

JONATHAN DIDN'T BELIEVE he'd survive the week, nor did he want to when he was laid in the bed where Amelia had died. Mrs. Goodwin in her abrupt efficient manner refused to let him have his way. "Amelia has to wait a while for your company," she explained. "I understand there are people in this world who you have a duty to first."

Jonathan did survive, but it was too dangerous to remain near New York City, so in very slow stages he was moved towards his parent's trading post north of Fort Pitt. He wanted desperately to make Elizabeth and Lady Beatrice aware of Cunningham's threat. Written communication would be compromising, so he asked people who might have an acquaintance in the city to inquire. Somewhere along the way, Jonathan received a pass recommending that this hero be treated with the utmost respect and care. Somewhere along the way, he learned that Cornwallis had surrendered at Yorktown and that Clinton's relief force had landed too late and in the wrong place to be of assistance.

His parents took him in. His mother, Madame

Corinne, her face still beautiful though lined, shook her head and said in a voice heavily accented because of emotion, "A new man, we make you."

Becoming that new man was two years off. During his long convalescence, he tried to obtain news from New York. A direct letter to his brother William or Elizabeth might implicate them in his spying activity. Gabriel had disappeared likely because his close connection to the spy Jonathan Asher put him at risk. Jonathan tried writing to the Goodwins asking them to look into the welfare of Emma and Daniel. The letters elicited no response. They did receive two letters from William. The missives did not acknowledge Jonathan's existence and said absolutely nothing about Emma and Daniel although they still worked out of the house on Jacob Street. Jonathan sensed they were bitter about his betrayal of the loyalist cause.

On inquiring about his house and farm in Toms River, he learned that residence had been burned to the ground by the British. Gabriel's wife and children had disappeared. Hamilton was kind enough to include inquiries in the communications with General Carleton, now the head of the British troops in New York. The fate of two orphans among the thousand orphans was not of sufficient importance to merit an investigation.

Twice Jonathan attempted to return. Both times he was carted back too exhausted and broken to continue. Finally, a letter came from the Goodwins, saying they were afraid to enter the city because it was noted the deaths of three officers and their daughter seemed connected.

CHAPTER 43

DECEMBER 1783

JONATHAN ARRIVED AT the empty Goodwin farm on a Sunday morning. They were at a church service four miles away. Jonathan did not wait for the Goodwins to come back from the service but left a note thanking them for the care they had given him when he was smuggled out of New York. With a stab of acute pain, he remembered his amazing first dinner at the house with Amelia blushing every other bite, Mr. Goodwin questioning his right to exist, and Mrs. Goodwin asking in her startlingly direct manner whether he was going to marry their daughter or not. Afraid for the safety of Elizabeth and the children, he hurried on.

This was one of the many frustrations on his return journey, a slow journey due to his not completely healed injuries. Jonathan required a cane to walk and rode with difficulty. Occasionally, his jaw would ache so much that he couldn't eat. Worse was that the closer he came to New York, the thicker the rumors filled the air about the terrible treatment meted out to loyalists. They were losing their property and sometimes their lives to mobs of vengeful Patriots. If Cunningham hadn't gotten to the children, the Patriot mobs might have done the job by burning out Elizabeth's millinery.

Jonathan believed his worst fears were realized when he saw the pile of ashes and charred timbers where the millinery once stood. He knocked on his brother's door, thanking God the house was still standing. William and Nancy both answered and stared at him with thunder in their faces. Trying to keep his voice calm, Jonathan asked what happened to the millinery and the children.

"The Littletons left a month before it was burned," Nancy explained, frowning at her traitorous brother-in-law. "The mob half tore it down when they were plundering but found nothing of value. They made quite a hullabaloo about tarring and feathering the father and son who were long gone. Fortunate for the Littletons that they were setting themselves up at Halifax when it all happened. The mob was going to do the same to us, but then word got out William was your brother, and you had helped General Washington, so we were left alone, even though a British Colonel Goshen purchased this residence from your confiscated property." Nancy shook her head, seemingly disappointed at not being burned out.

"And Emma and Daniel?" Jonathan asked, heart in his throat.

"I didn't see them the last month before they left, but I thought they were hiding inside, afraid of the rabble and riot." Nancy couldn't keep sympathy out of her voice.

"Did Miss Elizabeth leave a message?" Jonathan asked, not giving the strange purchaser of the house a second thought.

"Oh, I been remiss," Nancy exclaimed. "Miss Eliza-beth left a letter for you."

He tore it open and read:

"Dear Mr. Asher,

Enclosed is the deed to my shop to pay you back for your money which my family will need to start their new life. If there is any deficit when you sell the millinery and property, then contact my aunt in Halifax, and I will compensate you for the difference as soon as I am able. I am so sorry, and I pray to God for you to forgive me. I could not stay if I wanted Percy and Father to survive the mobs and Stephanie to go where she might restore her reputation. Emma and Daniel didn't want to accompany us."

Jonathan's hands began to sweat.

"I begged them, but they insisted you would return, for you said you would and you always kept your word to them. I am ashamed to say they are still a little bit afraid of Percy, although he has greatly improved. I went to see if Millicent could take them in. When I arrived at General Arnold's house, it was vacant. Mrs. Arnold was so fond of Millicent that I doubt she would leave New York without her. I learned about a group of charitable-minded gentlemen and their wives who planned to turn the Sugar House into an almshouse. I took Emma and Daniel there, and the director promised to care for them well. I gave them a hundred guineas and have

enclosed the receipt, so you know where they are and that they're well cared for.

"Lord Edgar has gallantly proposed to me again, and I have decided to accept his hand. Lady Beatrice, who seems to be able to arrange so many things, promises to fix the difficulties of Percy and Stephanie. Her plans for Edgar and me make me dizzy.

I feel the deepest gratitude to you for preserving Lord Edgar's life. It is a debt beyond my ability to repay. I can only say you hold a place in my heart no other man can ever take. Here I am crying. I have been so wretched to you.

With the greatest affection, Elizabeth."

Jonathan's first feeling was pity. Elizabeth would always hold a place in his heart too. Such a waste of beauty and courage on unworthy recipients. He could clearly see that to the end of her days she would be taking care of and making allowances for her brother and sister and likely the hapless Lord Edgar.

Then he saw the receipt from the backers of the almshouse and his hand trembled. Scrawled across it begging to be noticed was the large signature of Provost Cunningham.

Courage and beauty and betrayal. Lord have mercy on Emma and Daniel, he prayed.

Jonathan took a coach to the Sugar House. With all the filth built up from years of housing prisoners, it was one of the few truly abandoned buildings in New York. He talked to the new owner, a man all smiles and optimism as he supervised the clean-up. "Turn this into a place for orphans. What a crazy idea! And no money in it. I am already spending more on lye and vinegar than the building itself cost me."

Jonathan's sole hope rested on that Daniel, who had proven himself resourceful, could have escaped the provost. The next morning Jonathan started his search for the children. He began walking, his cane clacking on every other step, along the dockyards on the East River, down to the Battery, turning up Broadway to the Bowling Green, passing the Provost House and Arnold's residence, all the while desperately scanning the faces of the children. The task seemed impossible. His leg ached terribly. The dread in his heart was like that of his premonition of Amelia's fate after he saw her three murderers in the tavern.

He passed the burnt scar of the Canvas Town and his dilapidated warehouse. At least twenty people now called it home. When Jonathan questioned them, they claimed a British colonel Goshen owned the place, but he was in Halifax, and when would he ever be coming back? Most of the darkies, they informed him, had gone to Halifax also. Wasn't it funny that some of their former masters came looking for them, expecting their slaves to be waiting around to go back into servitude?

As he searched, Jonathan could not suppress the bitter thought that Emma and Daniel wouldn't have marked graves. Bodies of the poor were thrown into the river or buried by the dozens in pits. Cunningham would think it a good day's work to have punished and killed them as revenge. Jonathan did not regret killing Hogwood and

Hoffman, but he would undo his vengeance, his spying, everything for the lives of those dear children. Mercy was perhaps only a temporary gesture against the crushing machinery of time but, without it, humanity was empty. This final indignity of namelessness for two precious spirits angered him beyond reason.

Jonathan was still remembered by tavern keepers and shopowners as a loyalist and British officer. Most satisfied themselves with glares, although a hostler who recognized Jonathan warned that he should take care because, by and by, his boys will find where he lives and burn him out. He spotted Davina and almost approached her, then noticed she was leading a small boy by the hand.

Jonathan methodically retraced his steps, going up and down each street, forcing his bad leg to keep up with his good, stopping only when the pain became unbearable, occasionally calling out Emma and Daniel's names to the backs of children who were always too young to be them. More than two years had passed and Emma and Daniel, if alive, would be older and different. Hopeless, he returned to Bowling Green. He slept on the Green wrapped in three blankets against the cold with several hundred vagrants who had nowhere else to sleep including a dozen children huddling together. Maybe Emma and Daniel would appear during the night and join the other homeless children. Sometime in between his fitful dreams, he realized that of the six of his properties that he visited, three were owned by the fictitious Colonel Goshen who could never reclaim them. Unlike Elizabeth, Gabriel had made sure that he could recover half his property. The consolation was small, yet it was good to know that a few men exceeded the trust placed in them.

That morning, Jonathan shuddered at his next task, which was to discover whether those houses that specialized in selling the sexual favors of children still existed and search for Emma and Daniel there. He found such an establishment. The dirty half-naked children on narrow cots stared at him with fearful eyes. He forced himself to inspect every face, aware that if he discovered Emma and Daniel, not all the fine clothes, good food, and love in the world could erase the betrayal and hurt. He sat down on the street and gave dry heaving sobs afterward. With difficulty, Jonathan stood. He could not get the stench of the place out of his nose and lungs for the rest of the day as he retraced his steps a third time.

Near evening, he saw a Dutchman vending confections he used to buy for the children on their Sunday outings. The Dutchman would be the hundredth person Jonathan questioned that day, but at least the vendor might remember the faces of Emma and Daniel. He approached the man who, likely recalling that Jonathan once wore a British uniform, stared at him warily.

"Sir, do you remember…" Jonathan felt a tug on the back of his coat.

"An apple, sir." He turned around. Emma screamed and dropped the apple and ran away.

He followed, propelling the bad leg forward with his cane, shouting and waving his arms. Around the corner, he discovered Millicent at a cart arguing with a man over a bruised apple with a bite out of it. A much taller Daniel stood a few feet off with his fists clenched in case they were needed. Emma bounced into Millicent, then into the man dislodging the apple, cried again, and pointed, "Father!"

"Thank God!" Jonathan said, staring at the faces of Daniel and Emma who seemed more distressed than pleased to see him. The dissatisfied buyer of the apple retreated, this scene too confusing for his dispute.

Millicent unaccountably blushed, then said, "Mr. Jonathan Asher, may I offer you an apple?"

"The children—you took them in? Elizabeth wrote that you left with the Arnolds."

"Emmy and Danny and I, we were all cast out into this brave new world. Peggy would have taken me to London, but General Arnold suspected, and I made a promise to you, and I knew you would return to see whether I kept my word. In the meantime, your children and I become great friends, selling apples every day, Emmy teaching me how to read."

"Does your husband mind? I must express my thanks to him," Jonathan said.

"My marriage was annulled." Millicent smiled weakly. "For imbecility because Terence had once witnessed me conversing with Thomas in his grave, and who else but an imbecile would talk to her dead brother's grave. I believe his parents, who wanted their son to marry a lady of his station, were behind it all." She continued in bitterness. "They were the ones who purchased the loan for the mill, making it impossible for Terence to get ahead with such a poor choice of wife. In any event, he was ill with a catarrh he could never shake, and they were able to nurse him and feed him. I could do one or t'other."

"Daniel and Emma appear in very good health."

Millicent blushed again at the comment. "You—or I might say me because I am the only Colonel Goshen people have ever seen—gave Emma and Daniel a deed to our house. Also, the colonel was kind enough to make a gift of two hundred guineas, of which over one hundred eighty remain to help them in the future. We live with Dr. Smith and his wife who pay rent and their two children. My brothers feed my brood Thursdays and Sundays, and for the last year a mysterious basket from the country arrives every month with clothes, so I can claim we are as fortunate and as well cared for as any vagabond in New York."

"We don't want to leave Millie," Emma exclaimed. "She's fun."

"I'm just a big playmate for them. Come. I'm sure Dr. Smith will be delighted to see you, although, as you likely know, he still expresses his pleasure by grumbling louder than usual."

Jonathan didn't quite know how to phrase the next question. "Provost Cunningham who signed the receipt for the orphanage wanted to do the children harm to avenge what I had once done to him. How did the children get away from the provost?"

"I arrived at the millinery just after Cunningham collected the children, pretending to represent citizens desiring to create a society for the relief of widows, orphans, and the poor. When Elizabeth told me the name and described how proper a gentleman he was, I didn't even tell my sweet friend what a horrible mistake she had made. I went to my room, collected my pistol, and proceeded directly to the Provost House intending to introduce myself as Colonel Goshen's sister and then shoot the devil Cunningham between the eyes.

"When I arrived there, I met this fat man at the door with a monkey on his shoulder leading Emma and Daniel away. He seemed to know who I was and gave me Emma and Daniel and a hundred guineas. 'Take care of them, will you, madam,' he said and blushed bright red. When I asked about Cunningham, the man made the strange comment that the provost didn't like his monkey. Lucretia, I mean Mrs. Smith, later told me that her brother informed a personage with an interest in the welfare of the children what was happening, and this personage, who must have been the fat fellow with the monkey, swore he would remedy the problem."

Jonathan insisted on buying the rest of the apples and then accompanied Millicent to Emma and Daniel's house. Dr. Reginald Smith, having his consultation on the first story, was there with Lucretia and their son and new daughter. Millicent immediately started to help Dr. Smith's wife prepare the meal. Daniel and Emma shyly gazed at him and answered his awkward questions awkwardly.

The dinner began as a stiff affair—in part because Dr. Smith was always stiff, in part because there was so much to say yet seemingly no polite way to get at it. Jonathan, regretting that Smith was a teetotaler, experienced an increasing feeling of sadness and oppression.

Millicent bravely hung on to her smiles and kept up her small jokes. She constantly glanced at Jonathan's leg as if she wanted to fix it. Every few minutes Lucretia jumped up to check the baby who was sound asleep. Dr. Smith repeated last Sunday's sermon given at the Congregational church he attended, word for word. This went on until just before dessert a rap sounded on the door. When Millicent answered, Mrs. Goodwin swept in without waiting for an invitation.

She surveyed the company, her sharp birdlike eyes dissatisfied. "Well, I see from your downcast demeanors, it hasn't happened yet."

"What hasn't happened?" Jonathan inquired.

She snorted. "'It' hasn't happened."

"I am mystified about the nature of 'it,'" Jonathan said, annoyed.

"Am I to spell 'it' out for you?" Mrs. Goodwin asked in disbelief.

Jonathan sighed. "I'm afraid you must."

She addressed Millicent. "Forgive me for speaking for this dolt. I am Mrs. Goodwin. My information is that you are no longer married."

Millicent hung her head embarrassed, no smile now. "Yes."

"Good riddance to that squinty-eyed tin-headed fool. Now, as for this fool. He is a good man. He was engaged to my Amelia who was the best girl put on earth—you can forgive a mother for saying that, but she was. Now, he was too shy or too doltish to declare his love for Amelia, so I had to intervene. I'm here to do it again for him for I'm afraid he is backward in these matters."

"I fear you are mistaken. Mr. Jonathan Asher doesn't harbor great affection for me."

"Of course, he loves you. I know he gets an ox-like expression on his face and knows not what to say. That means he loves you, and you have to get used to it."

"I don't believe Millicent holds me in the same regard," Jonathan interrupted.

At this Mrs. Goodwin turned red, her small eyes started out of her head, and declared in a voice like ice being chipped away with a hammer: "The lady puts her life in danger to rescue you from the cruelest provost marshal and the most notorious prison in New York and then takes in your children for nearly two years and gives them as good a care as the best of mothers and you dare suggest she doesn't love you. What must a woman do to prove she loves you?"

"Jonathan loved Elizabeth more than he could ever love me." Millicent quickly peeked at him as if trying to ascertain the truth of this statement.

"Let's put to the side that this Elizabeth stole his money for her own ends and is never coming back to New York and talk about love. Nay, we won't. We will leave you two to figure it out. I'll be back within the hour to see how much progress you make."

Jonathan and Millicent remained in the room somewhat stunned as the others filed out.

"She is a strange forceful woman. You must admit you don't truly love me," Millicent said softly.

Jonathan nodded. "If only you had not been married. I wouldn't allow myself to nurture such an affection for another man's wife."

"I'm not married now," Millicent whispered.

"No," Jonathan mused, trying to come to grips with this new state of affairs. "But you were always so…"

"Don't say it. I hated war profiteers—hated them while they rode around in their fine coaches with their fat bellies, powdered wigs, silk stockings, and snuff-stained fingers, yet you weren't like them, and I didn't hate you even though I tried, and how could I know you weren't what you seemed…"

"How could I know…"

"That my marriage would be annulled because I was an imbecile."

"That you're definitely not."

"Well, thank you, Mr. Asher. You always were quite extravagant with your compliments."

Jonathan gave a cry of exasperation that appeared to startle her. "Since you insist I compliment you, Millicent, an act which all the women in my life apparently think I have difficulty performing, I will do so now. I could not conceive of a lovelier woman to spend my life with—good sense, good humor, beauty, gentleness, grace, kindness, spirit, wisdom, courage, fortitude—no man could be more fortunate than to have your hand in marriage."

"You still haven't said you loved me."

"By all that is sacred…"

Millicent began to laugh. "I always secretly thought Elizabeth fortunate in you as her suitor."

"Well, Miss Millicent, don't you dare interrupt me. Do me the great honor of becoming my wife, and if you say no, I'll, I'll…"

"Well, Mr. Jonathan Asher," she cut him off, smiling and snuffling. "You need not finish the sentence. I do accept with all the joy of my heart."

End

If you have enjoyed this book, please be so kind to take the time to write a review:

amazon.com

THE SULIOTE MAIDEN

NATHAN'S STORY I

CHAPTER ONE

NATHAN HELPED HIS mother carry his sister, Thomasina, down the stairs on a cot and then transfer her gently to the settee next to the fireplace. His mother returned upstairs to see to one of the hundred chores she hadn't had time to do, leaving Nathan and Thomasina alone. He jabbed the log with a poker, sending up a storm of sparks that he knew always gave his sister pleasure, and after seeing her smile in the orange light, retreated to a stool in a dark corner. He disliked the heat as much as Thomasina loved it. He felt Thomasina's eyes on him and heard her sigh. She beckoned to him to come closer.

"What is weighing you down, Mister Nate?" She asked as he settled himself in a chair beside her. Mister Nate was her pet name for him.

"Nothing, Tommy," he replied. Tommy being his special name for her which she enjoyed immensely.

"I've had nothing to do in my life except be sick and observe you, and I'm very good at both of those enterprises, Mister Nate. Don't turn away so I can't see your face. What is eating you?"

Nathan knelt on the hearth and poked the fire again sending up more sparks although he knew it was futile to hide from her. "The British landed in the Chesapeake," he said glumly.

"Does that make you angry?" He heard a smile in her voice.

"I want to go to war," he declared. There he had said it. He wasn't surprised by her reaction.

Thomasina laughed, screwing up her face. Everybody said her face was beautiful. He couldn't judge. She was just his sister. After she finished laughing, she said, "I may not know much, but I know a twelve-year-old boy can't go to war."

"Why not? They do all the time," Nathan argued. "I could be a drummer boy or even a powder monkey in the navy."

"And get yourself killed and leave your poor sick sister without her entertainment. How heartless of you!" Thomasina had an irritating habit of finding something wrong in whatever he said.

"You like making fun of me." She was also aggravating because the more seriously he took himself, the less she did so.

"I do for I love you, and I feel I done you great harm by being sick and taking up all of mother's attention." Thomasina had become serious.

Nathan protested. "They can't think of anything to say to me except correct what I'm doing wrong or remind me to do my chores."

"Emma called you the forgotten child because between me and her ailments, mother hasn't two minutes to spare for you. And father with this war and no trade with England, he has to figure out how to keep us housed, fed, and clothed."

"Emma should keep her mind on her own children," he replied unfairly. Emma and her brother Daniel had been taken in by their father during the War of Independence. She was thirty years older than Nathan, had a half-blind tailor as a husband and five well-behaved children of her own, and, much to his annoyance, alternately acted like a sister, mother, or aunt to him as it suited her.

"Emma is correct. And mama cried when she called you the forgotten child and said she would try to do better."

"I want to be forgotten by them so I can live my life." Nathan held the opinion that parents were inconvenient except for providing food, clothes, and lodging. That wasn't to say he didn't love them, but such sentiment rarely has room to be indulged in with somebody who is always telling you what to do.

"You don't want to be bothered out of your daydreams," Thomasina observed with painful accuracy.

"That's it. They discussed having one of our brothers take you in, then they said you were my best companion, and it would break my heart, which it would. So, you see I am selfish and want you all to myself."

His parents had had five children, three sons—Alfred, Thomas, Jonathan—and two daughters—Beatrice and Alice—between the years 1785 and 91 and had possessed the energy to raise them well with love and discipline. Then five years later Thomasina came into the family and was ill from her first days. Four years later, Nathan arrived, a surprise because their mother had believed she was well past childbearing. Nathan's appearance coincided with a change in the family's fortune. They were still considered well-off, but his father seemed continually selling property to make ends meet.

"Well, I still want to go to war, then when I come back, I'll have more interesting stories to tell you." This seemed good reasoning until he articulated it.

"Unless you die. Wait for the next war. I might be in my grave by then, so I wouldn't have to grieve you." Nathan did not like it when his sister mentioned her terrible illness even in jest.

"Does it hurt, Tommy… Your illness?" He asked.

"Some days not much. Other days… I don't want to think about those."

He took her hand and gazed at the face that others said was beautiful. He could see that her eyes were special—soft brown pools of comfort and warmth. "Maybe if I become Catholic and light a candle for you that would help."

Thomasina smiled. "You know I pray for you."

393

"Why do I need prayers?" He asked defensively.

Thomasina stared at him as if she couldn't believe he had just asked that question. "You wander about too shy and too proud to make friends. You come and go as you please as if you were a boarder here, not a son. I am the only one who mends your clothes, and I am very poor at it. You're hardly given any chores. You hardly gone to school. The Trevelyan brothers won't stop bullying you. I don't think anybody really knows you except for me and maybe Emma."

"Then, no one will miss me when I go to war." That seemed to Nathan a happy coincidence.

"You think Emma and I are nobody?" Thomasina was unreasonably angry because he hadn't expressed himself well.

"I didn't mean that."

"Don't you understand how impossible going to war is for you?" She grimaced. A part of her was hurting.

Nathan didn't.

After making sure Thomasina was comfortable and creeping upstairs to confirm what he had expected to find—his mother in an exhausted doze holding her swollen twisted hands in her lap, Nathan sneaked out the door. He planned to go down to the docks by Maiden Lane and play, which meant for him daydreaming. He loved the outdoors in all weathers. On this day, the late afternoon simmered in the summer sun, unfortunately with less warmth than Thomasina needed. The air smelled saltier than usual. Gulls squawked as they picked at the leavings near the docks. The taverns and the shops, the shouts of sailors getting underway or the teamsters loading, the carts, and wagons filled to the near tipping with casks and crates all became actors and props in his daydreams. Nathan felt a great adventure was in the offing, and instead of an anonymous boy, he became the hero. Life was best at these times

He had not experienced war, of course, but he thought of it most every day. To go into battle seemed the greatest adventure a man could undertake, so he read every book he could find about it, dreamed about it, and in his hours of lonely play imagined himself a general or a colonel strategizing a brilliant victory or a cavalry officer constantly performing a heroic deed. His father had the good fortune to be in a war—the great Revolutionary War, but oddly hadn't been a soldier, or at least that was what he said and little else. Daniel claimed his father had been a British soldier, but actually tricked everybody by being on Washington's side. That seemed a little dishonest to Nathan, and he was not alone in that opinion, but most people admired his father. His mother, well, she hated war. She had lost a brother. She could not talk about war without getting angry at both sides involved, although she got angry about practically nothing else.

When the British landed, it was a dream come true. Nathan now began to immerse himself in a daydream about how he as a lowly drummer boy saved the life of a general. This pleasurable train of thought was suddenly interrupted by a rotten squash splatting on the back of his head. He looked around for which of the Trevelyan brothers had hurled it. A vendor of corn wouldn't meet his eye. A mother hugged a young child close to her dress. As usual, nobody appeared although the rotten-fruit missile had come from the direction of a dirty alleyway.

He was sport for the Trevelyan brothers, although it could be said they were more afraid of him than he was of the six of them. So, they hurled their missiles, usually spoiled fruit, but occasionally stones or hunks of wet manure, and fled. A year ago, they had cornered Nathan behind an abandoned warehouse with the intention of doing him great harm, the four older ones—Sweden, Brogue, Sharon, and Tristan—who seemed like trunks of stout oaks cut off at six feet, the two younger—Kyle and Kinchin—resembling little rat terriers—swift and sharp-toothed. The six of them had first thrown him against the wall and slugged him a couple of times in the stomach making him vomit. Sweden and Brogue were dragging him across the muddy cobblestones pulling off his shoes while the rest held on to his queue joking that they wanted to see his head come off when Daniel appeared with his father. The six brothers turned to face the two adults and grinned. They liked the odds. Then eight teamsters who worked with his father also turned the corner.

"Care for a tussle?" His father said, lurching forward with the help of his cane.

"'Tisn't fair," the eldest, who for some obscure reason was called Sweden, answered.

"And what you were doing was?" Daniel asked.

"We was just funning around," Brogue insisted.

"Giving my son a black eye isn't funning around. Tell you what. You seem the stoutest and strongest, Sweden, in the interests of fairness take me on, one on one." Nathan's father, Jonathan Asher, stood nose to nose with

Sweden. Although used a cane to walk because of injuries in war, there wasn't a teamster who could beat him in arm-wrestling.

"My father will break every bone in your body if you hurt me," Sweden took a step back.

"Let's go ask your father if he wants to participate," Jonathan Asher suggested.

Mr. Trevelyan was drinking at a nearby tavern and had fame as a brawler, yet Sweden wavered, then shrugged his shoulders, "We were just funning around."

"If you attack my son again, with the help of my men, I'll publicly take down your britches on the Bowling Green and cane every single one of you. Any who doubts me, speak up, and I'll prove I can do it now."

The Trevelyan brothers sneered at Nathan from a distance for a month or so. Then, deciding his father's threat was merely hot air, they ambushed him again, swarming from an alleyway with swinging cudgels and wet handfuls of manure. Father was away in Connecticut. By the time Daniel arrived with a bevy of teamsters, they had torn off Nathan's pants and punched and kicked him black and blue. Teamsters drag, haul, lift all day, therefore are stronger than toughs and hit and kick harder than toughs and are familiar with all the dockside fighting tricks. Blood was shed, and at the end of the melee, four of the Trevelyan brothers were bound and dragged to the Bowling Green, the two rat terriers having escaped. Their father staggered out of the tavern from where he was rousted so he could watch the punishment of his sons. Bent over the pedestal where once stood the statue of George III, in front of him and all the passersby, Sweden, Brogue, Sharon, and

Tristan each had his breeches taken down and was caned twenty-five times.

"Next time I'll brand you on your bums," Daniel declared to the crumpled whimpering Trevelyans afterward.

The brothers still stalked him and, with immeasurable glee, they would have killed him, but they were afraid.

Nathan wasn't considered a promising scholar by the master of the school run by the Dutch Reformed Church and was caned almost weekly for his wandering thoughts. He was worse at church. His father threatened to nail his feet to the floor so he wouldn't wriggle so much. He should have been good at games but managed not to be.

Nathan's father did display fondness for his youngest son, which was moderated by a sense he was not doing right by him. When not overwhelmed by his affairs, Jonathan Asher would alternately threaten or promise to install him in the warehouse. He had done so with his brother Alfred, who was eighteen years older than Nathan. Alfred took naturally to being a merchant and had a prosperous business in his own right. He had even sailed to China in a ship he owned a sixteenth part in. Traveling to China seemed almost as good as going to war to Nathan. Before the present conflict, his father had taken him into his warehouse once to see whether he had any aptitude or interest in his trade. Nathan demonstrated neither. He did not like the stale salty air, the dark aisles, the oppressively tall stacks of merchandise, and given the choice between daydreaming and counting, the former always prevailed. Seeing bolts of silk from China, next to crates of tea from India, next to bags of coffee from Columbia did spark in

Nathan a desire to take a berth on a ship that his father owned a portion of and see those places. That was scotched because after his father took him in a small boat out into the harbor on a day of light breezes, Nathan was violently ill for three days afterward.

On a rare free day, his father taught him how to use a fowling piece, a beautiful gun of polished maple, light enough that a boy could hold steady. Two months then passed and it seemed increasingly unlikely his father would have another free day, so Nathan sneaked the weapon outdoors late one night to play and accidentally shot out the window of a neighbor. Amends were made, and he was forbidden the use of the piece for the rest of his life, although he could swear his mother was trying not to laugh when the neighbor displayed the wig, which being blown off the wig stand, had a big hole in the center.

CHAPTER 2

The embattled chronically underfunded Federal government requested that the States call up their militia to help in the war effort. The States started to comply, but then the concerned officials decided it might be more judicious if their armed boys stayed nearby to defend local interests. A newly formed militia spent its time idling at the North and West Batteries guarding the harbor. The best the New York authorities could do for the national cause was to suggest to their populace that men not inspired by the responsibility of protecting hearth and home in the militia could volunteer and join the struggle in Maryland. The Federal Government also made an urgent request for supplies. Nathan's father complained a merchant would go broke dealing with the government. Payment was slow, and if there were a change of parties in the meantime, the person who promised to pay might be replaced by an official who had no intention of wasting government money on the favorites of a defeated party. However, pricked by a patriotic guilty conscience, he purchased six hundred pairs of boots from Connecticut to deliver to the army facing the British, supposing he'd get his money eventually.

Nathan had spent weeks pondering the problem of how to join the National army. He attributed to the hand of God that the means arrived at this doorstep so to speak in the form of three wagons loaded with boots. He told Thomasina and his mother that he was traveling with his father who was leaving that afternoon for Connecticut to procure more boots. They believed him and didn't bother to check with Nathan's father who was departing from the warehouse. Six days would pass before the truth would be out. Meanwhile, Nathan hid in the wagon under a tarp with the boots. The smell of the blacking made his head swim, but he found a small rent in the tarp where he positioned his nose to get fresh air.

They joined a caravan of forty-five other wagons plus two hundred young men motivated by patriotism, lack of work, or boredom to join the national cause. Unfortunately, on the first day, Nathan heard walking beside his wagon the distinctive shrill voices of the four older Trevelyan brothers speculating openly how much plunder could be gotten off a dead British soldier and deciding that even a redcoat with a musket ball hole should be worth a pint of ale.

For more information about the **SONS OF THE NEW WORLD** series, my other novels, and access to free stories visit my website *www.jamesshort.me* and go to MY FICTION page.

BIO

I am the author of the **Sons of the New World** which includes **Brides of the Gauntlet, What the River of the Cherokee Did Not Tell, Jonathan's Story I** and **The Shadow Patriot, Jonathan's Story II** (Coming out in August 2022.) In 2023 I will publish **The Suliote Maiden, Nathan's Story I**, the fourth novel in the series. Also available on Amazon is **Where Fortune Lies**, a Romeo and Juliet story that plays out in a small town on the Pacific Coast which features a buried treasure, a ghost, and a cat burglar.

I graduated from UCLA with a bachelor's degree in Spanish after taking a circuitous route through the University of Santa Cruz and the University of Barcelona. I am married with two grown daughters. In an alternate universe where my life went wrong, I would be devoting the long hours of my prison sentence to translating **Don Quixote** into English.

LINKS:

BRIDES OF THE GAUNTLET

https://www.amazon.com/dp/B08ZJMLNWJ

WHAT THE RIVER OF THE CHEROKEE
DID NOT TELL

https://www.amazon.com/dp/B09TQ1Q7ZP

WHERE FORTUNE LIES

https://www.amazon.com/dp/B07R7CRYC1

TWITTER

James Short

@JAMESSH35099520

Made in the USA
Middletown, DE
20 March 2023

27165094R00243